T0285309

CHANGE *of* HEART

A MINER & MULVILLE
MEDICAL THRILLER

Cristina LePort, M.D.

bancroft
press

Cover & Interior Design: TracyCopesCreative.com
Author photo: Brystan Studios (Aliso Viejo, CA)

Change *of* Heart
978-1-61088-659-8 HC
9781610886604 PB
978-1-61088-661-1 Ebook
978-1-61088-662-8 PDF Ebook
978-1-61088-663-5 Audiobook

Published by Bancroft Press
"Books that Enlighten"
(818) 275-3061
4527 Glenwood Avenue
La Crescenta, CA 91214
www.bancroftpress.com

Printed in the United States of America

To Peter, the love of my life.

CHAPTER 1
THE VICTIM

The bullet carrying Amy Winter's name whooshed through her hair at a speed of fifteen hundred feet per second, burned a jagged hole into her smooth 24-year-old flesh, burst through the thin layer of her temporal muscle, and shattered the temporal bone. Protective membranes melted away and cerebrospinal fluid gushed out, merging with spurting blood. Amy's knowledge of biology and chemistry dissolved with the pulverization of her hippocampus. Her bubbly personality disappeared with her temporal lobe, followed by the loss of motor function, language, problem solving, judgment, and socio-sexual behavior—all wiped out by the shockwave crushing her frontal lobes.

Amy Winter the person was no more, but her heart kept on beating.

At 5:38 a.m., the colors of dawn were brightening the clear October sky when Kirk Miner arrived at the crime scene. The garbled sounds of disapproval from Aurora, his wife of over sixteen years, still resonated in his ears. She had voiced them from the other side of their bed half an hour earlier, when he had gotten the call. Kirk would have to make sure to remain only a consultant in the case. Not only that, but he would have to keep his excitement in check and leave the policing to the police. At least he would try, as he had promised Aurora. He had to admit that past failures to keep that promise had gotten him into some very close calls during the past few years.

The N.Y. Medical Center parking lot was crawling with blue uniforms.

Black and white police cars flashing red and blue lights called his attention to an area walled off by yellow crime-scene tape. Kirk parked his Subaru SUV behind a black sedan he recognized as belonging to his friend John Spencer, the new captain of the NYPD Manhattan division. He noticed John's tall and athletic figure standing next to a black Mini Cooper at the center of the crime scene. John always reminded him of a leopard ready to leap into action. Kirk lifted the yellow tape and ducked, stepping into the action as well.

"What have you got?" Kirk retrieved his PI identification card and held it up for a young policeman guarding the perimeter of the crime scene. "Captain Spencer called me."

"This way."

Kirk followed him to the Mini. The driver's seat was empty, testifying to the recent removal of the victim. Medics acted faster than medical examiners. The victim must still be alive.

John turned after hearing what the young policeman had to say. "Kirk," he said, "thanks for getting in so quickly."

"Hi, Captain." He stepped closer. "I thought you were promoted to paper pusher. What got you out of bed so early?"

John's clear blue eyes drooped from lack of sleep and his usual high-strung vitality wasn't quite there. Strands of gray peppered the black hair at his temple. The man had barely hit 40. The new rank of Captain had to be taking its toll already.

"Ah," John sighed. "Where's the fun if you can't smell the shit and get your hands dirty?"

"I'm not surprised. You never struck me as desk-job material."

"How's the family?"

"'Cept for Peter's growing pains, not too bad." Kirk pointed his chin at the car. "What's up?"

"Twenty-two-year-old female with gunshot wound to the head." John turned to the young uniform at his side and pointed at Kirk. "This is private investigator Kirk Miner. He's known as 'The Medical Detective,' because of his extensive medical knowledge. It's like having Sherlock Holmes and Dr.

Watson in one brain."

"Wow," Kirk said. "Just to hear that makes it worth getting up at the crack of dawn. But why am I here really?"

"The victim, one Amy Winter, has a typed and signed note to donate her organs." John retrieved a clear plastic evidence bag from a backpack at his feet and handed it to Kirk. "Left on the passenger seat, next to her pocketbook. Seems like she drove all the way from New Jersey to kill herself here. But no mention in the note about why she'd blow out her brains. Just the organ donation."

"An organ donation letter?" Kirk smiled. "I'm flattered by how much you miss me."

John knew precisely how to shove Kirk into a case, at which point Kirk was always happy to help his former mentor. But most of all, Kirk loved doing the work. The bread and butter part of his PI practice was like a pleasant, leisurely jog, but the periodic criminal case consultation was the all-out challenge, the limits-testing, reinvigorating sprint he needed to keep him on his toes.

After leaving the police force almost eight years ago, and only a few years of PI work, Kirk needed these cases like the air he gasped into his lungs after one of those runs, when he leaned forward, bent at his waist, massaging his painfully engorged spleen, looking down with pride at the countless bleachers he had just climbed, together with his son, at the college sport camp. If only he could make Aurora understand how good it felt.

"For today, you can thank the FBI," John said.

"The FBI? Why would they be interested in this case?"

"Apparently it's because of the hospital." John pointed his thumb at the building behind him. "It's on their radar because of some unsolved cybercrime."

"You don't mean last year's hacking of hospital records?"

"That's it."

"The New York Medical Center was one of them? I don't remember seeing anything about that."

"Yeah. They kept it out of the press, but they were hacked all right."

3

Spencer nodded. "And Director Mulville wants first peek at all violent crimes associated with NYMC. After finding out about the donor business, he asked me to call you. You're getting famous."

"Mulville?" Kirk's brows went up.

"He wants you to work with his cybercrime agent," John said. "He'll call to explain. He also wants you to act as liaison with the police."

"Wait a minute," Kirk said. "In Mulville's vocabulary, that means I'm going to manage the investigation instead of the Police."

"You got it." John again nodded, this time pointing his finger at Kirk. "He wants the Police to back off. And I'm not crying about it. Trust me, we've got enough business as it is."

Kirk nodded. Great. Aurora would be delighted to hear.

He examined the blood-smeared paper. Only one typed sentence: *I donate my organs for transplant.* He stared at the illegible signature. Something begged for attention, but Kirk couldn't pinpoint what it was.

"The $40 million question is: Did she pull the trigger?" Kirk said.

"Yeah," John said. "Amy's poor parents are on their way from somewhere in Ohio. In her wallet, we found a picture of Amy with another young woman. We're trying to identify and contact that other woman. Hopefully, we'll find out something."

From his bomber jacket pocket, Kirk retrieved a pair of plastic gloves and pulled them on. He peered through the open driver-side door. The window was down. Inside, on the passenger's seat, sat a small brown leather pocketbook covered with grayish and blood-red droplets.

The spray of the same material coated the passenger side front window. Blood's pungent smell entered Kirk's nostrils, forcing him to recall how it had been produced. Small particles generated odors by clinging to receptors inside the nose. He was inhaling small parts of the woman's brain. The thought, on an empty stomach, made him feel queasy. Kirk stood up and took a deep breath of fresh air.

"Any weapons or bullets?"

"This was on the driver's seat between the victim and the door." John produced a second evidence bag from his backpack. "A Ruger. A woman's gun. Small, concealable, and accurate."

Kirk reached for the bag and wrapped his hand around the plastic covering the grip's checkered frame. In his mind, the weapon's light weight and John's words triggered an image of a beautiful young woman, Amy Winter, with no future.

"The bullet," John went on, "ended up embedded next to the ceiling, on the car's front passenger side. No other bullets found in the gun."

"Why next to the ceiling?" Kirk lifted his eyes from the gun.

"It must have hit her cellphone." John handed Kirk a plastic-wrapped iPhone with a dazzling pink case. "She must've been holding the phone to her ear when the bullet exited. We found the phone on the car floor between the two back seats. Screen's shattered, phone's dead."

Kirk examined the phone. The black screen bore a bloody diagonal fracture from top to bottom. That would have been the direction of the exiting bullet grazing a phone glued to the woman's right ear. Who in hell would she be chatting with while killing herself?

"Who discovered the victim?" Kirk said.

"A man called the hospital ER and 9-1-1 at about the same time." John extracted a smartphone from his sport jacket and scrolled through his notes. "The call to the ER was registered at 4:41a.m. I'm not sure how precise that is. The 9-1-1 call came in at 4:42."

Kirk placed his index finger on the phone's volume button. Nothing happened. Then his thumb pressed the reset button several times. After the third try, the screen lit up. A key piece of a puzzle fell into place, making Kirk feel almost giddy with excitement.

"I'm afraid we're not dealing with an attempted suicide," Kirk said, turning the face of the phone toward John, "but an attempted murder."

"I agree." John's brows went up. "But how can you be so sure without any forensics?"

"Several things," Kirk said. "The note was added later, after the shot. Smears of blood, instead of sprays. Poor attempt by the shooter to make us believe the note was on the seat before the bullet hit."

"Yeah," John said, "that's been bothering me also. You've come a long way from your training over ribs and beer."

Kirk smiled at the memory of their favorite pub. It seemed a long time ago when Kirk decided to leave the police force and John helped him get started as a private investigator. John was more than a mentor. He always cared about Kirk, but cared even more after Kirk's near-fatal car accident years ago. John had become as protective as an older brother.

The image of the dark pub dissipated and Kirk refocused on the victim's note.

"I'm no calligrapher," he said, "but, from the slanting of the signature, I think the victim is right-handed. A right-handed person would shoot her right side."

"If it's actually her signature," John said.

"The shooter could have forced her to sign at gun point," Kirk said. "Either way, it would point to attempted murder."

"What else?"

"We've got the exact time of the shooting," Kirk said, waving the plastic-clad phone. "Here in this frozen, undead iPhone."

John grabbed the evidence bag. He stared at the fractured, frozen screen. His lips stretched into a grin.

"The bullet froze the time at 4:43," Kirk said. "One minute *after* the 9-1-1 call. The man called *before* the shooting occurred. It's unlikely someone would notice the shooter, figure out what he was going to do, call the police, and leave without talking to them."

"The witness could have left because he was afraid the shooter would come after him," John said.

"Or perhaps," Kirk said, "the caller knew the shooting would occur because he himself was the shooter. And he wanted the victim to be found as soon as possible."

John referred again to his notes. "The caller said that someone *had been* shot. Not someone is going to shoot, or is shooting, somebody. The woman had gun powder residue on her left hand, but the shooter could've placed the gun in her hand before throwing it in the car. We've got a few prints on the handle. I bet they're all from her. But I still think you're right."

Kirk nodded. "The shooter made sure she would be rescued in time for her organs to be saved for donation and subsequent transplant."

Kirk turned toward the hospital ER entrance. A vivid memory materialized. A plastic bracelet around his wrist, from six years ago, in a different hospital. The bracelet classifying him as an organ donor. After his prolonged coma, doctors had given up on Kirk. Luckily for him, he had woken up and retained his organs.

The woman who had crossed the ER threshold earlier that morning wouldn't be so lucky. Someone wanted her organs badly enough to put a bullet in her brain.

CHAPTER 2
BLOOM

Charlotte Bloom closed her computer and pressed her palms against her shut eyelids. Not even noon, and boredom had already made her sleepy. She reached out for a tall paper cup on her cluttered desk and poured the leftover cold coffee into her mouth. She stretched her neck and turned her head side to side, peeking into the two workspaces on each side of her cubicle. Both empty. No chance of a chatting break with the woman who had survived the same grueling 20 months of Quantico training. Or the cute new guy from DC who had just joined the team.

She looked up at the ceiling and stared at a large brown spot, the result of a past water leak. She sighed, bent down under her desk to dispose of the coffee container, then picked up the phone while opening a file on her desktop.

After several rings, a woman's raspy voice answered. "Who is this?" The Italian accent came through from just those few words: Mrs. Mezzapelle, an 85-year-old victim of vishing.

"It's Charlotte Bloom," Bloom said after taking a deep breath. She wanted to project her voice with authority. "From the FBI. We spoke last week."

"Did you find my money?"

"Mrs. Mezzapelle." Bloom paused. "Unfortunately, it may take some time. We confirmed that the call you received a month ago was definitely not from the IRS."

"But I spoke with an agent! He said he was with them. How was I supposed to know?"

"I'm sorry." Bloom searched for the best words. "Usually, the IRS doesn't accept gift cards as payments."

Heavy breathing followed. "One thousand dollars I paid him! And he said it was a discount."

"We're doing everything we can to find this crook…and recover your money. I assure you. I'll call you again as soon as we know more."

Bloom shook her head, sorry for the poor woman. After hanging up, she slid open her desk's top drawer. A shining FBI badge seemed to wink at her in mockery. The final test she had to pass at Quantico flashed into her mind. She had stood, eyes shut, in front of a uniformed man holding a can of pepper spray. Before she knew it, her face was on fire. But to pass this test, she had to open at least one eye, attack a punching bag, and defend herself against an assailant trying to take her gun out of its holster. She had earned that badge.

Now an FBI Special Agent, Cybercrime Division, she had been probationary for almost two years. Where were the national security cyber intrusions, the investigations of terrorist organizations, and the intelligence operations sponsored by foreign governments mentioned in the FBI's job description? Instead, she was assigned to online fraud.

She slammed the drawer shut. After lunch, she would speak with Director Jack Mulville about her dissatisfaction. He should know she was ready for real assignments. Getting up from her desk, she fetched her backpack from the floor and slid her gray jacket off the back of the chair. She wiggled into both as she walked to the elevator.

After a descent marked by a series of pings, she exited into the lobby. Before heading to the covered parking lot, her fist closed around her keys, several blades protruding between her fingers, according to her self-defense training. You never knew when a disgruntled perp would decide to preempt an investigation or an arrest. Mulville had insisted she take private Karate lessons over and above what the FBI required. She had complied, working hard to achieve black belt status. She couldn't wait to put her skills to work in challenging cases.

Her ponytail swung as she walked all the way across the garage and to the back wall. Having reached her black Mitsubishi. she stopped cold when her heart thumped out of rhythm for several beats and a wave of dizziness forced her to hold on to the side of a nearby SUV. The damn lightheadedness again! Twice this week alone. She took several deep breaths. The dizziness intensified. No. She couldn't faint. Not now.

Trying to blot out the bright dots dancing in front of her eyes, she shook her head, sealed her mouth, and pushed air down into her chest. The thumping subsided; the dizziness disappeared. Before driving off, she would have to get a sandwich from the local food truck.

Charlotte sat on a bench in front of her building, chewing on a pastrami on rye but not savoring it. In about two months, her probation would finally be over. No more "Probie" Bloom, but full-fledged FBI Cyber Special Agent Bloom. She had come a long way, and was so close. No way some stupid heart-rhythm glitch would get in her way. If discovered, a problem like that would likely disqualify her from any FBI field position. She couldn't let anyone know. Not even Mulville. Most of all, not Mulville.

Thank God she'd already passed the lie-detector test months ago. "Are you aware of anything that would interfere with your work as an agent?" At that happy time, her answer had been a truthful "No." Perhaps, with the right assignment, she could speed things up and graduate before...

That doctor, a month and a half ago, had warned about possible progression of the heart problem if it went untreated. How could she win this race when, under the current circumstances, she probably shouldn't even be driving? She swallowed and clenched her teeth.

Dr. Zayne Wilder looked up into the bathroom mirror and ran a sweaty hand through his unruly dark hair. He took his time washing his hands and drying them on paper towels, then he straightened his white coat collar and stepped out into the hall. As he walked through the corridor, glancing at the pictures of former chiefs of staff in hopes of finding inspiration, a familiar quivering started in the pit of his stomach. He stopped in front of a door labelled "Family Conference Room." After a deep breath, he pushed down on the handle and entered.

On a brown leather couch, a middle-aged man with a potbelly and receding hairline huddled with a frail-looking woman with mousey, dark-rooted blonde hair. Amy Winter's parents stood up holding hands, and lifted tired, puffy eyes full of pain and bewilderment.

"I'm Dr. McCarty." Zayne cleared his voice and offered his hand in salute and comfort. "A heart surgeon."

"Something's wrong with her heart now?" The man's voice carried a tinge of resentment.

"No. Nothing wrong with her heart." Zayne directed all his empathy to the man's eyes. The poor father would rather focus on a new problem than accept the agonizing reality of facts. That nothing much could hurt his daughter any longer, because everything was already lost. "I'm very sorry about your daughter. Thanks for meeting me this morning. Please, sit down so we can talk."

"Joe Winter."

"Martha Winter." The two murmured their names in introduction, while shaking the doctor's hand, then took the same position on the couch, clenching each other's hand again.

Zayne's task suddenly revealed itself to be much harder than anticipated. He expected an uphill battle, but now, instead of starting from way up the hill, he identified the parents' position as located at the base, miles from where he stood. Today, Zayne was facing the most impenetrable of all barriers. Parents' heartbreak. He sighed.

"This morning," Zayne went on in a soft voice, "we did another scan of Amy's brain. As the neurologist already explained to you, her brain, due to the extensive trauma she suffered, is not functioning any longer."

He paused to assess the parents' ability to follow his reasoning, hoping to spot any body language confirming agreement with his statement. He saw only blank stares. His chest tightened as he got ready to pronounce the preamble to the difficult request he had come to make.

"Your daughter is being kept alive by the tube in her throat and the respirator. The neurologist has declared your daughter brain dead. That means there is no chance that she'll ever wake up again. I'm so sorry."

Tears streamed down the mother's cheeks. The father placed his arm around her shoulders. Procuring hearts for transplants wasn't Zayne's favorite task. Talking to relatives about the death of a loved one didn't get any easier with experience. Talking to parents about their child as an organ donor required great diplomacy on his part—he needed to focus on his other patient, the potential recipient. Zayne was glad he could count on his fingers such cases in his experience. From his lab coat, he took out a folded paper.

"Why do we need to talk to a heart surgeon?" the father asked, tightening the hug around his wife.

"Your daughter wanted to donate her organs." After pushing aside a few magazines, Zayne unfolded the paper and placed it on a coffee table in front of the couch. He rotated the document to orient it toward the couple. "I'd like to get your consent so, according to her wishes, we can proceed to harvest her organs as soon as possible. I have a patient, a young woman just like your daughter, who's dying due to heart failure. She's a good match for your daughter's heart."

"How do you know she's a good match?" the father asked. "Who gave you permission to check it?"

"Your daughter is a blood donor," Zayne explained. "And she's also a pre-med student who participated in a study about donor compatibility, so we have her genetic information on file."

The father removed his arm from the mother's shoulder and reached out for the paper. Zayne retrieved a pen from his breast pocket, uncapped it, and offered it to him. The man ignored him and kept on reading in silence. The mother leaned forward and tilted her head to get a better view.

"We can't believe our girl took her own life," she said, after lifting her gaze. "We need time to understand what happened."

"We can't just let her go." The father shook his head. "No matter what you tell us."

Zayne knew when not to insist. It was inhumane to ask relatives for permission to cut up loved ones before they even had the time to accept their death. But this was the cruel rule of the organ donation game. He had learned to balance the urgency of his need to acquire organs, against the expected reluctance of relatives to relinquish the last shred of hope for their loved ones' recovery. Better to let things simmer and come back later.

"I understand," Zayne said, but he knew he didn't. In his 36 years of life, he had never incurred a loss of that kind. "I'll leave the consent with you. You call me when you think you may be ready, or if you have any questions. But please, keep in mind that the window of opportunity may close at any time. Your daughter's condition is unpredictable. Her heart may suddenly give out. If that happens, we won't be able to save the other patient and honor your daughter's last wish."

The father rose, pulling up the mother by the hand. He dropped the consent form back on the desk top. They shuffled to the door. Before exiting, the man turned.

"I'm sorry, Doctor," he said. "I know you're doing your job, and we'll take all this into consideration, but for now we need to be with our daughter, while she's still with us."

The door closed softly. Zayne sighed. His patient would have to wait a little longer for a new heart. He bent down, retrieved the consent form, folded it, and put it back in his pocket.

On the 11th floor of the FBI Headquarters, Bloom stood still and stared at the name on the door: *Director Jack Mulville.* She pulled at her ponytail and tucked her shirt collar inside her suit jacket. Her watch showed 1:29 P.M. At exactly 1:30, after a deep breath, she knocked twice.

"Come." Mulville's voice never ceased to intimidate her.

She stepped into the office. Mulville's bulkiness protruded from behind a large desk covered with files and papers. He had always reminded her of a mountain. His clothes seemed too small to contain him, as if on the verge of ripping, like the garments of a transforming Incredible Hulk. She wanted him always to be on her side.

He sat with his back to the stunning Manhattan view. Bloom had wondered why he had placed his desk in that unfavorable position. For at least a minute, Mulville shuffled papers before lifting his icy blue eyes. He smiled. Mulville didn't smile very often, but he did at her, sometimes.

"Bloom," he said, pointing at a chair across his desk, "how's your investigation coming along?"

"I followed the leads as far as some place in India. Waiting for the perp to go at it again. Chances of getting anywhere at this point are pretty slim." Bloom dropped onto the chair's worn fabric. "Did you read my report?"

He nodded too quickly to be truthful. She lifted her head and locked her eyes on the blue slits in front of her. Had he risen too high on the ladder to know she'd closed the case two days ago?

"I need a real case," she said. "Soon. I'm ready for it. I think you know that."

Mulville stared at her. Now she could see the white surrounding the blue of his eyes.

"Have you forgotten the first time you asked me to work for the FBI?" she asked, channeling her anger and fear into boldness. "When I helped you save the Country, five years ago, while working as a lowly hospital clerk to pay for my college tuition?"

"No, I haven't forgotten the second 9/11. And you did help. But those were exceptionally chaotic times, where almost everybody who could help were nowhere to be found. This is the real world." He made a sweeping gesture with his Karate-stubby hands.

"And now I'm a trained agent who's wasting time investigating the vishing and phishing targeted at little old ladies."

Mulville's head jerked back as if hit by a shockwave. Perhaps she had gone too far. She had been mostly immune from his semi-violent reactions, so far, but the director was unpredictable in his mood swings, and there was always a first.

"Well, well," Mulville said, nodding, his lips tightening, "you're ready to screw up a real case and get fucking shot or killed, aren't you?"

The last words struck her as out of place between an FBI Director and an agent on probation. Like it or not, she was his special project, ever since that eventful time five years ago, when fate had brought her and Mulville together, forging a bond that only life or death events can cement.

"No sir," she said, directing her chin at Mulville's thick and muscular neck. "I'm ready to solve a real cyber case. That's what I'm trained for, and what I'm good at."

"Says who?"

"Me." She hoped that the heat she felt rising from her chest wouldn't cause her to blush. "I need a real case to prove it."

What kind of conversation was this? Crowding her mind were memories of Mulville counselling her about college courses, attending her graduation, and reviewing her FBI application. She was more than his special project. She sensed a particular connection between the two of them, something that made her feel warm inside and, she suspected, made grumpy old Mulville feel uncomfortable. Originating during extreme circumstances, the bond had grown. It filled the need of both a fatherless young woman and a childless, middle-aged man. Was this bond compromising her career?

Mulville looked her in the eye and tilted his head. Then his mouth stretched into a grin.

"Look what just came in." His hand reached down inside a file cabinet to his right, and his fingers walked across several file folders until they stopped. He extracted a single paper, holding it between his index and middle finger, and handed it to her.

Bloom closed her hand around the thin paper. A wave of excitement made her stomach rumble. She hoped Mulville didn't hear the noise. She steadied the paper between her shaky fingers, read the few sentences, and sighed.

"But how's this a cybercrime?" she said, keeping her tone from rising above the respectful range. "It's a homicide made to look like a suicide. Why do we even need to get involved?"

"Calm down." Mulville put out his palm. "This happened in front of NYMC."

She looked at him expectantly.

"Last year, several hospitals in New York and other major cities were victims of cybercrimes. Someone hacked into their medical records and paralyzed their systems. In order to get back control, the institutions paid hefty ransoms. The New York Medical Center was one of them. Unlike other hospitals, they managed to keep their name out of the press."

"I know about the hacking," Bloom said, straightening her back against the uncomfortable chair. "For a short time, I was shadowing one of the investigators. The suspect was a mobster, right? What was his name?"

"Santo Montepulciano." Mulville nodded. "We tried very hard, but we just couldn't pin it to him."

"So, you think this may be connected to the past breach?" Bloom lifted the hand clenching the paper.

"That's where you come in," Mulville said. "The victim has a letter giving permission for organ donation. I want you to determine if this involves someone with illegal access to patient information."

"What evidence do we have that Montepulciano was the mastermind of the original hacking?"

Mulville opened a drawer and retrieved another file. He opened it and skimmed the documents inside. "We were able to track the hacking to a

Vincent Gonnella, who we know has been doing business with the Montepulciano crime family in the past. Unfortunately, he was orchestrating the takeover from somewhere in the Bahamas and we were never able to physically locate him."

"Before this case, I never heard of Santo Montepulciano," Bloom said. "I remember reading stuff about another Montepulciano being killed a couple of years ago."

"That was Santo's brother, Vincenzo." Mulville pointed the closed file at her. "He succeeded his father as head of the business."

"The business?"

"Mostly drugs and prostitution," Mulville said. "Vincenzo died under unclear circumstances. Food poisoning maybe. Most likely someone did him in in order to take his place."

"Santo?" Bloom said, her brow rising.

"I don't think so." Mulville shook his head. "Santo Montepulciano kept a relatively low profile while his father and then his brother were in charge of the Family."

"Did the guy do any time?"

"Santo did some time a few years ago, for drug trafficking and such."

"What kind of drugs?"

"Mostly pot," Mulville said. "No proof for the rest of the crap—cocaine or speed. Had a very good lawyer. Got out in only a couple of months. Supposedly moved on to some legitimate occupation. Want to know what it is?"

"What?" Bloom grinned. "Computer stuff?"

"You got it. He owns an IT consulting company." Mulville handed Bloom the file. "What a coincidence, right? All seems legit, and not just a laundering façade. Even pays taxes."

Bloom reached out for the file and held it together with the homicide document.

"After his brother died," Mulville went on, "the hospital hacking started. It was as if Santo Montepulciano had to do something substantial to prove himself worthy of his new position as Family Boss."

"Like steering the family business toward something new," Bloom said. "Much more promising than the stuff mobsters did in prior decades."

"Exactly. A few of his competitors disappeared from circulation. One we fished out of the Hudson with cement shoes. Likely a revenge for his brother's death. None of which we could prove. Now Santo Montepulciano has a few layers of stooges ready to take the fall for him."

"Can I have a copy of this file?" Bloom said, waving the documents.

"It's all yours."

"This is great," Bloom said, as a rush of adrenaline made her hands tingle. "Thanks."

"This is a hands-on case," Mulville whispered, eyes narrower than usual. "Your hands could get very dirty. And not only your hands ... and not only dirty."

She nodded.

"I'm serious." He pointed at the file. "You may think you're ready, but you're still very green. The fact that you think you're ready shows what a rookie you are. Only reason I'm allowing this so soon is that Kirk Miner is on the case. I spoke with him and—"

"Miner? The detective who worked with you on the second 9/11?"

"One and the same."

"With all due respect, Director," she said looking at him in the eye, "I don't need a babysitter."

"Miner is on the case as a liaison with the NYPD," Mulville said. He cleared his voice. "And also his medical knowledge may be useful dealing with transplants and hospital stuff. Listen, if you don't want the case, plenty other agents will try to grab it."

"You," she said, a lightness expanding in her chest. "You had already decided to assign me this case, hadn't you?"

Mulville's slit eyes gave her a poker look. Bloom's heart responded with a short flutter.

CHAPTER 3
THE PHONE

To enter the NYMC's Intensive Care Unit, Kirk held up his ID card for the charge nurse to see.

"Mr. Miner," said the tall woman in scrubs and a buzz-cut. "The police told us to expect you. A young woman is with the patient now. This way."

He followed the nurse's swift steps to one of the rooms. A glass door slid open as she approached, stepping aside to let Kirk enter. The bed stood surrounded by monitors on one side and a hissing respirator on the other. Amy Winter lay under the covers, her bandaged head on the pillow, an endotracheal tube protruding from her mouth, and several lines and catheters tethered to her body. Looking at the number of bags hanging from the nearby pole, Kirk figured she was on several medication drips to keep her blood pressure above shock level. He checked the monitor: 100/70. Just adequate to perfuse the kidneys and other organs as a bridge to organ donation. The heart-tracing looked steady and regular, as if belonging to a normal, healthy body.

Next to Amy sat a red-haired young woman with her head bowed as if in prayer, holding Amy's hand in hers. She lifted her head toward Kirk. Her eyes were green and shiny.

"Please don't get up," Kirk said. He introduced himself. "Are you her friend?"

"Best friend." She nodded. "And roommate for the past two years."

Kirk dragged a stool from the side wall to the bedside and sat down. He unzipped his black leather jacket, took a business card from his shirt pocket, and handed it to the girl. She glanced at it, then stashed it into a small black pocketbook at the foot of the bed. For now, Kirk decided to forgo taking notes on his tablet.

"I'm very sorry about your friend," Kirk said. "What's your name?"

"Casey."

"Casey, I wonder if you can help us find out what happened."

"She didn't do it." Anger colored her voice, as if she had to defend her friend from a stranger's accusations. Her hand tapped the victim's limp hand. "I've known her since first grade. She's the most alive and positive person I've ever met. She was just accepted at NYU Med school. And she'd made a hair appointment for next week, with my hairdresser, the evening before… Why would she make a hair appointment and then blow her brains out?"

She burst into a new round of tears and loud sobs. Kirk placed a hand on the bed, next to the best friends' joined hands. Casey turned back to Amy.

"I agree with you," Kirk whispered. "We're considering every possibility. You're helping me already."

As she began to wipe away her tears, Kirk reached for a tissue from a box near the night table and handed it to her. She blew her nose and seemed to recompose herself, ready to be questioned.

"Is Amy right- or left-handed?" Kirk asked.

"Right-handed," she said after a few seconds of consideration.

"Do you know how she ended up in the hospital parking lot at four o'clock in the morning?"

"She's a regular blood donor." Casey said it with a friend's pride. "Sometimes they need her type. I heard her talking on the phone—probably the hospital. She has some universal type of blood…"

"Type O?" Kirk said. "People with type O can donate to all types. This is very useful. Casey, did you happen to hear what she said? Are you sure it was the hospital?"

"I was sleeping. The call woke me up. I couldn't hear the other end. She left, and I went back to sleep."

Kirk nodded. He looked at Casey's green blood-shot eyes.

"Did she talk to you later? Did she call you?"

She stared at him. Kirk watched her thinking. Her wide-open eyes revealed sudden distress. Then, in a brusque motion, her hand disappeared into her pocketbook and she retrieved a cellphone.

"She left me a message," she said without looking at the screen. New tears filled her eyes. "I… I haven't listened to it yet. I just couldn't. How did you know?"

"You didn't tell the police about the message?"

"I didn't know about it at the time," she said, wiping her eyes with the tissue. "At night, I keep the phone on airplane mode. The police came to the house while I was still sleeping… to tell me about Amy. I rushed here. I didn't see it until later. Then I just couldn't. Why?"

"Casey, let's listen to Amy's message together." Kirk pointed at the phone.

She stared at the back wall for a moment, pondering. She sighed. Then she nodded. Her fingers swiped and clicked. She looked up at Kirk, wide eyed. Her mouth tightened.

"Listen," Amy's voice from the phone said, "I grabbed your keys by mistake. But I'll be back on time. What? Someone is here—"

A muffled thumping interrupted the conversation, followed by silence. Kirk felt his stomach sinking. He watched Casey realize the call's awful meaning.

"My God!" She covered her face with her hands, phone still clenched. "She left me a message while—while—"

"I'm so sorry you have to go through this," Kirk whispered. "Did you talk to the police at all?"

"A little," she said. "I was too freaked out. Someone is supposed to come back today to interview me. I thought it was you."

"I need to borrow your phone." Kirk lifted his palm. "It's evidence. And yes, I'm working with the police."

Casey looked at her phone, then at Kirk. Her hand shook. "But I can't be without it."

"Just for a short time. We need to download the call. I'll make sure you get it right back. And we're going to need a statement. About this call, and everything else you told me."

After a last reluctant look, she handed over the phone. Kirk's eyes scrutinized the screen until they fixed on what he was looking for. The time of the interrupted call—4:43 a.m. Kirk's breath caught.

"Another thing you could help me with, Casey." Kirk extracted a copy of the suicide note from his pocket. Trying to hide the bloody smears as much as possible, he oriented the paper so she could see it best. "Is this Amy's signature? Can you tell?"

Casey didn't reach for the note. She recoiled. Kirk placed the paper closer, under her wet eyes. "It must be so hard for you. I'm so sorry."

"I… I'm not sure. You should ask her parents. They were here earlier. They're talking with the doctors. Should be back any time now."

Kirk couldn't wait to walk out of the hospital and, even for just a moment, take a deep breath, away from the smell of antiseptics, disease, and death. As the door finally swooshed closed behind him, he patted the bagged phone through his leather jacket. John would be pleased about his findings. To figure out who Amy was talking with at the time of her death, he wouldn't have to wait for Forensics to retrieve data from the broken phone.

His steps slowed at the sight of a man and woman coming through the main ICU entrance and approaching the victim's room. Jeans and sweatshirts, bowed heads, shiny and swollen eyes. Amy's parents, probably wearing the same clothes they wore on the plane from Ohio.

Kirk stopped, watched them enter their daughter's room, and retraced his steps. He stood outside the room and watched the roommate again crying while hugging and talking to them, likely about the missed phone call. She seemed animated, but the parents looked less affected by the news than Kirk had expected. With eyes fixed on the pale face and the bandaged head, hands clenched around flaccid hands, perhaps nothing at this time could make much difference to them.

Kirk entered the room and introduced himself by handing out another business card. "I'm so sorry about your daughter."

Glazed eyes turned to him. "Joe Winter, "the husband said, as if his name didn't matter. "My wife Martha."

"I'm working with the FBI and the police," Kirk said, shaking their limp hands in turn, "trying to figure out what happened. One thing you may be able to help me with is to determine if the note we found at the scene was signed by your daughter or not."

This got the father's attention. He nodded, his mouth bent into an inverted crescent, eyes questioning. The mother touched the victim's forehead as if checking her temperature, something she must have done so many times in past years. This time, her daughter's medical situation wasn't going to get any better with TLC. Kirk diverted his gaze and extracted the copy of the note from his jacket pocket.

"Here it is," he said, extending the paper for the parents to view. "Do you recognize her signature?"

The father took the paper and glanced at it. Muscles tightened over his cheeks. He turned to his wife, placing the note directly under her eyes.

"Absolutely not," she said with indignation. "That's not her writing."

"Are you sure?" Kirk said.

"Sure I'm sure," Martha Winter said. "She's my daughter."

"Would you have a sample…"

The woman was already at work, rummaging through her backpack. She pulled out a paperback with something sticking out from within the pages—sort of a bookmark. Her fingers closed around it and she produced a postcard. A beach scene.

"This," she said, pointing to the back of the card, "is her signature."

Kirk examined the card. The name was readily legible, very different than the scribble on the note. Of course, with the new evidence provided by the phone call, Kirk didn't expect the scribble to be the girl's signature. There had been no time for any conversation between the girl and the shooter. At first approach, he had gunned her down in cold blood.

"It's a card she sent me from Hawaii last year." The woman sobbed. "She was so happy to go."

"I need to borrow this." Kirk waved the card. "To compare. We'll return it as soon as possible."

"What does this mean?" The father's voice rose as his hand moved around to include the note. "Someone shot our daughter?"

"Mr. Winter," Kirk said, "we're investigating all possibilities."

All eyes were on Kirk now. He saw fear, anger, and accusations. How could he blame them?

"And the only thing *they* worry about," the father said, pointing his finger at the door, "is ripping out her heart."

"What do you mean, Mr. Winter?" Kirk suspected he knew, but wanted to give the man the chance to vent.

"*They* want us to give permission to take her heart and give it to somebody else."

Kirk nodded. He could see Joe Winter's point of view.

"After our Amy donated her blood so many times to help sick people, that doctor isn't even curious to find out who would want to kill her. Our Amy wanted to become a doctor herself, so she could help others. The first doctor in our family. Our only baby." The furrow in the middle of Joe's forehead deepened, and his mouth tightened in what seemed to be an expression of anger. But soon his face crumpled and he lost the battle with his emotions. His wife patted and caressed his shuddering back while he hid his pain with the palms of his hands.

Failing to come up with any comforting words, Kirk watched them in respectful silence until a buzzing from his belt made him reach for his phone. As he recognized her as the initiator of the incoming call, he smiled at the picture of Aurora. He glanced at the Winters couple, still in the process of comforting each other, and sent an automatic replay to Aurora, promising a call back later.

After several minutes and some more assurance that he would do what he could to find out the truth, Kirk told Amy's parents to call him if there was anything he could do to help. He left the room, walked out of the ICU, stopped in the corridor leading to the hospital exit, and dialed Aurora.

"Hi." Her voice never failed to stir something pleasant in him. "When are you coming home?"

"I'm still working." He checked the time—3:14 p.m.. Where had the day gone? "Wrapping up now. Should be home in a half hour."

"We've got the meeting at the college campus. I'm here already."

Kirk's stomach collapsed in a knot while his hands tingled all the way to his fingertips. *The meeting!*

"You left early today," she said with the controlled calm Kirk knew she used to hide her frustration. "I couldn't remind you. The training for parents of chemically-dependent children. It's about to start. Right now."

"Jesus," Kirk said. He sighed. "I'll drive right over. I just got this case to work with the FBI. I'm basically in charge of the police investigation."

"Great!" Her voice sounded an octave higher. "I thought that the purpose of being a consultant was to have more time for your family."

"I'm trying."

"It's not working," she said. "It's just like when you were with the police. Nothing else matters."

"Listen, honey," Kirk said as softly as he could manage, "we both know the meeting is a waste of time. Carrying a bottle of vodka while walking to a party doesn't make Peter an alcoholic. It makes him naïve. His so-called older friends used him."

"He's fifteen!" she shouted. "Walking around a college campus carrying booze can get him expelled, no matter how smart he is."

"I know."

"The deal is we *both* have to attend. The entire meeting. If you're not here, it doesn't count. That *is* the deal. And I gave up half of my day-shift for this. I swapped it for night-time, thank you very much."

Damn! He had forgotten. The meeting to prevent Peter's expulsion from college. What kind of father would do that?

"I'm coming over. Right now."

Kirk hung up and rushed toward the hospital exit. While jogging to his car, he called John.

"Spencer."

Kirk took a few deep breaths, unlocked the SUV door, pressed the phone between shoulder and lower jaw in order to fasten his seat belt, and related the recent findings.

"If it wasn't suicide," John said, "the next step is to find out who could benefit from her organs."

"Yes," Kirk said. "Doctors are already pressuring the parents to donate their daughter's organs, in particular her heart. I'll find out who they need it for."

Kirk hung up, clenched the steering wheel, started the car, and tried to focus on driving. As he crossed the Brooklyn Bridge, the image of Amy Winter flashed in his mind. Luckily for him, Kirk had to worry about Peter, a fifteen-year-old college freshman genius who had violated campus rules. The Winters had to worry about their only daughter, a pre-med student with a dead brain.

For the rest of the trip, Kirk mourned not only the destruction of Amy's young life, but also the possible waste of her healthy organs. Because of all the legal implications and obstacles, Amy's heart, kidneys, and pancreas may be left to rot with the rest of her beautiful body instead of infusing new life into as many as three dying patients.

CHAPTER 4
THE CHAIN

Kirk checked the time as he inhaled the smell of disinfectant in the corridor leading to the ICU. The day before, after nearly missing the meeting on his "chemically dependent child," he called and asked to speak with Dr. Zayne Wilder, the cardiothoracic surgeon requesting Amy's heart for transplant.

The best way to do that, the charge nurse had suggested, was to catch him at the end of ICU rounds. At 8:05 a.m., Kirk figured he had a good chance. He walked by the room where Amy rested peacefully, all her tracing and colorful lines fluttering and changing shapes, testifying to the fact she was still alive, albeit in a vegetative condition. "A living cadaver"—that was what an article Kirk had recently read called this kind of brain-dead patient. Applying that description to the beautiful young woman made him cringe.

He stopped outside a room crowded by four white-clad doctors and two nurses. As he glanced through the glass wall, Kirk recognized the charge nurse with the buzz haircut and managed to get her attention by waving his hand. Pointing to himself and then the group of doctors, he reminded her of his request. The charge nurse fingered a tall man with curly black hair talking to the rest of the team huddled around him. Kirk assumed the acting leader to be Dr. Zayne Wilder.

At the center of the room, a pale young woman propped up by pillows in the hospital bed listened to Dr. Wilder, presumably explaining some forthcoming heart surgery. Under the thin hospital gown, her chest moved with frequent short breaths, sucking in the oxygen flowing into her nostrils through plastic prongs and tubing. Her face seemed relaxed, her mouth shaped into a tenuous smile. She seemed happy about something. Kirk stepped back and waited.

"Mr. Miner." The charge nurse had exited the room ahead of the group and approached. "Dr. Wilder has a moment now and can see you in his office. This way, please."

Kirk followed her to a cluttered, windowless room dominated by a wooden desk, an office chair, and two cushioned seats. Kirk sat down on one of the guest chairs and surveyed most of the diplomas hanging on the wall in front of him. Since medical school, Dr. Wilder had spent about ten years preparing for his present job. Kirk calculated his age to be somewhere in the mid-thirties or up. The skill needed to do heart transplants required long training and dedication.

"Mr. Miner." Dr. Wilder entered offering him his hand. "How can I help you?"

After a strong hand shake, the doctor sat on his chair and placed both palms down on the desk, as if he could lift himself up and leave at any time. Kirk retrieved his tablet for notes and offered the doctor one of his cards.

"Thanks for seeing me," Kirk said. "I'm helping the FBI investigate the shooting of Amy Winter."

"You mean the attempted suicide?" The doctor's thick brows rose. "I heard about the investigation. I'm not sure why—"

Kirk straightened his back against the chair. "We have reason to believe it might not have been a suicide."

"Someone tried to kill her?" Dr. Wilder eyes widened.

"We're looking at all the possibilities," Kirk said. "In the interest of time, I'll be brief. Mr. and Mrs. Winter, Amy's parents, told me you approached them about the heart donation."

The doctor's head moved into a barely perceptible nod.

"Can you tell me anything about the recipient?"

With gray-blue eyes, Dr. Wilder stared at him under furrowed brows. His hand went to lift a light-blue surgical cap off his tall forehead. Kirk knew what was coming—almighty privacy, the sacred doctor-patient relationship, and half a dozen agencies, all interfering with Kirk's ability to investigate the person who could benefit from getting Amy's heart.

"Mr. Miner," the doctor started, his palms rising from the desk and fanning out to convey helplessness, "I can't discuss—"

"I understand." Kirk lifted his own hands in a conceding gesture. "Can you at least tell me about how the heart came to be allocated? Take me through the process. And please, call me Kirk."

A personal touch sometimes broke the ice. Better leave the threat of a search warrants for last. Zayne Wilder seemed more relaxed and at ease with the last question.

"What I can tell you, Kirk," the doctor said, "is that my patient is a young woman who developed a cardiomyopathy—that is, a failing heart after giving birth. She's at the end of the line. She needs to get a heart or a LVAD, a left ventricular assist device. That's a mechanical pump that takes over part of the heart's function—as soon as possible. She's dying."

"How do you choose the patients for transplant?" Kirk asked.

He watched the doctor pushing against the desk and leaning back against his ergonomic chair. He seemed ready to run. Kirk needed to clarify the question.

"I mean," Kirk said, "is there a waiting list, a computerized search for the best match, some other process?"

"Yes." Dr. Wilder let his chair spring back and he sat forward again. "We have a registry, like a list, shared nationwide. We match recipients and donors according to size, blood type, and tissue compatibility."

Kirk noticed something flickering in the surgeon's eyes. There was more. Perhaps too much for the doctor to explain. But Kirk knew something about medicine. And he needed to know what the doctor was withholding.

"Anything else relevant," he pushed on, "about this particular patient?"

"Well," Dr. Wilder said, looking side to side, as if he needed some privacy to say more. "My patient is part of the chain."

"The chain?" Kirk felt his heart accelerate from the excitement of hitting a promising topic. "You mean a chain donation? I know they do something like that for kidneys."

Dr. Wilder lifted his brows. He seemed surprised about the extent of Kirk's medical knowledge. Perhaps he would be more generous with his time.

"Yes," he said. "For decades, we've had chain donations for kidneys.

What do you know about it, Kirk?"

"A patient in need, on their own, may have found a relative willing to donate a kidney, but the kidney is not compatible with that particular patient. The kidney of the would-be donor, however, may be compatible with some other patient."

"Exactly. We have hundreds of patients swapping kidneys back and forth—in effect, multiple donor-recipient pairs resulting in hundreds of great matches and exchanges. These are called domino-paired donor exchanges. We use computer algorithms to maximize the efficiency of these chains."

"But how can you apply this method to hearts?" Kirk said. "You can't just donate your heart the way you can donate a kidney."

"Of course not." Dr. Wilder smiled. "Anyway, two years ago, we started a special program—a chain donation of hearts ... with some modifications, of course. Each patient signs up together with a potential donor, even if that person's heart isn't compatible with the patient he signs up with. When a donor dies, the patients in the chain get priority, as long as we have a compatible match."

"But don't you have to be in pretty desperate shape to get a heart?"

"Patients in the chain get priority for hearts from donors in the chain," the doctor said, "even if they aren't as ill as other patients outside the chain. I mean, everyone who signs up is bad enough to need a heart, but the urgency may be different. Also, the chain is nationwide."

"Nationwide?" Kirk said. "As far as I know, a heart lasts about four to six hours outside a body. How can you get a heart from across country in time?"

"We use a special heart box." The doctor grinned. "It's a box with a pump that recycles blood and nutrients into the beating heart. Outside the body."

"The heart can beat outside the body, in a box?" Kirk's eyes widened. "How long can the heart last this way?"

"If you replace the nutrients and blood," the doctor said, "many hours. We can ship a heart across the country, and it arrives nice and warm. Because of the need to match blood and tissue type, the probability of a complete match, including HLA genes, between a random donor's heart and a recipient is less than 1.5 percent. However, in a pool of one thousand subjects, the chance of finding compatible donor–recipient pairs increases to 60 percent. And now we have more than 500 people in our chain database."

"About the database," Kirk said. "Who has access to it?"

Dr. Wilder pushed a strand of hair off his forehead and into his cap. He picked up a paper clip from his desk and rolled it around his long fingers. He shook his head.

"No one has access to the entire database," he said. "Patients and donors get matched by computer algorithms. Doctors get notified. I only have access to the data of my patients and their possible donors as they become available. Patients and donors are identified not by name but by the letters P or D followed by a number."

"Could anyone have hacked the system?"

The paper clip fell to the desktop. The doctor stared at the back wall for a moment. He bit his lower lip. Dr Wilder new about the hospital's hacking.

"As a matter of fact," he whispered, staring at Kirk as if swearing him into confidence, "the hospital's general database was hacked last year. We managed to keep it confidential, but the hospital paid a ransom. The FBI suspected some local mobster, but no arrest was made."

To keep up with the information the surgeon was providing, Kirk's fingers were flying across the tablet's keyboard. He felt like a doctor himself—a doctor who had just discovered the possible cause of a patient's symptoms. He had to continue probing.

"Who did you say they suspected? And why?"

The surgeon's face seemed to turn a shade whiter. Kirk wondered if it was the effect of the halogen light. Or perhaps it was fear. La Mano Nera, the black hand, a type of Italian Mafia extortion racket, flashed into Kirk's mind. In the early 1900s, they went around extorting protection fees from local businesses. If a cyber-equivalent of the Mano Nera had hacked the hospital database, the doctor had the right to be scared.

"I…" the doctor said. "I don't remember the name. Perhaps it's better you get this information straight from the FBI. Or the police."

"Fair enough," Kirk said. "Do you think it's possible someone shot Amy

Winter because of the chain?"

Dr. Wilder's color returned. He shook his head. His mouth formed a downturned crescent.

"No," he said. "No chance. Amy Winter isn't part of the chain."

"But then why would your patient get her heart?"

"My patient is so ill that she would get any compatible heart available. She's at the top of the list independent of the chain."

"I see," Kirk said.

"Despite her note, we're not even sure if Amy Winter is a donor," Wilder said.

"I know. It seems that the signature is a fake. The mother didn't recognize Amy's signature."

"To make a long story short," Wilder said, "if the parents don't agree to the donation, my patient will have to get some other form of treatment. The donor she signed up with—her father- in-law, is already dead, but his heart went to another patient, according to compatibility."

"P1's donor (D1) is DEAD," Kirk typed on his tablet. The doctor stood up announcing the end of the meeting. He stepped toward the door. Kirk had one last request.

"Could you arrange for me to meet your patient's family?" he asked. Then he added, "Without a warrant?"

"May I ask you why would you want that?" The doctor stopped short of the door.

"To check for any connection with Amy Winter's shooting," Kirk said. "Routine question for this particular case."

Dr. Wilder extracted a phone, lifted a finger in Kirk's direction, and stepped out into the corridor. Kirk heard him struggling with Spanish, then switching to English. After a brief conversation, the Doctor came back. P1's family had accepted Kirk's request to meet later that afternoon.

Kirk thanked the doctor and left the hospital. He had a few hours to kill before meeting Margarita Herrera's husband, who came home from his construction job at around 4 pm. The sky, full of deep gray clouds, looked ominous. As he walked to his car, an icy wind made him bundle up, which reminded him it was time to upgrade from the leather jacket to the down jacket. He dialed Aurora.

"Hey," she said. "What's up?"

"About lunch?" Kirk said. "I got time to spare. I can meet you at the Chinese place across from your hospital. When can you take lunch? "

"Around 2. Can you wait?"

"For you, always."

He listened to the silence, then heard a giggle.

"Okay. See you then," she said.

By the time he got to the SUV, his fingertips and his nose felt numb. He entered the car, started the engine, turned the heat up to max, drove to the Brooklyn Medical Center, and parked in the hospital lot. To get in, he used a card kept from his time moonlighting as a security guard to supplement his scanty income from his PI practice.

He walked to Hong Fat, his and Aurora's favorite Chinese restaurant. The smell of soy sauce welcomed him as the door jingled. The line for orders ran across the entire entrance. Lunch-goers from the hospital were dressed in all different-colored scrubs. He couldn't wait to see his favorite—Aurora's purple ones. He poured himself hot tea from the counter, found a table with a view of the hospital entrance, and watched for Aurora to come out to meet him. After a few minutes, his phone buzzed—an unknown number with an out-of-state area code. He hated robo-calls, but he couldn't risk missing somebody important one. He answered.

"Mr. Miner?" a male voice said.

"Speaking."

"Joe Winter." The tone made the words sound like a shout. "You said I could call you if I needed help."

"What's happening?"

"They're forcing us to sign the consent for our daughter's heart. That's what happening."

"What are you talking about?' Kirk said. "Who's forcing you? How?"

"I don't know." He sounded more subdued. "I got a call."

"Who called you?"

"I don't know. A man. He said we needed to sign the paper. Otherwise… something was going to happen. To Martha. What's going on? I'm going to sue that doctor, the hospital, everybody."

"Mr. Winter," Kirk said, "don't sign anything. That call is not from the doctor or the hospital. To make sure nothing happens to you or your wife, I'll send the police. Where are you now?"

Kirk lifted his eyes up. Aurora was standing there, next to the table, in her purple scrubs with a smile on her face. Kirk touched her cheek. He pulled out a pen from his shirt pocket and scribbled Winter's location on a napkin.

"Hold on a moment," he said, muting the call.

"Why don't you order?" Kirk said, pointing at the line. "Just get me a chicken chow mein. And the tea. I'll be done in a moment."

Aurora nodded and went to the end of the line. Kirk unmuted the phone.

"Sorry," he said.

"Listen," Joe Winter said, "With my girl like that, I don't give a damn if I live or die. But Martha? They're threatening my Martha. And how did they even know my number?"

"Mr. Winter," Kirk said, "don't erase the call. We need the number, so the police can try to find who called you. I'm going to go now, so I can call the police for you."

Kirk ended the call and dialed John. John agreed to send someone to investigate the development. After leaving a message for Dr. Wilder, Kirk joined Aurora. Someone wanted Amy Winter's heart to go to a certain patient. Very badly.

At a quarter to four, Kirk parked his car in a metered slot and looked in the direction of the Harlem River public housing complex in Spanish Harlem. The four- and five-story apartment buildings huddled together as if supporting and comforting each other. Each of different color and shape, all with cracked and smog-discolored paint, barred windows, and some with shattered glass. Multicolored graffiti covered the street-level walls. A faint smell of garbage lingered in the air despite a small joint advertising pizza slices for two bucks.

As locking it, Kirk wondered about the chances he would find his car undamaged after his interview. He looked around the deserted street. The tired barking of a dog resonated in the distance. Kirk grabbed his usual black leather jacket and, looking for street numbers, walked toward the buildings.

He entered a dark, grimy lobby reeking of fried grease and found the apartment he was looking for on the ground floor. The doorbell didn't work. Kirk knocked on a thin wooden door he could easily kick down on his first try. Moments later, he heard shuffling steps, followed by an inquiry in Spanish. Kirk announced his name and showed his ID, unsure if anybody was looking through the opaque peephole. He heard locks clicking, followed by the screeching sound of the door opening, then the face of a Hispanic woman with black hair in a bun. She nodded, unsmiling, at his credential and stepped aside, though obviously reluctant to let Kirk in.

As he crossed the threshold, Kirk noticed that the woman was holding an infant girl, busy sucking milk from a bottle. The infant looked well-kept, clean, and happy. The woman wore a loose and discolored housedress covered by a stained apron. She led Kirk into a room serving as dining-room, living-room, and kitchen.

The room was spotless. In a corner, a couch opened into a bed neatly covered by a cheerful blanket. The comforting smell of home-made soup came from a bubbling pot on the range. She pointed at one of the four chairs surrounding a square wooden table and Kirk sat down. The woman sat on a chair across from him and continued to feed the baby. When she got to the burping part, she looked up at Kirk.

"She's beautiful," Kirk said, smiling. "How old is she?"

"Six months?" she said, questioning her English. "Seis."

Kirk nodded and smiled again.

"Young mister should be here soon." Her English was broken, and she spoke with a heavy Spanish accent. "Working. Margarita, the mom, is sick. Hospital."

"Who are you?" Kirk asked. "A friend? A relative?"

"Friend," she said. Her face looked aged more by adversity than time. Her dark eyes looked watery, as if they hadn't been dry in a long time. "I was friend of Carlos, the old mister. He died."

Margarita Herrera's father-in-law, the one who had signed up for the chain with Wilder's patient, had died. Kirk retrieved his notes and wrote down the man's name, confirming the spelling with the woman. Tears welled in her tired eyes. She got up and placed the sleeping baby on the couch, covering her with the blanket, then returned to her chair.

"What happened to Carlos?" Kirk asked.

Screeching announced the reopening of the door. A young, muscular Hispanic man wearing dusty working clothes stepped in and looked at Kirk with puzzlement. The woman spoke to him in Spanish. He nodded.

"Ramon Herrera," he said, offering Kirk his hand. "I see you met Dolores."

Kirk felt relief to hear Ramon's fine English. The man checked on the baby and, confirming her to be sound asleep, sat down next to Kirk.

"Dolores was my father's girlfriend."

The woman nodded.

"Could you tell me how your father died?" Kirk asked.

Ramon looked straight at him. His deep eyes carried bitterness. Kirk, suddenly feeling warm, removed his jacket.

"He was depressed." Ramon spoke with a firm voice. "Got divorced, lost his job, too old to find anything. He had only us, me, my wife, and the new granddaughter. And Dolores. But then my wife got so sick. Heart problem. I was so unhappy… He couldn't take it no more."

"And then?" Kirk said, anticipating another piece of the puzzle falling into place.

"He started to act strange." Ramon pointed to the woman. "He left her. Said he had no time for girlfriends. Not sure what he meant. How could he be so busy, with nothing to do all day? Before we realized how depressed he was, he went and killed himself."

Ramon's voice broke into a quick sob. Kirk nodded. He felt for the son, but he needed to know more about the father.

"I'm very sorry," Kirk said. "But how exactly did he die?"

Ramon closed his eyes. Kirk waited. Ramon looked at him and sighed.

"He shot himself in the head," Ramon whispered. "With his rifle."

"I'm so sorry," Kirk said.

Ramon wiped tears from his eyes. Kirk nodded. He glanced at Dolores, who sat with her head bowed.

"Where was he?" Kirk said. "At home?"

"No. He did it in Boston." Ramon shook his head. "He took the train and went to Boston to die. I'll never know why he did it there. I was just too worried about Margarita. I should have seen it coming."

Tears were streaming down Ramon's cheeks now. Dolores placed a hand on his back.

"It's not your fault he died," Kirk said in a soothing tone. "That's why I'm investigating this. To make sure nobody *made* him do it. He was a heart-donor, right?"

"That's another thing." Ramon opened his palms. "I had no idea he'd signed up like that, with my wife. If I knew he wanted to kill himself..."

"Okay." Dolores whispered. "No mas."

"I'm so sorry," Kirk said, "but it's very important. Did your dad sign up for the special transplant program called chain, together with your wife?"

"I didn't know nothing about it," Ramon said, shaking his hand as if defending himself. "After he died, they told me he had donated his heart. But it was no good for my wife."

"What happened to his heart?"

"How would I know?" Ramon said. "I only know they took it and gave it to someone else. He couldn't even give it to my wife. What kind of fucking deal is that? You'll have to ask the stupid doctors about that."

Ramon's hands were shaking. His voice had risen an octave. The baby started to cry. Dolores went to fetch her.

"Are you sure," Kirk said, his heartbeat accelerating in his chest, "that nobody offered your father any compensation?"

"What?"

"I mean… money. You know, to give up his heart to someone."

Ramon's head tilted back. He looked down at Kirk, his mouth tightening into a line. Kirk stiffened and leaned back on his chair.

"Where's the fucking money?" Ramon said, making a sweeping gesture with his hand. "We don't have a pot to piss in. Go ahead, search the house. It won't take long. But hurry and leave, before I bash your teeth in."

Kirk apologized, stood up, thanked Ramon and Dolores, and left without any handshaking. He rushed across the street. His car looked intact. As Kirk drove off, one question demanded an answer in his mind: Where in Boston had Carlos Herrera placed a rifle to his head and pulled the trigger?

Kirk poured himself a cup of coffee. His turn to make breakfast today. Aurora was working the day shift at the Brooklyn Medical Center and had left earlier, by subway. He eyed the hot cakes piled on a plate. Good opportunity for a father-son talk. Peter ran out of his room, hopped downstairs, stuffed a pancake into his mouth, and rushed toward the door, dragging along his overstuffed backpack.

"Where you going?" Kirk said. "I can take you."

"I'm taking the subway with my friend," Peter said without turning. "Alan."

The William Tell Overture filled Kirk's ears. John's ring tone. Kirk put the coffee mug down.

"Okay." He waived at Peter. "See you later."

Kirk touched the screen. "Hi. What'd you find?"

"I found something very interesting," John said. "I think you're on the right track."

"About Herrera's death?"

"Yes," John said. "It happened about two months ago. Definitely suicide. GSW to the temple. In this case, the note was his. No doubt about it. Hand written in Spanish, full of details about being depressed. Authentic signature."

"So?" Kirk sighed, his budding excitement deflated. "What's interesting about it?"

"Patience," John said. "You asked me where the man shot himself. Now here's the interesting part."

Kirk reached for his cup and took another sip. John waited. Kirk knew he was grinning.

"I'm already on pins and needles, and I need to meet Dr. Wilder and the cybercrime FBI agent at lunch time," Kirk said. "Do you think you can give me the info by then?"

"Mulville's not coming?" John said. "I talked to him, Captain to Director. He said he'd brief you. But I guess it'll be just you and his newbie cyber-crime expert."

"Mulville already talked to me," Kirk said. "Don't change the fucking subject, please. Right now, I have no time for shooting the breeze. Where was D1? I mean Carlos Herrera when he shot himself?"

"Now it's Donor1 and Patient1?" John said. "Okay. Mr. Herrera shot himself at 55 Fruit St. in Boston, Massachusetts."

"Should I drop my freaking jaw?" Kirk took a calming breath. "Please, get a life. I can't be your only entertainment. What's so interesting about that address?"

"That," John said, "is the address of Massachusetts General Hospital. The man shot himself in front of Mass General. How's that for a place to commit suicide, if you want to donate your heart?"

CHAPTER 5
P1 AND D1

Kirk Miner stood in the NYMC lobby and looked outside, through the revolving glass door. After observing for some time the quivering mass of business people and workers shuttling to and from lunch, he noticed a petite woman emerging from the pack and hurrying toward the hospital entrance. She wore a white shirt under a tailored black suit. A golden round pin on the right lapel caught the morning's rays. The straight posture, the lifted chin, and the purposeful, steady stride were more than ably managed despite her high heels and bulky briefcase. From the auburn ponytail swinging side to side with each hurried step, he recognized her. The ponytail was the only thing left of the Charlotte Bloom Kirk had met five years earlier. The college girl he knew, the one hopping around in sneakers while working as a hospital clerk, had blossomed into the confident-looking FBI cyber special-agent meeting him today.

"Hello," she said, stepping from the revolving door, putting out her free hand, and smiling. "Kirk Miner, right?"

"Just Kirk." He inhaled a faint scent of perfume. "We met once, years ago, after … the attack."

She nodded.

"Dr. Wilder is expecting us," he said, walking toward the elevators. She moved to his side, heels clicking on the shiny linoleum. Kirk thought about the contents of her big briefcase. Probably a fancy computer, able to hack into all kinds of systems. Holding the elevator door open, he made a sweeping gesture of invitation and stepped in after her. "The goal today is to get access to the patients' database, so we can investigate the relationship of the victim to the possible recipient, if any. I assume you know the situation."

"Director Mulville briefed me." She tapped her black case.

"Did he tell you about the threat to Amy Winter's father?"

Bloom nodded.

"As expected, the phone number led nowhere—likely a throwaway," Kirk said. "But this adds to the theory that the shooting was planned to procure a heart."

"Sure," Bloom said. "As for the access to the chain database, good luck with that."

She was right and Kirk knew it. He was up against HIPAA, the Health Insurance Portability and Accountability Act, legislation protecting data privacy and security for all medical information.

"I know," Kirk said. "To maintain, privacy HIPAA would gladly place paper bags over the heads of all patients sitting in doctors' waiting rooms."

Bloom chuckled.

"I heard from my neurologist that even doctors have to waste time asking for their patients' hospital room numbers, because all the lists of names have been eliminated from the screens," Kirk said. "Here we are."

He stepped out of the elevator and walked to Dr. Wilder's office. Before he knocked at the door, Kirk turned to Bloom and whispered: "Captain Spencer made it clear. No chance for getting a search warrant yet, since we have no suspect and lack sufficient probable cause. We'll have to work it out somehow. You and I."

The door swung open and Zayne Wilder appeared. The doctor's mouth tensed.

"Kirk," he said, shaking his head. "Sorry, but something has come up and I have very limited time today."

"This is FBI special agent Charlotte Bloom." Kirk pointed at Bloom, standing at his side. "She's our FBI cyber expert."

The doctor's head pivoted toward Bloom and his chin moved up and down. He took her offered hand. His eyes widened for an instant as he carefully examined her lapel pin, her badge, and her face as if confirming her ID. His mouth relaxed into a smile. Perhaps there was a chance.

The doctor stepped aside and his hand went into a sweep, pointing at the two chairs in front of his desk. Kirk and Bloom sat, while the doctor went around to his ergonomic chair.

"Kirk," Wilder said, "thanks for the heads-up about that strange call Mr. Winters got. I can't believe this is happening. We already had enough problems getting their consent. Now they think the hospital is doing this. What did you find out?"

"Unfortunately nothing yet about the call," Kirk said. "But it adds to the suspicions."

"What suspicions?" Wilder said. His gaze turned to Bloom. She seemed oblivious to the doctor's attention, busily extracting a bulky computer from her briefcase and bringing it back to life after positioning it on her lap.

"What prompted this meeting," Kirk started, "besides that call to Mr. Winters, was something I learned about Carlos Herrera, the father-in-law of your patient Margarita Herrera."

"He's dead," the doctor said. "I told you at our first meeting."

"Yes." Kirk nodded. "What's interesting is how he died. He shot himself right in his temple."

Wilder nodded but remained silent, awaiting Kirk's point.

"He was a simple man," Kirk went on, "according to his son, whom I met. But he seemed to know exactly where to shoot himself—specifically how to avoid the medulla oblongata—so his heart would keep on beating despite the death of his brain. Most important, he did right in front of Mass General's emergency room. So doctors could get to him immediately and harvest his organs, including his heart, for donation, in accordance with his express wishes, which appeared in a note complete with his authentic, hand written signature."

"So?" Wilder's voice sounded edgier now.

"You don't find that a little too convenient?" Bloom said, lifting her eyes from the computer screen. "I mean, the daughter-in-law desperately needs a heart and the donor who signed up on your chain with her kills himself. Not too coincidental?"

"Not at all." The doctor's voice sounded softer. "He wasn't a match for his daughter-in-law. Just because he's dead doesn't mean she's guaranteed a donation. For signing on to the chain, Margarita Herrera merely gets priority matching to the chain's donors. Now, chain or no chain, she's sick enough to qualify for the first acceptable match available. In order to get a heart, she didn't need her father-in-law to die."

"Could someone have arranged Amy Winter's murder on behalf of your patient?" Bloom asked. "You know, in exchange for her father-in-law's heart donation?"

The doctor flinched. Bloom demonstrated good questioning skills. Kirk decided to let her go as far as she could.

"I find it hard to believe," the doctor said.

"I reviewed the FBI investigation of last year's hacking of your hospital's medical records, allegedly pulled off by the known mobster Santo Montepulciano," Bloom said. "I wonder if we can establish any relationship between him and Margarita Herrera, or her father-in-law for that matter, or the patient who got Carlos Herrera's heart."

Wilder's eye widened. Bloom busied herself with the keyboard.

"Here is Santo Montepulciano," she said, turning her computer so both Kirk and the doctor could see the photo—a muscular man in his late fifties with slicked-back hair, a receding hairline, and a well-groomed mustache. A subtle mocking smile parted the full lips and suggested defiance. He reminded Kirk of some famous actor impersonating a mobster beating poor victims to death to the rhapsodic sounds of famous operas covering up their screams.

"No children," she said. "Never married. An older sibling, now dead."

"My patient is a Cuban immigrant," Wilder said with an apologetic tone. "How can she be related to an Italian-American mobster?"

"You never know," she said, lifting her brows without wrinkling her forehead. "Perhaps some illegitimate relationship. Or maybe a payment was made to facilitate the donation. Nothing to do with a familial relationship."

"No," the doctor said. "Nothing like that. The proof is that my patient now refuses to receive a heart transplant, even if a donor may be available."

"She does?" Kirk saw his theory spiraling downward, as if sucked into a black hole. "But why? You said she's dying."

"She took herself off the list." Wilder's hands spread and dropped in a

46

sign of utter frustration. "I have no rational explanation. She wants an LVAD—a left ventricular assist device—instead. I'm having a hard time convincing her that such a decision is insane. I could understand if she was older. But at her age, she should go for a transplant as soon as possible."

Kirk straightened up in his chair. A dying woman refusing a life-saving organ. This sounded more and more like an offer she couldn't refuse.

"Who's the next in line?" Bloom said, her fingers hovered over her keyboard. "I mean, who would get the available heart if your patient refuses?"

Bloom had stolen Kirk's next question. Great job. Dr. Wilder didn't make any motion to look at the famous chain database on his computer screen.

"Nobody, for now." The doctor shook his head. "I mean, I don't know. Since the authenticity of Amy Winter's note is now in dispute, we don't have consent to harvest the heart yet. We can't match her until we're sure the parents are okay with the donation. If and when we have consent, and only then, will the computer tell us who's next in line,."

The doctor gave Bloom a quick sympathetic smile.

"Could you at least look at your database?" she insisted. "Is another patient in the chain a match for Amy Winter's heart? When you first searched for a matching recipient, you must have seen all the possible patient names."

"Well," Wilder said with a sigh. His eyes darted side to side. "When my patient started to express doubts about wanting the surgery, I kind of looked. And yes the computer showed another possible recipient in the chain. But instead of a number, I only got a series of hashtags. It was the strangest thing. It's never happened to me before. And no name. And I can't go back and manipulate the system again."

"Who got Carlos Herrera's heart?" Kirk asked. "Could the recipient of *his* heart be related to Montepulciano?"

"I doubt it," the doctor said after turning to his computer and scrolling through names on the screen. "His heart went to a patient in the chain. A 50-year-old man with coronary artery disease, a business executive from Washington DC. That's all I can tell you. And only because this man got a heart from a donor who signed up with one of my patients."

Kirk wrote in his tablet "D1(Carlos Herrera) to P2. Not much to go on without knowing the name. Thanks to HIPAA." The silence in the room was broken only by the soft keyboard tapping of Bloom's fingers. Dr. Wilder stood up.

"Back to my patients," he said.

"Would it be possible for us to talk to Margarita Herrera for a moment?" Kirk said.

"Why? She has no breaths to spare." Wilder's tone carried defiance.

"I'd like to make sure she's freely choosing to get an assist device instead of a transplant. I don't see why she would want to plug herself into an electrical socket like a vacuum cleaner and live with the high risk of clots, strokes, and bleeding." Kirk spoke in a soft but grave tone. "I'd like to rule out the possibility that someone coerced or seduced her decision."

Kirk paced in front of the ICU, his chin dropping to his chest, to avoid looking at Margarita Herrera. Moments earlier, when glancing up at her, he had recoiled in sadness. After just a few days, her complexion looked grayer, her breathing more labored, her lips more purple. In the journey from life to death, she looked much closer to the latter. And now the doctor sat inside the room at her bedside, asking for the interview on his behalf. Kirk doubted she would be up for it. But Wilder turned, a sad smile on his face, and waved in both Kirk and Bloom.

They entered the room, heads bowed to the gravely ill woman. The doctor made the introductions. The lifting of her lids was the only movement Kirk noticed, her only sign of life and alertness.

"Thanks for seeing us, Mrs. Herrera," Bloom said. "It's very important."

Her lids closed in acknowledgment. Kirk pulled a chair next to the bed, opposite the doctor. Bloom remained standing.

"We understand you have decided against having a heart transplant, even if a heart may be available now," Kirk said. He waited for the slightest nod. "Did anybody talk to you, trying to convince you not to have the surgery? To give up the new heart?"

He stopped and waited for a sign of understanding. The patient's eyes remained closed. Her chest struggled to expand under her hospital gown. The heartbeat on the monitor accelerated with erratic beats. A gurgling sound came from her throat. Kirk feared she would go into cardiac arrest. Wilder stared at him, shaking his head in slow motion.

"We can come back later," Kirk said as he rose. "Sorry to bother you."

A thin and feeble hand rose from the bed. The patient opened her eyes. They were large, brown eyes. Kirk imagined the passion those eyes must have conveyed in an earlier time. Now he saw only emptiness.

"No," she said, her voice unexpectedly clear and firm. "Nobody talked to me. I'm scared of surgery—all the problems, all the medicines." She waved her hand to indicate everything a heart transplant would entail.

Kirk considered himself a decent judge of truth-telling, but the grave illness in this case acted as a barrier. He couldn't tell. The woman looked resigned. Perhaps when compared to the present suffering, death could appear desirable to her, better than struggling for every bit of air to enter her waterlogged lungs. But then, why refuse the lifeline of a new heart?

The swoosh of a door interrupted his analysis. A nurse rushed in and approached the doctor.

"Code blue," she whispered. "You better come."

"I gotta go," the doctor said, springing from the chair. "We'll have to finish this later. Sorry."

He signaled Kirk and Bloom out of the room, and followed the nurse, running to the code blue site. The patient showed no reaction. Her lids dropped to insulate her again from the outside world. Kirk and Bloom thanked her and walked back to the elevator.

Zayne Wilder approached the room of the code blue. He saw an intubated woman surrounded by scrub-clad hospital personnel working to revive her. Her body jerked at every crunch of her breast bone. The EKG tracing showed only the large spikes of the resuscitation efforts, spaced over an unwrinkled string of nothingness, like mountains sticking up from a deadly desert.

"Sudden cardiac arrest," the ER doctor running the code said, looking up at Zayne. "Flatline."

Calls for epinephrine, calcium, and defibrillation filled the room. Something was very wrong. Not just for the poor human being in front of Zayne. Something was wrong inside his own head. His body wasn't reacting according to the circumstances. During his years as a surgeon, he had witnessed many cardiac arrests and other deadly emergencies. A detached calm would shield the fear and the anxiety like a lid on a boiling pot, allowing him to make dispassionate decisions and tend to his highly technical and delicate work.

This time, Zayne could feel his heart pounding against his ribcage. His face and neck heated up in a flash. He looked around to see if anyone was detecting anything unusual on his face. Nobody seemed to pay any attention to him, busily carrying on the tasks he normally would be assigning. What was happening to him?

Zayne did something he had never done before: He stepped back, knowing that it was the best decision at the moment. His mind simply wasn't tuned to the patient's best interest. His mind was too busy determining the reason for his sudden physical problems. As he stood against the back wall, an incongruous image dominated his mind. Zayne fought to suppress the distraction. He bit his lower lip, trying to coerce his brain to focus on the pain. No matter what he did, nothing helped.

The image of the lovely woman with intelligent eyes and commanding voice under a golden FBI pin remained in his consciousness—a stubborn presence in his moment of helplessness.

CHAPTER 6
THE DATABASE

Kirk tore off the end of a crusty baguette and used it to sop up the sauce remaining on his plate. Buddy, his Dalmatian, nudged his leg with great insistence. Kirk retrieved a meatball from the pot, brought it to his lips, assessed the temperature, bit off half, and fed the rest to Buddy. The dog's lips retracted, showing sharp teeth that seized the food with controlled gentleness. Nothing like a home-made meal after a long, stressful day. Kirk looked at Aurora and smiled. Brutus, his golden mutt, growled from Kirk's other side.

"Your spaghetti is the best." Kirk said, patting his stomach. "And the wine hit the spot." He took a sip of Sangiovese, savored it in his mouth, swallowed it, and exhaled with pleasure. Good thing it wasn't Montepulciano wine.

Kirk looked at Peter, sitting next to Aurora instead of his usual spot across from her. Totally focused on his plate, Peter had managed to avoid eye contact with Kirk all evening. As a matter of fact, Peter had successfully avoided spending time with Dad since the vodka episode on campus.

Earlier that afternoon, Kirk had come through the front door, changed into his sweats for his usual evening run, and knocked at Peter's bedroom door.

"Ready to go?"

Loud tapping and rapping music reached him from inside Peter's room.

"Too much homework!" Peter shouted from the other side of the closed door.

Kirk had hoped to use the run as an opportunity to talk to him about the vodka incident. He knocked again.

"Doesn't sound like home work," he said through a crack in the door. "Can I come in to talk?"

"Whatever."

Kirk entered the room, stepped over a pair of discarded jeans and a t-shirt, and sat on the unmade bed next to the wooden desk. On the wall, a neon poster of a game Kirk didn't know hung next to the periodic table. A computer screen showed complicated math and physics formulas Kirk didn't understand. The computer was also the source of the uncanny music. How could a brain capable of such intellectual feats appreciate that crap?

"Cut the music, please," Kirk said, thinking that the term shouldn't apply to the screeching sound. "We need to talk."

Peter picked up a remote control and hit the off button. The noise subsided.

"Look at me," Kirk said, swiveling in Peter's chair. "Tell me more about the vodka. The truth, so I can help."

"Nothing to tell," Peter said. "I was carrying the bottle. That's all."

"How much do you drink?"

"I don't."

"You tell me you never tried?"

"Once," Peter said. "I got sick from it. Okay?"

Kirk bit his lower lip.

"I should just move back home," Peter said. "Most kids in my dorm are busier getting drunk and stoned than studying."

"That's your decision," Kirk said. "Breaking the law isn't an option. It can get on your record and ruin your ability to pursue certain careers, get good jobs…You make a bad choice, you suffer the consequences."

"I know," Peter said. "Are we done? I need to study now."

Kirk left the room. Gone were the days when Kirk built robots with Peter and joined him for rollercoaster rides. In all fairness, he couldn't expect Peter to open up about sensitive subjects just because Kirk showed interest in his world for a few minutes He needed to spend more time with his son—more meaningful time.

Kirk did his run alone. Pushing himself to the limit failed to lift the layer of sadness that still coated his insides and weighed him down.

"What are you thinking?" Aurora said.

"I'm wondering how you found the time to cook," he said. "Didn't you work the day shift?"

"Yeah. I like the surgical unit. And I can stay on day shift for the rest of the year," she said, taking a sip from her glass and checking the ruby-red color against the light. "I had sauce and meatballs in the freezer from last month."

"Smart, and a great cook." He smiled. "Sorry I haven't been much help the past few days."

He looked at the cluttered kitchen. He loved his house. Life was good. He handed a meatball to Brutus.

"Hard day?" Aurora patted his free hand and gave him a sympathetic smile. "Want to talk about it?"

With a different woman, he would still be in the dog house after forgetting the stupid parents' meeting. Aurora yelled and screamed, but she always got it all out at once. No build-up of repressed feelings. They had already completed their "all-out" session after the meeting. She wasn't holding a grudge any more. He loved her for that. And he was looking forward to showing her how much. After sixteen years of marriage, Aurora never failed to stir excitement in his body, no matter how tired he felt.

"It's a very sad case," he said. "A young woman with a gunshot to the head. Someone made it look like suicide. She's basically brain dead. And another woman is dying of a heart condition, waiting for a heart transplant."

"Sounds like something good can come out of something terrible," Peter said, looking up from an improvised ice-cream sundae with chocolate smeared lips.

"It's complicated," Kirk said, pleased at Peter's interest. "The victim's family isn't consenting to the transplant."

"Why not?" Peter said. "If she's brain dead, at least her other organs can go to people who need them."

At times when he felt as tired as tonight, Kirk would regret having started such a serious conversation, thus foregoing needed after-dinner relaxation. But this was Peter's way to reconnect. Aurora got up and collected the dishes, leaving the two alone at the table. Only the clicking of silverware and the running of water broke the silence, as Kirk tried to formulate a suitable answer. His heaviness lifted.

"Is this the case from NY Medical Center?" Aurora asked, rinsing the dishes and placing them in the open dishwasher.

"How did you hear about it?" Kirk said, nodding.

"I thought that's already over," Aurora said, a deep frown creasing her forehead. She held a dirty dish in mid-air.

"What's over?" Kirk replaced his glass on the table. "What are you talking about?"

Aurora placed the dish inside the dishwasher, dried her hands on her apron, came back to the table, and sat down. Kirk saw what looked like sympathy in her large brown eyes.

"You haven't heard?" she asked. "I thought you—being on the case—would know."

"Heard what?" Kirk said. "How do you know more about this than I do?"

"My friend," she said. "She works registry and was in the NYMC ICU today,. We spoke on the phone, about meeting for lunch next week. She told me about the cardiac arrest they had just worked on."

She must be talking about the code blue that ended the interview with the doctor this morning. Who had coded? Kirk didn't know. He fought a wave of indigestion.

"The gunshot victim you mentioned." Aurora hesitated. "I'm afraid she's dead.."

Kirk's breath sounded like a whistle. Anger boiled inside him. His case of attempted murder had been upgraded to homicide and this was the way he was finding out? He wiped his mouth with a napkin and loosened his shirt collar. Aurora stepped near him.

"I love you," she said. Her lips touched his cheek. She always knew what he needed and when.

"Me too," Kirk said. He gave her a quick smile. "Hold that thought, please. I need to make a call. Sorry."

Kirk got up, left the dining room, and walked to the living room. Buddy followed closely, his nails clicking against the wooden floor. The living room curved to the right, where a long narrow desk hugged the wall in front of an office chair. The desktop was a sheet of metal dominated by a large computer screen. His home office. Kirk sat on his chair. On the wall in front of him, above his computer, his Police Academy diploma saluted him. It had taken him a few years to be able to look at it without experiencing pangs of regret. Now, with Aurora constantly trying to limit his risk, he was starting to again doubt his decision to quit the force. Aurora's picture on his desk melted his anger down to a manageable level. Kirk pulled out his phone from his belt holster. His finger hovered over John Spencer's number, but an incoming call took precedence. He stopped dialing and answered instead.

"It's Bloom." Her voice didn't convey any urgency or surprise. "Should we talk about the next step?"

"Do you know that Amy Winter is dead? The code blue, when we left the hospital." Kirk kept his voice calm. "That was her dying. But I was never notified."

"Dr. Wilder called me." She paused. Kirk took a deep breath to manage his frustration. "He said the poor woman's brain herniated because of swelling from the gunshot trauma. What a waste."

Kirk remained silent.

"You didn't know?" Bloom said. "I should have called you. Sorry."

"Never mind," he said. "FBI gets on the case and everyone else takes second place. It figures."

He felt immediately sorry about the statement. Bloom had sounded concerned and respectful. Her first real case carried a lot of weight in her budding career. She was likely still unaware of the squabbles between the police and the FBI. She represented a big asset. Better for Kirk to work with someone fully focused on the case than with an experienced FBI agent more worried about looking good on the job.

"The doctor told me he notified the police." No shyness in her voice. "I assumed he meant you. Or I would have called you."

She sounded upfront and honest. No use explaining or arguing.

"Next time," he said. "Now we have more urgent problems to worry about."

"Like who's next?"

"Exactly," Kirk said. "Someone went to all the trouble of shooting Amy Winter, then forced Herrera to refuse the heart so the heart would go to another patient. Winter's death brings us back to square one. The killer needs to find a new victim. Soon. Before the patient waiting for the heart dies as well."

"To find out who's next, we need the chain list," Bloom said. Now. Do you think Amy's death makes it easier to get a warrant?"

"You can try, but I don't think we can pull it off. It all rests on the hacking, which the FBI couldn't pin on Montepulciano. We need to convince the good doctor to voluntarily hand over the list."

"Perhaps I should try alone, in the morning," she said. "I think I might have a ... a connection."

"I think you're right." Kirk chuckled. "You may be the next best thing to a warrant. Call me after you meet."

He ended the call and walked back to the dining room. Peter's idea of dessert looked great. Kirk would have a sundae too, but his would be made with extra chocolate syrup.

The small closet door slid open with a squeak. In her plush white bathrobe, Bloom stood barefoot and inspected her clothes, getting ready for a 12:30 meeting with Dr. Wilder that he hadn't hesitated to grant. *A connection?* The detective's chuckle came to mind. She blushed. She had to keep all this highly professional.

She swept aside a black, low-cut, body-hugging tube. This wasn't a date but a quest for a database. She smiled. The red woolen dress was good for Christmas. She reached for a blue-green long-sleeved dress, opened her robe, and draped the dress on her shapely figure. The v- shaped neck provided just the right amount of exposure. Still professional. Someone had once done her colors, telling her what looked good with her hair shade and skin complexion. In that respect, this dress was a clear winner.

She dropped the robe to the floor, put on a simple nude bra, and matching no-show panties, then slipped the dress over her head and smoothed it down over her breasts and narrow waist. Perfect. She spent a few extra minutes on her makeup, choosing a not-too-bright lipstick. Next she rushed to the door, grabbing her jacket off the wall hanger. Before leaving, though, she took a last glance in the hall mirror. Her hand went to the back of her head and untied the hair band. Her hair fanned out on her shoulders. Auburn. That was the name of the color she had read about in a fashion blog. She looked—beautiful. Heat spread to her cheeks.

Was she crazy? With all that was going on in her life, was she trying to draw a man into it? Of course not. Again, this wasn't a date. This was an expedition in search of the chain database. She shrugged, reached out for the FBI badge on top of the wall table, and headed for the door.

The young doctor's handshake lasted a moment longer than necessary. His hand felt strong. A hand used to hold living hearts and stitch arteries. She registered a subtle heat wave rising from her neck. He wore dark green scrubs and sneakers. Bloom thanked him for his time and sat in the same office chair she had occupied the day before.

"What can I do for you, Agent Bloom?" The doctor sat back, as if he had all the time in the world. "I guess you have a homicide on your hands now."

"Doctor," she said, her eyes locked onto his, "we strongly suspect that Amy Winter was killed for the purpose of procuring a heart for a patient. Likely for *your* patient, Herrera."

"But that's impossible," he said. "You know my patient refused the transplant."

"Nevertheless," Bloom said, "we have to assume that someone wanted that transplant to occur badly enough to kill for it. What other reason could there be for this murder, for the way it was executed?"

She paused to let her statement sink in. The doctor seemed deep in thought, looking at her. The thought he might be considering her freely flowing auburn hair caught her by surprise. The heatwave intensified. She should have left her hair tied up in something.

"What do you mean, exactly?" The doctor leaned forward.

"The murderer," she explained, "shot the victim right in the temple and smack in front of the hospital. So the ER could get the patient right away and place her on a respirator, keep her organs alive and well."

The doctor eyes turned to the back wall. Good. At least he was concentrating on the facts of the case instead of her.

"Do you really believe that?" he said, looking back at her from under his thick brows. "I doubt very much the murderer chose the exact spot. And isn't the temple where people usually shoot others so they can die quickly?"

"In at least 50 percent of garden-variety homicides," she said, in the most professional tone she could muster, "we see more than one shot. Often to both head *and* chest. If the purpose is just killing, people usually want to make sure the victim dies. Here, I think the purpose was to provide you with a heart. Also, the entry spot of the bullet was almost exactly the same as the entry spot in Carlos Herrera's brain when he committed suicide. Also executed right in front of a hospital. Too many coincidences, don't you think?"

The doctor stared at her again, but now with bewilderment.

"How would this murder and that suicide be connected?" he said. "Despite the similarities, I just don't see how. I'm sorry."

He looked sorry. But the feeling didn't help her or any potential future victims.

"Detective Miner and I are investigating any possible connection," she said. "Right now, we don't have any good reason for Amy Winter's murder, except for a heart donation. Now, with Amy dead and her heart gone, we're concerned that the killer may try again. If we could access the list of potential donors, and see who else is compatible with your patient, we may be able to predict who could be next, take precautions—"

"Sorry." The doctor waved his hand. "The database is protected by patient privacy. You would need a warrant."

"If we had enough for a warrant," she said, staring into his handsome gray eyes, "I'd be in possession of the database right now instead of looking at you."

"I'm glad something good came from it." He grinned. "Or from the lack of it, I should say."

Bloom bit her lip not to smile back.

"You wouldn't want another donor from your chain to die prematurely, would you? Because sure as hell the blood would be on your hands." The words burst out of her mouth like a glove striking his stubbly face.

The doctor's eyes widened. Muscles tightened over his cheeks. Her strike had caught him by surprise. Bloom saw the chance of any amicable connection quickly fade.

"Listen," the doctor whispered, looking side to side, "I can see your point. And of course, I certainly don't want anyone else to die. But even if I totally agree with your assessment of the situation, a HIPAA violation of this kind could cause me to lose my doctor's license."

He checked his phone and scrolled through several items. He bent down on his computer and started typing. Bloom stared at his dark chest hair appearing within the green V of his scrubs After less than a minute, he stopped and pushed back from his desk.

"I need to go," he said. "Sorry if I can't see you out."

He didn't wave her out. He didn't wait for her to leave. Instead, he left and pulled the door closed. Bloom sat frozen, wondering what it all meant. Her harsh words must have gotten to the doctor. Great way of conducting an interview. She tried chasing Zayne's image from her mind so she could focus on her next step. When had Dr. Wilder become Zayne?

She stuffed her computer into its case. What was she going to tell Kirk? And Mulville? She should have had Kirk Miner right there with her, sitting on the other chair. She could have learned how to coerce doctors into releasing key information without a warrant. What was she thinking? Was she hoping to charm the handsome young doctor into violating hospital policies, laws, and ethical principles and handing over his career on a platter? No. She had honestly tried plead her case professionally. But she had failed.

She stood and got ready to leave. But something on the doctor's desk grabbed her attention. His computer was still open. She looked back at the door. Closed. The doctor had showed no intention of coming back. Yet he had left her there. Alone. With his open computer. She rushed to the other side of the desk. On the screen, a word document displayed two lines of letters, numbers, and punctuation characters—a username and a password. Zayne had come through.

For a moment she felt breathless. Suddenly the Word document disappeared and she was staring at smears of green, yellow, and a thin rim of red. A beautiful aurora borealis. The screen saver. *No, no.* She tapped the keyboard repeatedly to no avail. A blank rectangle in the middle of the aurora's red rim requested a password.

"Shit!" she said through clenched teeth, slamming her hands on the desk.

How stupid could she be? Why had it taken so long for her to understand that Zayne had given her a chance at access the chain database? And now what? She couldn't just call him back and have him acknowledge his HIPAA violation.

She stepped back to the other side of the desk, grabbed her computer bag, and brought it next to the doctor's computer. She sat on the doctor's chair and rummaged through her bulky bag until she found what she needed. She retrieved a disk, a special disk player, a USB and other cables, and connected her equipment to the doctor's computer. She went through a multiple-step program aimed at bypassing the password to unlock the screen. Her lips pursed, she took several deep breaths, repeatedly glancing at the closed door, listening for footsteps, while her fingers worked the keyboard. She heard only the far pinning of the elevators.

Her heart pounded against her chest. She detected only a regular, albeit fast, rhythm. After several seemingly endless minutes, the Word document reappeared on the screen. She seized her phone and snapped a picture. Then she disconnected her equipment, placed it back inside her bag, checked around to make sure everything was as meant to be, and got ready to leave. Stopping at the door, she cracked it open and peered outside. After making sure nobody was around to see her exiting the office, she left and walked at a purposely slow pace toward the elevators.

As she rushed to her car, Bloom detected no trace of the embarrassment she had experienced earlier while talking to Zayne. She let the motor running idle and rested her forehead on her hands while holding the cold steering wheel. Honesty required her to admit that she had wanted him to notice her hair. She felt an attraction to the doctor. It wasn't just his strong jawline and the deeply set eyes she usually liked in a man. She thought about the way he looked at her, with respectful interest; about how he had acknowledged her professionally, despite her brusqueness, to the point of putting his career on the line in the interest of saving people.

That showed unusual courage. The realization made her feel light. But also sad. Under regular circumstances, she would try to get to know the doctor better—much better. But her life didn't qualify as normal.

On the drive back to the FBI quarters, she recomposed herself and tried to rid her mind of the dangerous distraction Zayne Wilder had become. The introspection didn't last long.

As she parked her Mitsubishi in the designated spot of the underground garage, her side vision picked up something that flushed the lightness away with a flood of adrenaline. A shadow. A few yards from her. She turned to face it. The shadow disappeared behind a column. A chill ran down her back as she stared at a pair of black leather shoes protruding from the hiding place. A man. Watching her. Could someone know what she was up to and want to stop her?

She surveilled the area and saw nobody walking to or from a car. She was alone with a stalker. She looked back at the man's shoes. Still there, motionless. Perhaps he was waiting for someone else, and the excitement about her new assignment was feeding her mind scary scenarios. After one last look at the immobile shoes, she restarted the engine and drove outside the garage and around the block. When she returned, the man was gone.

Bloom exited her car and walked toward the column. The usual faint smell of oil and gasoline hung in the stuffy air. Nothing on the ground caught her attention. As she stood where the man had hidden, a strange scent entered her nostrils. A masculine fragrance, like an aftershave. Who on Earth would still wear something like that? Older men. The image of Santo Montepulciano flashed into her mind.

Her heart tapped her ribcage like a hammer all the way up to her office.

CHAPTER 7
THE NEXT DONOR

At FBI headquarters in New York, Bloom sat in the director's meeting room and retrieved her phone, placing it on the desk next to her computer. She found the picture of Zayne's desktop and entered the URL on her computer's screen. A request for username and password followed. She complied, feeding the computer the typed symbols. She was in. After adding the precious information to her list of passwords, she mentally thanked Zayne and deleted the incriminating picture, as she assumed the doctor expected her to do.

"Fucking good job with the doc, Rookie," said Mulville from the chair next to her.

Bloom hadn't heard him approaching from behind. She glanced at him, hating that, after several years, she still blushed at his rudeness. Curses and offensive statements had likely flown out of Mulville's mouth, escaping censoring and defying social pressure, for most of his 40-plus years. What counted was that, underneath everything, Mulville would kill to protect her.

"Thanks," she whispered, eyes fixed on the scrolling letters and numbers.

"What am I looking at?" he said.

"The chain's patients." She pointed at the screen. "They're named under the hospital that requested the transplant listing. So, for example, here is the first—"

A series of knocks on the door caused Mulville to turn around.

"Miner," he said. "Come in. If not Miner, we're busy."

"I came as soon as I heard," Kirk said, walking in. He closed the door and approached. "I can't believe the doctor gave it up."

"The official story is that he didn't," Bloom said, glancing back at Miner. "The way it happened would fall back on me and only me."

"Great," Mulville said. "What have you got?"

"Mr. Miner," she said, "I mean, Kirk. This is your P1 patient, Margarita Herrera. Her number is 142."

She pointed at one of the NYMC listings for Dr. Wilder. P142 was listed as having signed up with D142. The name, address, and phone numbers of patient and donor followed. In this case, they were the same last name and address. Next to D142, the word DECEASED stood out in red capital letters.

"That's the address in Spanish Harlem where I met her husband," Kirk said. "When I asked him if anyone had offered his father money to commit suicide, he offered me to bash my teeth in."

"Oh boy." Mulville chuckled. "I couldn't have done any worse myself."

"Seriously," Kirk said, leaning toward the screen. "We need to find out who else in the chain is a possible donor for Margarita Herrera."

Bloom took a breath. She typed the question about other suitable donors for the same N142 patient and waited. A circling icon briefly dominated the screen. Then something flashed in the middle: D348, Carl Baker. Address and phone number followed. He lived in Hartford, Connecticut.

"Check him out," Mulville said. "He could be our next victim."

Bloom went to work. The warmth of Mulville's breath on her neck reminded her that this was the time to show her competence. She accessed the Crime Information Center and searched for criminal, traffic, court, and arrest records. Next she checked police reports. Unsatisfied by the lack of results, she checked for mentions in the media. Soon, an article appeared on her screen. "Small hedge fund broker allegedly involved in shady money laundering."

"Carl Baker has been busy," Kirk said, pointing at the article on her desktop.

"Allegedly is the word," Mulville said. "I vaguely remember this case. Wait."

His stubby thumbs went to work on his phone. After a few attempts, he stopped to read. He nodded and grunted a couple of times.

"We never proved it," he said. "The important thing to learn here is that our potential donor isn't afraid of dirtying his hands."

"Good to know," Kirk said. "What I don't understand is why someone killed a woman outside the chain, when this guy was already signed up and ready to go. If someone was looking for a good match for Margarita Herrera, why didn't they kill Baker? Unless…Baker is connected to the person doing the killing, so they bypassed him. Was Baker a suspect in connection with Montepulciano's money laundering?"

"As I said," Mulville said, his voice resounding with annoyance and defeat, "we couldn't prove anything. The wine man didn't come up. Anything is possible, but we have to deal with facts."

Bloom kept on typing. She needed something. Now. She switched her focus to Montepulciano. She conducted the same extensive search she had used for Baker.

"Look," she said. "About Montepulciano. Besides the short jail time for a drug conviction and the NYMC's alleged hacking, there is an old rape charge. Twenty-six years ago."

The clicking of keys filled the silence. Mulville sighed again. The pressure cooker was getting ready to explode, unless she gave him something relevant and useful. Now.

"Charges were dismissed," Bloom said. "The woman, an ex-girlfriend, later changed her story to consensual sex."

"Sure," Kirk said. "What method did he use to refresh her memory?"

"Can we cut this useless crap?" Mulville said. "Go back to Baker."

"He's a widower," Bloom said, clicking along. "His wife was the patient he signed up with. She died last month during a heart transplant. He has a fifteen-year-old daughter."

"Poor man," Kirk said. "He may be on the list for an accident in the near future. I wonder what happens if a patient dies during a transplant. Can the donor who signed up with her withdraw from the chain? By the way, where was his wife's transplant done?"

"Hartford University," Bloom said. "She lived near there with her husband. Why he's still on the list as a donor I guess is a question for Dr. Wilder. There may be rules."

"Here's the much more important question," Mulville said. "Is there a connection between Montepulciano and Margarita Herrera?".

"Why don't you follow up on this with the doctor?" Kirk said to Bloom. "Meantime, I'll talk to Baker about possible protection."

A warm feeling spread to Bloom's neck. "Sure." Bloom avoided looking at Mulville, afraid she'd see a smirk on his face.

At 9:53 the following morning, Kirk rode the elevator up to Carl Baker's office in downtown Hartford. The drive from New York had taken him just under three hours. Flying would have taken only half an hour but, all in, would have taken him just as long. Besides, he didn't mind driving.

Kirk stopped at Baker's floor and walked to an opaque glass door displaying several business names. Second in line on the alphabetized list was "Carl Baker, Investments Inc." The door slid open and Kirk stepped into a round reception area. There a young woman with excessive makeup and shoulder-length blond hair interrupted her nail filing to greet him. She asked him for his name and the purpose of his visit.

The circular area stood surrounded by several doors with their business names displayed on them. Kirk wondered what kind of hedge fund manager would run his business from a shared office space and with a shared receptionist. How small was Carl Baker's hedge fund? Veneer for money-laundering seemed more and more plausible.

"Kirk Miner PI, working with the FBI and the NYPD. I'm here to see Mr. Baker." He surrendered his card to the brightly manicured hand. "I called yesterday. My appointment is at 10."

He was told to sit in the common waiting area, while the receptionist handled a few phone calls. Almost fifteen minutes later, after reading most of an outdated Sports Illustrated magazine, Kirk got up and inquired about the delay.

"Mr. Baker apologizes." The receptionist's blue-lined green eyes conveyed regret. "He's being detained and just notified me he won't be able to get back here today. Perhaps you can reschedule for a later date. He's a very busy man."

Kirk sighed. He understood the drill. Money launderer Carl Baker didn't want to meet and shoot the breeze with a nobody detective about an ongoing investigation.

"Okay," Kirk said. "When would the next opening be?"

"Mr. Baker is booked for the next couple of months. How's December second at 10 a.m.?"

"Sounds great." Kirk took the appointment card. "I hope Mr. Baker makes it back on time for his next appointment. Thanks."

Kirk walked out, thinking of a funny coaster he kept in his home office. *How about never? Does never work for you?* But Kirk knew how to handle the Bakers of this world. He rode the elevator down to the lobby, sat on a comfortable couch with a clear view of the elevator doors, and dialed Baker's office, holding the phone a foot from his mouth, and tapping it with his fingers to mimic static.

"Mr. Higgins from England." Kirk used his best English accent. "Is Mr. Baker available to talk about possible investments?"

"Let me check," the receptionist said.

Soothing music followed. Kirk had his answer. He hung up, slid deeper into the couch's overstuffed pillows, and waited. At the touch of his thumb, Carl Baker's picture appeared on his phone screen: a portly man in his fifties with thick dark hair and a smile forged just for the official picture on his website. Kirk studied it, then turned his gaze to the elevators. He hoped that Baker would take lunch outside his office, but would wait for him as long as it took.

The wait was shorter than expected. At 11:43, Baker hopped out of the elevator and headed for the exit. Kirk sprang from the couch and barred the man's way.

"Mr. Baker," he said. "I'm Kirk Miner. I think we need to talk about your safety."

"Miner?" Baker looked up at the ceiling as if he was trying to remember.

"Please," Kirk sad, "cut the crap so maybe you'll survive."

"What are you talking about?" Baker glanced around as if looking for someone with a weapon pointed at him, or more likely for a security guard. "Who in the hell are you?"

"I'm your ten o'clock appointment, asshole," Kirk said in a calm voice. "Trying to save your ass, despite yourself. Can we talk?"

Baker sighed. His hand rose in a sign of frustration, but he walked with Kirk to the couch.

"I'll give you five minutes," Baker said, sitting down. "Talk fast."

Kirk sat next to him and told him about Margarita Herrera and Amy Winter, her potential donor. He explained how Baker was also a match for Herrera, and therefore a potential next victim. Baker's eyes widened. He leaned forward, abdomen extruding over his spread legs. A thin film of sweat made his corrugated brow glisten.

"Listen," Baker said, wiping his forehead with his pocket handkerchief, "the only reason I signed up for that system as a donor was my wife, who's dead. They fucked up her surgery and she's gone. I don't see any way I would be a target."

"You're still on the list," Kirk said.

"Fine." Baker made a sweep of his hand. "I'll take myself off. Since my wife died, I assumed I would be off already. I never bothered to check. It **didn't occur to me that someone was going to kill me.**"

"I don't think it's that simple," Kirk said. "They know you're a match for this patient and they seem to want her transplant done as soon as possible."

"They who?" Baker asked. "What the fuck are you talking about?"

"Did anyone approach you about all this?" Kirk said.

"About what?"

"About the chain," Kirk said. "Did anyone threaten you, or offer you money for your family, or a timely organ for your wife, in exchange for—"

"Are you insane?" Baker made a circle in the air with his finger. "No. No one asked me to do myself in."

"Regardless," Kirk said, "I recommend you accept police protection. Think what would happen to your daughter if you should die."

"What do you know about my daughter?" Baker at last seemed engaged. "Leave my daughter out of all this."

"I'm only trying to make you see the problem you're facing," Kirk said.

"Okay." Baker stood up. "I'm going to call the hospital and take myself off the donors list. That's all. I'm not going to lose my privacy for this BS. Now, I'd like you to leave. I'm late for a real meeting."

He got up, turned around, and left the building. Kirk watched him go. He asked himself what illegal business was so important that he'd forgo protection and risk his life for it. Money laundering didn't seem quite enough.

CHAPTER 8
IT'S ONLY COFFEE

Bloom peeked through the coffee shop window. At three o'clock in the afternoon, the lunch crowd had retreated, and most of the usual customers sandwiched between chair and laptop had departed for the day. Her eyes found Zayne Wilder seated at a back table for two, sipping a tall beverage and looking at his phone. A gray sport jacket and a light blue shirt had replaced scrubs and white coat. No stranger would identify him as a cardio-thoracic surgeon. He looked much more like a young man waiting for a first, non-committal date, where two people talk for the first time over coffee to decide whether to escalate to lunch, dinner, or something hotter altogether. Something warm lifted and spread in Bloom's chest. She had to keep in mind that none of the above constituted the purpose of their meeting today. She pushed the door open and stepped in.

He immediately waved her over, revealing where his focus had been all along, and it wasn't his emails or phone messages. Feeling she owed something in return, she gave up on ordering and joined him at once. He stood like a gentleman.

"Thanks for meeting me," she said. His handshake was warm and strong. "I won't take too long."

He glanced at his phone, shut it down, and sat again. His hands crossed and the long surgeon's fingers went to support his chin. The gray eyes took her in with obvious approval and perhaps a touch of playfulness.

"I needed a lift." He pointed at his coffee. "The coffee shop is a bit more private than the hospital cafeteria. And here the coffee actually tastes like coffee. Are you having anything?"

She shook her head, pulled her computer out of the briefcase, and opened it onto the table. At the moment, no files needed to be opened and there was no need for notes. The screen offered protection and the trappings of professionalism.

"Thanks for…" she started, but a flag in her mind made her stop. "We spoke to Carl Baker, another possible donor for your patient. He doesn't want any protection. His wife was a patient of some medical group in Connecticut who apparently died during transplant. We were wondering: Does he have to stay in the chain?"

Zayne's eyes swept the surroundings as if checking for witnesses. He took a sip of his beverage and sighed. Then his hand came up and landed on hers, not with the uncertainty of a first date, but with the authority of a commander directing a recruit.

"Listen," he said, looking her in the eye. "No names. I know nothing about this. We only get involved when our patients are concerned. Privacy in medicine is an absolute. It'll snuff out our license at any infraction. I count on your complete discretion."

She remained still, conscious only of the warm pressure of his hand on hers. After a moment, she realized he expected an answer and she nodded. The hand went away, back to the paper container.

"People don't sign in or drop off as organ donors just because they no longer have a relative who needs an organ," he said. "The chain is a tool to increase organ donations. Optimally, a donor has the satisfaction of seeing the patient he signed up with get a heart. In this case, he's obliged to remain a donor for the rest of his life. If the patient dies without getting successfully transplanted, the donor who signed up with that patient usually remains on the list, but in theory he could opt out. Just like he can opt out any time before the patient gets a heart. They both can leave, together."

Bloom nodded. She looked at the 3D FBI logo rotating on her computer screen and collected her thoughts before asking her next question—the real reason for the meeting. She took the computer onto her lap, slumped down on her seat, and lowered her head, as if searching for information on her screen. The doctor started fidgeting with his phone again. This could be the last chunk of time he was willing to give her. She might as well really piss him off.

"There is something else Detective Miner and I need," she said. Then, she added as an afterthought: "This request comes directly from the FBI director."

She looked up at him. Zayne's brows rose. She swallowed.

"We're still wondering if there's any relationship between your patient and the mobster who allegedly hacked the hospital system last year."

The doctor's gray eyes turned to her like gun barrels. She stared at them. A breath exited Zayne's pursed lips.

"I told you." His hand made a sweep. "Very unlikely."

"Not as unlikely as last time we spoke," she said. "About twenty-six years ago, some woman accused Santo Montepulciano of rape. An ex-girlfriend. Charges were dismissed after she changed her story. The case is sealed, to protect possible the vic's identity.

"And?"

"Your patient is 25 years old." She said it as if the deduction was self-evident. "You do the math."

Now Zayne looked at her from under raised brows. She had his attention. But his shoulders came up in a sign of futility.

"Even if that was actually the case," he said, opening his hands, "what would you want from me? I don't see how I can help you find out for sure if Montepulciano and Margarita Herrera are somehow related."

"There *could* be a way."

"How?"

"If and when we were to get DNA from Montepulciano," she said, as if there was no chance, "would you let us compare it with your patient's?"

From the look on Zayne's face, she knew she had gone too far. Would he suspect her of disregarding his ethical boundaries and using him for her own purposes?

"Come on," he whispered, as if he was embarrassed for her. "You know better than that. Without a warrant, my hands are tied. I could lose everything. Besides, even if you're right, without a warrant, without permission, I'm sure there would be serious legal repercussions. Such as not being able to use the evidence—etcetera."

"We don't meet the probable cause criteria for a warrant. I checked with my director. It's a long shot," she said. "I have no idea if we even have any DNA on file for him. If we do the test off the books and it's negative, nobody has to know. If it's positive, we'll work to get more evidence to get a warrant and make it legal."

He looked at her in silence. His eyes narrowed and a touch of playfulness resurfaced. Bloom liked it much better than the frustration she had witnessed and the anger she had feared.

"I would be willing to discuss this further," he said. "Over dinner."

Her mind wanted to do somersaults. But with a burst of pounding, her heart warned her, and she felt the need to hold on to her chair. The computer slid off her lap and fell to the ground with an unhealthy clunk.

"Are you okay?" Zayne leaped to her side.

"Yes." A pressure in her throat made it difficult to breathe. "I'm fine."

She bent to retrieve her computer, checked the intact screen, commented on her good luck, but couldn't fool the doctor. His finger clamped onto her wrist, forcing her to sit back straight. She watched his forehead twitch as he took her pulse. The fluttering inside her chest intensified, riding the tide of adrenaline flowing into her veins. She pulled her wrist away.

"We should do an EKG," he said. "Even better, a Holter monitor, to document this rapid heartbeat. How long have you had it?"

"Long enough that I know how to stop it." She coughed and tapped her chest with her fist. "Gone."

He shook his head, eyes full of concern.

"It's bad enough we're working together on an investigation," she said, fetching her computer and securing it in her bag. "If you're my doctor, it's going to be impossible."

"What are you talking about?"

"We can't go on a date," she said, getting up from the chair. Sudden heat set her cheeks on fire. Her mind tried to retrace the doctor's words, begging for a confirmation that he had used the D word first. He hadn't. "Not if you're my doctor. I have my own doctor."

"What is your doctor doing about that?" He pointed at her chest. She became conscious of her breasts, now under the doctor's scrutiny. If only they constituted adequate distraction from her abnormal heart beat. "Did you have an echocardiogram, an ultrasound? A stress test?"

"I'm serious," she said. "If we're to have dinner, or any other conversation, or meeting, my medical history is off limits."

He gave her a schemer's grin that spelled victory. But the gray eyes telegraphed unease. She had opened this door to achieve the goal she had come for, in exchange for a date with a man she liked. Was this a surrender of her professionalism? And how was she going to hide her heart problem from an MD? A heart specialist, on top of everything?

"Fair enough," he said. "I'll pick you up Saturday evening at 7:30."

The following morning, while in his sedan's passenger seat, Kirk battled the New York rush hour traffic. He glanced at Peter, holding the steering wheel. Hard to believe his son had a learner's permit and was on his way to driving alone in the near future.

"Not very smart," Kirk said, "driving to NYU at 7:30 a.m., is it?"

Peter glanced at him with that special look that warned he knew better than his old man. Unruly hair shook as Peter's head jerked back to the stop-and-go traffic. Way to dodge an answer by following Dad's instructions to the letter. Always keep your eyes on the road.

"How am I supposed to get my license?" Peter said. "I need to put in the time. And I need to be at NYU at eight o'clock. I'm working on a tractor beam a little bit like the one described in those old sci-fi programs, the ones you like to watch on TV."

"Star Trek?"

"Yeah. 'Cept we're two centuries earlier than predicted."

"Wow," Kirk said. His son never failed to impress him. "You need to tell me more about it later. Now I need to be at the FBI Manhattan office. I'm already late."

The last two sentences didn't resonate well. Kirk had to make more time for Peter, understand him better, encourage him, appreciate his strengths, offer suggestions to mitigate his weaknesses. But the interview with Baker crept into his mind. Why had that idiot refused protection? He must be hiding something, but what was worth risking your life over? Unless.... The change of light to a deep green forced Kirk to refocus on the task at hand. The car rolled forward for several minutes, while Baker kept on returning to Kirk's mind. Then the car came to a stop. He noticed the glass building with the NYU sign, and watched Peter put the car on reverse.

"Here," Peter said, completing a perfect parallel parking job in a no-stop area. "Gotta go."

Peter kissed him on the cheek and was gone in a flash. Kirk checked the time. Bloom would wonder what had happened to him. He crossed over to the driver's seat and drove away. Three quarters of an hour later, he had traveled a distance that should have taken him eleven minutes according to his GPS. He rushed from the covered parking, through the metal detector, to the elevator, into the corridor, and up to Bloom's desk.

Bloom didn't turn away from her computer, even after Kirk announced himself. Her ponytail wavered as she read from the screen and clicked her mouse. A half-eaten power bar sat next to her computer. The data from the transplant chain must have been as absorbing as his interview with Baker. Kirk stood behind her and watched her work.

"Hi, Kirk. Look here," she said pointing at the screen. "These two columns show the patients and the donors they signed up with. All 504."

"Not many names," Kirk said. "Mostly numbers."

"Yes, of course. Zayne—I mean Dr. Wilder—only has access to his own patients and the donors who signed up with them."

"Right," Kirk said. He looked over the divider and grabbed a chair from the empty cubicle beside Bloom's. He dragged it around and sat next to Bloom. "And the names in red?"

"Dead," she said. "And I added the cause of death."

Miner counted 92 deaths on the patient list and 21 on the donor list. According to the doctor, the chain had been in existence for about two years.

"Amazing," he whispered.

"Thanks." She turned, a grin lighting up her face. "It doesn't take long, if you know the tricks."

He nodded, smiling back. Kirk didn't want to disappoint her by revealing the real source of his amazement. His eyes lingered on the red names.

"Something else is also amazing." He pointed at the lists.

"I agree," she said. "But you go first."

"For starters," he said, "the number of violent deaths on the donor list seems pretty high to me. Let's check how this compares to the general donors pool."

"Already done," she said. Bloom's mouse went to a file on the desktop. She clicked it open. A pie chart filled the screen. She read the notation below. "Trauma victims constitute between 55% and 77% of total heart donors. That's the same percentage as in the chain. Ten out of 21 are trauma vics. Very common in the case of organ donations. The best donors are healthy, young, and, unfortunately for them, dying accidentally."

"But here," Kirk said, pointing at the screen, "in the chain database, many deaths are caused by gunshot wounds to the head, mostly deemed suicides and most during the last year."

"Patients sustaining fatal gunshot wounds to the head," she continued reading, "are often young, without associated comorbidities, and are potentially ideal transplantation candidates as well. No wonder organ donors are frequently GSW victims."

"Yes," he said. "But there's a problem here. The chain is made up of people who sign up for it, not of people already dead on arrival to the ER. Check the rate of suicide in the general population."

He waited as Bloom did her search. Something in the transplant chain didn't add up. The last click gave them the answer.

"The annual age-adjusted suicide rate," she announced, "is 13.42 per 100,000 individuals."

"In the last year," Kirk said, pointing at the screen, "there were six suicides out of 500 individuals. That's almost 100 times the general population's rate."

"All since the hacking." She looked back at him, nodding.

Bloom was the best. Most FBI agents Kirk had dealt with in the past would have spent time trying to justify their failure to come to the right conclusion first. Not Bloom. She had readily accepted his point and moved on to the next step of the investigation. The rookie had a future.

"And there is more."

"Yes?" She turned to him.

"Look at the patients' column," he said. The adrenaline rush made his heart speed up. "Eighty-seven deaths out of five hundred patients in two years. That's a small number, isn't it?"

She searched for an article on the rate of death while waiting for a heart transplant. Her finger scrolled to the conclusion. She nodded.

"It should be about 12 per 100 patients per year," she said. She counted in silence. "Translated to 500 patients, it should be 120 in 2 years. In the chain, we have 55 deaths the first year and 37 the second year."

Kirk nodded. "Dramatic death rate drop last year. People are getting transplanted more often."

"It gets even better," she said. "It seems that all these donors committing suicide know how to shoot themselves in such a way as to keep their heart beating. To the temple. Massive damage to both hemispheres of the brain, but the brain stem is spared, so the heart keeps on beating. And none of the hearts got wasted with some shot to the chest. Which, by the way, is a fairly common way to commit suicide by GSW."

"Mr. Herrera," Kirk said, "the father-in-law of Wilder's patient, acted as if he was following instructions on how to avoid his Medulla Oblongata. A bullet hits that organ and the breathing stops. The heart follows in a few minutes unless the patient is immediately intubated and placed on a respirator. It's very suspicious."

Bloom's fingers started to move at great speed. Soon the FBI's, NYPD's and other cities' violent crimes and suicides databases appeared.

When that didn't yield the information she was looking for, newspapers articles started to populate her screen. Kirk wondered what was so urgent that wasn't yet obvious. He remained silent, afraid to disrupt something that felt promising. After several minutes of searching, while her computer crunched data, Bloom swiveled in her chair to face him.

"I'm matching the data I was able to extract from the chain database about the dead donors, with the information listed by the Police, the FBI, and various newspapers. Often the person's name isn't listed on the chain list, but using the date and time of death and the city, I'm able to identify many of the victims. Then I'm getting more detail from the FBI, Police, and newspaper articles about the exact location of the deaths."

After a few long minutes, new data appeared of her screen. She scrolled and studied the results of her search. A grin highlighted her face. "Most of these people shot themselves either in front of, or really close to, a hospital," she said, winking.

"We need to talk to the good doctor about this," Kirk said. "He must be so happy to see how well his chain system is working. Too bad it looks like someone is cranking up the handle to help it along."

"Perhaps," she said, "with this evidence, we'll be able to get a warrant to officially explore the chain database. By the way, from the looks of this, Baker may really need protection."

"The moron refused everything," Kirk said.

She shook her head in sympathy. Her eyes unfocused and turned to the back of the room. She seemed to be considering something.

"What happened with the doctor when you met?" Kirk asked.

"I asked him to compare Montepulciano's DNA with the DNA from Margarita Herrera, his patient. To see if she's related to the mobster."

"And?"

"He said no." She tapped her fingers on the desk. "But then he agreed to discuss it further. Do we have any DNA on him?"

Kirk shook her head. "Not at the FBI lab. But with that old rape charge, they may have it at the police department. I'll call my friend John. But I doubt it. Usually, if charges are dismissed, the evidence is destroyed after five years max."

"How can we get it? Do you think we have probable cause now—enough for a warrant?"

"Not with Montepulciano's cybercrime charges already dismissed," Kirk said. "I think we should have a talk with the guy ourselves."

"With him?"

Kirk nodded while dialing Spencer. He confirmed Kirk's prediction. Bloom swiveled back toward the computer screen and opened all available material on Santo Montepulciano.

"This is very helpful," Kirk said. "Great work. With everything you discovered today. And with Dr. Wilder."

"Yeah. Thanks."

Kirk wondered why she sounded like she felt sorry. A good break in finding such important information shouldn't be greeted with a feeling that comes across as sadness. Something was going on in Bloom's mind. Something she wasn't willing to share.

CHAPTER 9
MONTEPULCIANO

The entrance to Santo Montepulciano's office reminded Kirk of a spa. Not that Kirk was one to get facials or massages, but once during an investigation at an upscale hotel, he had checked out the amenities. He stared at the opaque sheath of glass. At the center, surrounded by a white cloud, the owner's name appeared together with the words "IT Consulting."

Before entering the office, Kirk went to look for the floor's men's room. He walked around in the opposite direction of the elevator, passing several offices until he spotted the restroom sign. He entered the men's room and, finding the two stalls empty and the wash area deserted, he extracted a plastic kit from his jacket pocket, peeled the plastic off the top, and retrieved a small pouch, leaving behind a Dacron hand wipe sealed in a clear wrap, which he put back in his pocket. He scrubbed his hands for two whole minutes with a yellowish cleaner from the pouch. The smell of alcohol reached his nostrils and made him clear his throat. After drying his hands in the air, Kirk went back to the office entrance.

As he looked for a handle to grab or a button to touch, the glass parted and he stepped into a large room furnished with a plush chairs and a couch arrangement straight out of a designer's magazine. The spa came back to mind. A petite secretary with a Botox-paralyzed forehead and augmented lips waved him in from behind a marble-topped counter reaching up to her neck. Kirk approached and deposited his card into a small hand with nails looking like red claws.

"Welcome, Mr. Miner." Her smile flashed perfect, white teeth. "Have a seat. Mr. Montepulciano will join you shortly."

She spoke into the phone on her desk. After a few minutes, an invisible door opened in the wooden-paneled back wall and the silhouette of a man appeared. Behind the man, Kirk viewed blue sky over New York City sky-scrapers, through the wall-to-wall window of a large room. His IT business must be booming.

Kirk recognized Montepulciano from the computer image brought up by Bloom. The secretary handed him Kirk's card, motioned Kirk to follow, and returned to her desk. Kirk stepped up to Montepulciano. Shorter than Kirk's 5' 11," the muscular man projected a squat appearance. Kirk had imag-ined him taller. Montepulciano flashed a disarming smile and pumped Kirk's hand with a powerful squeeze as he introduced himself. Kirk kept the hand-shaking going for as long as he could, admiring the black designer suit, the crisp white shirt, and the multicolored tie. A matching handkerchief peeked out of the man's jacket pocket and completed his impeccable outfit.

"Please come in." Montepulciano stepped aside and motioned Kirk into the office. "Make yourself comfortable. Coffee? Water?"

"No thank you." Kirk's sneakers found resistance against the tan plush carpet as he stepped toward the skyscrapers and sat on one of two gold-stud-ded black leather chairs across a massive block-like mahogany desk that would have looked perfect in a lawyer's office. Montepulciano sat on a matching executive office chair on the opposite site of the desk. A poor plaster reproduction of the "Last Supper" hung above Montepulciano's chair, placing him under Jesus' blessings every time he sat at his desk. Very appro-priate for someone named Saint.

"What can I do for the police today? Mr. ..." The mobster glanced at the PI's business card, then looked Kirk in the eye. His mouth stretched into the same mocking smile Kirk remembered from the picture. "Mr Miner, NYPD consultant."

Montepulciano parted his upturned hands in the disarming gesture of someone with nothing to hide. A little too cooperative. Kirk sat up straight.

"We're investigating the shooting of a young woman, Amy Winter," Kirk said. "In front of NYMC a few days ago. She left a note donating her organs. Her heart is a match for a patient named Margarita Herrera."

Montepulciano's brows went up together with his shoulders.

"We were wondering," Kirk went on, "if you might be related to

Margarita Herrera."

"What the fuck?" Montepulciano sat back. He sighed. A droplet spurted from his lip. "Sorry, but this is so out of the blue, I don't know what to say. What makes you think I might be involved, or related, as you say? Who is she anyway?"

Kirk congratulated himself on his choice of tactic. He had gone for the shake-the-tree-see-what-falls-out method. Montepulciano sounded shaken.

"A 25-year-old Cuban immigrant," Kirk said. "Do you have any children, Mr. Montepulciano?"

"I don't see how this is relevant, or any of your business. As a matter of fact I don't." Montepulciano shared a sleezy conspiratorial smile. "At least, not that I know of."

"Are you sure?" Kirk kept any irony out of his tone.

"What's that supposed to mean?"

A reddish tinge suffused the mobster's cheeks. Had the mention of children struck a chord? Time to shake the tree a little harder.

"Sometimes children are born without the father's knowledge," Kirk said. "For example, is it possible that the woman you raped in 1998—"

"That was no rape." The words seeped through clenched teeth. Montepulciano's index finger tilted side to side to emphasize his comment. "That was my freaking ex-girlfriend. Is this what it's all about? Extortion from that bitch? Get out of here and go tell her to call my lawyer."

"Sorry," Kirk said. "I meant, is it possible your girlfriend from 1998 got pregnant and perhaps you have a daughter?"

Montepulciano turned to look at the sky through the large window. When his eyes spun back to Kirk, they projected rage. A cold ripple spread along Kirk's spine.

"Even if that were the case, I couldn't give a flying fuck." The back of Montepulciano's fingertips scraped under his chin. It reminded Kirk of a book he had seen once in a bookstore: how to speak Italian using only hand gestures. "And now you have two minutes to explain what makes you think I have anything to do with a *murder*, or managing heart transplants for that matter."

The mobster pulled back his shirt sleeve held together by dollar-sign cufflinks, eyed the exposed Rolex, and started timing. Kirk leaned forward and took a calming breath.

"A year or so ago," Kirk said, "you were accused of hacking into NYMC's records. It's the same hospital Amy Winter died in. We think the heart transplant database might have been compromised. We suspect the shooting might have been done to provide a heart for transplant."

"Wait a minute." Montepulciano leaned forward, both elbows on his desk, his index finger pointed at the desk top. "I was cleared of all charges. You have no right to even mention it, let alone hold that against me. Perhaps you should talk to my lawyer. We're done here."

Montepulciano pushed himself up from his chair. Kirk couldn't leave without a second handshake. He had to get what information he could from the interview, but remain friendly enough to shake hands again at the end.

"Listen," Kirk said, "we don't need lawyers. Between you and me, I thought it was far-fetched bullshit. I'm actually here to clear you. Where were you on Tuesday this week between 3 and 6 a.m.?"

"Tuesday?" Montepulciano looked at the ceiling. "I was in Florida. My ninety-one-year old mother is in a place there. I went to visit."

"That's nice," Kirk said. "Do you go there often?"

"Not really." Montepulciano's mouth stretched into a line and his cheeks muscles contracted several times. "But what business is that of yours?"

It was about time to visit the old lady. The Florida trip sounded more like a planned alibi. Still, the purpose of the interview wasn't to call the mobster's bluff. Montepulciano didn't look to be in the best of moods. Kirk had to quit pushing ahead with accusatory questions.

"I understand, believe me." He gave the mobster a most sympathetic smile. "When my mother was in one of those places, I couldn't take it either. Too depressing."

Montepulciano stared at him, his wide open eyes like piercing rods. The suggestion of a smirk conveyed *you've got to be kidding* as a silent answer. It was now or never. Kirk stood up without touching the chair's upholstery.

"Well," he said, "that should clear the air for you. Sorry for the trouble."

Kirk put out his hand. The mobster stood and looked around as if searching for a way to avoid the handshake. Kirk's breath caught. Montepulciano's hand didn't move.

"So we're done?" Montepulciano came around the desk.

"I think we're done." Kirk extended his open hand a few inches further. "Thanks for your cooperation."

The relief of being off the hook did the trick. Montepulciano grabbed Kirk's hand. Kirk felt the tension in the man's muscles relax as a film of sweat transferred from the mobster's palm to his own. Kirk counted four seconds before letting go and exhaled with a jolt of triumph.

"Next time, you'll have to call my lawyer," the mobster said, putting forward his perfunctory smile while waving Kirk to the door and back to the lobby.

Keeping his hand in the air, Kirk rushed to the bathroom and locked himself inside a stall. With his left hand, he removed the kit again. Now, using the special Dacron polyester wipe, he swiped his right hand over and over, then placed the wipe in a sterile evidence container, sealed it, and labeled it. The sweat had been icing on the cake. Kirk walked out confident that in the evidence bag he carried enough biological material to extract Santo Montepulciano's DNA.

CHAPTER 10
FIRST DATE

This was a date; Bloom had no doubt about it. The dim light of the Manhattan French Bistro imparted a red glow to the two wine glasses standing on a crisp, white table cloth. Across from her, on this fine Saturday night, Zayne Wilder looked less and less like a doctor. His wild dark-brown hair lay coerced into a neat partition by a recent shower. A black suede jacket and neatly pressed tan trousers replaced his uniform-like scrubs. An open collared light-green shirt made his eyes look grayer. Bloom remembered reading that only three percent of the population had gray eyes. This fact suffused Zayne with an exotic aura and made Bloom conscious of her breathing.

She picked up her glass and took a healthy sip of Cabernet. She skipped swishing the wine around her mouth, the way she had learned during wine tasting. Instead, she swallowed it at once, hoping that the alcohol would help redirect her focus away from Zayne's exotic features and more toward her investigatory task. That wine could help was obviously wrong; it merely confirmed the hopelessness of her predicament.

"How did you get into the FBI?" Zayne said.

"I always wanted to do something important with my life," Bloom said. "I didn't know what it would be until I had the chance to work with Director Mulville about five years ago. Well, he was just an agent then. And I was still in college, working as a clerk in a Washington hospital. It was insane. We had to find the nuclear biscuit—you know the nuclear codes—before the—"

"What?" Zayne said. "You were involved in the second 9/11? Are you kidding me?"

"No kidding. I was." She relished the awe in his eyes. "And, right on the spot, Mulville offered me a job with the FBI. I mean he needed my help then and there, but he said it could become for real, in the future, you know, if I was interested. After I saw what was at stake and how important FBI work can be, I knew I wanted to be part of it, to fight the bad guys."

"What a story," Zayne said. "You helped save millions. Including me. I was here, in New York, at the time."

He smiled. The laugh lines that gathered at the side of his nose made him look younger. She wished he kept on smiling, knowing that she was the reason.

"After I finished college," she said, "Mulville helped me with the paperwork, pushed me along, mentored me. And I always loved the cyber stuff. I was lucky because the FBI cyber-crimes division was starting and recruiting just when I finished training."

"Very impressive." He looked past her as if searching for a new topic of conversation. "What about your parents? Did they encourage you?"

"My father died when I was ten," she said.

"I'm sorry."

"He was an accountant. But I remember him as a fun-loving man who liked to make toys for me because he couldn't afford to buy them. I still have a wooden train he carved—I think he would have preferred a boy over a girl."

Zayne smiled.

She shook her head. "One day, he suddenly had a fatal heart attack. He was only 42."

His eyelids dropped. The sympathy she saw in his eyes melted something inside her.

"For years," she said, "my mother worked two jobs: in a factory, making ice cream containers, and as a waitress, on weekends. Soon, for everything she did and is doing for me, I'll be able to give her back a little."

"That sounds like a good plan." His hand landed on hers and she saw his eyes steadying on hers again. His pupils seemed larger. The pity she had noticed at the mention of her father had faded.

"What about you?" she said, keeping her gaze away from their hands. "How did you decide to be a heart surgeon?"

"My father was a general surgeon," he said it as if that explained everything. "I guess I never thought of doing anything else. Then one day, while rotating through cardiothoracic surgery, the attending let me hold a heart. A human heart, in my hands. They were transplanting it. I felt … so happy, to be part of such a difficult and critical procedure, to fight against death and disease. That was my moment. I knew I wanted to transplant hearts and become great at it. And I wanted to experience that feeling every day for the rest of my life. So I fell in love with my work."

"You're lucky." She looked at his hand, covering hers. The surgeon's hand. The hand that held quivering hearts and fixed them. She wanted to feel his hands all over her body. "Not many people love their work."

"I don't see how one can work forty or fifty years not liking what he does." He shook his head. "Life is to be enjoyed. Work is one of the most important parts of life."

She wanted to enjoy the warmth she felt inside. She wished she had no agenda for the night other than getting to know Zayne Wilder better. But if she left the difficult part for last, the evening might end up worse.

"It's so true." She had to leave time to go back to regular date conversation. She withdrew her hand to pick up her glass and to take another sip of wine.

"There is something I need to tell you," she said. "I kinda want to get it out of the way, so we can enjoy the rest of the evening."

He nodded.

"We were able to secure a DNA sample from Santo Montepulciano," she said, putting her wine glass back on the table. She bent down to retrieve the evidence bag from the pocketbook at her feet. "I hope you can check his DNA against your patient's."

She extended her hand across the table. Zayne held his glass to his lips. His eyes, staring into hers, carried only dreamy approval. The evidence bag entered his field of vision and tore him away from his trance. Bloom felt a jab of remorse.

"I have to say," Zayne whispered, "I admire your determination."

He took the bag and examined it under a candle-like fixture at the center of their table. His surgeon's fingers flattened the plastic to bring Kirk's swipe into better view. He squinted to read the label. When he glanced at her again, his lids narrowed.

"Where did you get this?" he asked, his voice betraying a hint of reproach. "It's nothing like the cheek swabs we usually get."

"You don't wanna know." She let go of a nervous chuckle. "What you should know is that Kirk Miner and I have noticed several unusual things about your transplant chain. It looks more and more like someone may be messing with it, and Montepulciano is the top candidate."

"I doubt it," Zayne said, shaking his head. "Can we talk about this? If I remember correctly, that was what we agreed to do today. Discuss it."

"Listen," she said, straightening up on her chair, "you have an excessive number of suicidal donors in your chain. Most of them shoot themselves in the temple, in the one perfect spot to avoid cardiac arrest, and near a hospital, to facilitate their quick rescue and subsequent heart donation. If you want, I can show you the data. We have enough to get a warrant for your chain. At least you don't have to worry about that anymore. Now we have to find out who's responsible. And the answer may be in that bag. For that DNA, though, we can't get a warrant because last year the FBI didn't have enough evidence for cybercrime charges to stick to Montepulciano. So, it's up to you. Do you want him to continue to mess with your chain database?"

"Are you sure?" he whispered.

She nodded emphatically.

"This is terrible, if it's true. I guess it's possible that what's happening now is related to the hacking of the hospital records last year."

"I think that's the case." She looked at him with as much empathy he had shown her. "If you want, I can take you through the data analysis."

He nodded and placed the bag into his jacket pocket. "I'll put a rush on losing my license. And my career."

Bloom bit her lip. "Thanks." She took a deep breath and another sip of wine. "It may help us find out the truth and straighten out your transplant database."

The waiter brought their entrees, and for a while they ate in silence. Bloom focused on her plate. Was Zayne still thinking about her part of the deal—that is, their date? Or, like an evil fairy godmother, had she turned their date *and* his career into shit? She wanted to disappear under the table and crawl her way out of the restaurant. Did Zayne hate her for using him, and getting a free dinner to boot?

But it wasn't true. She was actually helping him. His chain was under attack. She hoped he could see that. Under different circumstances, she would be fantasizing about going home with him, right now. The only thing she wanted to think of at the moment was standing against a cool wall, pinned by Zayne's taut body, his full lips on her mouth, his tongue—

"Wake up." Zayne was talking now.

He snapped his fingers as if he were a hypnotist bringing a subject out of a trance. He wanted conversation. The date must still be on.

"I understand that, by solving the case, you're trying to help me," he said. "I certainly don't want anything illegal threatening my patients. And I can relate to how much you love your job."

The professional appreciation made her feel particularly sexy.

"I think there are two major loves in life," he said, pushing back from his steak. "Your work and your soul mate. And, if you're lucky enough to find what you're looking for in both fields, the intensity of the feelings is about the same."

"And you think that goes even for a woman?" she said.

"Of course." His chuckle made her regret her question. "A human being of either sex *must* have a life purpose *independent* of his or her relationships."

"Many men can't stand an accomplished woman. They say they want her, but in reality they feel castrated."

"I'm glad I'm not many men," he said, his hand finding hers again.

"Me too," she said.

Her hand felt good under his. Nothing like a heart doctor's healing touch to keep away a fluttering heart. Only a healthy heartbeat pulsated in her throat, fueled by the exciting light squeeze of her hand.

Soon the dinner plates were gone and the waiter asked about dessert. She withdrew her hand to look at the menu. Zayne settled on the chocolate soufflé, which gave them an extra twenty minutes together.

Three quarters of an hour later, a paid restaurant bill sat on the chocolate-soiled tablecloth. The dinner was over. Something relaxed in the pit of her stomach, replacing the pleasant tension that had been with her for most of the evening.

"Time to go," he said, getting up. He held her jacket and she pushed her arms into the sleeves, then tightened her belt with a quick, final gesture. "I'll walk you to your car."

He held open the door of the restaurant. Avoiding any contact, she passed by him, keenly aware of her fragile resolve. There had to be a way to be with this man without giving up her career. How could she trust him with her problem? As a doctor, he would immediately insist on subjecting her to tests and treatments, as he had already suggested during their coffee shop meeting.

A *personally* involved doctor would be impossible to handle. Before she knew it, Mulville would find out about her condition and place her on administrative duty. Permanently. She needed time to think, figure out how to hide her cardiac problem from a heart doctor, while seeing him socially. She let go a bittersweet chuckle.

His hand took charge of hers the moment they stepped on the sidewalk. The clear night felt crisp on her hot skin. The city looked particularly alive with lights, cars, and people. The city that never sleeps. She never wanted to sleep tonight. He colored her world. Simply walking at his side turned into an exhilarating experience that made her feel light, like on a roller coaster ride. Just a taste of what a relationship with Zayne could be. She thought of an Italian song she liked, about a man who goes back with his girl to all the places he has travelled to by himself. In the song, everything was new and much more beautiful as he relived the experiences with her.

She had never been so sad to see her car at the end of the block. They approached it slowly and stopped next to the driver's side door.

"I guess you got what you came for," he said, winking.

His sentence hit her stomach, alleviating her of all prior pleasantness. Perhaps she'd be better off if Zayne saw her as a bitchy, opportunistic FBI agent. It would make her life easier. But something rebelled inside.

"Not yet," she whispered, leaning back against the cold car door. "Not everything I came for."

She lifted her head, her mouth in full view. His mouth's corners lifted. His lips looked dangerously inviting. His eyes widened. She closed her eyes, afraid of the rising intensity. She felt his arms around her and his mouth pressed on hers with all the boldness she had invited. His tongue tasted of chocolate. The kiss ended too soon. His arms released her. *What? Just a good night kiss?* The night was over. She turned to her car, hoping not to show her disappointment.

She opened the door and sat behind the wheel. The door slammed shut. He gave her the same narrow-eyed look he had used in the restaurant, after she had handed over the evidence bag. An *is that all there is* look. No, it wasn't all there was. She wanted much more. She turned on the engine and rolled down her window.

"So," he said, leaning in, so close that she inhaled—*what did they call the sex-scent-chemicals?*—pheromones. "I'll see you later?"

It had been a long time since her last date. Months and months of FBI training stretched behind her. She had gone entire life without dating *this* kind of man. A man able to appreciate her not just for her looks, but for who she was and what she did. She couldn't risk letting him go. She needed it. And she deserved it. Only once. Then she would wait during the next two months, until her promotion to full FBI agent.

"You could keep on seeing me now," she whispered, unlocking the passenger door. "If you wish."

His eyes gave her a flash of surprise. Heat rose to her face. He nodded and smiled.

"I'm parked across the way." He pointed to a black Avalon on the other side of the street. "Follow me."

During the short ride, she battled to keep any negative thoughts out of her mind. Losing that battle would mean turning around and going back to her Brooklyn apartment and likely never seeing Zayne again, except in her FBI agent function. As she followed him to his Manhattan apartment, a few blocks from NYMC, she took a few cleansing breaths. She was so near the hospital. If something happened to her heart, she would be in good hands and in a good place. She wasn't totally crazy—only partially insane.

The lobby was unmanned and smelled of curry and other Indian spices. They rode in the elevator without touching or looking at each other. He waved her out like a gentleman, and they walked side by side to his door. He fumbled with a few locks, and they were in.

"It's a rental from the hospital," he explained in an apologetic tone. "For people in training and doctors starting practice. I'm looking for my own place."

The one-bedroom place was sparsely furnished with a cozy black couch and two matching armchairs crowded around a glass coffee table. She saw the bedroom through an open door. The bed was made. What were the chances that a super-busy cardiac surgeon, a bachelor, had make his bed? Had he prepared for the possibility? The thought made her tremble with anticipation.

"Would you like anything to drink?" he asked.

No, she didn't need anything else to drink. Too much alcohol could trigger arrhythmias.

"No thanks," she said. "I think I had too much wine already."

Zayne smiled, as if in total agreement. He took her by the hand and brought her to his bedroom. In the dim light, her black dress hit the floor next to Zayne's shirt. Looking at Zayne's hairy chest and muscular abdomen gave her heart a few extra beats. But the doctor took charge. The lovemaking seemed to happen in slow motion. It was as if he knew, as a doctor, the right amount of excitement to impart without overstimulating her heart. She was safe in his hands. She could let go. And she did.

The rapid pulse in her throat jolted her away from the post-coital languor. Damn. She had fallen asleep rather than leave while she was ahead. And now her heart was acting up. And Zayne was very close. She could smell his scent. In the dim street light filtering through the blinds, she saw him propped up on his elbow, eyes open and focused not on her face, but on her neck.

"What are you doing?" She gasped. "Are you examining me?"

"It's not like that." He looked at her more closely, eyebrows drawn together. "I can't help it if I'm a doctor. You're having ventricular tachycardia. I can tell, just looking at your neck veins. They bulge with every abnormal beat of your heart. The heart is trying to pump blood against closed valves. Instead, the blood backs up into the veins. It's dangerous. If it goes on, your heart could go into ventricular fibrillation and arrest. The only reason you're not passing out now is that you're lying down. We need to call 911."

She took a breath and pushed hard into her chest. It didn't work. She clenched her hand into a fist and punched her sternum. The rhythm normalized. She exhaled.

"No," she said. "It's gone. Don't call anyone. Please."

He looked at her as if waiting for a further explanation. But that was the thing she couldn't give him. He had to understand. She had given him her body, for God's sake! Wasn't that enough?

"Arrhythmias can be sign of serious heart problems." His voice carried the gentleness of seasoned bedside manners. "I can help you. I can refer you to the best cardiologist I know."

"I can't," she said. "If they find out I have a problem with arrhythmias, my career with the FBI is done. I need to hold on for two months."

"Two months? What happens then?"

"My probation is over. The probation is for two years. I have only two months to go. You can't tell anyone. Until I'm set as a real FBI agent."

"Listen." He squeezed her arm. "I don't want anything to happen to you. Do you know what's wrong with your heart? You said you have a doctor."

"I know you care," she said, getting up and gathering her bra, panties, and dress from the floor. "I do too. I mean I care about me. And you. But for now, my job takes priority. I need to focus on that."

"Where are you going?" he said, his voice becoming shrill. "You can't just hop up and leave, after ventricular tachycardia. I want to see you again. I need you to stay alive."

The staying-alive line chilled her skin. She chuckled sadly while struggling with the bra hooks behind her back. She gave up and stuffed her bra in her pocketbook.

"Listen," she said, pulling her dress down to cover her naked body. "You have to trust me. For the next two months, I have to focus only on my work. I can't go to doctors, or on dates. Most of all, I can't go on dates with doctors. I hope you can wait for me. I really want you to."

She kissed his open mouth, grabbed her pocketbook from the bedroom floor, walked through the living room to the front door, and left, before Zayne could recover from the surprise. The image she carried to the elevator was Zayne's large gray eyes full of bewilderment and hurt. Would she ever be with him again, the way they had been tonight? Tears of doubt streamed down her cheeks as she walked out of the elevator, through the small lobby, and outside the front door into the cold night.

CHAPTER 11
DNA

Saturday night wine and the lack of sleep took a toll. And Sunday had not provided Bloom with the needed rest either. On Monday morning, stuck in Manhattan rush-hour traffic, she yawned and gulped down several sips of her large latte. Her head bobbed and jolted at the sound of a ping. After a glance at her phone stuck to the dashboard, she slammed on the brakes to avoid hitting the car in front of her. A text message lit up the screen. From Zayne, again. Counting phone messages and texts, this was the twelfth message since their date. Weren't doctors busy saving lives? Where did he find the time to torment her? She was still trying to formulate a plan of action. So far, silence seemed the best response. At last, she reached the FBI building. Seeing the time, she sighed. She had to hurry up.

As she parked, her gaze went instinctively to the column at the side of her car, as she had done coming and going every day since first noticing the hidden man. Today, her breath caught in her throat as her eyes landed on the familiar black shoes. The stalker was back.

Bloom kept her head low as she glanced up and sideways at the pillar. The halogen light shone from behind cast a linear outline. But the straight line bulged out into an irregular shape indicating a human shadow. She had just about had it.

Bloom stretched her arm and grabbed the Kevlar vest from the passenger's seat. Glad that she had left her jacket on the back seat, she squeezed her upper body into the straps without straightening up or lifting her head above the side window. Her hand reached out again and opened the glove compartment. Her gun fell onto the car floor with a muffled thump.

"Shit."

With great effort, she extended her arm until her finger reached the

Glock. She retrieved it, clutched the grip's cold metal, and took a deep breath. Eyes locked on the shadow, she steadied the gun barrel onto her left forearm, as Mulville had shown her many times during the past few years. The thought of her mentor brought her comfort and doubt at the same time. What would Mulville tell her to do now?

While her thumb unlocked the safety and cocked the hammer, sweat poured down her back and she saw hair sticking up on the exposed part of her wrist. She was ready. But for what? Should she really confront the man? What if he was armed and waiting for her to leave the safety of her car? Perhaps she should call for back-up. But the man hadn't done anything threatening. Not yet. Except for stalking. Was stalking threatening enough to justify her behavior? Her neck hurt from the twisted position. The gun felt cold and heavy. Mulville was right. She was a foolish, inexperienced rookie.

As if mocking her, the shadow retreated behind the column. Bloom's hand tensed up around the gun. Then she saw the figure shrinking, as the man walked away from her. He moved swiftly, hands deep into the pockets of a black coat, head covered by an old-fashioned, brimmed, black hat, the dressy black shoes shining under the ceiling light.

The buzzing of her phone made her fingers twitch. Bloom took a cleansing breath and ordered her trigger finger to stand down. She straightened up and looked at the screen. Zayne was calling again. She was going to let the call go to voicemail, but his last text forced her to answer. The DNA results were in. Already. She put the gun back into the glove compartment.

"Hey," she said. "What's up?"

"Hello to you too," the doctor said. "I've been trying to get you for a while."

"Sorry." She really was sorry. No good solution in sight. "I had a great time, and I want to do it again. Give me two months. But what's with the DNA? The sooner I solve this case, the closer I may get to my promotion, and the sooner we can have a second date."

"If our relationship depends on this," he said, "I'm afraid we should forget about it. No luck. No match. Not even close. Your mobster has nothing to do with my patient, as I already told you and Miner. Have a nice day."

The call ended. Something went amiss inside her as well. No more lightness in her chest while thinking about Zayne's enticing eyes. No look-ing forward to future dates. There was no easy or gentle way to hold passion back. Only an equally strong negative emotion could do the job. She had done it to Zayne—forced him to hold back the feelings he was developing for her. The accomplishment didn't bring her any pleasure. She'd much rather be in Zayne's arms.

The renewed buzzing of her phone reminded her that Kirk Miner was waiting for her to report on her meeting with Zayne. She shrugged the painful thoughts away, exchanged the Kevlar for her jacket, grabbed her backpack, and stepped out of the car. The faint scent of the stalker's after-shave reached her nostrils and made her shiver.

Bloom exited the elevator and approached a small waiting area marked by a faded rug with the round FBI logo. The sight of the Bureau's symbol always gave her an uplifting feeling of pride, for being part of such group, performing critical, life-or-death work. Today, she felt like wiping her feet on it.

Kirk held two large coffee containers and was sipping his latte. He nod-ded without smiling and offered her one without leaving his armchair. His roman nose imparted an aura of pride without arrogance. The more she got to know Kirk, the more she liked him, despite Mulville's warning her about the unlikelihood of any smooth FBI-police interactions. Perhaps, as a PI, Kirk was a once-removed veteran of the police department. More likely, suspicion boosted by paranoia often obfuscated Mulville's judgment.

Bloom took the paper cup, sipped the lukewarm contents, and forced a thankful smile.

"So sorry I'm late." She glanced at her watch and shook her head. "I sat in traffic for at least half an hour. Then the doctor called. Let's go in."

"I hope your news is better than mine." Kirk followed her to her work-ing space and dumped his paper cup in her waste basket. He sat next to her while she took out her computer. "Tell me."

He looked away as she brought the computer to life with her password. She had to put forward her Plan B. Kirk and Mulville would then discuss her performance. She opened the chain database using Zayne's username and password. Images of Zayne's sexy body flashed into her mind and brought her a hurtful pang.

"Baker, D3, is also a match to Margarita Herrera, P1." Her fingers flew across the keyboard searching the chain. "I'm looking for other patients matching D3, Baker. Do you remember? Zayne said there was another patient who would have gotten the heart if Herrera refused? This patient should show up as a possible match to Baker as well, because Baker is also a match to Herrera. Do you follow?"

"Yes," Kirk said. "You're looking for a second patient who could have been a recipient of Amy Winter's heart after Herrera refused it."

"Exactly," she said. "But none shows up. No other patients in the chain could be a recipient of Amy Winter's heart. Or of Baker's. I searched the entire database."

"But Dr. Wilder said another patient in the chain matched Amy Winter," Kirk said. "You're saying *that* patient could be Montepulciano's real target? Boy, that's a bit far removed, isn't it?"

"Yes, it is," she said. "We need to call the doctor and get that patient's name. I'm still convinced Montepulciano has something to do with this. We just got to find the connection."

Kirk picked up her phone and handed it to her. Little did he know that she was the last person Dr. Wilder, after her icy treatment, would want to chat with at the moment. She waved her hand to indicate he should make the call, but Kirk didn't budge. She sighed and dialed.

"Hello, Charlotte," Zayne said. "What do you need now?"

Fire set in her throat and cheeks. She couldn't look at Kirk, who would report to Mulville. She could just imagine how Mulville would react if *he* found out what happened between her and Zayne.

"Listen, please." She got up and walked away from her desk, her mouth on the cold screen, whispering. "I'm in my office with Detective Miner. We're wondering if you can tell us a bit more about that patient in the chain you mentioned as a possible second recipient for Amy Winter's heart. Shouldn't this patient show up as a match to Baker's as well?"

"Good to know I have a witness," Zayne said. "Do you need another date for that?"

She pressed her hands on her face. This wasn't happening. She definitely didn't deserve it. Good thing she had placed some distance from Kirk.

"Please," she said. "Don't joke about this."

"You listen." Zayne's voice carried all the irritation and anger she feared. "For the record, I'm not acknowledging anything you say, and I don't have any idea how you came to know all this. But in the interest of saving people's lives, I'll check my database again."

"We have a warrant for the chain database. I'm sending it to you, so you don't have to risk your license for this info. And now I'm going back to Kirk Miner. Please let's keep this professional."

Bloom glanced at Kirk. She approached him again and nodded. "He's checking," she mouthed.

They stared at the unanswered question on their screen until Zayne came back.

"That patient is gone," he said. "Not there anymore. Must have died. Unfortunately, it happens more often than not in this business. And now I got to scrub for my next patient. Otherwise, we'll have one more death on our hands."

Bloom reported the answer to Kirk.

"Doctor," Kirk said, leaning forward toward the phone, "you need to hear this."

Kirk motioned Bloom to place the call on speaker.

"In the last year," Kirk said, "there were six suicides out of 500 individuals in your chain, all since the hacking of the hospital's database. That's more than one-hundred times the rate in the general population, according to Agent Bloom. You have a big problem, and we're trying to solve it. But we need your help."

Bloom nodded in gratitude for giving her credit. Kirk was on her side. Hopefully, Zayne would take into account her good intentions. Silence followed. A long silence.

"I understand," Zayne said finally. "Agent Bloom made me aware of this fact during our last…meeting. But these numbers are incredible."

"So," Kirk said, "nothing we can do to find out who she or he is, or was?"

"A woman," Zayne said. "I remember she was a woman, about 25, and her blood type was A."

"Any way we can check Montepulciano's DNA against this woman's?" Kirk said.

"Wow," Zayne said. "No. No access to such data. I don't even see her on the list now."

"Do you remember where she was from?" Bloom asked. "We're trying to save lives too."

After a short pause, Zayne came back. "You might be able to get an ID from the enrolling hospital. I think she was from the Cleveland Clinic. And now I really gotta go."

The call ended. The mention of the Cleveland Clinic gave Bloom a jolt. It was where she had consulted a cardiologist about her arrhythmia. She had gone to Ohio for fear of being discovered in New York by New York doctors as unfit to serve in the FBI. She was familiar with the Cleveland Clinic; it wasn't too far from her old home in Ohio. Perhaps Bloom could use this to her advantage. But for that she needed privacy.

"Good questions, Kirk," she said.

Kirk smiled, but the smile froze on his face as he stared at Bloom. "What's wrong? Not feeling well?"

"No," she said. "I'm okay. I know someone at the Cleveland Clinic. I need to search a bit and will let you know if I come up with a doctor I can call."

"Good idea." Kirk slapped his hands on the desk, got up, and grabbed his leather jacket from the back of the chair. "In the world of sacred privacy, it's always good to utilize any clout you may have to get useful info."

She watched him walk out in his noiseless sneakers. She had never seen him wearing anything but those. She looked at her black pumps. Good only for sitting at a computer desk. At least she had Kirk to cover the running-after-the-bad-guys part of the job, if and when the time for that came.

The phone shifted in her sweating hand as she dialed the Cleveland Clinic and listened to a litany of offered services, spanning all medical specialties, while she waited to be connected to the Cardiology Clinic. She considered using her FBI credentials instead of her connection as a patient.

"Charlotte Bloom, FBI," she said. Then she asked for her doctor.

"Charlotte," a kind male voice said, interrupting the soothing on-hold music after another short wait. "I'm so glad you called. I was worried about you. How are you?"

"Fine, Doctor. I'm fine." Her heart missed a beat as if to defy her words. She suppressed a surging fear, fueled by the memory of the warnings the same professional voice had conveyed a few months ago. "I'm not calling about me. It's about a case I'm working on. I need your help."

"Oh." The word sounded like something deflating. "But it's already too long. Soon, very soon, it could be too late."

"Doctor," she said, cutting to the chase, "I'm trying to solve a murder here, and to prevent future ones, if possible. We have reason to suspect someone is hacking and manipulating the heart transplant database called chain."

"What does the database have to do with your murder case?" the doctor said, his tone implying puzzlement.

"We suspect someone might have a special interest in one of the patients and is trying to provide her with a heart by facilitating the death of a matching donor."

"Facilitating?" the doctor said. "How?"

She couldn't allow the conversation to bog down in the details. She had to give the essential points, and only the essential ones. Just as Kirk had done.

"We think a patient listed by the Cleveland Clinic may be the daughter of a man connected to the New York Mafia."

"Whose daughter?" The doctor's voice rose an octave.

"That information," she said, "I can't divulge because it's part of an ongoing investigation. Today I'm asking you to share the name of the patient you listed in the chain."

So much for the freaking HIPAA. Bloom had tried to preempt the doctor's objections the best she could. Murder versus patient privacy: That was the choice.

"You're going to need a warrant." He sounded as if that was his final answer.

"See if you can answer only one question first," she came back. "To see if a warrant is really, well, warranted."

She heard him chuckle. Good sign. Here was her chance.

"I only need to know," she said, followed by a long deep breath, "if you recently listed a 25-year-old woman in the chain. Someone who subsequently died, or was taken off the chain for whatever reason. If so, we'll need to get her data, to see if her DNA matches our suspect's."

"Okay," the doctor said after a short pause. "I might be able to answer the first part. Hold on a moment."

She heard the clicking of fingers on a keyboard. Much better than what she had feared would happen, such as a long, music-filled hold, or worse, dismissal with the promise of a future call.

"Sorry," the doctor said. "No such patient."

"What?" She couldn't believe it. "No 25-year-old woman from the Cleveland Clinic? Ever?"

"It's an easy question to answer." The doctor sounded ominously sure. "We just started to sign people up to the chain last month. Our first patient doesn't even come close to what you're mentioning. For starters, he's a man. So far, he's the only patient we've listed on the chain. Probably the last one, after what you're telling me now."

"Do you have any donor without a related patient in the chain? In case the patient he signed up with has died?"

"No." The doctor didn't hesitate. "Only the one I told you about, with his donor. That's all."

"Would you know if a patient was signed up, and then died or was taken off by someone else?" Bloom's voice rose. "Who else has access to the chain at your clinic?"

"Of course I would know." She heard him chuckle again. But this time it transmitted annoyance. "As the head of Cardiology, I'm the only one who has final say on the matter. And the only one with access to the various transplant databases."

Great. No more signing up on the chain for Cleveland Clinic's patients.

Detective Bloom had just become a hindrance to future heart transplants. And all this for a theory that was looking more and more far-fetched every day. Except she trusted Zayne's memory. And Dr. Zayne Wilder had seen a 25-year-old patient from the Cleveland Clinic listed on the chain. Besides, her suspect was an expert hacker, or someone who worked with expert hackers, and thus was able to make patients appear and disappear.

After thanking her doctor and renewing the promise of becoming more compliant with his recommendations, she phoned Kirk and recounted her conversation.

"Well," Kirk said, "I agree with you and tend to believe Dr. Wilder, given the Cleveland Clinic inability to protect the hospital against hackers like Montepulciano and his men. But all this doesn't make any sense. Montepulciano isn't a doctor with a patient in desperate need of a heart. The patient, if she exists, has to get onto the list via some doctor, some program. Besides, no one was able to prove anything about Montepulciano."

The next step became clear in her mind. She and Kirk made a good team. Mulville would be proud of how much she was learning.

"You should talk to your captain friend, Spencer. See if we can find out anything about the mobster's ex-girlfriend. Perhaps we can come at this case from the mother's angle instead of the father's."

"Good idea," Kirk said. "We don't really have much else to go on, since a secret patient and donor connection are dead ends, so to speak."

She smiled at the phone screen, as she imagined Kirk winking at her. At least something promising had emerged from her work, something for her to focus on, instead of the disaster her personal life had turned into.

CHAPTER 12
RIBS AND BEER

The thick wooden door cracked open, as if complaining about Kirk's long absence. Kirk's favorite Celtic Pub stood across from the Prospect Park Police Station, former headquarters of former NYPD detective, now captain, John Spencer. He spotted John in their usual booth against the back wall. The choice of a table with view of the entrance and most of the room was one of the first rules his friend had taught Kirk over ribs and beer. John had stood by Kirk during his training to become a policeman, and then the transition from a short career in the Police to private investigator.

Kirk might owe John his marriage, too. Aurora had been unable to adjust to the role of a cop's wife. As a nurse often assigned to the trauma unit of the Brooklyn Medical Center, she was constantly reminded of a cop's daily dangers. She spent most days wondering if the kiss she had given Kirk that morning had been the last one. John had suggested the transition to private investigator.

But recently Kirk's job wasn't good enough to keep Aurora happy either. He had missed John. Their pub dinners had ceased to take place, mainly due to John's promotion and his move to Manhattan.

John sat in front of his favorite blonde on tap, drawing imaginary circles with his finger on a shamrock-shaped coaster. His face looked serious but lit up with a smile as soon as his eyes found Kirk.

"Too long, man." John got up from the bench and clasped his hand with the same energy Kirk remembered from the past. There was hope yet for the captain. "I missed this place."

"Tell me about it." Kirk took off his jacket and sat on the opposite bench of the dark green leather booth. "Between work and shuttling Peter around to all his activities, not much time left for this great stuff."

"How is he doing? Taking college courses now?"

"Right," Kirk said, and shook his head. "One of the subjects seems to be booze. He was picked up on campus walking to a party with a bottle of vodka."

John let go of a soft whistle.

"Aurora and I had to waste our time attending a meeting for the parents of the *chemically dependent*," Kirk said it as if he had a bad taste in his mouth.

"Great." John sighed.

"I don't think he's really drinking," Kirk said. "I think his older pals just made him carry the bottle."

"Do you really believe that?" John said, his blue eyes questioning Kirk from under lifted brows. "What did *you* do when you were in college?"

"Yeah. I hear you. He says he isn't. Problem is Peter isn't even 16 yet and he's around college-age people. I don't believe he's got a serious problem. Or maybe I'm naïve. I feel I should spend more time with him. Really find out what he's up to."

"Maybe you should," John said. "It's an important time in his life, I think. Pretty unusual."

"It is." An uncomfortable feeling started at the pit of Kirk's stomach. It nagged Kirk every time he felt guilty about his shortfalls with Aurora or Peter. John gave him a sympathetic smile.

"To tell you the truth," John said, "I wished I had your problems."

"Do you mean kids?" Kirk said. "You still have time to have kids."

"Not easy finding the right woman. And I'm getting old."

They both refused a menu from an unknown waitress and ordered the Miner-Spencer special of ribs and fries with blonde ale on tap. John got a refill. The sound of the clinking frosted glasses was overwhelmed by some fans cheering a basketball score. Everything sounded just the way it ought to. And the beer went down cold and soothing.

"So," John said, his blue eyes sparkling with happy mockery, "time to tell me what's so serious to warrant an over-the-ribs-and-beer session. You got me worried."

"Still the same case," Kirk said. "The patient who was supposed to get the heart all of a sudden refused it. Now the heart—"

"Wait a moment." John lifted his palm. "Now that the FBI took over the investigation, I'm just an interested bystander."

Great. Kirk was on his own with an FBI probe against the NY Mob. Good chance of ending up in some meat grinder. The *remains*, forensic people called them. Aurora and Peter's faces came to mind.

"So, what am I still doing on this case?" Kirk said. "I'm *a liaison* with the Police. Shouldn't I report?"

"Exactly." John pointed at him and winked. "That's how I know what's going on with this case. Go on. Act as the liaison you are. Also, Mulville will kill you if you quit and leave Bloom alone. Of course, if you need me, I'm here."

"Great to know." Kirk nodded. "The FBI girl is green but very good."

"What about Amy Winter's heart?"

"That heart," Kirk said, "after Dr. Wilder's patient, Margarita Herrera, refused the transplant, would have gone to this other patient, listed by the Cleveland Clinic."

"But you already told me that Amy Winter died," John said. "I guess we don't have to worry about the Winters any more. But someone tried to force them to consent to the donation."

"Yes," Kirk said. "And after Amy's death, this second patient has disappeared from the list. And the Cleveland Clinic has no record of ever listing her."

"How do you know about this second patient?"

"Right after Margarita Herrera refused the heart, Dr. Wilder saw this other woman listed as a number and various hashtags only. But now we can't see her in the database anymore."

The waiter brought two slabs of succulent ribs with sides of fries. Kirk inhaled deeply and let the memories flood his brain.

"Strange how nostalgia can filter away any anxiety and other negative feelings," Kirk said.

"What do you mean?"

"Most of the time we met here was to discuss difficult cases—the ones which would keep me up at night and stress me out during the day. But when I'm here now, I only remember the good feelings. You know, the friendship, the trust, and my gratitude for you being there for me."

"Thanks," John said. "I love this place."

The noise of drinks being shaken drifted from the bar. The smell of beer and fried food filled the air.

"So, what's up that cannot be discussed over the phone?" John said. "Shoot."

"We think that *the second* patient may be connected to Montepulciano, and he may have forced Margarita Herrera to refuse the heart."

"I already told you." John took a large bite of rib. The BBQ sauce colored his chin and upper lip. He chewed and swallowed. "We don't have any DNA from him. And even if we did, I'm not sure we could use it."

"About the DNA," Kirk said. Time to decide whether to tell John about his stunt. Coming clean with his friend won out.

John stopped chewing and held two sauce-dripping ribs in mid-air. His brows rose over wide eyes fixed on Kirk. "You did what?" John whispered. "After all I taught you. That'll only make sure the prick *doesn't* go to jail."

"Eat," Kirk said, waving his palm down. "DNA was no match. Margarita Herrera isn't related to the mobster. But what we need to know now is if Montepulciano's ex-girlfriend had a child after the rape. If she did, maybe her daughter is the real heart recipient. Maybe she's the second patient. Do you know who the girlfriend was and where she may be after 25 years?"

They ate in silence. John seemed wrapped in thought. Kirk hoped John had the answer and was debating whether or not to disclose the information. So he waited.

"Luckily for you, the DNA match came out negative," John said at last. He took a long sip of beer and wiped his hands and face clean with his napkin. "It would have been inadmissible."

"I took a gamble," Kirk said. "What about the former girlfriend?"

"The girlfriend's name is sealed for privacy. That's why it didn't show up in the file I gave you. Girlfriend doesn't want to be found. I can imagine why not."

Kirk looked John in the eye. Despite the captainship, this was still his friend John, man of inexhaustible resources and elastic rules, when possible and when necessary. Like right now.

"Listen." Kirk put down his last well-polished rib bone and wiped his mouth with a wet towel. "I'm afraid we're at the end of the line with the doctor. We have several dead ends. That's all... unless we can talk to the girlfriend, and even that is a long shot. Only thing clear to me and Bloom is that all the anomalies with this transplant database started after the hack."

John looked at him in a strange way now—a you've-got-to-be-kidding kind of look. Perhaps he had a point. As he told the story, Kirk had to admit that it sounded pretty fantastic to him as well. John smiled.

"Look, I see your point," John said. "I hate that fucking slob, Montepulciano, and wish I could put him down for good for all his sins. But we *are* the law. We don't have the luxury of acting on whims. I don't know. I think you're stretching this pretty thin."

The only thing to look forward to was dessert. The waitress came back, got the order, and refilled their beer mugs. They drank in silence.

The apple pie was a half-foot tall slice smothered in ice-cream. Kirk shifted his focus to the cold and sweet taste he remembered so well, hoping that the wave of disappointment wouldn't wipe away the calming effect of beer. But something was happening. John was looking at him like old times again, and there was the familiar spark in his eyes—the spark that preceded putting one over on the system. John still had his back.

"Listen," John said, as if revealing a secret, "from the original interview, I might still have the girlfriend's name and old address somewhere."

"How?" Kirk said. "You must've been a teenager when that case went down."

"It's kinda true—I started a few years later than that. But when we got Montepulciano for drugs, I reviewed the prior rape file. In it was a paper with the name and address of the woman. And an old picture. I should've destroyed it, but I wanted to talk to the woman myself, to see if I could find out about his past drug smuggling, so we could put him away for longer. She had changed her name but, with facial recognition, I was able to track her down. At least I thought so. With an old black and white picture, we can't be 100 percent sure that it's her, unless she confirms. She denied everything and didn't want anything to do with us. For years, she hid in a small town in Ohio, out in the sticks. More recently she moved somewhere near Washington DC. I think it's her, and she got very upset I'd been able to find her. She's still scared of him."

"Great," Kirk said. "When I'm ahead, I shouldn't ask, but I had to know. What made you change your mind—I mean, right now?"

"There is something—how can I put it?—disarming about you," John said. He looked at him with the pride of a mentor. He took a mouthful of pie and a sip of beer as if he needed help to put forward his words. "Same stuff from another person would sound ridiculous, but coming from you, there might be something there. And I've been wanting to nail the son-of-a-bitch for too long. Rape, drug trafficking, hacking, and now murder? We gotta stop him."

Kirk felt lucky. John appreciated, and acknowledged, who Kirk was. His best friend.

"Thanks." Kirk bit his lip. "How should we go about this?"

"I'll call you and you'll pick up the info," Spencer said. "You didn't get it from me. If I'm asked, I'll deny everything. Best way, if you find her, would be to show up unannounced. Start telling her about the murder and see if she opens up, if she knows anything."

"I agree," Kirk said.

"I mean it, Miner. My ass is on the line. Don't fuck with it."

"No sir," Kirk said.

The waitress approached. Kirk handed her the bill with his credit card.

"Dinner's on me," he said.

John fumbled with his wallet. He extracted a credit card and placed it in the waitress' hand on top of Kirk's card. He looked at Kirk.

"We're splitting," he said. "No reason not to."

"None whatever." Kirk nodded at the waitress.

Kirk and John finished their drinks. After signing the credit card receipts, they slid out of the booth and left the restaurant. Several people were in line for the valet.

"I was thinking," Kirk said as they waited for their cars. "Perhaps Bloom should go talk to Montepulciano's ex. You know, woman to woman."

"I would leave Bloom out of this for now," John said. "The DNA shit is enough. If Mulville finds out we're involving her in shady crap, he might pull her."

CHAPTER 13
THE MOBSTER'S EX

The River Hill apartment complex in Washington D.C. was located a few miles east of the Potomac River. The three-story red brick building spread wide against a clear, breezy sky whose color matched the unusual blue of the doorframes. The setting reminded Kirk of a cheap motel, except for the surrounding well-manicured lawn, trees, and shrubs. And the different window coverings.

He got out of his car, crossed the street, and stretched. The four-hour drive from Brooklyn marked the beginning of this expedition. The call Joe Winter had received proved that someone somehow knew who was involved in the case at hand. Kirk wanted to be as inconspicuous as possible, until he got to talk to Marjorie Silverman—probably former Marsha Stevens, Montepulciano's ex-girlfriend—and assess her willingness to cooperate. Or, more likely, her unwillingness. He figured driving left behind less evidence than flying.

The pleasant scent of pines and grass accompanied him as he approached the main entrance. The cold wind bit through his clothes as he rushed to pull open the blue-framed door. Locked. And nobody around. He checked the time: 2:09 p.m.. If Marjorie worked, she would probably get home after 4. Last time John had verified her address was a few years back, but Kirk had confirmed it using DMV records.

By assuming a new identity, the woman had done a pretty decent job hiding. Why would she come out of her safe hiding now? He turned to an old-fashioned tenant list on the side of the door. 36 apartments. Marjorie Silverman lived in apartment N. 301, on the third floor. He rang the bell. No buzz.

He decided to wait by having lunch in a coffee shop across the street with a view of the building entrance. During a couple of hours of sipping lattes and nibbling on a salami sandwich on ciabatta bread, he had seen only a few people enter the building, and none of them looked like Marjorie Silverman. Kirk glanced again at the black and white picture John had provided. The woman had dark hair, thick brows over makeup-free eyes that revealed considerable determination. Not a classic beauty, but attractive in a strong kind of way.

At last, a petite woman in her late fifties parked a battered tan-colored Honda Civic in the tenants-designated area in front of the building, and headed for the entrance. She wore corduroy black pants and a dark trench coat. Her gait appeared swift and determined.

To catch up to her before she got to the door, Kirk dashed out of the coffee shop. He was going to wait for her to open the door, to assure his own entry into the building, but at the last minute something made him call out while she fished the keys out of a large brown pocketbook. Better to give her the choice to invite him into the building after hearing what he had rehearsed during the long car trip.

"Mrs. Silverman," Kirk said in a soft tone, walking up to her from the right side, holding one of his business cards and the police ID card in his extended hand.

The woman stopped moving, her hands still clenching her pocketbook. Dark inquisitive eyes searched Kirk's face for any sign of familiarity. After finding none, puzzlement filled the large eyes, followed by a flash of fear. Then, in a sudden change, as if at the push of a button, an automatic door of indifference dropped in front of her eyes.

"I don't need anything," she said, resuming her quest for the keys.

She was no longer young, as testified to by the grayish roots sticking out from the partition of her black wavy hair. Her deeply wrinkled forehead suggested lifelong worry. The still attractive features had survived not just natural aging, but the ravaging of sorrow and despair. The determination in her eyes was unchanged from her old picture. She had survived with obvious dignity.

"My name is Kirk Miner." Kirk waved his credentials. "I'm a private investigator."

She looked up again. Now Kirk saw only anger. The fear was his.

"Did he send you?" she said with straight lips.

"Nobody sent me," Kirk said, opening his arms, hand still holding his cards. "I'm coming on my own. I just need to ask you a few questions."

She reached out for the card and the ID and gave them a skeptical look. Kirk's glance conveyed all the compassion and respect he already felt for the woman.

"What do you want," she said, "from *Miss* Silverman?"

"Do you mind?" Kirk said, wrapping his arms around his chest to fend the evening chill. "Could we go inside? It's getting very cold out here."

"Okay," she hissed, "but you'll be brief and go home quickly."

She unlocked the door and let him into a small lobby in serious need of repainting and no room for any seating arrangements. The air smelled stale. The woman returned Kirk's police ID and placed the business card in her pocketbook.

"What do you want?" She looked around the deserted tiny lobby as if searching for listening ears.

"Thanks for talking with me," Kirk said. "All that we say today will be kept confidential.

I'm helping the police investigate the murder of a young woman. We suspect she was killed to facilitate the donation of her heart to a patient. We think the patient may be another young woman listed by the Cleveland Clinic. When the heart—"

"Stop," she said, her chin trembling. "Why are you telling me all this? What does this have to do with me? I don't know, and I don't care, and I gotta go ... now."

Her face looked paler. As she turned to rush for the stairs, her eyes told Kirk she knew a lot, and the knowledge terrified her.

"Wait," Kirk said. "Please. I need your help."

The woman started to climb the stairs. Kirk followed her. His heart thumped in his chest out of all proportion to the exertion.

"Marsha Stevens!" he shouted.

The clicking of her shoes on the tiled stairs immediately ceased. A heater hissed in the distance. Then breathing and a sob echoed in the staircase. Kirk climbed two steps at a time and found Marjorie on the third floor, sitting on the stairs, clenching her pocketbook in front of her as if it were a shield. She stared at the wall ahead. Her cheeks sagged. Her mouth, which Kirk thought could be full and beautiful under other circumstances, stretched and quivered with pain. Kirk sat down near her, making sure not to touch her.

"How do you know?" she said through clenched teeth.

"I don't," Kirk said, electing to go with the full truth, to encourage the woman to do the same. "That's why I need your help. Is your daughter sick?"

"I don't have a daughter." The woman shook her head. "I don't know what you're talking about."

"I know what happened to you 25 years ago," Kirk said. "I know you're scared to talk about it. I know how much that man can scare people."

Marjorie turned and looked him in the eye. "You know nothing."

"The man who hurt you 25 years ago," Kirk whispered, "will kill again, to save this young woman, who we think is his daughter. We need to stop him."

"I don't know any man," she said, her tone more resigned than aggressive. "Please leave me alone."

"Miss Silverman doesn't have a daughter. But what about Marsha Stevens' daughter?" Kirk asked, though it sounded more like a statement than a question.

"No. No. Stop!"

"Is Marsha's daughter also his daughter—Santo Montepulciano's daughter?"

"What difference does it make to you?" She shrugged.

"I'm afraid he's trying to provide a heart for a certain patient by killing innocent people," Kirk said. "If she's your daughter, we need your help to stop him."

Marjorie bit her lower lip. Her eyes remained fixed on the staircase. Kirk thought about his next question. He felt like he was walking in a mine field.

"Is she very sick?" he asked, his tone soothing. "What's her problem?"

She shook her head, her eyes closed, tears streaming down her cheeks. Then she turned to Kirk. Her eyes opened wide with despair.

"She'll die," she said. "Soon. Without a new heart. That's all I can tell you."

"Did you talk to Mr. Montepulciano about her?"

Marjorie placed her tear-streaked face in her hands. Her hands looked chafed and in desperate need of care. She shook her head again, this time more vigorously, as if she was trying to avoid hearing the question.

"Please," Kirk said, "if you tell me, I'll do everything I can to help you. As you know, we're dealing with a very dangerous man."

She lifted her face. Kirk watched her moist eyes assess him, deciding whether she could trust him, and his professed ability to safeguard her from Montepulciano. How could he expect the poor woman to trust him? His mouth felt dry.

"When she got ill, a while ago," she said, "I felt desperate. The wait on those organ lists is so long. I suspected he might have a way to push her ahead on the transplant list and keep her from dying. I lived in hiding much of my adult life, afraid he might find me ... find us. I risked my life to send him a hair sample from my daughter, for him to determine if he was her father. That was about a month ago. He got so mad, I thought he would send someone to kill me. He told me he didn't give a fuck. That's what he said about his dying daughter. As far as I know, he never bothered with the DNA test."

"He must have changed his mind," Kirk said. The mention of a possible DNA test a month ago raised questions in his mind about the event timeline, but he kept his focus on Marjorie. "He killed someone to give his daughter—your daughter—her heart."

She flinched.

"Who's your daughter?" Kirk said. "We need her name and location. So we can contact her. If we can connect her to Montepulciano, we may be able to stop him from future killings."

"You promised me," she said, shaking, "this would be private. He'll kill *me* if he finds out I'm talking to you. And you can't stop him anyway. Nobody can. You have no proof of anything. And if we stop him, my daughter will die."

"You don't need him," Kirk said. "There are great hospitals and doctors to help your daughter. I believe she was listed by the Cleveland Clinic."

Marjorie's mouth slacked. She cocked her head. Her wet eyes widened.

"The police *can* protect you."

Her face reddened. Her mouth and eyes tightened. Kirk was quickly concluding that nothing he could say would get Marjory back on his side. He swallowed acid and braced for what he knew was coming.

"Like they protected me 25 years ago," she whispered, "when I had to take back my accusations in order to survive?"

Kirk stared at the wall.

"And you're lying to me." She pointed at him. "You know a lot more than you're telling me. You leave my daughter out of this. I never meant for anyone to get killed. If he did it, he belongs in jail. That's where he's always belonged. For the past 25 years. No thanks to people like you. And now you better get out and go to work. Good night, Mr. Miner. Have a good life. Let me live mine in peace. Don't you dare bring my daughter into this. She knows nothing about anything, and if it doesn't stay that way, I swear, I'll sue the police, you, and everyone involved."

She got up and rushed to her door. Kirk remained seated, head in his hands. Behind Marjorie Silverman's door echoed the metallic sounds of several locks clicking into place.

CHAPTER 14
THE CHAIN

Bloom took a sip from her paper cup, hoping that the hot coffee would melt away the knot squeezing her chest since her last phone call with Zayne about the other possible recipient of Amy Winter's heart. She had never heard from him again. Nor had she expected to. Her life would never be the same.

She had to focus. Otherwise, she would lose the job she had already lost Zayne for. Kirk Miner was sitting in her office area, recounting his meeting with Montepulciano's ex-girlfriend.

"At least," Kirk concluded, "we know the mobster probably has a daughter who needs a heart transplant soon."

"But Montepulciano doesn't give a damn about her," Bloom said. "He's not even interested in finding out if he *has* a daughter, let alone helping her."

"Yeah. He told me the same thing in person." Kirk nodded. "A very nice family man."

"And why can't we determine the identity of the daughter on our own?" Bloom asked.

"The records have been officially sealed for the past 25 years," Kirk said. "I checked Marsha Stevens' past and couldn't find any records of her having a baby. I actually couldn't find anything at all. It's like she never existed."

Bloom shook her head. "How can you be sure she had a daughter?"

"Marsha Stevens admitted as much," Kirk said. "And she thinks Montepulciano is the father."

"What name does Marsha go by now?" Bloom said. "It should be very easy to find out if she has a daughter using her new name."

Kirk looked at her in silence. What was he thinking? This should be her turf. But John's advice about not involving Bloom returned to his mind.

"Marsha Stevens changed her name, erased her past, and went to great trouble to keep her and her daughter's privacy," he said. "I searched for a daughter bearing her new name and came up empty. I don't feel comfortable sharing Marsha's present name as yet. I promised the poor woman I'd keep her privacy."

Was Kirk holding back because he didn't trust her? But she had her own secrets as well.

And how did her stalker fit into this? Someone didn't want her to investigate. Or was this just one more unsupported theory? Bloom needed something solid to go on before sharing what could amount to a paranoid delusion. Hopefully the first solid thing she would encounter wouldn't be a bullet. She stared at her hands. Then something occurred to her.

"You mentioned that Marsha Stevens contacted Montepulciano about a month ago," Bloom said. "By then, several of the suicides had already happened. The hacking and the interference with the chain might have started independently of Montepulciano's daughter's illness. I think we're dealing with a hacking job for the purpose of facilitating transplants, but a hacking that had nothing to do with his daughter, at least at the beginning."

Kirk rubbed his chin, considering. She liked the fact that he never just dismissed her input, but took care to ponder, even if she was just a FBI probie. Working with Miner boosted her confidence.

"But if that's true," Kirk said, "what's in it for the mobster?"

Kirk was right. Montepulciano would have to be receiving some compensation to make all this effort and risk worth it. Mobsters didn't work pro-bono.

"I don't think the daughter's medical problem is a coincidence." Kirk smiled. "Coincidences in investigations are, as in medicine, very rare and never to be readily accepted. I think the daughter is real, and she complicated things for Montepulciano."

"And there is Amy Winter's shooting that needs explaining," Bloom said. "Outside the chain."

"That too," Kirk said. "Right now we should focus on finding out how Montepulciano is manipulating the chain. We need to follow the chain and see where it leads us. Let's get the names of as many people as possible, as patients or donors, who were involved in transplants."

Bloom liked this direction of the investigation. She would be immersed in what she did best, unravelling the different layers of the medical database. No more dangerous meetings with Dr. Wilder. She intertwined her fingers, cracked her knuckles, and went to work on her computer.

"Using the access from the doctor," she said, "I can only get names and addresses of the patients and donors Dr. Wilder listed. Let's see... Here's Donor 1, Carlos Herrera, father-in-law of Margarita Herrera."

A picture of a dark-skinned man in his late fifties appeared. His bushy mustache contrasted with the white of his teeth. The word "deceased," appearing below the smiling image in red letters, seemed incongruous. She scrolled down.

"His heart went to this patient." She clicked on a thumbnail to enlarge the head shot of a white man in his forties, wearing a dark suit, light shirt, and maroon tie.

"Mark Biddle. He's a 47-year-old man with coronary artery disease, severe cardiomyopathy, congestive heart failure, and a series of heart attacks. But something is strange."

"What?" Kirk said.

"It says here that D1, Herrera, shot himself in front of Mass. General Hospital, in Boston." Bloom pointed at the ledger under the Hispanic donor. "But the receiving patient is from Washington. If this suicide was arranged, why didn't the patient go to Washington to kill himself? This doesn't quite fit with our theory."

"That's not unusual nowadays," Kirk said. "The donor just had to make sure to be near a major hospital where they do heart transplants. They have that special heart box to ship the heart to the recipient's location, even if it's across the country."

"So," she said, "there's nothing wrong with this match?"

"Nothing wrong with our theory," Kirk sighed, "if Carlos Herrera was hard-pressed to kill himself. Who was the donor who signed up with Biddle, Patient 2? I'll call him Donor 2, or D2."

"I can't see that donor." Bloom huffed. "He or she has nothing to do with Zayne's patients."

Kirk looked at her expectantly.

"Well, we have a warrant for the database, so I'm allowed to search deeper, beyond what the doctor can tell us," she said, accessing the Metasploit framework and applying it to the database. Several minutes went by, filled with the clicking of keys.

"Mark Biddle signed up with his wife, Clara Biddle."

The red word DECEASED appeared under the picture of a frail-looking middle-aged woman with wispy blond air and clear blue eyes."

Bloom didn't stop typing. "What do you know? She committed suicide."

"Bingo!" Kirk said.

"Wait. I can't match her with any police report of violent death or newspaper stories. She must have used a method other than gunshot."

"We've got the name and address of Mr. Biddle," Kirk said. "Let's go to Washington and find out about Mrs. Biddle, the donor who signed up with him. And what price, if any, Biddle had to pay for his heart."

Great. A trip to Washington seemed precisely what the doctor ordered. Damn. She should stop thinking about or mentioning any doctors. On the computer, Bloom arranged flights for the following morning out of La Guardia to Reagan National.

"It's early, but I'm going home to pack." She stretched her arms above her head to release the tension in her shoulders.

"I'll go too," Kirk said, grabbing his jacket.

They rode the elevator together. Kirk checked the time on his phone.

"Maybe, while I'm packing, I can spend a couple of hours with my son."

"How old is he?"

"Fifteen," Kirk said, "going on twenty. Not all for the good, either. Early college."

"Wow. Must be hard to adjust."

"He's into physics and engineering." Kirk smiled.

"Must be on screen 24/7."

"Funny thing: Despite all the high-tech surrounding him, he always walks around with this yellow pad, jotting down his ideas."

"Use of paper is pretty unusual for kids today."

They exited the elevator and walked to the garage. *The garage.* The stalker hadn't resurfaced for the past few days. After her last stunt with the gun, Bloom couldn't find the courage to talk to Mulville about the matter. He would put her through the interrogation grinder and probably judge her reaction inadequate and inappropriate. But should she mention the stalker to Kirk? Her first impulse was to say "no." Then again, maybe it was time to get a second opinion about the man with the shiny shoes. And who was better than Kirk Miner?

The clicking of her pumps echoed in the garage as she kept up with Kirk's swift, silent- sneaker pace. Then she spotted the sign for "Employee & Guest Parking," with two bright red arrows pointing in opposite directions. The air felt chilling. From that spot, she had an unobstructed view of the familiar column to the right of her car. Next to the halogen light, the shadow line looked straight and uninterrupted.

"I'm down there." She pointed to the back wall, where her car was parked—a spot not visible in the dim light. "I'll see you at the airport."

"What's the matter?" Kirk asked, stopping. His detective's eyes drilled into hers with a trace of puzzlement. "Did you see something?"

She did. The man was far away already. He'd left after noticing her quasi-bodyguard. She took a breath to let Kirk know. She wanted to lift her arm and point at the shrinking stalker's figure, but her arm didn't budge. A cold sweat started in the back of her neck. What was she afraid of? Kirk wouldn't judge her unfit to be an agent for paying attention to her surroundings.

"I thought I saw someone watching me. I'm not sure if I'm making something out of nothing or if it's real."

Kirk looked in the same direction. The man was no longer visible.

"Nobody there now," she said. "I guess I'll see you tomorrow."

She waved goodbye. Bloom wondered why she was trembling. She walked to her car, clicked the door open, and sat down at the wheel before she could faint. Her heart was at it again. *This* was a secret she couldn't share with Kirk.

"Hey," Kirk said, stepping next to her car. He had followed her, and she hadn't noticed. "No one is there. Relax. Are you feeling okay?"

Still doing her breathing and her pushing-down routine, she nodded. *Please, make it stop.* It had to stop.

"You're sweating," Kirk said after touching her forehead, like a parent checking a child for a possible fever. "Should I take you to the hospital?"

"No!" She realized she had yelled. "Sorry. No, thanks. It's nothing a good night's sleep won't cure. I'm feeling much better."

"Sure?"

She nodded.

"It's normal to be uptight." He smiled. "This is your first real case. Besides, being vigilant and thinking of worst case scenarios is a very good practice, one that can save your life. It saved mine more than once. You do very good work."

"Thanks." She really meant it. "I'll see you tomorrow."

"Are you sure you can drive?" Kirk said. "I could take you."

"I'm too out of your way," she said. Kirk's eyes told her he wouldn't accept no for an answer. "I'll be fine. If it makes you happy, I'll take an Uber, and get my car after we come back."

After the Uber ride, she climbed the stoops of her apartment, one of a triplex off Fulton Street—in light traffic, a mere half-hour from the FBI's Manhattan FBI headquarters. Exhaustion took over along with depression. Normal people had best friends, parents, significant others to confide in. She hadn't had time to develop deep friendships. Only acquaintances she couldn't burden with her present dilemma. Her mother could only be informed with partial truths about her condition—Bloom had some irregular heartbeats and was under a doctor's care. Bloom couldn't risk having Mom appearing at her doorsteps to nag her. As far as her potential significant other, Zayne was part of the problem and far from the solution.

To get her keys, Bloom reached into her briefcase, but the corner of a white paper peeked out from under the "welcome" doormat in front of the old wooden door. She retrieved a pair of plastic gloves from the briefcase and pulled the blank envelope out into the open. No address or stamp. This was good FBI practice, not paranoia.

She opened the door, entered, shut it again, reset locks and alarm, and walked to the kitchen. Sitting at the counter, she inserted her gloved finger into the envelope, opened it, and extracted a folded sheet. She steadied her hands on the counter and read the brief typed note:

I know.

Let's meet. Before someone else dies.

Alone.

Pick a restaurant.

The note shook in her hand. Her vision blurred. She blinked several times. The words on the page sharpened again. She found a phone number at the bottom. She should text her willingness to meet to what she guessed was a throwaway phone. Coincidences don't happen often, as Kirk said. The message had to involve this transplant case. No doubt about that. Someone else was going to die. What did this person know? Did this person know the hacker's identity? Who would be the next victim? How?

She became aware of something familiar. She brought the note to her nose and inhaled deeply. Was she imagining things, or could she detect the same aftershave scent she had noticed in the garage? She placed the note back into the envelope, retrieved a plastic bag from her computer bag, and saved her evidence.

When she discarded the plastic gloves, her hands felt clammy but a strange calm took over while she walked to the refrigerator. She wondered why she didn't experience terror at the thought that the stalker knew where she lived and had no problem leaving her messages in the middle of the afternoon. What had pushed her depression and her doubts away? The note. Someone was messing with her and her first important case. She wasn't paranoid. She was a good agent.

She would cook herself dinner with the chicken breast she spotted in the meat box and drink some of the chilled white wine waiting for her on the refrigerator shelf. Later, she would plan her future—what to do, and whom to tell. Whatever her challenges, Charlotte Bloom was on her way out of probationary service, and fully ready to become a *real* FBI special agent.

CHAPTER 15
P2 AND D2

As he walked through the office of Tax Relief Inc. looking for Mark Biddle's cubicle, Kirk understood why the man had suffered multiple heart attacks. The room was a large warehouse. At least two dozen cubicles, separated by flimsy dividers, occupied the floor. In each workstation, a person sat at a computer, in front of a desk overwhelmed by papers. Kirk exchanged glances with Bloom, trotting at his side with her large briefcase. Biddle, P2, was a tax lawyer.

"I can't believe how much money is wasted," Kirk said, sweeping his hand all around. "Not just in taxes, but in trying to avoid them."

They followed the receptionist's directions to a cubicle in the back of the room bearing the name *Mark Biddle, Esq.* on the side of the partition. Kirk rehearsed his introduction in his head one more time. He'd been able to obtain an appointment for the following day as soon as he had mentioned the FBI and an important matter that required in-person handling.

"Mr. Biddle?" he said, knocking on the divider. "Kirk Miner. We spoke on the phone."

"Come in." A hand waved in the air.

The man Kirk remembered from a computer image stood up from behind a secretarial desk and came around to shake hands. In person, he looked at least ten years older, with a paler complexion, and a much thinner face, than in the picture. Kirk guessed a heart transplant could have that effect on people—or perhaps it was the disease he suffered from prior to the transplant. Kirk and Bloom stepped into the cubicle.

"I'm a private investigator with the New York Police and this is Agent Bloom, with the FBI."

"Please, sit down." Biddle pointed at two worn-out chairs. "What's going on?"

Biddle's color got worse, something Kirk would have guessed impossible. Kirk feared he might have to call an ambulance, or give the man CPR right there on the desk. Then he understood. Charlotte Bloom, an FBI agent, represented the worse possible nightmare in the tax-avoidance/evasion world.

"What do you want from me?" Biddle let himself down on his office chair as if he had to avoid fainting. "I didn't get any notice about any inspection of any client."

"Relax, Mr. Biddle." Kirk sat down and placed one of his cards on the desk. He pushed it past the paper piles that sat in seeming disarray right in front of Biddle. "We're not here to discuss taxes."

At the news, the man's pallor improved. Biddle seemed to come back to life. Kirk had to take his chances while he still rode the wave of Biddle's relief.

"What do you want?" Biddle repeated, his tone having lost any trace of meekness. "My time is very limited."

"We're investigating a possible mismanagement of a database for heart transplants," Kirk said. "We know you're part of this database and that you received a heart transplant last year."

"What the hell!" Biddle said angrily. "How did you get access to my medical records? This is a violation of privacy. I don't have to talk to you."

"True," Kirk said. "You don't have to. But we're dealing with one murder for sure, several questionable suicides, and a few possible murders. All geared to procure hearts for transplants. We expect indictments to result from our investigation. It would behoove you to cooperate and help us ferret out the truth. We only have a few questions about the circumstances of your transplant. If we can get to them, we'll be on our way in no time at all."

Biddle's hands tightened around the edges of his desk. His knuckles whitened. Kirk noticed his jugular veins bulging on his neck. He hoped Biddle wouldn't suffer permanent damage from this visit.

"Go ahead," Biddle conceded with a loud huff. "You have ten minutes until my next appointment. I still work for a living."

Kirk had to choose his questions well. He took a moment to think, as Bloom retrieved her computer and got ready to take notes.

"How long did it take you to get a heart?" Kirk asked. "From the moment you were listed?"

Biddle looked at the ceiling for an answer. He sighed. Kirk feared the answers he needed wouldn't happen.

"A couple of months," Biddle said after several long seconds. Kirk let go a breath.

"Were you in the hospital at the time?" Kirk said. "Did you require drips of intravenous medications to keep you going?"

Biddle shook his head.

"No?" Bloom said. "Meaning you weren't that sick?"

"I felt very weak," Biddle said, his tone subdued. "Couldn't work much. I wasn't dying yet, if that's what you mean."

"How did you sign up for the chain?' Kirk asked. "Did anyone approach you?"

"Yes." Biddle spoke as if his answer would vindicate him from being a suspect. "My doctor."

"What did he say?"

"The pills would soon stop working." Biddle combed his sparse hair with his hand. "He said he should list me for a heart transplant, so we had time to find a donor."

"We know someone had to sign up with you on the chain as a possible donor," Bloom said, "Who signed up with you?"

"My wife."

The all-capitals red word from the medical records flashed into Kirk's mind. He searched for the best way to prompt Biddle to explain. "What happened to her?"

Biddle's eyes became shiny. Then he seemed to regain control and every-thing in his gaze calmed down to a flat, unemotional stare.

"My wife is dead," he said.

"Sorry to hear," Kirk said. "How did she die?'

"She committed suicide," Biddle said without hesitation.

Kirk felt an adrenaline rush. He exchanged glances with Bloom, whose fingers clicked away on the keyboard, filling the silence.

"How did she commit suicide?" Bloom asked, lifting her head up from the keyboard.

"She went to Oregon," Biddle said. "For an assisted suicide. It's legal there."

Kirk lifted his head. This death didn't fit the usual pattern. His lips tightened.

"My wife was very sick," Biddle explained. He had gone from a reluctant interviewee to a man needing to unload his grief. "She had Huntington's Chorea."

Kirk was familiar with the disease. He glanced at Bloom. She had stopped typing, waiting for an explanation.

"By the time the genetic test showed she had the disease," Biddle went on, suppressing a sob, "it was too late. We were already married and very much in love. We decided not to have children, because of the 50 percent chance of transmission. Usually, it strikes after the age of 40, so we had some time to get used to the idea. But neither of us was prepared for the uncontrollable jerky movements, the clumsiness, the loss of coordination, and finally the terrible stiffness. She couldn't take it anymore."

As he digested the man's pain, Kirk felt like an impostor. A soreness spread in his throat. But someone could have taken advantage of this unfortunate couple. He had to go on.

"I'm so sorry for what you went through," Kirk said, struggling to put forward his next question. "But I have to ask, just to make sure: Did anyone offer you a deal: provide you with a heart to save your life, so long as your wife agreed to end hers?"

The tears on Biddle's pale face were real and sincere. Kirk felt guilty for inflicting additional pain. He bit his lip.

"No." Biddle shook his head with sadness. "I wouldn't have accepted any deal to shorten my darlin's life, no matter what. I tried to discourage her. In the end, she looked so miserable, I had to go along with her wishes."

"When did she start to mention suicide?" Bloom said, her voice loaded with sympathy.

"After my heart transplant," Biddle said. "It was like she had completed a mission. I was better, and she could let go."

Time for the tougher questions.

"Did you have to pay a fee," Kirk said, "in order to receive a heart?"

"No." Biddle's eyes widened.

"Do you have any reason to believe your wife paid money for your transplant?"

Kirk expected indignation. None came. Biddle slumped in his chair. He sighed.

"Not money," he said. "But after she died, I went through all her thinga. Clothes, jewels."

He had to stop talking to suppress a series of sobs. Kirk watched him relive the pain of sorting through and giving away his wife's personal items. His probing questions had rekindled Biddle's feelings of loss and despair that time had mercifully attenuated, the burning, gnawing pain that had plagued him in the aftermath of his soulmate's death. Kirk placed himself in his position. Even imagining how he would feel if Aurora were to die was too difficult to bear.

"What did you find?" Kirk asked, hoping that the investigation would become less uncomfortable.

"Some of her jewels were gone," Biddle said. "A diamond bracelet I gave her for our twentieth anniversary. And a ruby pendant. That one I gave her the day we got married. I wondered if someone stole them. I can't believe she would give them away. It's a mystery I'll go to my grave with. She was the only one who knew."

Time to go. Let the poor widower grieve. As for the missing jewels, Kirk had a good idea where they might have ended up.

Bloom and Kirk grabbed a taxi right outside the office building and rode in silence to Reagan Airport. While he sat waiting for the flight, Kirk went over the interview in his mind, wondering how much it had helped the investigation. Biddle seemed sincerely ignorant of any crooked deal.

"Up until now," Bloom said looking up from her computer, "I thought the price for the hearts, the condition for some of these patients to get a heart sooner than later, was the death of the donor who signed up with each patient. Now, I don't know any more. Do you think the wife paid someone to get Biddle a heart, and then killed herself?"

"Sure looks that way," Kirk said. "Although here the suicide seems appropriate. Biddle's wife's life was hell on earth. It doesn't quite fit the same pattern as Herrera. And he didn't pay any money for his daughter-in-law to get a heart, which she didn't want any way."

Bloom sighed, closing the computer.

The boarding for the LaGuardia flight was announced. Kirk remained seated, so as not to disrupt his thinking.

"I still think that someone is messing with the chain, facilitating heart donations," he said. "Probably Montepulciano, since he likely has access to the hospital records."

"I agree." Bloom stood up with her computer case and headed for the passenger line. Kirk followed.

"If this is this case," he said, "there has to be something in it for him. Either he wants a heart for someone he cares about, or money—lots of it— or both. Hence the money question."

"Follow the money," Bloom said, stepping onto the plane.

CHAPTER 16
THE PROBIE

Bloom clenched the backpack's straps and walked towards the director's office. The tapping of her heels was muffled by the gray carpet. With her rushing stride, her tight skirt stretched to the limit and sweat gathered in her armpits, soaking her tailored shirt and jacket. Today, she would finally come clean with the entire stalker issue.

Just before leaving her apartment, she stashed the plastic bag containing the mysterious note into one of the compartments of her computer case. Since receiving the note, her determination had kept all doubt in check ... until now. She turned the corner and Mulville's office appeared. Bloom paused in front of the director's door. Her resolution didn't falter. Her hand closed into a fist, ready to knock, but stopped in midair.

She could hear Kirk and Mulville inside, talking about the case. Darn. She was already late. Her life felt like a treadmill rolling at full speed. What gave her an adrenaline rush—when first receiving the case assignment—now overwhelmed her. Her unpredictable heart could strike at any time: its rapid fluttering could not only paralyze her, but relegate her to the sideline. She listened for any comments about her performance. Hearing none, Bloom knocked.

"Come," Mulville said.

She entered the room. The men glanced at her without interrupting their conversation. She sat down next to Kirk, and in front of Mulville, her blue tailored skirt pulled down to her knees, and listened to Kirk's recounting of the Biddle interview. Mulville's head moved side to side. From his desk, he picked up a pointed letter-opener the shape of a dagger and tested its sharpness on his index finger.

"It's likely she paid with the jewels so her husband could get a heart,"

Kirk said. "Somebody must be organizing, facilitating, and profiting from all this."

"After what you've told me, I'm not so sure any more," Mulville said, dropping the letter-opener and sweeping the air in dismissal. "For now, we should concentrate on solving the murder."

Kirk sat up straight. The PI seemed ready to defend his hypothesis. Good luck.

"Jack," Kirk said, "before we leave this path for good, I think we should at least check and see who got Mrs. Biddle's heart. Let's just go one step further."

"Bloom?" Mulville turned to her and relaxed back into his executive chair. "How quickly can you figure out who got the Mrs.'s heart?"

She opened the computer and entered Zayne's passwords. "Mrs. Biddle's heart went to a patient not from Dr. Wilder."

"Forget the doctor," Mulville said. "I think we've stretched him enough. If we go at him any harder, frigging HIPAA may come back to fuck him and us in the ass. Not worth it."

"We have a warrant for the chain," Bloom said. "I can get anything we need, without asking anyone."

"Waste of your time," Mulville said.

Bloom shifted in her chair. Her heart, still in a normal rhythm, started to pound. Then, whipped by adrenaline, it went into forceful contractions. She reached for the computer bag at her feet.

"With all due respect, Kirk may have a point." Bloom unzipped the pocket of the bag and extracted the plastic-enclosed note. She placed it on Mulville's desk and oriented it towards him. "Look at what I found under my doormat, day before yesterday."

Bloom felt like Cinderella displaying the second glass slipper to one and all. But Mulville was no Grand Duke. The blue slits of his eyes became wider as he read the note without touching it. Then his intense gaze found Bloom. A desire to run replaced her excitement.

"What the fuck is this?" Mulville pointed down at the note. "Tell me everything, Bloom."

"Nothing much to tell." She kept her voice calm and soothing. "I suspect it's from someone who's been watching me for several days. While I came and went, I noticed his shadow in the garage a few times,. He usually hides behind a column. One day I saw him walking away. A man with a fedora hat and shiny black shoes. Not very tall. Average weight."

"Why you didn't tell us this before?" Mulville's finger changed direction to aim at her chest like the muzzle of a gun.

"She told *me* about it." Prince Kirk came to Cinderella's rescue. "It wasn't clear if there was anything there. Until now."

"No," Mulville thundered. "Until the day *before* yesterday. Bloom, do you know the chance I'm taking in letting you investigate something like this Mafia-related case? And you Miner? What the fuck were *you* thinking?"

"Did you check the phone number from the note?" Kirk asked Bloom, ignoring Mulville's tantrum.

"The number is from one of those burner phone apps," Bloom said. "It creates disposable phone numbers, but you can use your own phone."

"What about prints?"

"No prints."

Now the difficult part. Kirk's presence made it a little easier. Better having a witness.

"Director." Bloom's voice sounded steady and clear. "I didn't want to report something without evidence. That much I heard you say over and over to other agents. I assumed it would apply to me. I appreciate your concern, but I wouldn't want to think you were worrying about me, and acting to keep me safe… you know, giving me special treatment."

Mulville's eyes rolled up toward the ceiling. He seemed speechless for a moment. That was a first for Bloom. This was her chance.

"I propose," she said, "I set up a meeting. And I should be wired."

"I propose," Mulville mocked her, his voice imitating hers, "you're freaking nuts. You should be sent back to cyber-fraud division as of yesterday."

"Wait a moment, please. Hear me out." Kirk came back on a white horse. "I think she has a plan here. Someone knows there will be more deaths. This is the first hard evidence we have that someone is screwing with the chain.

And he wants to talk to Bloom. If we plan it well, we can do it safely."

"How?" Mulville said, leaning on his desk in Kirk's direction. A soft spray of spit diffused in the air.

"He obviously wants the meeting in a public place," Kirk said. "Let's have it at ... I don't know ... Rockefeller Center."

"Too fucking busy," Mulville said. "Something goes wrong, there'll be mayhem. And he said a restaurant."

"The Boathouse in Central Park," Bloom said. She clicked on her keyboard. "Before lunch. On Saturday, it opens at 9:30. We can go tomorrow, at 10 or so."

"The place with the boats?" Mulville asked. He repositioned himself on his executive chair. "Where can we hide? Amidst the swans?"

"That's a good idea." Bloom tried twisting irony into flattery. "You and Kirk hide on a boat."

"I want full back-up right inside the park," Mulville groaned. "This doesn't mean I like it. I don't like it for shit. Something goes wrong, we'll have a blood bath."

"I'm not going to the O.K. Corral." Bloom pulled back a loose strand of hair from her forehead. "It's only a meeting to get some information."

"What do you know about that?" Mulville asked. "You were a freaking egg when the movie came out."

"I studied history," she said. "And I also like old movies. You can learn a lot from them."

Mulville's mass shifted in her direction. A stubby finger, pointed at her chest, was ready to strike. Bloom's heart skipped a beat. She took a deep breath to avert the usual flood of adrenaline that would follow.

"You know diddly squat about this guy." The deep voice filtered through Mulville's teeth like a hiss. "For all you know, he could be the next mass killer. What about the restaurant's customers? How would *you* like to make reservations for breakfast and be served a bullet between your eyes?"

"Director, sir," Bloom whispered. "I honestly don't think the man is out to kill anyone. He seems to want to *prevent* deaths. If he really wanted to kill me, he could have done it already. In the garage. Without witnesses."

"Exactly." Mulville's balled-up fist came crashing down on his desk. A bunch of paperclips in a mesh cup tinkled. "If the message is from the same man, you're risking your life for no fucking good reason that I can see."

"I chose a dangerous job." She looked up at the intimidating blue slits. "You can't protect me from the risk of belonging to the FBI. This is where I want to be."

"I need to know if this stunt is even worth it," Mulville said. He twirled his finger at Bloom. "Hack the chain, now!"

Bloom wiped a drop of sweat off her brow. She must find the information. At all costs, avoid having to get it from Zayne. She went to work.

Her future was on the line. Her fingers shook. She used Metasploit again, but she couldn't get past the backdoor she had installed to have easy future access. The hospital had instituted hacking protection since the blackmail, and the program had detected and eliminated her breach. She glanced up to see Mulville's and Kirk's eyes fixed on her. Waiting. She took a cleansing breath and cracked her fingers. Her backup plan was Nmap, used by hackers to gain access to uncontrolled ports on a system. The clicking of her keys resonated loudly in the otherwise silent room. After several minutes, she stopped and waited.

"I had to use a different method," she said, looking Mulville in the eye and trying to keep her voice from cracking. "It'll be a little longer."

"We've got a freaking warrant," he said. "Let's call the doctor."

No. How could she talk to Zayne? *I'm so sorry, really sorry. No it's not another date. It's just squeezing you for more information, using you to death, sucking your bones before spitting them out. Thank you very much.* Sweat again soaked her back.

"The doctor only has access to his own patients," she said with as much authority as she could muster. "I already checked all that *he* has access to. Mrs. Biddle's heart went to someone outside his practice. The doctor isn't going to know who it was."

"Take your time," Kirk said, leaning back in his chair. Mulville picked up a paper clip from the mesh cup and started bending it out of shape. Bloom tapped her fingers on the side of her keyboard. The answers to her prayers appeared.

"Oh my God," she said. "Mrs. Biddle's heart went to Mrs. Baker, the woman who died in surgery."

"Mrs. Baker? The wife of our Mr. Baker?" Kirk said. "The one who didn't want protection."

"We have a triple swap," she announced. "Donor 1, Carlos Herrera, killed himself and his heart went to Patient 2, Mr. Biddle. Mrs. Biddle, Donor 2, committed suicide and her heart went to Mrs. Baker, Patient 3, who died in surgery. Now, Mr. Baker, Donor 3, has to die to provide his heart to Patient 1, Margarita Herrera."

"So what?" Mulville said. "Matching groups of patients and donors is the exact purpose of the chain. That's the reason why it was created in the first place. Unless we prove that the donors were somehow *coerced* to commit suicide, we've got zilch."

"This is how to do it." Bloom pointed at the note on Mulville's desk. "This guy predicts more deaths in the future. We need to find out how he can know that. He obviously knows something we don't. He must know that some of these death *were* coerced."

Mulville nodded. His jaw tightened. He took a deep breath and pushed back from his desk. His biceps and triceps threatened to rip his shirt's sleeves. Bloom braced for some strong reaction to come.

"The chain was running smoothly," Mulville said with an unexpected calm, "until Mrs. Baker screwed things up by dying. If things are as you say, people are committing suicide and even unloading cash in order for their relatives to get a heart. Baker must be pretty pissed off, if he paid his dues and didn't get what he paid for. And now someone is also expecting him to commit suicide."

"More than pissed off," Kirk said. "He must be pretty scared. At least, he should be. I was wondering why the money was needed, on top of suicide, in order to assure transplant for the person one signed up with. Now I think I understand. People pay so that nobody can refuse to fulfill the condition they agreed to. It's like insurance. If someone hesitates to commit suicide after the relative has gotten the heart, the mobster steps in to make sure the deal is completed. That's how he makes his money. He's getting paid to enforce the rules he set up in the chain."

"But what about Herrera?" Bloom said. "He didn't pay any fee, as far as we know."

"No, he didn't." Kirk's smile conveyed a hint of pity. "He was the first donor in the loop, the one to start the domino reaction. The only one who couldn't see the relative he signed up with, his daughter-in-law, getting her heart transplant. He had no money, so he had to trust that the mobster would make sure that his daughter-in-law would actually get a heart. He just had to give up his. All the donors who come later in the swap, after the first donor, pay money to Montepulciano for the privilege of seeing their relatives get a heart. Of course, there is one pre-existing condition to people getting their hearts on time, as guaranteed. The death of the donor. After the heart for their own relative is secured, the donor agrees to commit suicide to provide his or her heart for a patient in the particular chain's loop."

"And there could be many more loops for patients like this one," Bloom said. "We just discovered one."

"But Margarita Herrera refused the heart." Mulville parted his palms in puzzlement. "Aren't we done? No need for blowing up any more brains."

"Unless," Bloom said, "Amy Winter's heart was really for someone else, someone important to Montepulciano."

"Hence," Kirk said, "forcing Herrera to refuse the heart, so that the other patient would get it. In this case, it's still an open season."

"Congratulations," Mulville said, pointing at Kirk. "That's the first sensible statement I've heard today. Did you want me to believe that all these shenanigan are to save random patients? There's a big difference between convincing somebody to commit suicide and pulling the trigger. There's got to be a stronger motive for Montepulciano to escalate from making offers one cannot refuse to murder. We've got *a murder* to explain."

"Yes," Bloom said. "Amy Winter's heart It's for the secret patient—Montepulciano's daughter."

"What daughter?" Mulville said, turning to Kirk. "In your stunt with the ex-girlfriend, she told you Montepulciano couldn't give a flying fuck about even finding out if there was a daughter. And didn't Montepulciano tell you this himself, when you talked to him?"

"Yes," Kirk said. "But we know from the ex-girlfriend that there *is* a daughter. And that she's got some heart condition. Can't be a coincidence. Let's assume the mobster took over and organized the chain, taking advantage of desperate patients, nudging donors with threats and promises. And making good money in the process. Everything was running smoothly, until a glitch in this delicate scheme: the death of P3, Baker's wife. Because his wife died, Baker may not be so eager to kill himself and become a donor. Montepulciano has to maintain his reputation in order to do business in the future. But all of a sudden, things get even more complicated. Montepulciano's daughter needs a heart. Now the wine man has much higher stakes. He's ready to kill for his daughter. And Baker may be a potential donor."

"But then why isn't Baker dead already?" Bloom said. "Why didn't Montepulciano kill Baker instead of Amy Winter?"

"Who knows?" Kirk said. "Maybe Baker's got a pass with the mobster. Maybe that's why he thinks he doesn't need protection."

"All good and dandy," Mulville said, "but no proof of anything. We need someone to break the chain, confess to the deal. Conveniently for Montepulciano, they're all dead."

"Not all," Kirk said. "Baker is still alive. He must know something and, now that Amy Winter is dead, her heart included, he doesn't realize how much at risk he runs."

"Much more at risk if he doesn't talk than if he does," Mulville grunted.

"I tried to convince him," Kirk said. "He refused."

"That settles it," Bloom said. "We're back to the writer of the note. He's willing to talk. Perhaps *he's* in the chain."

She heard no other objections. Her first real mission was about to start. This was the stuff she had dreamt about while spending sleepless nights, falling asleep while reading books, and long days taxing her small body to its limits, preparing for the assignments ahead. But why did her throat feel like she had swallowed a thorny cactus? Shouldn't she disclose her handicap? Lives were at stake here. Her own, first of all, but also Mulville's, and Kirk's, and all the back-up agents.'

If anything happened to her, Mulville wouldn't hesitate to risk his own life to save hers. He would push everyone to hell and back to do the same. She had no doubt whatsoever. Did she have the right to keep private the fact that her heart's electrical system was as dangerous as a downed power line in the middle of a blizzard?

"Fine." Mulville slapped the air in front of him, as if he was fighting. "Bloom, send the answer, now. Kirk, arrange for back-up. Call the restaurant. Something goes wrong, your ass is on the line."

Kirk nodded.

"Yes," Bloom whispered.

No time for unanswered questions. Bloom composed a text to send. It would include the meeting time—10 am tomorrow—and place: Loeb Boathouse, Central Park. She re-read the text twice. Her lungs sucked in air and she pushed it against her closed throat, as she did during episodes when her heart fluttered, even if now her heart stood silent and calm. She let a long out a long breath, then touched the *send* button.

Sleep didn't come easy that night.

CHAPTER 17
THE MEETING

Inside the Boathouse Restaurant, the clinking of silverware and diners' happy chatting was getting louder by the minute. Bloom sat at a table with full view of the lake. She took a sip of her refilled iced tea and looked out at the New York skyscrapers stacked against the crisp blue sky, behind the red-, yellow-, and orange-colored trees. She loved the Fall. Her eyes panned down to the few boats carrying happy tourists and couples in love... and Kirk and Mulville, somewhere out there, hiding from her view. She wished she were rowing on one of those shells, looking at Zayne Wilder's smile, with a loaded picnic basket and a bottle of wine stuck between their feet. The smell of fried bacon and cilantro reached her from a nearby table. Her stomach growled and reminded her that her only food since the previous evening meal was the honey in her tea.

She pulled back her shirt sleeve to check the time: 10:42. She wouldn't be eating lunch anytime soon. The stalker had stood her up. Doubt crept in like pointed claws on her skin and made her shudder. Perhaps the note had nothing to do with her stalker. Her phone message had gone unanswered, as expected. She had hoped that the person who had sent her the note would show up anyway. Did he spot her two bodyguards on the boat? How much backup had Mulville ordered?

Coming over, she had noticed several unmarked police sedans. The stalker would have seen them as well. Damn Mulville and his suffocating paternalistic attitude. She looked at the flow of people coming through the front door and noticed a loud group of middle-aged tourists perched on stools around the bar. No sign of the man with the fedora and the black shoes. No one approached her table.

She touched the first button of her gray jacket. Her digital wire lay beneath the button's smooth leather cover. The visual came through the pin-hole in the middle. The other two buttons had been camouflaged with a similar cover.

"Shit." From a tiny wireless device wedged inside her right ear, Mulville's voice thundered against her tympanic membrane. "What's going on?"

"Nothing," she said, startled. "How long before we call it?"

"Now," he ordered. "Go home. Enjoy the weekend. I sent a car to watch your place."

Great. A sitter was all she needed. Someone to watch every move she made and report to Daddy Mulville. But part of her didn't feel this way. Despite the iced tea, Bloom couldn't help experiencing a certain warmth in the pit of her stomach. She waved the waiter to her table, asked for the check, and made a trip to the ladies' room.

When she came back, a black leather folder beckoned her from the table, her spotless napkin folded in quarters on the upholstered chair. She pulled up the napkin. A white paper sticker winked at her in the middle of the green fabric. On it, a message etched in thick marker read simply: "I'll see you later." Her heart pounded, her knees buckled, and her palm flattened onto the table for support, as she turned her head all around, eyes wide open, taking in the entire dining room, searching for the old-fashioned fedora hat, the coat, the shiny shoes. Nothing.

She didn't know any longer whom she was looking for. She did her deep breathing. The answer reached her with a subtle but familiar whiff that catapulted her heart into a frightening frenzy. She inhaled deeply, ignoring her fear. *The stalker's aftershave.* Her date was her stalker. She used the napkin to retrieve the sticker and secured it in her spare evidence bag. She dropped it in her pocketbook, rummaging for her wallet and credit card. A sudden weakness forced her to sit down. She waved the bill folder at the waiter.

"Did you see anyone near my table?" she asked the server, suppressing the shrillness in her voice.

The man shook his head. "No ma'am. I was in the back. I can ask around. Something is wrong? Missing?"

"No, nothing missing." She sensed the need to chuckle. "Someone left me a message. Please ask if they saw anyone."

She knew the futility of her request. But she did ask the occupants of the nearby table the same question, with the same result. Nothing. Rewarding her waiter for his unproductive help, she signed her name on the bill and let Kirk and Mulville know she was leaving. She waded through throngs of fun-seeking tourists, relaxing New York couples, and gathered families, her body weighted down by discouragement like metal on a magnet.

As Bloom reached the steps to her apartment, Mulville's man took a bite of his hamburger and waved at her from his unmarked black sedan. Should she feel safer already? Her stomach protested the lack of food again. She made a mental inventory of the contents of her refrigerator. Her depression deepened. She would treat herself to pizza delivery and spend the weekend wallowing in pepperoni and cheese, wine, and reality TV shows. The more stupid the show, the better.

She bent to lift the doormat. Nothing hiding.

The apartment still smelled like the Chinese food she had eaten the previous night. It seemed like a long time ago. She dropped her gun and badge on the entry table, kicked off her heels, got out of her jacket, and laid it on a chair in the living room. As soon as she dropped herself onto the couch, the phone lit up in her hand and she quickly found the number of the pizza place on Fulton. She dug out her earpiece and placed it on a side table.

"Pizza Italy."

She took a breath to order her pepperoni pizza.

Suddenly, a large and strong hand, covered with surgical gloves, pressed against her lips, blocking her voice. And her breath. The aftershave's smell hit her, throwing her brain into a frenzy of fear.

She lifted her head backward to free her nose from the rubber-clad fingers. A second hand took the phone from her, hung up on the pizza place, and tossed the device on a nearby chair. Hair lifted on her arms. Her body started to shake. Dread spread inside her chest like ink dropped into water.

She raised her right arm and wrapped it around her attacker's arms. It seemed to happen automatically, as if she was still undergoing martial art training. Her left hand balled up and came around with all the speed and power that fear commanded. With a tight fist, she struck the man's face with a perfect front-two-knuckles punch. The crunch of cartilage and bone, followed by a moan, broke the silence. The grip on her cheeks relaxed. She slid off the couch, stepped back, and turned toward her assailant. Her hand reached for her jacket's button wire.

"Wait," the man mumbled, retrieving a handkerchief from his pocket and pressing it to his nose. Soaking up blood, it turned red almost immediately. "I wouldn't call for reinforcements right now."

Bloom's hand froze. Sleek receding hair and mustache. She knew the man. A picture from the article she had read on her computer flashed into her mind. Santo Montepulciano stared at her with piercing coal-black eyes, while tending to his bloody, broken nose. She had punched the mobster in the face. What would happen now? What came to mind was an image of feet set in cement.

"You won't get away with this," she said, her voice breaking. "The FBI is right outside. And I'm wired, so the FBI is listening. They'll be here in no time."

"They'd better not." The man's laugher filtered through the cloth. "Damn good karate chop, kiddo."

As he put the reddened handkerchief in his breast pocket, she moved to retrieve her discarded ear piece which sat on the side table. The man surprised her with his swiftness. He grabbed her arm and turned her around to face away from him. Her elbows came together at her back. Her shoulder sockets protested, just short of hurting. The stubby fingers reminded her of Mulville's.

"If you're interested in what I have to say," he whispered, his warm breath making the hair in the nape of her neck stand, "shut down the Feds. Now. And, please, stop playing cop and robber games. With me, of all people. If I wanted to kill you, we wouldn't be having this conversation."

The mobster could easily dislocate her shoulders. She nodded with unambiguous decisiveness.

"Gooood." He sounded as if he was talking to a defiant child. "I'm going to let you go, and you'll make sure the feed doesn't show my bloody face, while you reassure the Feds you're peachy good. Then we can talk like civilized adults, before you make me snuff the stooge outside."

The vice-like grip released her arms. Bloom worked her shoulders into place. She grabbed her ear piece and activated her wire button.

"Just reporting that I'm home safe," she said, surprised and proud at the firmness of her voice. She heard Mulville's grunt. "Have a nice weekend, Bloom. Out."

She tapped the button, folded her jacket inside-out, and placed it on the couch. With two fingers, Montepulciano picked it up by the collar, as if it were an infected animal. Without losing sight of her, he stuffed the wired garment in one of the kitchen drawers. He came back to the couch, retrieved his handkerchief from his pocket and checked his nose for blood. Finding none, he tapped his still gloved hand on the couch as an invitation for Bloom to sit.

Bloom sat across from him on a matching chair. Her heart's rhythm settled to a steady pounding, normal for the circumstances. She bit her lower lip as she looked at the man's poker face. Her hands felt cold and clammy.

"I'll tell you some facts," he said. "I hope, for your sake, you'll act accordingly. For the sake of your colleagues, I hope you keep your mouth shut and avoid unnecessary casualties."

"I know what you're up to," she said. "You want a heart for someone you care for. Killing isn't going to get it."

"Can't you ever shut up?" The frightening smirk from the computer image appeared on his face and gave Bloom the shudders. "Relax. No reason to pass out on me now. Just listen. I'm going to give you exclusive info on a platter. Easy."

Bloom looked at the discolored bluish rug under her bare feet and nodded. Her eyes stared at the man's shiny black shoes.

"I have a daughter." He said it like he was reading a story that concerned him not at all. "She needs a heart transplant. And she's going to get it. These are facts. Neither you nor your friends can prevent it."

"Did you kill the woman in front of the NYMC?" she asked, finding courage she didn't know she had.

"No," he said, looking straight at her.

The conversation reminded her of the Godfather movie scene, where Al Pacino rejects Satan during the christening of his godson and nephew, while his gang is decimating the rival mob in a bloodbath. Montepulciano sounded just as trustworthy.

"It will happen without further killing," he said. "You have my word. Drop all investigations until it's done. Just let it happen. Let it be."

"Sure." She chuckled. "You're the expert in making offers people can't refuse. Like the one you're making right now. Someone will commit suicide on demand, just like all those other donors in the chain. I'm curious. Why your sudden paternalistic interest? Isn't this the daughter of your old girlfriend? The one you didn't rape twenty-five years ago?"

For the first time, his face seemed stricken by emotion. His thick eyebrows gathered and united to form a mountain-shaped line. The bruised nose and reddened eyes made him seem to be on the verge of crying. His muscular arms rose and fell, as a breath heavy with sadness exited the barrel chest like a whine.

"I have no other children," he said. "I guess life has caught up with me. The fear of losing it. Of dying. I don't want my daughter to die. If she dies, nothing would be left of me when *I* die."

The man spoke as if he needed to convince her of his good intentions. His entire life had been a continuous hands-on succession of deception, corruption, dishonesty, and crime. All canned and sealed like fresh fruit marmalade in a jar, compartmentalized away on the shelf of family worship, honor, and integrity. It made her sick to her stomach. She should never forget it.

"I'm sorry for your daughter." She meant it, though her sympathy was more directed at his daughter's relationship to him than at her heart condition. "But we have a problem here."

He looked at her in silence, the poker face back in place, like a shutter slammed tight.

"I'll be honest also." She cleared her voice. Her hands closed into fists to force herself to continue before any second or third thoughts stifled her resolve. "I promise you, I'll do anything and everything to stop you."

She braced for what was to come, her feet firm against the rug, ready to sprint. She hoped that Mulville wouldn't have to curse her honorable behavior over her dead remains. Montepulciano seemed absorbed in thought, as if determining his next move.

"To make things easier for you," he said, acting as if making a concession, "I'm willing to share my daughter's identity with you."

"This isn't a negotiation," Bloom said. "Even if I get to talk to her, no matter how ill or pitiful she is, nothing will make me ignore your hacking of the hospital databases, depriving a young woman of her life and her future, then forcing a terminal patient to give up her only chance at life, so your daughter would get a heart. Knowing who your daughter is will only make it easier for me to stop you."

But Montepulciano wasn't listening any longer. He extracted a phone from his jacket, entered a password, touched a few keys, and put it back in his pocket. The man had prepared something for her. This wasn't a sudden decision reached while sitting on her couch. This was him carrying out a premeditated plan.

"I sent you what you and your Sherlock friend have been so desperately trying to get." He smiled. An ironic, threats-pregnant smile that made her stomach knot. "Do what you think is best with it."

He rose and walked to the front door. Bloom remined frozen, her legs hugging the couch while her gaze followed him to the door. She watched him open the coat closet. He took out his camel coat and his fedora hat and put them on. He came back to her.

"I hope you choose wisely," he said. "Your life depends on it."

His hand touched the slanted hat's rim in salute. The wooden floor squeaked as he walked away. The hammering of Bloom's heart accompanied the thud of the closing door.

CHAPTER 18
COLLATERAL DAMAGE

Saturday, shortly after 12 noon, Kirk Miner paced the sidewalk in front of NYMC. After his boating trip with Mulville earlier that morning, gray clouds gathered to cover most of the sky,. The temperature had dipped, and a cold breeze made him speed up his pace. He blew on his cold fingertips and shoved his hands into his coat pockets as he watched hordes of medical personnel come in and out of the hospital's main door. Several nurses and orderlies with different-colored scrubs chatted while hurrying to grab lunch.

Where was Aurora? He should have waited inside for her. After the Central Park fiasco, he needed a bit of quality time with his wife. And, after she heard of his morning plan, she signed up for a registry shift in the Manhattan hospital.

He saw her coming out of the revolving door, purple scrubs under a white dawn jacket. He could pick her out in a crowd just from the way she moved. He remembered the first time he saw her in the corridor of the Brooklyn Medical Center. He was still a policeman then. He had just brought an injured prisoner to the ER and was looking for a cup of coffee somewhere. She came toward him, blond curls swinging side to side in sync with her hips. Warmth rose from his chest and radiated upward and downward. The day his body didn't react in such a way looking at his wife, Kirk would know he had died. He loved her so much. Sixteen years and getting stronger.

"Hey." Warm lips touched his cold cheek. "What happened to your stake-out?"

"The guy we were waiting for didn't show up." Kirk peeked at the line extending outside a small sandwich place across the street and sighed. "All of a sudden, I had time on my hands. Good thing you were here today."

"So," she said grinning, "I'm second choice? Hell of a date."

Kirk smiled and locked onto her dark brown eyes. Tension released from his shoulders as he took her hand and they walked toward the sandwich place.

"I like that you called," she said.

"How long do you have?" he asked, his chin pointing at the waiting line.

Her hand tightened around his. He answered with a squeeze, suppressed a curse, and waited for her to find the good side of a long line with no time to eat. Leave it to Aurora.

"An hour," she said. "I took this shift because I knew you wouldn't be home. And Peter is studying with Alan. Let's do take-out and sit in the hospital waiting area. It's still better than cafeteria food."

The take-out line went faster than expected. He swung the food bag as they crossed the street hand in hand. An ambulance flashed and screeched its way to the emergency room entrance, forcing them to stop. The New York traffic rumbled all around as they resumed their short walk. She pulled his hand into a stop in front of the hospital entrance and faced him.

"I was worried about you today," she said. "It was more dangerous than you told me, wasn't it?"

He shook his head. "I don't think so. When you work in this field, you always have to be ready and plan for the worst, but we had enough backup to protect the President."

Aurora smiled. He saw the worry in her eyes dissipate. Her face came closer. Kirk felt her arm coming up on his shoulders and his head pulled down by her hand. He closed his eyes to enjoy her lips on his.

Suddenly, the crack of a whip hit his ear drums. Aurora jerked back. Glass-shattering sounds reverberated behind them. Wetness hit his face. An agonizing cry of pain filled the air. Aurora moaned in his ears. Her eyes widened with terror. The face that always reminded him of a cameo jewel twisted in shock and crumpled in anguish. Then Kirk noticed her hand. It stuck up in the air, dripping blood, the purple sleeve turning black. A gunshot wound!

He reached out for the wounded hand and wrapped Aurora into a protective embrace bringing her down to the pavement, his body shielding hers.

The aroma of pastrami reached him from the scattered sandwiches, mingled with the pungent, metallic scent of blood. Kirk's face leaned against Aurora's jacket as he cradled her in his arms on the hard concrete, his fingers compressing the open wound on the side of her hand. People around started to duck to the ground or run away, screaming, adding to the cacophony of sounds. Someone yelled at the guard in front of the hospital entrance that a woman had been shot.

Kirk looked at his fingers, which were covered in blood, thick and red and turning darker. As he hit the ground, he saw blood rushing out of Aurora. He had to stop it. He pressed down on her wound with renewed strength. She screamed. Blood kept on pouring.

A muscular young man rushed to them, wheeling a stretcher, lowered it, and helped Aurora onto it. Despite her ashen color, she was able to push up from the pavement with her legs. Kirk didn't let go of her hand until he felt fingers prying away his own fingers from her. Only then, when Aurora was safe on the gurney, on her way through the ER door, did Kirk turn and try to understand what had just happened.

A bullet had gone through Aurora's hand and shattered the hospital's glass entrance. Will she ever again be able to dispense medications, start intravenous lines, change bandages, comfort patients, ever again? The questions crammed his head and demanded instant answers. But he had to wait.

The cry of police sirens intensified. His breathing accelerated. He slowed it. A hand injury wasn't life threatening if properly tended to right away. Help was on the way. His friend John would take charge.

Kirk ran inside and closely followed his wife's gurney.

Bloom sat on the couch, face on her palms, taking deep, slow breaths.

The mobster was gone and she was still alive. She knew what her new mission was: facilitate the man's plan to procure a heart for his desperate daughter. Her own life depended on it.

Peeking through her fingers, she spotted her phone resting on the nearby chair. She rose to her feet despite an all-encompassing exhaustion pulling her back to the couch like a powerful rubber band. Her right hand hurt at the tiniest motion. She lifted and stretched her fingers to examine them. The knuckles of her index and middle fingers had turned a purple-bluish color from the impact with the mobster's nose. Her instructor would be proud of her.

She dragged herself to the phone and brought the screen back to life. After entering her password, texts came into view. She recognized the stalker's number. A message appeared with instructions on how to access a certain web page dealing with DNA-matching information. She shuffled to the kitchen and sat in front of her laptop. As she opened it, her phone buzzed in her hand and forced her to shift focus to the oncoming call. Kirk Miner.

She listened to the PI's fast recount, punctuated by accelerated breathing. Aurora. Shot. In surgery.

The mobster's words echoed in her mind. "For the sake of your colleagues, I hope you can prevent their interference." Her hands and legs started to tingle and a prickly sensation crawled all over her skin. Kirk was the target. Kirk's wife was collateral damage. The shooting was a message to Bloom. An example of what could happen if she made the wrong choice.

"I'll be right there," she said. "Does Mulville know?"

"He's coming."

Of course. What did she expect? She ended the call, found her Glock, badge, and pocketbook, and ran out. Mulville's man sat up straight and tracked her with puzzled eyes. She felt sorry for the guy. Surely her anxious exit must be causing him some concern. Would he follow her, notify the boss, or stay put to prevent any intrusion? The guy certainly wasn't very good at the prevention part. No matter what he decided, he would face Mulville's wrath. Wait until the Director found out that the mobster-stalker himself had sat on her couch that afternoon and made her an offer she had to refuse.

The front of the hospital was swarming with police and police vehicles. Bloom spotted a couple of antennas from news vehicles. People huddled outside the crime scene yellow tape. Inside, Bloom saw the chalk outline of a body and dried blood spatter. Aurora's. Her body. Her blood. Bloom's breath caught.

Mulville stood next to the entrance, a tall coffee in his hand, talking to Kirk. Bloom noticed the director's outfit: jeans and wind jacket instead of the familiar dark suit. *No time to shed his boating attire, I guess.* Kirk's tight mouth and the slow motion of his head made her pause. She wished she didn't have to tell them her own story. To alleviate a lump in the back of her throat, she swallowed hard. Flashing her badge, she gracefully ducked under the yellow tape.

"Bloom," Mulville said, irritation spurting from his glance. "What are you doing here? We got this. No cyber-stuff for you."

"Kirk, how is she? I'm so sorry," Bloom said. Then to Mulville. "Of course I want to be here."

"I called her." Kirk shook her hand. A large red stain spread on the front of his light blue shirt. A few droplets marked his forehead. "We should discuss what happened. With Aurora in surgery, best to keep my mind occupied on other stuff."

"What's to discuss?" Mulville flung the empty paper cup towards a nearby trash bin. "Nobody saw anything, but we know who did it. Mr. Montepulciano better have a good alibi. Better than the one he gave to you, Kirk, about the prodigal son dropping by his unfortunate mother during Amy Winter's shooting. They're picking him up as we speak. Captain Spencer and a SWAT team. Can't wait to put the fucking bastard in the slammer."

"Guy in his position doesn't get his hands dirty," Bloom said, feeling like someone had puncher her in her sternum. "He would send someone to do his dirty work."

"But why now?" Kirk said. "And why me? Assuming I was the target. And why did he miss? Did he *want* to miss?"

What could come from picking up the mobster at that moment? A man who didn't hesitate to send such a bloody message? What was she waiting for? Kirk stared into space, wondering about the answers to his many questions.

"I think that whoever shot at you wanted to miss." Bloom plunged in. "And Aurora's hand got in the way."

"She was trying to kiss me." Kirk's eyes filled with wetness. "She pulled me down and saved my life."

"It wasn't Montepulciano," Aurora said. "He has an alibi."

"Bloom," Mulville gave her any icy look that chilled her insides, "is there anything you need to tell us?"

"Montepulciano," Bloom said, clearing her throat, "was at the Boathouse."

"What are you talking about?" Mulville stepped closer. A few drops of saliva hit her cheek. She resisted the impulse to wipe her face. "You were alone the entire time. We never stopped watching you. And you didn't tell us you fucking spotted him. What's wrong with you?"

She stepped back. A deep breath didn't help much. She had to remain calm and professional, otherwise her heart would act up. If she fainted in front of the hospital, she had no way to avoid being admitted, much less scrutinized with all kind of revealing tests. Her career would be over before it began. Better to face Mulville's wrath and suffocating protectiveness.

"I didn't see him." She looked Mulville in the eye. Her hand reached inside her pocketbook. "He left me another message."

She handed the plastic-wrapped yellow sticker to Mulville. He seized it and studied the writing.

"When did this come in?" He pointed his finger at the evidence bag. "Talk."

"I found it on my chair, at the restaurant, after I came back from the bathroom, just before I left."

"And you kept it from us, as usual. At least the shooting gives us an excuse to pick up the bastard." Mulville talked into his wrist microphone contacting the SWAT team to find out the status of the mission, but got no answer. "What in the fuck are they waiting for? An invitation?"

"Jack, wait," Kirk said. "I think Bloom is trying to tell us something important here."

"Montepulciano has an alibi for this shooting," Bloom explained, her voice soft, calming, for herself more than Mulville. "He came to see me, after the Boathouse. At my apartment. I'm afraid the shooting was a threat, to show us what he can and will do, if we don't allow him to have what he wants."

Mulville was talking into his wrist again. The poor guy stationed in front of her building was getting his share of damnation. Bloom braced for her turn.

"Great job." Mulville shook his head. His shoulder drooped a bit. "I put a guy outside to protect you, and you're having high tea with a mobster right inside, without bothering to let us know anything. Are we on the same team?"

"It just happened," Bloom said. "Kirk called me. I knew you'd be here. And I'm letting you know everything now."

The theme of the original Star Trek series soared over the background cacophony of horns, ambulance sirens, chatting, shouting, Kirk's phone ringing. The PI's hand shook as he yanked it from his jacket pocket. News about Aurora? Bloom's breath caught.

"Miner here," Kirk said. "Hi, John. Nothing yet. Still in surgery."

Bloom exhaled. John was with the SWAT. Was Montepulciano in custody? If so, what would happen to her? What mess had she dug herself into? Hoping that a murderous mobster would go free? She stared at Kirk.

"Did you get him?" Kirk listened and his mouth tightened in a downturned twist. "It figures."

Montepulciano had escaped. Bloom hated herself for the relief flooding her chest. But there was more. Kirk's eyes widened, his forehead creased with several parallel wrinkles.

"Thanks," he said, and he ended the call. Then he turned to them. "Montepulciano is nowhere to be found. And the ballistics for Aurora's bullet don't match the gun used on Amy Winter. It was a 7.62 mm."

"Military sniper rifle?" Mulville whistled. "The fucker is ex-army? Of course, some shit you can get any time at the Mob's flea-market."

"Not that I believe him," Bloom said. "But he said he didn't shoot Amy Winter outside the hospital. He wants us to step back and not interfere. I guess he's got in place some poor suicidal donor."

Bloom gave a detailed recount of her meeting. Mulville stared at her. His cheek muscles tightened, as if he was chewing without moving his jaw.

"We can't just sit around waiting for people to blow out their brains at this psychopath's command. If we knew who the daughter was… That's where you should put your energy, Bloom. She must be listed in the system. Find her."

The sweat on Bloom's back cooled off. Her throat didn't hurt any longer. Calm had returned to her heart.

"Actually," she said, "Montepulciano sent me instructions on how to retrieve that information. I was just starting when Kirk called me."

"Why would he give you access to that?" Kirk said. "It doesn't make any sense."

"Maybe he wants us to know who she is, so we don't interfere," Bloom said.

"He's screwing with us," Mulville said with a gesture of dismissal. "Go and find out who she is. We'll put the screws to her, make her talk, until we get something solid to nail her dear daddy with."

"On it." Bloom had never felt happier about being dismissed. "Kirk, let me know about Aurora as soon as you hear."

Kirk nodded his thanks. Bloom turned to go. She couldn't wait to get back home to her computer and some food, though not necessarily in that order.

"Hey." Mulville's voice reached her from behind and startled her like a lashing whip. She stopped and turned to face the director again. "If he ever contacts you again, don't be shy with me or you're done. I'll upgrade the watch at your place."

She nodded. Between Mulville, the mobster, and her heart condition, she might already be done. She rushed home to her computer. It was the only thing that made her feel in control.

On her way home, she stopped at Pizza Italy and picked up a medium pie. The smell of sauce and oregano in the car hiked up her hunger to a ravenous level. At home, she rapidly exchanged her constricting tailored skirt and shirt for a soft cotton T shirt and pajama pants. The first bite of pizza hit the spot, quieting her growling stomach. A sip of cold beer smoothed her stressed mind's rough edges. Her toes, recovering from the painful high heels, comfortably spread inside soft booties. She brought the frosted bottle to her lips one more time, wiped her hands on a paper napkin, and grabbed her mouse.

In front of her, on the kitchen table, her phone displayed the text message with webpage, instructions, and password to access the document. She followed the steps, and soon she was navigating the website of a private company offering paternity tests for a modest price. She read the offered credentials and accreditations. All seemed legit. When prompted, she entered the password Montepulciano had provided. A page appeared, featuring four columns.

The column underlying the case number listed all the gene loci tested. The mother's name, in the second column, was blank. Santo Montepulciano's name appeared in the third column under "Purported Father", followed by a number ID. Underneath, The "Allele Called" column listed the purported father's alleles side by side with the purported child's "Called Alleles," listed in the fourth column under "Purported Child."

The comparison showed the similarities and differences of the two gene sets. Bloom noticed the xy listed at the top of Montepulciano's list and the xx for the daughter. At the bottom, in a blue bordered box, she read the results. The probability of paternity was listed at 99.9999%. Her eyes jumped up, looking for the child's name, but only an anonymous number teased her from the top of the last column. *Fuck!*

She went back to the text instructions. A second password—a jumble of letters, numbers, and symbols—was listed on the last line of the message. Where should she plug in this password? She went back to the paternity document. No slot to plug in the set of characters. She clicked on the words "Purported Child." A slot appeared. She typed in the password. After two attempts, she got it right.

At last, the illegitimate child's name appeared in the middle of the screen.

Charlotte Kristal Bloom

CHAPTER 19
THE DAUGHTER

Bloom's heart pounded as if calling out for help. She had to be dreaming and, if so, this constituted a nightmare. She shut and opened her eyes again, trying to wake up. But she *was* awake. She stared again at her computer screen. Her own name was shouting at her from the middle of the screen.

Bloom's body was covered in cold sweat. The pizza sat in her stomach like a brick, smell from the leftovers nauseated her and, by the way, her father was a New York gangster.

The headline flashed in her mind: "Strong ties revealed between Montepulciano crime family and FBI cyber agent." Right when she thought her FBI career was finished, things had just gotten a lot worse.

No. Montepulciano was screwing with her. He was a good hacker, as demonstrated by his criminal past. He could fake a stupid document like the one in front of her any time. But he couldn't fool her. No sir.

She grabbed her computer and rushed into the bedroom. She sat the laptop on her dresser, in front of a mirror, and searched for the picture she had previously saved. She studied Montepulciano's face, her finger stroking the mouse to enlarge the picture to the maximum the pixels allowed.

Her eyes lifted to the mirror in front of her. She studied her thick brows. Much money had gone to beauty parlors to shape the two bushes into submission and discourage their joining in the middle of her forehead. Her eyes snapped back to Montepulciano's joining brows. Her heart jumped. She shifted her attention to the full lips. Not her mother's. Her mother's lips were so thin, she joked with her about not having room to apply lipstick. Bloom's mouth mimicked a smile to allow for a fair comparison. Despite the fact that man's moustache hid his upper lip, the shape of his mouth seemed similar to hers. Shit. Was it possible?

What about his brain? Had she inherited 50 percent of his brain, together with 50 percent of his genes? What about the part that made him a ruthless criminal, able (happy even) to threaten, torture, and mercilessly kill innocent victims for profit? When would the rotten part of her brain resurface and take over her desire and choice to be moral, to do good, to fight for justice as an FBI agent? Could it be true? Could this scum of the earth, this piece of shit criminal, really be her father? She closed her eyes and swallowed bile.

Rushing back to the kitchen, she grabbed the beer, now lukewarm. She took a large gulp. Some of the frothy liquid flew from her nose. The bitter fruity scent penetrated her nostrils. The bubbles made her sneeze. She drained the bottle and belched softly. A rage-driven resolve rose from the pit of her stomach and calmed her. She refused to be a victim of anything or anyone. Not of disease, not of the powerful mobster. She would defeat both.

With a jerk of her hand, she wiped Montepulciano's text from her cellphone. But the fact remained: She couldn't dismiss the possibility that the document represented the truth. After all, several coincidences made it at least marginally plausible. Her age, 25. The fact that she also had a heart condition. Her father had died when she was a young girl. Could it be that the man she had called Dad wasn't her biological father? A rebellious "no" shouted inside her head, as memories of her childhood flooded her mind, arguing against this absurd possibility.

On her dad's lap, she had learned how to read at an early age. He had made her Christmas toys with his own hands. What about the hot nights, lying on the backyard grass looking at stars and planets, her dad pointing at Jupiter and Venus? Weren't all these instances much better proof of paternity than the stupid document in her computer? Besides, she refused to accept the possibility that her mother would keep such a secret from her.

The heat of anger rose from her chest to her face. She had to admit she couldn't rule out that possibility with certainty. But how could she verify that the document screaming from her laptop was false? She couldn't just swab her inner cheek, send the saliva specimen to the lab, and ask them to rush the comparison of her DNA with Montepulciano's.

"Hi, Zayne." The conversation played in her mind like a comedy. *"Could you please check my DNA against the mobster's? I need to see if I'm the daughter he kills people for, so I can add it to my credentials. Thank you very much."*

She snorted. Her gaze fell on her dark and silent phone. There was a way, without raising too many flags, to glimpse the truth,. She dialed Kirk's number, but she cut off the call after the first ring. She wiped sweat off her face, blew her nose on a paper napkin, and looked at the empty bottle of beer sitting on the table. Was she sober enough to talk to the PI, without revealing anything she would be sorry about in the morning? Actually, she had no choice. Going to sleep without knowing was not a good option in her tired mind.

She stood in the middle of her kitchen and performed a relaxing tai-chi routine from her martial art classes. She stood on one foot and went to the familiar motions without hesitation. Calm descended on her as the air expanded her lungs and hissed out her pursed lips. Now she was ready for her conversation.

"Hi, Bloom," Kirk's voice answered over a background of silverware drumming on plates. "What's up? Did you get the name?"

The clock on her phone screen showed 6:46 p.m.. Dinner time. She imagined Kirk and his son, eating at the kitchen table, staring at the empty seat that Aurora should occupy instead of the hospital bed, having been shot on Bloom's account. And Bloom couldn't even leave him alone to enjoy a peaceful family dinner.

"How's Aurora?" The information wasn't her priority to know. She bit her lip.

"She's okay," he said. "The surgery went well. The doctor thinks her hand will fully recover."

"Great." She gave it a few appropriate seconds before changing subject. "I'm still working on the name. I need the information you've got about the alleged mother—you know, the ex-girlfriend you talked to—to see if it all makes sense. I need her present name."

She wasn't accustomed to lying. Lies took on a life of their own and expanded like oil leaks, generating wider and wider circles of pollution. The more she explained the bogus reason for her request, the less plausible it sounded in her own mind. Kirk was an experienced detective. He would expose her for the liar she was. No wonder she might be a mobster's daughter. Her genes were already showing through.

"The information John gave me is strictly confidential," Kirk said. "The case is sealed. All of it was supposed to have been destroyed years ago."

Silence dominated the line for several seconds.

"Without it," she ventured, shifting on the chair, "I might not be able to get an answer."

Who was she kidding? Kirk would bury her with an avalanche of objections. She shouldn't have called him. Time to bail.

"Under the circumstances," Kirk said, a deep breath following, "I guess I could send it to you. It's just a name. And an old picture. For your eyes only, of course."

She thanked him and hung up, fearful that her unease and guilt would reveal her lie. She fidgeted with her hair, stood up, and walked to the sink for a glass of water, her phone and computer waiting on the kitchen table for the answer that might change her life. A ping announced a new email. She gasped. Water droplets flooded her trachea and sent her into a coughing frenzy.

Regardless, she rushed to the table and guided her mouse to open the new file. Still clearing her throat, her teary eyes too blurred to read words, she was only able to focus on an image. The picture of Santo Montepulciano's ex-girlfriend from 25 years ago. A young innocent woman raped by a monster.

Despite the poor quality of the print and the young age of the subject, Bloom had no doubt. The young woman smiling at her from the computer screen was indeed her own mother. Her mother, raped by her father, the famous New York gangster Santo Montepulciano. Bloom slammed the computer shut.

Mulville was waiting to find out the identity of Montepulciano's daughter. If she didn't come up with an answer, her work would be questioned, checked. She re-opened her computer. In a few minutes, she had hacked her way into the paternity test website. She located her name in the "Purported Child" slot. With a stroke of her mouse and a touch of a key, she erased her name and typed "inconclusive" in its place. She went back to the highly significant statistical data and erased them from the report. Now wasn't the time to focus on the fact that she had just actively sabotaged the investigation. She had something more pressing to do.

As the black Mitsubishi followed the road to Washington DC., green grassy fields zipped by. Hidden behind a gray curtain of clouds, the sunset dimmed the daylight, forcing Bloom to snap out of her trance and switch on the headlights. By the time she crossed into Delaware, darkness had taken over. The dashboard clock showed 10:52. For hours, she had been battling a storm of conflicting emotions dominated by intense anger. Her fingers, too tight around the steering wheel, protested with numbing pain. Dry tears prickled her face. Her chin remained high and pointed at the beams piercing the night. Her mother had lied to her for twenty-five years. Bloom had the right to feel what she felt. Bloom had the right to hate her. The car plowed ahead, like an unstoppable tank going to war.

The chances were 99.9999 percent that 50 percent of that monster's genes were inextricably intertwined in her chromosomes. How much of the badness was inherited, and how much was still left to exercise free-will? Bloom still refused to accept the new development. Just because a woman was raped by the mobster, it didn't necessarily follow that Bloom was the product.

Yet, it made sense in so many ways. Montepulciano didn't retaliate against Bloom after her blow to his nose. Under any other circumstances, he would have killed her, or made her wish he would. Instead, he had congratulated her on her martial art expertise. Also, he had said: "You better choose wisely. Your life may be at stake." Now the real meaning of that statement seemed crystal clear in Bloom's mind.

Who had told him about her heart? Her mother? How would she know? Bloom had made sure she didn't know the full severity of her illness. Bloom's mouth tightened and her teeth bit her lower lip. His legacy... *She* was his legacy.

Bright lights hit her eyes and shocked her out of her thoughts. She registered the presence of a large mass coming straight at her just before the blaring of a powerful horn hit her ear drums. Adrenaline flew, her hands jerked, and the oncoming car swerved to the right. The lights disappeared toward her left. She came to a stop at the side of the road, put on the emergency signal, and folded her head onto her arms, resting on the steering wheel.

Her heart pounded with a few ominous extra beats. She calmed it with deep slow breaths. She was an FBI special agent on a mission. She had to compartmentalize the fact that Charlotte Bloom was also the subject of the investigation.

Her heart flipped into a flutter. She interrupted the arrhythmia with the pushing-into-her-chest method. Her future, her career, if she had any left, and her life depended on her ability to investigate the matter with detachment. No one but Bloom could do the job without revealing her secret and undermining her goal. She had to take the difficult journey one small step at a time. Today, the first step was to talk to her mother. In order to do that, she had to remain alive. She had to focus on the road. A sense of calm and pride took over her as she contemplated the professionalism of her last few thoughts. She was again thinking like an FBI agent.

When she arrived at the River Hill apartment complex, the first thing she noticed was her mother's Honda parked in the designated space. Her mother would be surprised to see her so soon after her recent monthly visit, unannounced, and at such a late hour. Her phone now showed 12:07 a.m.. It was already tomorrow. With just a late-night intrusion, Mom would have a hard time getting up at 6 a.m. for her factory job. *Oh, stop it!*

She parked her car on the street and walked toward the familiar building. The night lights shone on the red bricks and the trees cast ominous shadows onto the manicured yard. The chill of the night air made her wish she had grabbed a heavy jacket instead of the flimsy sweatshirt she now zipped up to her neck. Her mother would remind her about her health.

She rang the bell next to the name "Silverman."

Her mother had changed her name after the rape. Add the reasons for that to the questions she already had for her. What about Bloom's name? Had that gotten changed too? She banged her fingertip on the metal several times. The delay got her anger boiling again, infusing needed adrenaline into her tired body.

"Who is it?" a weary familiar voice inquired from a rectangular panel beside the list of names.

Bloom took a breath, ready to shout her FBI credentials, savoring the effect on the sleepy voice. But the words in her mind underwent a transformation while riding between brain and vocal cords.

"Mom," she heard herself saying, "it's me. Open up. We need to talk."

"Charlie," her mother said. "What happened? Wait."

Charlie. Mom had no right to use her nickname any longer. She had betrayed Charlie forever and for good. At the buzzing of the door, Bloom barged into the building as if she had just kicked down the door. She ran up the few flights of stairs, and stopped in front of the door, just as her mother appeared. Wrapped in her old pink, fluffy oversized robe and barefoot, Mom looked smaller. Her face seemed paler. She was without the dark red lipstick she never failed to wear during their visits. This time, Mom hadn't bothered checking through the peep hole to verify the caller's identity, something she never failed to do, even when her daughter came to see her.

"What's the matter, honey?" Marjorie Silverman opened her arms, her voice projecting only love and concern. No trace of distress for the inconvenience of being summoned from sleep in the middle of the night. No worry about the difficulty she would incur waking up at the crack of dawn to drive to work. Only watchfulness over the most precious thing in her life, her Charlie. "Come here."

Bloom's feet felt glued to the corridor's thin carpet. She stared at the light and dark brown geometric design, then she looked up again. Twenty-five plus years ago, the small, frail woman in front of her had been raped. RAPED. That was a fact. In a flash, Bloom reviewed her mother's life through the dirty glass called rape. She saw a lonely young woman fighting a ruthless mobster, pounding his powerful chest with her small fists, then a large hand crushing her muffled cries for help. The same girl stared at the results of a positive pregnancy test and saw the rest of her life slipping away, falling by the side, like a head under a guillotine. Why hadn't she terminated the life begun in violence by a despicable human being? Bloom would have.

A single mom moved away to a small town in Ohio, hid her abdominal bump, hid her baby, and found a new life partner with a respectable name to fill the vacuum left by the menacing bully. Recently, the lonely widow had moved back to town. Why? To be near her precious, only daughter who wanted to be an FBI agent when she grew up. She risked her life to be near her.

Something crumbled inside Bloom. The raw anger drained out of her, washed out by the cold sweat that now covered her body, leaving only a strong need to accept the offered hug, even if only for a moment's rest.

"You're freezing," her mother said. Her hand rose to touch Bloom's forehead in the typical gesture Bloom had witnessed countless times over the years during the usual childhood ailments. "Come in. I'll make us some tea."

Bloom watched her mother shuffle on the kitchen linoleum floor, setting the water kettle on the range, reaching up for two cups and saucers from a cabinet, retrieving two old Lipton tea bags from the pantry smelling like spices, and getting plastic-wrapped lemon wedges from the refrigerator. She carried everything to the wooden table and sat on a chair across from Bloom. A long, heartfelt sigh exited the woman's pursed lips. Her dark brown eyes looked shiny. Her lower lip quivered. Something in her mother's demeanor begged for forgiveness.

Her mother knew why Bloom had come. Something she must have dreaded and expected for the past twenty-five years was happening now. It wasn't fair. Her mother had no right to preempt Bloom's rage, even before hearing what she had to say. From her mother's reaction, all of what Bloom dreaded the most had to be true. Anger, pain, and pity clashed inside her, playing her like a ping-pong ball with no purpose and no aim.

The kettle whistled. The mother rushed to fetch the hot water. After a longer than necessary period of time, she shuffled back carrying the kettle and took her time placing the tea bags inside the cups and pouring the hot water on them. They waited, watching the water turning darker.

"Who's my real father?" Bloom asked with the controlled calm practiced during her FBI training. "The truth. Now. Please."

"Did something happen?" No questioning or protest. Her mother knew what she was talking about. And her tone left no doubt that she was ready to protect her daughter to the end. "Did someone try to hurt you?"

"No, Mom." Bloom searched inside for fierceness. "Much worse than that. Someone's trying to save me. Is Santo Montepulciano my real father? The piece of shit bastard who raped you? Am I his freaking bastard daughter?"

Bloom watched her mother wince. Not about the cursing, although she hated cursing and Bloom had endured childhood time-outs for it on at least a few occasions. This was a much deeper and more serious grimace. Bloom braced herself for what was coming. The phrase "99.9999% possible" flashed in her mind like a neon sign.

"Yes," her mother whispered. She looked straight at Bloom. Tears welled in her lower eyelids. The solemnity in her face made it difficult for Bloom to pity her.

"What about Daddy?" The short word seemed to erase, rearrange, and rewrite Bloom's entire life. "He wasn't my real father? Did he even know? Or did you keep it a secret even from him?"

"Daddy, bless his soul, was the only other person to know the truth." Tears were flowing now, marking Marjorie's face. "I couldn't let anyone else know. Santo would've taken you. I'm sure of it. I had to protect you. I gave you a new family, and a good name, instead of a rotten one."

Silence helped the words sink into Bloom's mind. It argued her mother's case like a defense lawyer in front of a judge and jury. The warm tea soothed her aching throat. Her mother had prepared the hot beverage for her. Mom always knew what she needed. From change of diapers to ignorance of the truth about being a mobster's daughter. No, that latter one was different, much different. Her mother had no right to keep all this from her. Anger was boiling up again like water in a pot after uncooked spaghetti is added and the flame is boosted.

"Did you tell that bastard about my heart?!" Bloom shouted. "After I told you to keep it secret, to keep your mouth shut, you went and told *him*, of all people!"

The rumbling of the refrigerator startled her like a thunder warning her of a forthcoming storm.

"I had to." Marjorie's tone was anything but apologetic. "I didn't want you to die."

"Who said anything about me dying?!" Bloom yelled. "I told you I had extra heart beats. Those don't kill people. Unless you involve the Mob."

Her mother's shoulder slumped. She looked smaller, shrunken.

"I knew you weren't telling me the truth," Marjorie said. Bloom noticed that her mother avoided using the word "lying. "After the first time, you never took me with you to the doctor."

"So how did you find out?"

"I went back to the doctor by myself. I begged him to tell me how bad your problem was. He told me you weren't taking your illness seriously. But nothing more."

Her mother took a sip of tea and replaced the cup on the saucer. She reached for a paper napkin and wiped her eyes. She blew her nose, crumpled the napkin, and placed it on the saucer next to the cup. Bloom waited.

"I knew his nurse," Marjorie said. "One of the few friends I had in Ohio. She told me what the doctor wrote in the chart. That he told you you needed a heart transplant, or the worst could happen…in a matter of months. Charlie, baby, what's wrong with your heart?"

"If I could," Bloom said, "I would have told you already. I didn't want *this* to happen."

"You know it's very difficult to get a heart," Marjorie said. "And you didn't even want to be listed. I felt desperate. With nobody to turn to. From what I read in the newspapers last year, I knew your father has a way to get into hospital computers. I figured he could push you up on the list, before you—"

"Hacking, Mom," Bloom interrupted. "The technical term is hacking. He knows how to hack. So, you told him I was his daughter. How did he take it? Was he ecstatic?"

"He cursed and yelled at me. The way you're yelling at me now." She looked immediately sorry for the last statement. "I've never seen him so mad. I thought for sure he was going to kill me. I left him some hair from your brush, in case he wanted to check if I was telling the truth. After his reaction, I didn't expect anything to happen. When the detective came to see me, I had no idea Santo was killing people to get you a heart. I never meant anything like that to happen."

Bloom looked at the woman in front of her and knew there was no punishment on earth Bloom could inflict on her that could be worse than what her mother had already dealt to herself. And all her mother had done was to risk her own life to protect her daughter from a bad name, kidnapping by a gangster, and a deadly disease.

"You meant well," Bloom said. "But you destroyed my life."

"How?" The mother's shiny eyes lifted to meet hers. "I only wanted to help you. I worked all my life, and you're what I've lived for. All my life."

"I don't doubt it." Bloom shook her head. "But I told you before, if the FBI finds out about my heart before I finish my probation time, I'm done. I guess now it doesn't matter anymore. I have a much worse problem than that. Gaining a mobster father isn't a good career boost."

"That's why I protected you from the truth. I love you, Charlie." No whining. Only her solemn dignity. She stood by her intentions and her actions. "You're all I have."

Agent Bloom had accomplished her mission. But she couldn't leave her mother like that. Mom was right. She had given Bloom 25 years free of threats and worries. She had delayed the inevitable truth as long as she could, like a soldier, risking her life dodging bullets, and providing cover for her comrades. She observed her mother's stooped posture, her lowered gaze. She listened to her silence. Marjorie Silverman didn't deserve that kind of punishment.

Bloom stood and walked around the table. She took her mother in her arms and placed her own face against the old and fluffy pink robe she knew so well.

"I don't want you to die." Marjorie Silverman sobbed, patting her back.

"Neither do I." Bloom cried with her.

CHAPTER 21
P####

Bloom took a long sip of her large latte, the only breakfast she had opted for, and refocused on driving without dozing off. She should have left the night before. Lying in the spare bedroom, staring at the ceiling, hadn't done her any good, except feeding into the fire of her anger, whose target was getting harder and harder to identify. Arguing with Mom about not getting on the road after their emotional meeting had left her more exhausted than ever.

But she couldn't fall asleep without a plan. One thing stood clear in her jumbled mind—under no circumstances could she reveal to Kirk or Mulville her newly discovered paternal relationship. Never. Meanwhile, she hoped that her failure to discover the mobster's daughter would be excused.

Her default ring tone filled the car's silence. Damn. 'Unknown caller' made her sigh in relief. Not Kirk, and not Mulville. She touched the phone to answer.

"Hi sweetie." The man's sentimental voice betrayed an ominous undertone. "Did my credentials check out?"

The car burst forward as Bloom's foot jerked on the accelerator. Trees enlarged to occupy most of the front window. Bloom's hands tightened on the steering wheel and swung to the left. The car swerved back onto the road.

"Shit!" she shouted. She looked for a place to stop. She drove on until she saw a side road. She turned onto it and stopped at the curb. "Damn you. Go back where you came from. Out of my life."

"Sorry." How often did Santo Montepulciano say that word? Was he making the rare exception because she was his daughter? Another small fragment of evidence in favor of Bloom's father-daughter relationship. As if she needed more proof. "I see I caught you at a bad time. Don't need any car accidents on my account. I can call later."

"Say what you have to say now." Bloom eyed the phone with loathing, as if it were a real person. "Quick. Before I hang up on you forever."

Static followed. Bloom's face heated up though cold air seeped into the car. She took a calming breath.

"You better not be wired," he warned, his voice having lost any semblance of cordiality, "unless you want me added to your FBI CV. Not very good for your career if the police and the FBI find out we're connected."

"My father is dead!" she shouted, knowing that yelling didn't make what she said any more convincing to either of them. "It's a little late for you to jump into the picture. If you care about me, the best you can do now is to leave me alone."

"I signed you up on the chain." He went on as if she hadn't uttered a word. "You're the patient without a number—the patient with only the hashtag symbols. I protected your identity. I even removed you when no heart was available any longer."

"You, you…" Bloom searched for words to release the pressure bottled up inside her chest, like gas in a volcano agitated by scuffing tectonic plates. "Screw you. You have no right. I went out of town, to the Cleveland Clinic, to keep this private. And I refused to be listed for transplant. How in hell can I be listed on the chain without my consent and no donor?"

Her question by now sounded rhetorical. Bloom guessed the answer even before hearing it. The air smelled stuffy. The car's confinement gave her an uncomfortable feeling of claustrophobia.

"I am the donor," Montepulciano said. "You and me will appear as hashtags only—no names, no real info, just as a place-saver until a heart becomes available. I want you to accept the heart when it becomes available."

The mere mention of the two of them together in the same sentence, much less part of the same plan, made Bloom queasy with disgust. She had to stop this. But how could she stop a New York gangster who had risen to power by drowning or burying his competiti into the Hudson, who had beaten dozens of big hospitals into submission, and who had even forced several people to commit suicide? She was stuck. Trapped.

"You're insane." It was all she could say in protest.

"Why?" He came across as cheerful now, as if he was having a good time. "You almost got your heart. If it weren't for the fucking lawyers …"

"You killed that woman for me?"

"You have no evidence of that, and I already answered that question," he said. "But, for what it's worth, I did not."

"You took over the heart transplant chain to make money," she said, as if she were a prosecutor in a court of law. "You forced people to kill themselves and others. And you threatened that poor patient, Margarita Herrera. You made her refuse Amy Winter's heart and accept that mechanical device instead. All for me. I have news for you. I don't want it. I don't want a freaking heart under these conditions. Actually, coming from you, I don't want it under any circumstances. I'd rather be dead."

Silence. Bloom looked at the screen. She heard deep breathing, uncertain if it was his or her own.

"Did you send someone to kill Kirk Miner?" she said.

"No," he said without hesitation. "Only one way for this nonsense to stop once and for all, and it's up to you. Get your heart. Just let it happen. All this will stop. I'll make it all go away."

"You'll stop all killings," she said, "*and* your interference with the hospital database?"

"Yes."

"So," she said, touching the phone screen to start recording, "you're admitting that you are interfering with the chain and forcing people to commit suicide?'

"Of course not." He chuckled. "And, if you want to continue this conversation, stop recording it."

His tone would have been appropriate for a business negotiation. But for Montepulciano, this was how he always got his way. An offer regular people couldn't refuse…or else.

"It's a federal crime," she said, "to threaten an FBI agent."

"I'm doing no such thing." The soft loving tone was back again. "I'm trying to *save* your life. It's not my fault if other people are involved in this equation. I warned you about your friends' safety. You didn't listen."

So the life of Kirk Miner and Director Mulville's might indeed be at stake after all. The man really meant it. She chewed on her lower lip as she got ready to take a new approach.

"Listen," she said, stopping the useless recording, "even if it were all legal and possible, I need to wait a little longer. I can't do it just yet. My career is at stake. If anyone finds out I'm medically unfit for work, I'm done. You have to give me time."

"Your life comes first." He sounded like a father now. The bastard really knew how to play the part. "You have only months to live, and you know it. Dead people can't worry about their careers."

"What do you care?" she insisted, as her last attempt at reasoning slipped away. "You didn't give a damn about me for twenty-five years. What's two months longer?"

"All those years, I had no idea you even existed," he said. "I first learned of you when your mother came to see me. I'll never forgive her for keeping you a secret."

Montepulciano's wrath was what her poor mother had faced head on in order to protect her all those years. She fought back tears. Now it was Bloom's turn to protect her.

"I swear to you," she said in her best agent's tone, "I'll investigate and arrest you if, as I suspect, you're responsible for all these crimes. And don't bother killing anyone else for my sake. I won't admit I'm ill, let alone accept a heart transplant."

No further threats came. Had Montepulciano acceded to her wishes? More likely he was planning how to coerce her, or worse, how to silence her. Though her hair lifted at the nape of her neck and she started shaking, she managed to control her voice.

"And make sure that nothing happens to my mother," she added. "If she so much as slips and falls, I'll hold you responsible and come knocking at your door—me and an FBI SWAT team."

Hanging up felt as good as silencing her adversary with a punch to the face. If she was heading for hell anyway, she might as well ride in, head held high. She relaxed against the seat and savored the moment with the rest of her lukewarm latte. Soon enough, she would have to come up with a plan on how to handle Kirk Miner and Director Mulville.

CHAPTER 22
DONOR

It was past noon when Bloom pulled up in front of her building, parking just behind the black sedan driven by her FBI-sitter. She waved at the middle-aged man. The upgrade to a more experienced agent, as Mulville had insisted on doing, didn't reassure her in the least. And she had no idea yet what to tell Mulville or Kirk about Montepulciano. Or about the identity of his secret daughter. Her colleagues had the right to know the risk they were running on her account. Every minute of her silence could result in injury or even death, as demonstrated by Aurora's shooting. But the secret about her father was inexorably tied to the secret of her illness. Bloom's mind was in no condition to do anything at the moment but shut down and sleep.

She climbed the stairs, entered her apartment, peeled off her jeans, exchanged a sweat shirt for her favorite sleeping shirt, and crawled under the covers. Just before falling asleep, she checked her cellphone one more time. Two messages from Mulville and one from Kirk in the past hour alone. She typed the same answer to both, telling them she needed until tomorrow to complete her investigation. Exhaustion numbed any feeling of guilt about withholding the truth.

She jolted awake. Not by a noise or a light. A thought.

Her phone showed 5:52 A M. She had been asleep for longer than fourteen hours. That's what stress did to people. She threw the covers off the bed and walked to the kitchen while fastening her robe. After starting the coffee machine, she went into the bathroom and took a long, hot shower. As her back muscles relaxed under the soothing water massage, Bloom realized the torture she had endured. Her mind relaxed as well, loosening her memory. During her sleep, she'd dreamt of Aurora's shooting, with Kirk's words playin again and again in her mind: "She pulled me down and saved my life."

A moment before the gunshot, Aurora's hand had grabbed Kirk and made him bend down to kiss her. If that hadn't occurred, the path of the bullet would have been directly though Kirk's head instead of Aurora's hand. This was no warning shot. The shooter hadn't missed on purpose. The shooter wanted to blow out Kirk's brain.

She stepped out of the shower, towel dried, wrapped the damp towel around her hair and her robe around her body, and rushed back to the kitchen. Armed with a fresh cup of coffee, she woke up her computer. She tailored a search that, she hoped, would answer the urgent inquiry hammering her mind. At last, a spreadsheet appeared showing a list of names with corresponding genetic data. Her breath stopped in her throat while she scrolled down the alphabetized list to find what she was looking for. Her eyes locked onto a name. Her breath came out like a soft whistle.

She saved her work, closed the top, and ran to the bedroom to dress. A look at the clock made her slow down. Where would Kirk be at 7:30 in the morning? She could think of only one place. Good. She needed to talk to him alone as soon as possible.

Kirk stood by the hospital bed and handed Aurora a container of hot tea. Despite the mass of bandages and splints her right hand had become, she attempted to sit up from the pile of pillows supporting the hand. Kirk didn't miss the futile struggle, the automatic response from a nervous system that hadn't yet registered or fully accepted the injury. He cringed, and grabbed Aurora's free and functional left hand.

"How're you doing?" he whispered.

She closed her puffy eyes and nodded. The attempt of a reassuring smile flashed and morphed into a grimace as the pain to her injured hand travelled through the nerves and reached her brain.

"Hurts bad?" Kirk bent to touch her forehead with his lips. "You're sweating."

"It's the stupid pain meds," she said, reaching for the paper cup. "I hope I can stop the narcotics today. I want to go home."

He watched her take a sip of the hot beverage, hoping to see enjoyment on her face. Her predicament was all due to his damn work. Montepulciano would pay for every moment of Aurora's suffering.

"I'm so sorry." He ran his finger over her smooth cheek and stopped to play with her blonde curls.

To make him feel better, the way only she could, Aurora took a breath before leveling her complaint. A buzzing from his belt intruded. Kirk cursed. He checked his phone. Bloom. Was about time. What had she been up to, other than determining the identity of Montepulciano's daughter? Mulville was right. The daughter was the key to the mobster's eventual imprisonment. That was the last and only clue left to follow. Kirk couldn't wait to hear. But not now. Now was his time with Aurora. He placed the phone back into his belt and turned his attention back to his wife.

She seemed to enjoy the tea made according to her preference—with added honey. Her head rose from the pillow and her lips closed around the rim for one more small sip before handing the cup back to Kirk.

"Take your call. Go get the bad guys," she said. Her chin came up, pointing at her mangled hand—her nurse's hand. "Punish them for this."

Kirk nodded and looked at the phone again. A text. Bloom urgently needed him. Now. He texted her his location, pulled a chair over to the bed, and sat down. He took his wife's good hand in his and kissed it.

Bloom showed up half an hour later, laptop in hand. Her hair smelled fresh and she looked rested and crisp in her blue suit and white shirt. Whatever she had been up to for the past couple days didn't seem so bad. She exchanged a greeting with Aurora. Then her eyes took in the room, as if looking for something. Kirk got the message. Privacy was what she was looking for. She didn't want Aurora to be alarmed or upset by their discussion. Neither did Kirk.

"Why don't you rest?" he told Aurora with another stroke of her cheek. "Bloom and I will step outside for a moment to regroup. I'll be right back."

Bloom led the way to a small and deserted doctor-patient conference room at the end of the corridor. A couch and two matching chairs huddled around a wooden coffee table covered with magazines. A window without curtains let the daylight in and onto the bare walls. This was a room for news, some good—a successful surgery, some bad—death, now or looming in the near future. What did Bloom have in store for Kirk? He sat and watched her setting up the computer on the coffee table. Her face didn't give away any clues. Her fingers knew where to stir into cyber-space to arrive at a certain spreadsheet.

"Last night I couldn't stop wondering why they shot at you," Bloom said, as she stopped typing. "I finally came to the conclusion that they missed you only because Aurora pulled you down."

Kirke nodded. "I know."

"She saved your life. They didn't want to miss. They wanted to kill you."

Somebody had tried to kill him. Kirk had suspected it all long. But hearing it spelled out made his skin tingle.

"I don't know anything more than you or Mulville," he said. "And this investigation wouldn't stop if I weren't around. You're the leading FBI investigator. So, why me?"

"Exactly." Bloom's brows rose. "And why now?"

"And?" Kirk waited.

"I think I found the answer." Bloom stifled a sad little chuckle. "Together with a lot more questions."

Bloom turned the computer screen toward Kirk. Her palm came up in an inviting gesture. Kirk leaned forward and placed his palms on the table. He perused a spreadsheet consisting of names and genetic data.

"Help me out, here." He pointed at the screen, impatience breaking through. "What am I looking at?"

"A list of people designated as possible organ donors." She tapped and stroked her mouse. The names scrolled down. She stopped at the letter M. "Check it out."

Kirk's eyes ran down the names. The third one on the list made his throat clamp down: "Kirk Miner." Right next to his date of birth.

"That's me." His voice cracked. "What list is this? I'm not listed as a donor anywhere."

The light of understanding shone on Bloom's face. She had found answers to some of her questions. Now Kirk needed answers too.

"You're not listed *now*," she said. She pointed at the screen. "This is an *in*active list."

Kirk stared at the spreadsheet. He gasped.

"These are people who were listed as donors in the past, but aren't in the donor pool any longer."

She looked at him, waiting for an explanation. They both knew that by the word "listed," Bloom didn't refer to the pink dot with which people mark their driver's licenses to indicate a desire to donate their organs in case of accidental death. The genetic data next to each name on the chart meant that the people on the list had been evaluated by some organ-donation team. It meant that they had spent some time in a condition that had led the team to presume them brain dead. Kirk guessed that very few of the people on the list had woken up.

"Years ago," Kirk said, "I was in a terrible car accident. I was in a coma for two months. Nobody expected me to recover. I had to undergo experimental brain surgery. Hence my listing as a potential organ donor. But then I woke up. And they took me off the list."

"Yet, here you are," she said, pointing at the screen, her mouth stretched. "If I can find you, any worth-a-damn hacker can find you too."

"Great." Kirk's hand went up in frustration. "What about patient privacy? Where's HIPAA when we need it?"

"Yeah." Bloom smiled.

"And why is my name in bold letters?" Kirk's voice sounded an octave higher than normal.

"You've recently been upgraded," she said, sounding like the expert she had become. "You're now appearing on all active donors' lists as well. If anything should happen to you, your organs would be up for grabs."

"So this is why…," Kirk asked in a whisper, "why they tried blowing my brains out? Because I'm a match for…somebody? Whom?"

Kirk remembered Amy Winter, a universal blood donor, according to the friend he had met in the hospital. Something didn't add up. Bloom looked at him with puzzled eyes.

"I'm blood type A," Kirk explained. "The GSW victim, Amy Winter, and Patient 1, Margarita Herrera, who was supposed to get her heart, were both type O—universal donors. My heart wouldn't be a match for Herrera. So, why did they try to kill me?"

Bloom turned the computer and checked out the chart. She leaned closer to the screen, typed, and scrolled, her lips pinched together. After a while, she sat back in her chair, as if she had come up with an answer. The answer didn't help her. Her color drained to a dreadful pale gray. Kirk touched her hand. Icy.

"Bloom!" he shouted. He squeezed and shook her hand. He summoned his medical expertise. His fingers went for her pulse. It was there, but faster than normal, as expected under stressful circumstances. "Stop hyperventilating or you're going to pass out. Hold your breath for a moment, then breathe slowly."

"I'm okay," she said. "I just realized who's your match."

"Who?"

"The secret patient," Bloom said. "The one that disappeared after the victim died. I remember the doctor mentioning that she was type A, just like you."

"It makes sense," Kirk said. "Amy Winter was a universal donor. She could have been a donor for Herrera, and also for the secret patient."

"That's why she was chosen." Bloom had recovered most of her color. Her breathing seemed more controlled. "Montepulciano's plan was to convince Herrera to refuse Amy's heart, so it would go to the secret patient instead. He had it all planned out."

Something occurred to Kirk. He had to steady himself against the back of his chair. He followed the same instruction he had just given Bloom. He took a deep, slow breath.

"Let's assume that what you're saying is true," he said, looking around the room as if he could find answers, "that they tried to kill me to get a heart for the secret patient. It means that now they're just worrying about finding a heart for her, and only her, as soon as possible. Is she Montepulciano's daughter, for sure?"

"Yes," Bloom said. Was it a speck of pity Kirk saw in her eyes? "And yes. You are a match for the mobster's daughter. I'm so sorry."

Kirk felt sorry too. And trapped. Like a meat cow whose only destination was the slaughterhouse.

"You have to hide," Bloom said. "Montepulciano was crystal clear. He'll do anything to save his daughter. She's the most important thing in his sorry life. He'll stop at nothing."

Hiding was Bloom's solution? That just about wrapped up how precarious Kirk's predicament had become. And why would an FBI agent suggest such a passive surrender? He might have an idea about that.

"Tell me," Kirk said. "Who's this secret patient? Did you find out the name of Montepulciano's daughter?"

"No." Bloom said it too quickly, as if she was in a hurry to dismiss the crucial question. "What Montepulciano told me was all BS. The document I found was inconclusive. Montepulciano had no intention of revealing anything. And he denied any killing, or forcing people to commit suicide, just like he denied hacking the hospital's system. Only thing we can do is play it safe and hope he makes a mistake."

"So," Kirk said, looking Bloom in the eye, "there's no way to figure out who that secret patient is—not even with all your tricks?"

"I'm afraid not." She directed her gaze to the tiled floor.

"Too bad." Kirk sighed. "Perhaps I can help."

Bloom lifted her eyes. "How?" Her eyes dilated. "I'm the one who spoke with Montepulciano."

She fidgeted with her ponytail. Her breath was speeding up again. Kirk had to be careful not to stress her too much.

"Yes," Kirk said. "But I'm the one at the highest risk of dying. And I'm not going to hide. And neither should you."

Bloom looked at Kirk.

"I know who the secret patient is," Kirk said.

Bloom's eyes got wider. She jerked up on her chair as if she had just experienced an electric jolt.

"Who?" she said, her voice fading.

"You."

CHAPTER 23
LIFE OR DEATH

Kirk knew her secret. He had revealed it not in triumph, like a cold winner crushing his competitors, or a prosecutor exposing a lie. He had said it as a compassionate friend who understood and offered a helping hand.

"Me? The secret patient?" Bloom said. A prickly sensation spread from her chest to her fingertips. "How can you say that?"

"Bloom." Kirk placed his fingers under her chin and lifted her head. Her eyes were now level with his. "I'm a private investigator. I went and talked to Montepulciano's ex-girlfriend. She has a daughter in need of a heart."

"So?"

"I knew from John that Marsha Stevens' name for the past twenty-five years has been Marjorie Silverman."

Bloom gasped. Betrayed by her own mother? She shook her head.

"Marjorie never mentioned your name," Kirk said, as if he had read Bloom's mind. "I checked her background. Marjorie Silverman's deceased husband's name was Bloom. She's your mother."

Kirk let go of her chin. For a moment, adrenaline flowed into her veins, and she got ready to protest. But then her shoulders slumped. She checked out the floor one more time.

"Why didn't you tell me earlier that you knew?" Bloom said. "I've been wondering why you kept secrets from me. I thought you didn't trust me."

"I thought I was helping you," Kirk said. "By not giving you something more to worry about. Now I think I was wrong."

"So," Bloom said, "why tell me now?"

"Now Mulville has you up against the wall. I want you to know you can trust me as much as I trust you."

Bloom nodded.

"Why do you need a heart?"

"No, please," she whispered, her hands twitching. "I can't tell anyone until about two months from now. Please."

"What happens in two months?"

"I become an actual special agent," she said, lifting up her head. "My probation will be over."

"Your mother said you need a heart soon, otherwise you're going to die." Kirk spoke softly. "How soon is soon?"

"I'm good," she said with a firm voice. "I have several months. I'm under care at the Cleveland Clinic, of all places. They know what they're doing, so you don't need to be concerned. Nobody needs to know or to worry about me."

"What about Mulville?" Kirk's brows rose. "He cares so much about you. He'll never forgive me, or you, if anything happens."

"You can't tell Mulville about this," she snapped. "Most of all Mulville. Let me handle him."

"If something happens to you," Kirk said with a sad chuckle, "you'll be lucky to die. I'm going to be the one to face Mulville."

Bloom's eyes narrowed as she pondered the matter.

"We'll talk to him together," she said. "I'll let him know everything I found out. But no word about my medical problem. Or my ties to the New York mob."

Though that left off the plate just about everything, Kirk nodded anyway. Bloom could only hope that once they were in Mulville's presence, she could reveal the truth without too much collateral damage.

Mulville sat at his desk, a paperclip twirling around his karate-primed finger tips. From the look of the mangled paper clip, the director didn't appear to be in a good mood.

Bloom and Kirk faced him from the two guest chairs. Kirk straightened his back against the hard metal and wondered if the FBI director had purposefully chosen uncomfortable seating arrangements to keep his meetings short. At 12:25 in the afternoon, the three of them had been at it for half an hour, mostly discussing Kirk's role as a possible donor. The remnants of a bagel on Mulville's desk gave the room the faint smell of toasted bread. Kirk felt pangs of hunger. He had forgone lunch with Aurora for this dreadful meeting.

"Bloom," Mulville said after a prolonged silence, "you're telling me that after two days of hard work, and with Montepulciano's instructions, the only new information you came up is that the anonymous and fleeting patient with the four hashtag symbols is Montepulciano's daughter? Correct me if I'm wrong, but didn't we know this already? You told us this at the hospital, after Kirk's wife got shot. You also told us Montepulciano was letting you know his daughter's name. So, who's his freaking daughter?"

Mulville nailed Bloom with his gaze. Kirk saw droplets of sweat appearing on the probie's upper lip. He leaned forward and scrounged in his head for something to give Bloom time to come up with an answer."

"The instructions he left lead to an unconclusive paternity document," Bloom said. "I'm still working it from different angles. I'll let you know as soon as I have something."

"We need to know now," Mulville said, pointing the paperclip at her. "*Before* they do Kirk in and give her his heart. Send me the info he gave you, so I can have someone else give it a shot."

Bloom nodded. She gave Kirk a quick glance.

"Otherwise, he didn't admit to anything," Mulville said. "And even if he did, without a freaking wire, which you didn't bother to wear, we got zilch."

Mulville turned to Kirk. "Since you're the one with the medical knowledge, please explain something to me. What is this, a convention of perfect donors? We've got Herrera with her match Baker, but also another match in Amy Winter. And all are also a match for Montepulciano's daughter? And now, even you, Kirk, are a match for her. And they say there's a shortage of hearts. Patients are dying waiting for people to drop dead, so they can take their heart."

"It's not like that." Kirk felt his stomach relax at the possibility of diving into a scientific issue. "Amy Winter was blood type O, just like D3—that is, Baker. They're universal donors, so their heart could go not only to Herrera, but also to Montepulciano's daughter, who's type A. But then there are the HLA genes to consider to determine if a donor is a good match."

"English," Mulville said. "Bottom line. English."

"As Dr. Wilder explained it to me," Kirk said, "a complete HLA match just by chance is very unlikely. The probability that a random donor and a recipient will be good matches is less than 1.5 percent. But in a large pool, you can find several possible donors—recipient pairs with two HLA mismatches or less—that are a good match, like the ones we're talking about here."

"I get it." Mulville threw the unlucky paperclip into a wastebasket in the corner of the room. He must have played basketball in college. "Nothing like looking for live and well matches and arranging for their early demise to crank up a notch or two the number of happy transplants."

"Precisely." Mulville's statement stirred Kirk's unease. "About that: My blood type is A. My heart can go to the mobster's daughter, but not to Herrera."

"They're not even trying to mask their intentions any longer," Bloom said, exchanging a glance with Kirk with the concern of someone who knew the whole story. "No more patients refusing the heart so it can go to Montepulciano's daughter, who's second in line."

"What do you two know that I don't?" Mulville asked, looking at both of them in turn.

Mulville didn't miss a beat. Bloom looked paralyzed. Kirk's back went into a painful spasm. He tightened his lips.

"Nothing," she said. "That's all."

"I swear." Mulville pointed a finger at Kirk and Bloom in turn. "If I ever discover you're holding back shit . . ."

The distant city traffic noise was the only answer to the unfinished threat. Bloom and Kirk knew what would follow. Bloom would be looking for another job. Kirk would never again collaborate with the FBI. The resolve he saw in Bloom's eyes told Kirk she hadn't changed her plan. She focused on her computer's screen and remained silent.

"Can't you just take him off the active donor list?" Mulville asked Bloom, pointing at Kirk. "Before someone blows his brains out for good?"

"I already did," Bloom said. "But I'm not sure it'll do any good. This hacker can put him back any time he feels like it."

"I'm going to try to talk to that moron Baker again," Kirk said, "even if maybe it'd be easier to let Montepulciano blow out his brains instead of mine. That would solve all our problems, and most of all mine. But Baker may be the only chance we have left to nail Montepulciano. I think he's hiding something."

"And as soon as we're done here," Bloom said, "I'm going to track the different cyber signals to see if I can come up with the origin of the hack into the inactive donor file. If we can prove it came from Montepulciano, it'll give us a solid basis to subpoena his electronics."

"Okay," Mulville groaned. "We're done here."

Bloom sat in the kitchen of the small Brooklyn apartment, the remnants of her dinner on a plate next to an empty wine glass. Before going back to her computer, she wrapped her robe around her body and reveled in the wine's mellowing effect. Her head fell back, stretching the neck muscles. She pressed one hand to her stomach. The extra tension that had plagued her for the past few days was subsiding. Kirk's hearing of her relationship with Montepulciano had allowed her to share her burden, instead of holding everything inside. She could count on his discretion with Mulville.

Now, the best she could do was to figure out how Kirk's name had gone from the inactive to the active donor's list. If only she could come up with some hard evidence.

Bloom cracked her knuckles and went to work. After several searches and queries, the computer started churning out data. Bloom poured herself some more vino and took it to the couch. A familiar sound startled her and she had to steady her hand in order not to spill red wine on the carpet.

It took Bloom a moment to realize that the sound hadn't come from her computer, but from the doorbell. She placed her glass on the coffee table and walked to the door. Who would visit at this hour in the evening, especially without calling first? She hoped the FBI guy outside had screened her visitor. She blinked and placed her right eye against the door's peep-hole. Zayne Wilder stood a foot from her, separated only by air and the width of her door. Her hand went to her hair. She thought about her face: no makeup and covered by moisturizer. He wore a sport's jacket over a sweater and tight jeans. He bit his lower lip. She had touched and tasted his lips. The memory of his naked body moving over hers wiped off any worries about hair, homey robe, and makeup-free face.

Had something happened at the hospital so urgent and important he had to come and report to the FBI in person? What about phones? She mocked herself for her foolishness. She saw him shifting his weight from one foot to the other, as if he was fighting a desire to leave. *No, please, don't leave.* She hurried to unfasten the two new locks installed since Montepulciano's home invasion, and opened the door.

Did she detect a shade of red on his face? The color went well with his gray eyes. He stepped closer without asking. He must have read something on her face. Everything she had suppressed during the past few days unleashed inside her. In advance, she mentally decided to go along with anything he could wanted from her. She stepped aside. But he didn't go far. He embraced her at the door and wouldn't let her move. His mouth locked on hers, his hands busy removing her robe.

She kicked the door closed. They moved together and collapsed on the couch. She fumbled with his belt and removed his clothes. His hands traced her face, neck, and breasts, as if he had to relearn her shape to make her his again. He belonged there, with her, inside her. No protests came from her. Totally absorbed by the excitement and pleasure his body gave her, she felt pride knowing that his intense reaction came from her, and her alone.

For the longest time, they held on to each other. No need to talk, only feel. The unmistakable ping of the computer pulled her from her dreams and Zayne's embrace. Her computer had answers. She picked up Zane's arm from her shoulder and placed it on the couch. He mumbled some unrecognizable sounds, turned on his side, and resumed his soft snoring. Bloom smiled, admired his well-defined back muscles, rhythmically moving with his breath. She covered him with a blanket they had been sharing.

The computer tugged her attention from the kitchen, but drying sweat chilled her naked body and she went to retrieve her robe from the entry. She walked back to the kitchen and her eyes locked on the lighted screen as she approached the kitchen table and sat. She stared at the new information leaping at her. A blue dot pointed at the origin of the hacking into the inactive donor's database. Bloom clicked on the dot to get an address.

What she saw released adrenaline into her weary body. Her heart started to pound. Her neck pulsated at every beat. She took a breath and pushed it down into her chest, but this time the pounding only accelerated. Her head felt heavy and lights started dancing in front of her eyes. She took deeper breaths, but dizziness struck. Soon the lights would go out. The cardiologist had warned her. Ventricular tachycardia doesn't allow your heart to fill properly. Your blood pressure falls. Brain and heart don't get enough oxygen and eventually shut down. The rapid heartbeat deteriorates into ventricular fibrillation.

From computer searches, she knew what a VF rhythm looked and felt like. The image flashed into her failing mind now—the rhythm of an unfortunate patient. A jagged, irregular line, like a drawing by a shaking hand. Her heart wouldn't beat or squeeze any longer. Her heart muscle would just wiggle—flaccid, without power. She was going to die.

The thought didn't frighten her as much as she had imagined it would. Lack of oxygen acted mercifully. She remembered the end of the patient's monitor. A flat line.

That was the last image in her mind.

Zayne stirred on the couch, trying to recapture his ecstasy-filled dream. Something had pulled him out of his bliss with the abruptness of thunder. The sound was real; it wasn't in his head or part of his fantasy. Something had crashed somewhere. He sat up, shook himself awake, and realized he was alone. Charlotte. Where was she?

Adrenaline jolted him like a defibrillator shock. He leaped up, fully naked, and looked across the living room into the kitchen. He froze. His heart paused. His sweaty hands grabbed the phone from the night table and dialed 911. He kept the call on speaker while he rushed to the limp body that lay on the kitchen floor.

"Charlotte!" he shouted, as if his voice could revive her heart. He turned her around, her body heavy and lifeless. He placed his cheek against her mouth. No breath. He searched for a pulse, no matter how feeble, on the side of her neck. *Please. Please.* Nothing. Only stillness. The 911 operator came on the line and Zayne communicated the gravity of the emergency, his location, and his qualifications. His voice broke with the rhythm of his CPR compressions. With strong hands, he pressed hard on the fragile breast bone, his fingers touching the soft breasts he had kissed only hours ago. The pleasure he had experienced seemed part of another time and place.

Why hadn't he done what he knew he should have done the first time he had made love to her and noticed her arrhythmia? He was a doctor. A cardiac surgeon, of all things. Instead, he had made love to her again, placing her at risk. He had acted like the coward he was. When was the last time he had done what a patient wanted, despite knowing how detrimental that could be? Never. He had never done that in his entire career. But he had done it with her. He had gone along with Charlotte, fearful of losing her. And the result of his spineless decision lay under his hands right now. He *was* losing her. Maybe he had lost her already.

Tears streamed down his cheeks and fell onto Charlotte's lifeless body like rain drops. Would she ever be able to see rain fall again? He ground his teeth against fatigue and continued his resuscitation efforts.

What was he thinking? After days and days of hesitation, he had come to her apartment with the idea of seeing her and convincing her to immediately seek the treatment she needed for whatever heart condition she suffered from. He should have had his priorities straight. Or perhaps he did. Since the day she had first come to his office with Miner, his priority had always been this woman. Her intensity. The intelligence in her eyes. Her love for her work. Just like his own love for surgery.

Something about her made him unable to wait for months to hold her and love her again. He had placed *his* wants before *her* needs. And now he would *never* have her again. The ambulance's siren, getting louder and louder, whined in the distance. He let a deep breath go. Help was on the way. *Please, hurry.*

The whine stopped. The sound of scurrying, heavy steps came from outside the front door, announcing the medics' arrival. Zayne looked from his life-sustaining hands to the door locks. He gave Charlotte a few powerful CPR crunches and rushed to open the door. His naked body reclaimed his attention and he cursed himself for caring about something so irrelevant at the moment. He unlocked the door, and quickly went back to kneel at Bloom's side, returning to his CPR.

A young man and a younger woman in black uniforms bearing their names rushed in carrying a stretcher and medical equipment. Suppressing the impulse to shield his naked body from the eyes of strangers, he identified himself, grabbed the defibrillator patches, and stuck them to Bloom's chest. His stomach sank with sickness as he stared at the wiggly line of ventricular fibrillation appearing on the monitor, despite the fact that he had expected, no—more than that—he had hoped for it. A wiggly line, under the circumstances, is easier to convert to a good rhythm than a flat one. Medics were busy administering oxygen with a mask connected to a pump and trying to get intravenous access, piercing Charlotte's neck. For the first time, Zayne noticed his hickeys there. Heat rose to his cheeks.

"Everybody off!" he shouted, as he pushed the red shock button.

Bloom's body jolted up, her muscle contracting as if there was life in her. But then she went flaccid again. Zayne shocked her a second time. For a moment, The wiggly line became a giant wave, registering the defibrillator's shock. Zayne held his breath. But the deadly wiggling was back.

"Epinephrine!" he ordered.

From the hand of the woman medic, he took the syringe with the long needle. He felt for a space at the left side of the sternum, between two ribs. For a moment, he suppressed all feelings and thoughts about how important this woman was to him, to allow for Zayne Wilder, MD to take over. He plunged the needle into Bloom's chest, deep into her sick heart, and delivered the drug. He shocked her again. The wiggly line went away. In its place, Zayne saw the beautiful tracing of a normal rhythm. Tears blurred his vision.

"I got a pulse," the male medic said.

But the battle wasn't over. Bloom's chest wasn't moving. No discernible breathing. Zayne wiped his eyes and grabbed an endotracheal tube and a laryngoscope from the medic's box. He gently inserted the dull blade between Bloom's teeth and lifted up her tongue. The V of the vocal cords saluted him. The tube went in. He inflated the balloon to keep it in place and connected the tube to the oxygen tank. He sighed and wiped sweat from his forehead and upper lip. His hands still shaking, he reached for a stethoscope from the neck of the female medic and pulled it off her without asking. He inserted the tips into his ears and placed the bell on Bloom's chest.

The sounds of breathing reached him from both sides, reassured that the tube was in good position and both lungs were ventilated. He recalled Bloom's objections to his examining her. He was the only doctor available. The one in charge of saving her life. He moved the stethoscope's diaphragm to the left of the sternum, under her left breast, and listened to her heart. He heard normal heart sounds. S1 and S2.

But there was more—something he had read about in the medical textbooks, but only encountered in patients on a couple of occasions. More than a few times, he had made sure that every intern, resident, and medical student went to the unfortunate patient and listened. *No. Not here. Not now. Not Charlotte.*

"Ready to move her to the stretcher, Doc," the male medic said. The narrow ambulance gurney, lowered to the floor, sat next to him, covered with blankets and straps ready to embrace Bloom's body.

"Go." Zayne stood, picking up a blanket and wrapping it around his waist. He watched the medics enveloping the precious cargo. "I'll grab my clothes."

He dressed in the bedroom while the medics carried Bloom outside to the waiting ambulance. Carrying his backpack, he rushed to the front door, passing through the kitchen. His eyes glanced at the open computer on the table. Something had triggered Bloom's arrhythmia. He grabbed Blook's computer and stuffed it into his backpack. As he locked the door behind him and ran downstairs, the adrenaline of anger rose inside him. He hoped that in the near future he could yell at Charlotte for having kept such secret from him. A secret she might still pay for with her life.

CHAPTER 24
HEART CONDITION

A rhythmic beeping reached Bloom from a dark, faraway emptiness. Raw pain was her first sensation. Her throat and lungs burned like fire. The image of a flatlining heart came back to her mind and sent a chill through her body. She needed air. A hissing sound accompanied the expansion of her lungs and lit up her chest with a sharp pain. She was alive.

She opened her eyes to a stark hospital room. Her gaze moved closer to her body. A hose began in her mouth and disappeared into a machine. A respirator. She was intubated in some intensive care unit. An overwhelming sensation of choking came over her. She desperately wanted to cough. The beeping accelerated as she tried to suck in air. The hissing stopped and an alarm screeched from the machine. A door swooshed open and a female nurse rushed in.

"Charlotte," she said. "Relax. Let the machine breathe for you. Soon we may be able to pull the tube out from your throat. If you fight it, we may have to sedate you again, and it will take longer."

Bloom looked at the young woman in scrubs. What did she know about what it felt like to have a plastic tube jammed down her throat? What about Zayne? Where was Zayne? Bloom moved her hand to the breathing tube and made a gesture as if she wanted to pull it out. The nurse's eyes dilated.

"No," the nurse said, her voice firm. "Don't pull. The inflated cuff will damage your trachea. I don't want to restrain you. Let me call Dr. Wilder and see if we can give you a trial off the respirator."

Bloom nodded several times. She tried to relax her tense muscles. With every breath the respirator pumped into her lungs, her chest registered sharp jabs of pain from both sides. She closed her eyes. What she saw, as a flash in her mind, was her laptop's screen displaying the name and address of the hacker. Her eyes jerked open. She had to talk to Kirk. Now. She pushed herself off the bed, but went only a few inches before the alarm sounded again. The nurse gave her a menacing stare. Bloom mimicked holding a phone to her ear.

How long had she been asleep? Perhaps it was already too late. She had to warn Kirk. Somebody had to listen to her. For that, her tube had to go.

"Dr. Wilder is on his way," the nurse said. "Relax."

Time moved in slow motion. Bloom closed her eyes and tried to calm her mind. It was no use. Images of Kirk Miner's head blown out by a bullet wouldn't leave her. This time Aurora's hand wouldn't be there to save him. The nurse stood watching every move she made. No way to escape, call, warn.

At last, the door parted again and Zayne entered. A smile lit his face. His hand wrapped around hers. She squeezed his hand with all her strength.

"Charlotte," he said, kissing her hand, despite the nurse's puzzled look. "You're awake."

Zayne instructed the nurse to disconnect the respirator. The hose disappeared, but the tube was still jammed into her throat. Bloom had to talk to him. She had to call Mulville. Or Kirk would die. She withdrew her hand from his and again gestured about removing the endotracheal tube.

"Yes," Zayne said. "In a few minutes, we'll get rid of it. You suffered some heart damage during the CPR. You had fluids in your lungs, but we got rid of it with diuretics. You should be able to breathe on your own now. We'll see if you can do without the respirator in the next half hour or so."

Heart damage? Fluid in the lungs? Her heart was failing. All this treatment required time. Lots of time. Too long. Half an hour? She didn't have half an hour. She grabbed Zayne's top scrub and pulled him toward her. He smiled. What was he thinking? She shook her head, pointing at her mouth. He made a calming sign, both palms down, stood up, and dismissed the nurse, who finally stopped staring and left. Alone with Bloom, Zayne extracted his stethoscope and went through the motions of examining her heart. No. She couldn't allow him. Not her heart. She pushed his hands away and shook her head.

"Charlotte," he whispered, stethoscope stuck in his ears and bell held up in his hand. "You don't want me to examine you? What are you afraid of?"

She watched him wide-eyed. He asked questions she couldn't answer. She had no time for explanations and no way to talk with the damn tube in her throat. Right now, the thing she was most afraid of was Kirk taking a bullet to his head.

"That I could hear something wrong? Find out why you have deadly arrhythmias?" Zayne went on without mercy. She had no time to even hate him for it. "Too late. I already heard it. Yesterday, when we brought you back, after you almost died. You have an extra heart sound. It's called the tumor plop. You have a heart tumor."

She had almost died. Yesterday. It was only one day ago. She might still have time to save Kirk. Everything else was lost for her.

"I took an ultrasound of your heart." Zayne turned to a computer screen at her bedside, ant swiveled it around, so she could see it. Zayne touched several keys and several images appeared on the screen. "If you were a regular patient, I would wait until you're extubated to talk to you. But, since it's you, and I know how you feel about this, I figure the only way you're going to hear me is if you can't talk. Look at your heart, Charlotte."

Son of a bitch. She looked.

"Here it is." The surgeon's long index finger traced a mass the size of a walnut, connected to the inside heart's wall by a stalk. The blob danced up and down and seemed ready to detach. "It's attached to the septum, the part that divides the left and right side of the heart. It causes short-circuits in the conduction system, which are the heart cells in charge of transmitting the electrical impulse that makes the heart contract. That's why you get arrhythmias. Mostly extra beats and ventricular tachycardia. If it lasts too long, it deteriorates into ventricular fibrillation, a fatal arrhythmia. Like yesterday. I had to do CPR on you. We shocked you several times to keep you alive."

In his beautiful tear-filled eyes, she saw the agony he must have endured as well as how much he cared. She nodded. She had almost died. He had saved her life.

"Also, the tumor is right at the level of the mitral valve. It moves up and down." Zayne's fingers mimicked the mass's to-and-fro motion. "This motion is what causes the tumor plop, an extra sound, when the tumor slaps against the valve. If it gets stuck right in the middle of the valve, it blocks the entire circulation, and it may bring the heart to a sudden stop. That's how people die. The ones who don't get treatment on time."

Her eyes stared at the contracting heart pushing and pulling the tumor up and down. The tumor seemed larger than it had been just six or seven weeks ago, when the doctor at the Cleveland Clinic had shown it to her. Sweat poured out of her pores. The beat of Bloom's heart accelerated.

Zayne's mouth tightened. His fingers again touched the screen. Muffled heart sounds filled the room. Her heartbeat. The three rhythmic noises sounded like a galloping horse. The third muffled beat occurred when the mass struggled through the valve opening, paused for an interminable moment, and then snapped into the other side, pulling on the stalk as if desperately trying to free itself. Sweat drenched her body. Her heart rate accelerated as loathing for Dr. Wilder's ruthlessness clashed with her longing for Zayne's love.

"At first," he said, pointing at the screen again, "I thought it would be easy to surgically remove it, since usually a tumor plop is caused by a myxoma, a benign and resectable tumor."

Benign? What was benign about a tumor that caused life-threatening arrhythmias, threatened to obstruct the mitral valve at any time, and could kill you on the spot, which was probably what had happened once already? But Bloom didn't have the luxury of dwelling on this now.

"Unfortunately, yours is a very unusual tumor," Zayne said. "The base has infiltrated a large part of the heart muscle. Given the location and the size, the tumor cannot be removed without killing you. And, if we don't remove it fully, it may come back. So, we need to find you a donor quickly. Hopefully, it's an unusual fibroma, but we're not going to know for sure if it's cancer until and unless we remove your heart and send it to Pathology. I'd rather line you up with a donor while you're still alive."

Heat rose from her chest. She wished she could slap his face, but her hands, tethered to intravenous lines, couldn't reach him. He looked at her as if he was expecting an answer. Or perhaps he was studying her reaction to his words. Little did he know that, whether she wanted it or not, she might soon have a donor.

"But you already knew all that, didn't you?" Zayne said.

The last sentence threw her over the edge. She sat up and tried to pry the tube out of her mouth. The heart-beeping went into a frenzy. Zayne grabbed her wrists and forced her against the mattress.

"Calm down," he said. "I don't want anything else to happen. I'll remove the tube now."

She nodded. Zayne called the respiratory therapist. He used a small syringe to deflate the cuff and instructed Bloom to take a deep breath and exhale. He pulled the tube out. She coughed. Her ribs felt as if they were breaking anew. She opened her mouth to talk, but only a rasping sound came out, like the grating of sand paper.

"Easy." Zayne sat on her bed. Across the thin cover, the warmth of his body came through. "We can talk about all this again, after you rest."

"No!" She shook her head, pleased that she could hear her own voice. "I need to talk to Mulville. Now."

"Mulville already knows you're here," Zayne said. He rose to go. "I told him you fainted. I didn't mention the v-fib arrest part. I'll leave it to you to explain what you want. Luckily, I can stay out of this. Doctor-patient privilege."

"Wait!" She grabbed his hand. "Kirk's walking into a trap. I need to warn him. I need to send Mulville. I need my phone."

Zayne sat down again. She had his attention now.

"What's going on?" He took her hand between both his and looked her in the eye. "What did you discover that sent you into cardiac arrest?"

"Long story." She spoke fast, explaining about Kirk Miner and the inactive donor database.

"I was able to find out who did it. Who hacked into the inactive donor list. I got my answer just before I passed out."

"That's great," Zayne said. "Who was he? Montepulciano?"

"No," she said. "Not him."

"Who else?"

"Carl Baker."

"Baker?"

"The guy with the wife who died during transplant. He's the one who upgraded Miner to active donor. And Kirk is planning to go to Hartford to meet him. Sometime today. He has a meeting with the person who tried to kill him."

CHAPTER 25
CARL BAKER

Earlier that morning, as Bloom continued to lie unconscious and intubated in the ICU, Santo Montepulciano walked briskly from the parking lot to his Manhattan office, his cell phone sandwiched between ear and hand. He grinned as his lawyer's reassuring words calmed his mind. The glass front door parted in front of him, welcoming his return, and he strode across the lobby toward the elevators. He was free to go back to his urgent business. And urgent it was. Charlotte was in the hospital. Her illness was much more serious than the silly girl had wanted people to believe. Was she worth risking his life and freedom? The poor girl's heart had stopped, or so his informer told him, after seeing the paramedics transporting her out of her apartment. At this point, he felt he had to see this through to the end. He just hoped it wouldn't be her end, nor, most of all, his own.

As he went to put his phone back in his pocket, buzzing and vibrations announced a new incoming call. Montepulciano frowned as he noticed the unknown caller.

"Yes." As used as he was to throw-away devices, he never volunteered his identity. "Speak."

"Baker." Carl Baker's voice came through loud and clear. "This is secure. We need to talk."

Montepulciano stopped walking. His mouth tensed as he turned around, walked back into the lobby, and slumped onto a well-padded couch. His eyes surveilled the area. Nobody within earshot. Perfect for the conversation he anticipated.

"Listen, Santo," Baker said. The sound of his name more or less announced the plea Montepulciano was expecting. "We've known each other for at least ten years. I've always considered you my friend."

Montepulciano rolled his eyes toward the ceiling and stared at the brass and glass light fixtures. At his best, Baker had been helpful with his hacking, but his usefulness had run out a while ago. There was only one way he could still deliver anything of value. As a heart donor.

"We worked together," Baker said, his voice betraying a slight crack, "on the hospital hacking and then—"

"Are you insane?" the mobster interrupted him. "Shut the fuck up."

"Relax. It's secure. If you want to talk in person, I can come in. I'm in town. Right outside your building."

"Then come the fuck in."

Montepulciano turned toward the front door and spotted Baker's chubby outline against the light streaming in from the front entrance. Suits didn't fit Baker's body well. The hanging abdomen spread the jacket open and made the good quality garment look shrunken or undersized. Baker walked with slouched shoulders. The balding head, camouflaged by a hair flap, bowed toward the floor, as if he was doing penitence. Penitence he deserved. He shuffled toward the couch and sat on a matching chair across from Montepulciano, but not before lowering his head even more in respectful salute. Montepulciano didn't budge.

"I wanted to touch base," he whispered, retrieving his pocket handkerchief and wiping his forehead, "so we're on the same page."

Montepulciano stared at him. Baker looked pathetic. Whatever little respect Montepulciano had for the man was long since gone.

"When my wife got ill," Baker said, "I greatly appreciated you helping with the transplant list. You told us to go ahead and sign up for the chain, and we did. When we realized the wait was going to be too long for my poor wife, you provided a way to facilitate procuring a heart for her. But I always understood we would find a way…a way to… spare me."

"You understood incorrectly." The mobster took pride in his judgmental tone. "We made a contract. For your wife to get a heart, there was a condition. Your heart. It had to be available for the next patient."

"But my wife is dead," Baker said, intertwining his fingers as if in prayer. "I have no obligations. And I have a daughter. What's going to happen to *her* if I die. You can't possibly expect me to commit suicide and turn my daughter into an orphan."

"Sorry. Not my fault that your wife died." Montepulciano shifted to a more comfortable position. "I fulfilled my responsibility. The condition remains. You're wasting my time."

"I tried." Baker made eye contact for only a brief moment before going back to studying the carpet. "Even if I thought I didn't have any obligation, I got you a good match for the patient I'm supposed to be a donor for. Not my fault the stupid lawyers wasted her heart. Amy Winter died, just like my wife. I fulfilled my responsibility."

"You did not." The mobster let his words sink in for a moment. The pinging of elevators filled the silence. "It's still your responsibility to fulfill your obligation. I don't care how you do it. It's your problem. You have to provide me with a heart, or else…"

"But what's the hurry?" Baker replied. "Margarita Herrera got an artificial pump. She can live for a while with it. You wanted her to refuse the heart. Why?"

This is why morons didn't live long. Natural selection. Especially in the mob's world.

"I'm going to make believe I didn't hear this." Montepulciano shook his head slowly. "You really don't get the business model, do you? I have a reputation to protect. Who's going to sign up for the freaking chain in the future if I don't enforce the rules?"

"With all due respect," Baker said, lifting his head, "your attitude seems to have changed. You've never been so adamant about any patient. I know there is something else going on. The heart you need isn't for Herrera. It's for that special patient with no name or number. The one you had me add from the Cleveland Clinic. That's why you had me lean on Herrera to refuse the heart. I've been working on another donor who's only a match for her and not for Herrera. Why is she so important to you?"

"None of your business." The air around Montepulciano felt warm and stuffy. "Your business is to provide a good match. You're perfect for it."

"Listen," Baker said, "who's this patient? I'm asking you. I could find out if I hack into the Cleveland Clinic database and search her background."

"Try it." Montepulciano's chest burned with the fire of anger. But he had to give this loser a hook of hope to keep him from snooping around in forbidden territory. "You'll be dead before you can get into the database. I haven't killed you because I'd like to continue our collaboration. But if you don't find a substitute by end of tomorrow, I got no choice."

"At least, confirm this much," Baker said. "A donor who's a perfect match for your special patient, but not for Herrera. Would he do?"

Montepulciano nodded.

"Great." Baker pushed himself up from the padded chair. "I might solve the problem sooner than you think."

Zayne sat on Bloom's hospital bed looking puzzled. "Your phone isn't here," he said, handing her his.

Bloom's hands shook as she dialed the director.

"Mulville," the gruff voice said. "How's she doing, Doctor? I'm on my way."

Bloom looked at the phone and remembered she was holding Zayne's device. She could feel Mulville's distress … about her.

"It's Bloom. I'm fine," she said. "Don't come here. Kirk Miner is in danger. He needs backup."

"Bloom! Are you okay?"

"Yes," she said. "Please, listen. Kirk needs you. Now."

"Where the fuck is he going all by himself?"

"To see Carl Baker."

"What the heck?" she imagined the typical saliva spray out of Mulville's mouth, grateful that the conversation wasn't in person. "What about *I don't give a flying fuck* does Miner not understand? If Baker wants to drop dead, let him."

"At the last meeting," she said, "Kirk told us he wanted to talk to Baker to see if he was involved. He is. Baker is the one who hacked into the inactive transplant database and picked Kirk as an organ donor for Montepulciano's daughter. And now Kirk doesn't even suspect he's walking into a trap. And I can't get in touch with him. His phone goes to voice mail. He may be in trouble already."

She waited. Bloom had no idea what to expect from Mulville. Praise or curse seemed equally possible. She rested her forehead on her hand. Her forehead felt wet and cold.

"Son of a bitch," Mulville said. Bloom waited to find out who was the target of the curse. "Baker is looking for a substitute donor to take his place. Anything new about who the bastard daughter is? Montepulciano's paternity document was a joke. Why did he even send it if it was inconclusive? Have you made any progress on the ex-girlfriend side?"

The new insult hit her by surprise, like a slap in the face. What would Mulville think when he found out that his favorite recruit was the bastard he was looking for? And what about Zayne? How would he feel about dating Montepulciano's daughter? The mere thought made her stomach pour out acid.

"Not yet," she said. "I've been too busy passing out, remember?"

Bloom wanted to take back the last words as soon as they flew out of her mouth. Mulville didn't deserve that kind of sarcasm. Besides, she should try to eliminate the event from Mulville's mind, not remind him of it. She hoped he would let go of this line of questioning.

"Where is Kirk Miner now?" Mulville said. Bloom sighed in relief at the change of subject.

"If he's meeting Baker, he should be at Baker's home, or office," she said, her voice trailing down, reluctant to utter an uncomfortable truth. "Hartford, Connecticut."

"Hartford?" Mulville's agitation came through the speakerphone. "Great. When we find out where he is, one backup coming up. Freaking idiot. We have to mobilize the local police."

Bloom inhaled deeply. The cool oxygen hissed from the plastic tubing and penetrated her nostrils, energizing her recovering brain. What if the meeting wasn't in Connecticut?

"Wait!" she shouted as she looked around for her belongings. "I got no answer from Kirk, but let me see if I can locate his phone."

She looked at Zayne. "Did you by any chance take my computer with you?" she asked.

The grin on Zayne's face was the best news Bloom got after waking up alive. "Quick, get it. Now."

Zayne left the room and came back in less than a minute. He handed over her computer with the gesture of a waiter presenting her with dinner. Bloom's excitement and reassurance dimmed as she remembered her recent loss of consciousness. She had crashed to the floor. Had her computer gone down with her? Kirk's life was on the line.

Her hands trembled as she touched a key, leaving behind a film of wetness. The computer came back to life. She sighed. Adrenaline flooded her blood and whipped her body and mind to work. After entering the necessary passwords, a blue dot appeared on the screen. Her jaw fell, leaving her mouth open with a O of surprise. She turned to Zayne's phone, still on the call to Mulville.

"Director," she said "Kirk isn't in Connecticut. He's right here."

"Right where, Bloom?" he said in his usual condescending voice. "I need to know yesterday."

"He's inside the Fitzgerald Hotel," she said. "A half a block from NYMC."

"Shit!" Mulville said. Bloom understood and knew what was coming. "He's got Kirk all ready to go. Right in front of the hospital. Montepulciano's daughter could be close by as well."

"Not necessarily," Bloom said. She tried to swallow, but her mouth felt dry. "With that heart box, they can ship the heart across the country."

"Nah," Mulville said. "There's a reason why Baker is meeting Miner in New York, near the NYMC."

The phone went dead. Mulville's last words played in Bloom's mind. She looked up, her eyes locked onto Zayne's. The gray irises pointed directly at her. She watched the last piece of a puzzle fall into place inside Zayne's mind. She pulled her covers up to her neck, but there was nowhere to hide from the truth.

From the side window, Kirk Miner looked at the blue patch of sky and cursed. He sat on an uncomfortable hard-back chair in a room on the 9th floor of the Fitzgerald Hotel in Manhattan. In front of him, Carl Baker occupied the only cushioned chair.

"How can I help you today, Mr. Miner?" Baker smiled. He wore a dark blue business suit, a white shirt, and a red tie. If he only had a small American flag lapel pin, he'd have looked like your usual politician. His flashing teeth were already right for the role. "You said you had new information for me."

"I do," Kirk said. "Thanks for offering to meet in the city. Less travelling for me."

"No prob." Baker made an accommodating gesture. "I have other business here today."

What about that? Kirk had wondered about meeting in the city. He thought it plausible for a money-launderer to conduct business in New York City.

But this time Baker had seemed more agreeable to meet him. Perhaps too agreeable. A big change since his first conversation at the guy's office. That alone had raised flags in Kirk's mind. The hotel room was guarded by a muscular and armed goon. The rough hands had frisked every inch of Kirk's body and retrieved his gun and cell phone. That was when Kirk started to realize what was going on.

Baker was supposed to be a victim. One of the many victims of

Montepulciano's scheme. It was Baker's turn to graciously commit suicide, so that the next patient in line would get his heart. But Baker had refused protection, and now his attitude had changed. Kirk had looked at this the wrong way. Baker's wife had died. Now Montepulciano wanted Baker to die, to keep his part of the bargain. Kirk reviewed Baker's criminal record. He didn't seem like a submissive and obedient pawn. Not even to a powerful mobster.

"We've reason to believe," Kirk said, "that you may be at much higher risk than previously suspected."

Baker leaned forward, his forehead gathered in a multitude of wrinkles, his abundant abdomen protruding between open legs. Kirk's words had fueled his attention. So far, so good.

"And why is that?" Baker asked. "I already told you about my wife. And after we spoke the first time, I took myself off the list of donors. Case closed."

But Baker didn't act as if he really believed his case was closed. He shifted in his chair and his hand went through the flap of hair covering the bald spot on the top of his head. He took a sip from a glass of water. Even before his wife's death, Baker must have had a Plan B to save his own skin. Somewhere along the way, Baker had shed his victim status like an old snake's skin. Now his transformation was complete. Baker was the killer desperately looking for someone to take his place as an organ donor.

Under the light hospital bed cover, Bloom's body shivered in cold sweat. Her laptop pressed down on her legs.

"It's you, isn't it?" Zayne said, his eyes wider, his mouth showing the strain of controlling his emotions. "You're Montepulciano's daughter."

Inside her chest, Bloom felt her future breaking into pieces. Zayne stared at her now, his mouth open in a round shape of disbelief and rebellion. How could she blame him?

"No," he said after hearing no protest or denial from her. "Not you, of all people."

She closed her eyes, afraid of seeing him recoil. But his tone had sounded gentle, soothing. She felt his hand on her clammy forehead, stroking her hair. She reopened her eyes to see Zayne sitting on her bed. He removed her laptop and came closer. His arms embraced her and she felt his strength as he pulled her close.

"I'm so sorry," he whispered. "I'm here for you."

She nodded against his neck. She inhaled a fresh scent of soap mixed with his unique personal fragrance. The pleasure of their lovemaking flashed in her mind. But the adrenaline forced her to change focus. She would worry about her problems later. Her mission was to save Kirk.

She pulled back from Zayne's arms, threw her covers off, and stood up, her flimsy hospital gown fluttering around her naked thighs. A pinch in her left wrist and a pulling around her neck reminded her that she was still tethered to intravenous catheters, monitor leads, and the oxygen tubes. Fighting a wave of dizziness, she steadied herself against the bed. Her right hand came up and removed the oxygen tubing from her face and dropped it to the floor. Then she went to lift the tape holding her intravenous line in place and clenched the catheter. With a firm pull, she extracted the bloody plastic twig from her body and discarded it as well. The sharp pain she experienced shocked and unsteadied her. The rapid beeping from the monitor reminded her of the leads and electrodes stuck to her chest.

"What are you doing?" Zayne's voice seemed oddly distant, as if coming from a different dimension. "Stop! You're in no condition…"

"Please," she said, her voice as steady and powerful as she could muster. "Don't try to hold me back. I'm the only one who can stop these lunatics."

"You?" To bring her to her senses, Zayne grabbed her arm and shook her. "You should be on your way to the OR to get a heart. If you're not, you'll soon be unable to fix anything. And why you? Why are you the one to save the day?"

Bloom looked at his hand around her arm. It would be so easy to grab it and twist it into a wrist lock. But it belonged to Zayne. Bloom wanted to kiss that hand. Heat rose from her electrodes-studded chest. The beeping of her heart accelerated.

"I am Santo Montepulciano's daughter, for God's sake." She pressed her thumb to the site of her line, now oozing blood. For the first time in her life, she had used something she had always despised, the *Do you know who I am?* tactic. She had never utilized her FBI authority in such fashion. But now she had exploited her most despised credentials, to silence and neutralize Zayne, of all people. "Let go of my arm. I don't want to hurt you."

Zayne stared at her, mouth agape. His finger's pressure lightened. The heart monitor seemed to protest with several ominous extra beats from her tired, overworked ventricle. She silenced it by pulling the wires off her chest. The wiggly line went flat. She had to act quickly, before Zayne recovered from the shock. She pulled away from Zayne's hand and dashed out of the room.

Her eyes roamed around until they found what she was looking for. She ducked past the nurse's station and disappeared into the women's locker room. She rushed past the wall of lockers and the bathroom and stopped in front of the line of shelves holding piles of different colored scrubs. The small blue scrubs fitted her perfectly. She pulled the orange strings around her waist, combed her hair with her hands, checked her wrist for any residual bleeding, and, finding none, exited through the back door into a corridor leading directly to the elevators.

As soon as she exited the hospital, she located the Fitzgerald Hotel on the right, across the street, and at the end of the block. On the sidewalk, she started to run, squinting against the excessive midday sun light, ignoring the noon traffic's cacophony, bumping into the business- attired lunchtime crowd. She stopped across the street, in front of the hotel. Her right hand went to her side, feeling for her badge and weapon, rubbing instead against the smoothness of an empty cotton garment. What was she thinking? Her cardiac arrest must have fried a good part of her brain. *I'll have to do this with my bare hands. That's what karate training was for. Karate. Empty hands.* She sighed, jumping off the curb.

A screech jolted her. An ambulance came straight at her. Bloom stepped back onto the curb, but she collided with something as concrete as a wall. A vice-like squeeze clamped down onto her shoulder. The ambulance swooshed by her with a deafening clanking sound. She looked up and stared into the upside-down blue slits she knew so well.

"What the fuck?" Mulville said. "What do you think you're doing? Weren't you busy in the hospital, passing out?"

Mulville steadied her onto her feet. She turned and saw a four-person SWAT team following him. Everyone stopped behind the powerful barrier put up by Mulville's extended arms. The director had come out himself to rescue Kirk.

"I'm all done fainting," Bloom said. "Kirk needs us. Now. And I need a gun."

"You are in no condition to come back to work," Mulville said. He pointed in the direction of the hospital. "That's where you belong."

"The doctor released me," she said. "This is my mission. I called this back-up, didn't I?"

She saw no sarcasm in his narrowed eyes. Only hinted at was a new kind of pride, as he bent down and lifted his sweat pants' left leg to reveal a concealed holster. Mulville pulled out a Glock 17 and handed it to her.

"Follow me," he ordered, pushing Bloom behind him, to the end of the line-up.

But nothing could quash her excitement. Director Mulville needed her at his side. He trusted her to perform the job she had so painstakingly trained for. She wasn't his favorite trainee any more. She was Charlotte Bloom, FBI special agent. She trotted across the street to Kirk Miner's rescue.

Deprived of his tools for survival—his gun and cell phone—Kirk sat in the mediocre hotel room with cheerful curtains, matching blanket, and the smell of smoke-camouflaging air freshener. He took a deep breath, but the air flooding his lungs felt stuffy and unsatisfying. This meeting was a mistake. Perhaps the worst mistake of his career. A weight expanded into his chest as the images of Aurora and Peter came to him.

"We believe Montepulciano is manipulating the donor-patient chain," Kirk said. "He's manipulating the process by forcing donors to commit suicide."

"Damn it," Baker said, sitting back in his chair again. He exhaled through pursed lips. "Tell me something new. You sound like a broken record."

"Let me finish," Kirk said. "Something has changed, and it's made the search for a heart especially urgent for Montepulciano. Personal."

"*Personal?*" Baker leaned over again. His hand shook as he gulped down the rest of his water. "How so?"

A knock at the door startled Kirk. As he answered, Baker looked annoyed. The bodyguard's plump face squeezed through the cracked door.

"A call came through his phone," he barked. "No name, but a local number."

"You didn't shut off the fucking phone?!" Baker shouted at the man, then turned to Kirk. "If you came with baggage, we're done here."

Kirk straightened his spine against the hard chair. Either Bloom or Mulville was looking for him. He would have recognized the number. But he had Baker where he wanted him, and would have dreaded the call, afraid it would undermine his mission. Now, circumstances had changed and the tables had turned. Baker had Kirk where he wanted him. The phone call rekindled Kirk's hope like a life-saver thrown to a drowning man. The phone had been on. Had Bloom located his position?

"No," Kirk said. "No back-up. Of course not. I came alone to warn you…

to offer you protection. Believe me, you're gonna need it."

Baker's hand gave the goon a wave of dismissal. At the click of the closing door, Kirk released a short, noiseless breath. He hoped the pounding of his heart remained undetected.

"Why in hell would I need protection now?" Baker said. "The patient who needed the heart refused it. Last I heard, she was getting one of those artificial pumps."

"She's not the one Montepulciano is worried about," Kirk said, purposefully dragging out the revelation to gain time. "He's looking for a heart for a different patient."

"That much I figured out," Baker said. "I know all about the secret patient he wants the heart for."

"Do you know she's a close relative of Montepulciano?"

"What kind of close relative?" Baker said.

A pearly drop shone on Baker's forehead. This wasn't an act. Baker didn't know.

"His daughter," Kirk said, going for the kill. "Santo Montepulciano is looking for a heart for his own daughter. He'll never stop until she gets a transplant. You're a perfect match. And you're up, because he made sure your wife got a heart. He doesn't give a damn if your wife died."

He watched Baker. His wide watery eyes reminded Kirk of two eggs cooked over easy. An unhealthy gray pallor washed over his face.

"His daughter?" Baker's eyes dilated. Then suspicion chased away Baker's surprise. "What daughter? Santo hasn't got any fucking children."

"None that *you* know of." Kirk needed to convince him of the truth. Baker needed to understand that he and Kirk were both Montepulciano's targets. He had to get him to cooperate. The PI's own life was at stake. He summoned all his powers of persuasion. "The secret patient next on the transplant list, after Margarita Herrera. That's his daughter. Your match."

"And you know this how?"

"Montepulciano told one of the FBI agents working the case."

Baker smiled. Not a good sign. Kirk wanted him scared, not amused. He shifted his weight on the hard chair.

"You want me to believe," Baker said, "that Montepulciano went and talked to the Feds? About his freaking daughter?"

"Yes." Kirk said, "He threatened us. Told us to back off and let the chain procure the heart. Then, for good measure, he tried to kill me."

"Why aren't you running around to arrest him?" Baker said, "instead of talking to me?"

Now came the question: What was Baker guilty of? How much did he have to lose if he cooperated in taking Montepulciano down? Kirk swallowed, but the tightness in his throat didn't lessen.

"As I said, I'm here to warn you. But you need to come clean. Only way we can protect you. You've got to help us take down Montepulciano."

"His own daughter," Baker said, eyes staring at the floor, talking to himself, as if understanding something for the first time. "He needs it for his own daughter."

Was Baker working for Montepulciano, or had he split up with him and was operating solo? Was he responsible for Amy Winter's death? And what about Aurora's shooting? Who had pulled the trigger? The more Kirk thought about all this, the more it seemed Baker might be in too deep to make a deal.

"What do you know about this, Carl?" Kirk asked. "We can help you only if you help us. We're not interested in your petty money-laundering. We're interested in putting away a murderer. Who killed the young woman in front of NYMC? Who took the shot that almost killed my wife? Talk. This is private. Just you and me."

If Baker himself was responsible for Amy Winter's murder and the attempt against Kirk's life, why would he cooperate? The question resonated in Kirk's mind and made his stomach churn. Would Baker try to kill Kirk again? The appointment at a hotel right in front of the hospital took on a different light now. If Baker killed him then and there, Kirk's heart could be promptly harvested. More pearls of sweat appeared on Baker's spacious forehead. Kirk hoped he would faint. That would greatly simplify Kirk's situation.

"What's the matter?" Kirk said. "Are you all right?"

Kirk got up and went to the sink. He found two glasses next to the faucet and filled one with water for himself. The cool liquid soothed his throat. On an impulse, he filled the second glass for Baker. When he handed the glass to Baker, the man looked better already. His color had come back. He looked like someone who had come to a decision. Kirk sat down.

"Thanks for explaining all this to me," Baker said, his voice steady and calm. "Things make a lot more sense now. It really helped point me to the best solution."

His hand came up, as if to grab the water from Kirk. But the hand didn't open. It was gripping a gun aimed right at Kirk's face.

With Mulville and the SWAT team, Bloom rode the elevator to the 9th floor. The front desk had been very cooperative. The maid had noticed a man outside the door. Only one man to deal with before entering Baker's room. A plan took shape in Bloom's mind as floor numbers rolled past. Now was the moment to show what she had. If only her heart could behave for a little while longer.

"I'll take out the bodyguard," Bloom said, pointing at the blue scrubs she was wearing. "I can tell him someone called the front desk asking for a nurse. Then I'll tase him down."

Mulville turned to her. She watched him run through the alternatives. Bloom knew there were none.

"Kirk may be in danger already. We have to do this quietly," she said. "It's the best way."

Her scrubs fit the part perfectly. Mulville nodded. He addressed one of the men.

"Take off your vest, will you?" he said. Mulville's finger made a circle in the air. "You guys turn around. Bloom, put that Kevlar on, under the scrubs. Now."

She nodded. That was his way of accepting her proposal, of telling her she was mostly right. Bloom grabbed the bullet-proof vest from the male SWAT, turned her back to the five men, and strapped it onto her still painful rib cage. The crackling of the Velcro filled the silence and underlined her resolve.

The elevator door opened to a deserted corridor. Mulville handed her a taser. She placed it in her pants pocket, her gun hiding on the other side.

They exited in line, first Mulville, then Bloom, then the four men. A finger went to the director's mouth signaling silence. They walked sideways, flattened against the cold wall, the noise of their steps muffled by the cheap carpet. At the corner, Mulville put his hand out and pointed two fingers at his eyes to the corridor after the turn. One of the men produced a fiberscope, a thin instrument similar to the ones used by doctors to check the inside of hollow organs. Mulville placed his eye to it and bent the tip to turn the corner.

He faced Bloom and held up his finger to confirm the presence of one man. Then his finger curled as an invitation and pointed at the eye piece. Bloom stepped closer and looked through the scope. The man, dressed in black, a gun holster bulging at his side, was large and top-heavy with muscles. She calculated he was twice her weight.

Being the mobster's daughter wouldn't help her at all at this moment. She had to subdue him the moment she went near him. She contracted her arms' muscles to prevent them from twitching and answered Mulville's thumbs-up by repeating his gesture. Mulville took her by the shoulders. He didn't say anything. He just looked at her with his narrow blue eyes. Bloom nodded. The powerful hands pushed her along until she was first in line. It was up to her now.

Kirk looked inside the dark gun barrel and saw his own death. What would Aurora do without him? What about Peter, growing up without a father? His heart sank like a dead weight.

"Carl," he said with the calm of an expert psychologist, "what are you doing, man? I'm here to protect you."

"Thanks for making the choice easy for me," Baker said. "I don't need protection. I need to blow out your brains and get you to the hospital pronto."

"What are you talking about?" Kirk said, though he knew exactly what Baker meant. Montepulciano would stop at nothing to procure a heart for his daughter. Finding out the identity of the secret patient had convinced Baker of the futility—no, the stupidity—of antagonizing Montepulciano.

Everything made sense to Kirk as well. He shut down any thought of self-pity. He had to keep talking. He breathed. "Sure, you'll save yourself from Montepulciano, but you'll spend it in jail. I offer you the possibility of being alive and free. Free from Montepulciano. For good."

"Sorry, PI." Baker had his index finger on the trigger. "No time to debate. Got a deadline and nothing but time to lose. You and me are the best ones on the list to match his little girl. I have the gun. And I choose you."

Bloom took a deep breath and concentrated on playing her part. She shook her hair loose on her shoulder and straightened her back to push out a chest compressed by the unforgiving Kevlar. She stepped out into the corridor with the most alluring hip motion she could manage while carrying a gun and a taser in her pockets. Her arms went to the sides to show her empty hands and to cover up the bulges as much as possible. She needed to avoid frisking. Her life depended on it. Her hands felt cold from adrenaline.

The burly man's round face turned to her like a periscope. His hand went to his holster by instinct. Bloom bit down on her lip to fight the impulse to do the same. The incident in the garage flashed in her mind. No. She had to remain calm and controlled. Her heart pounded in her throat. She smiled.

The man had ruby cheeks and baggy eyes. She wondered if he drank. How could he maintain a strong body? He looked like a former bodybuilder on his way downhill due to alcohol and drugs. Hence his present employment. None of her business. She shouldn't underestimate him. She hoped he didn't have martial arts training. Given their difference in size, she wouldn't stand a chance if he did. The warning of her karate instructor resounded in her mind. The best way to win a fight is to avoid it. The second best way is to end it before it starts.

"Hey," she said approaching. "Someone from this room called the front desk for a nurse. Is someone sick?"

The guard sized her up and down. His professional alertness to potential danger melted away. In its place was an all-too-familiar demeaning gaze typical of scummy men in the presence of young and pretty women. He didn't judge her a worthy enemy. *Good job, Charlie.*

"I may be coming down with something," he said, his hand leaving his holster and going to massage his crotch. "Or perhaps, coming up. Wanna check it out, Nurse—what's your name?"

"Charlie," she said. Armed with a jolt of confidence, she stepped closer. So close that she could see hair coming out of the man's flattened nose. She speculated that he had once been a boxer and wondered how many times his nose had been broken. "Here's my card."

Her right hand moved to the taser gun. With a sweaty finger, she confirmed that the safety was off. The instructions on how to use the taser flashed in her mind. She brought it out in the open, pointing at the man's lower abdomen, in case he too was wearing a vest. Her hand turned twenty degrees to allow the maximum separation of the electrodes for the largest area of paralysis. She fired.

The tethered electrodes took off from the muzzle and stuck to the man's upper abdomen and right thigh. She wondered if the genitals were also electrically shocked. In any event, she hoped for the worse possible pain.

The man didn't have time to scream. His mouth opened, but only a strong gasp came out. He slumped to the ground with a muffled thump. She watched him on the carpeted floor, arms and legs jerking, teeth grinding, a primal guttural sound exiting his clenched mouth. His face turned as red as a beet, except for his lips, which looked purplish. Bloom wasn't sure if she was imagining it or if she smelled burnt meat.

She turned and saw Mulville and the SWAT team rushing in. Someone cuffed the incapacitated bodyguard, as Mulville shoved the tip of the fiber-scope under the door and squatted to examine the inside of the room. A grin spread on his stolid face. That was for her, Bloom had no doubt.

Mulville looked through the scope. At his gesture, the four men flattened both sides of the door and waited, weapons in hand. Bloom took third position from the door. This was the real thing, not a cyber search. Bullets mights fly. Decisions had to be made on the spot with a fraction of a second for assessment. Could her heart take the excitement? Would her illness, and her concealment of it, cause her any harm? Her breaths became shallower and more rapid. The air didn't seem to satisfy her lungs any longer.

She watched Mulville withdrawing his eye from the scope, his mouth in a grim expression. He turned a ninety degree angle and, with his hand, thumb, and index finger pointed at his forehead, signaled Kirk's predicament. Bloom's eyes widened. Mulville banged his palm against the door.

"FBI!" he shouted. "Drop your weapon and open the door."

He remained squatting at the side of the door, his eye returning to the scope.

Kirk continued to stare straight into the gun muzzle. Baker's finger remained on the trigger, ready to fire. Kirk held his breath. A muffled noise came from the direction of the front door—a thump, followed by a strange scratching sound. Kirk took in a gulp of air. Perhaps he had a chance.

"How are you going to avoid jail or worse?" he asked. "Everyone knows this is your room."

Baker shook his head, a diabolical grin spreading on his face. "Don't worry about me. I'll place this gun in my bodyguard's hand. And your gun will finish the job by taking care of your killer. It will look like you shot each other."

"I don't know about your bodyguard," Kirk said, pointing at the door. "He may not be available for your plan right now."

Baker stopped smiling. The muzzle of his gun grew even closer. Someone banged at the door.

Mulville's voice came through. "FBI! Drop your weapon and open the door."

Kirk rode a roller coaster of hope and fear. Would he be still standing in the end?

"Son of a bitch." Baker pushed the muzzle against Kirk's cheek and grabbed him by the left shoulder, turning him to use as a human shield. "Walk."

The soft flesh, sandwiched between metal and teeth, hurt. Kirk tasted his own blood. A glimpse at where the door met the floor was enough for Kirk to notice a round dot. A fiberscope's tip. Mulville could see them.

"You come in," Baker said, digging his fingertips into the front of Kirk's shoulder, "and I'll blow out Miner's head."

Mulville's voice had infused Kirk's muscles with eager strength. Baker pushed Kirk to take a few short side-steps away from the door. Now it was up to Kirk. He thought of Aurora and Peter and his two dogs' welcoming barks, tail wagging, and slobber.

"It's over," Kirk said, the gun preventing his mouth's full range of motion. "Listen to me. You don't want to add murder, or *another* murder, to the list. Better to deal, or you're not going to make it. You're looking at the needle at the end of this road, if they don't kill you now."

"Shut up," Baker said, his voice strained.

His jaw tightened. Tendons appeared on his neck. A ping came from his pocket. The sound of an arriving message. Baker grinned. He didn't bother checking his tablet.

"If I don't kill you, I'm dead anyway," Baker said. "But you're going to do it yourself. Call off your friends. Now. Or your family dies."

His family? What did Aurora and Peter have to do with this? Kirk had kissed them both goodbye less than an hour earlier. Before coming to the Fitzgerald, he had dropped Aurora off at her doctor's appointment near NYMC. He had dropped Peter off as well. He was supposed to walk to NYU. By now, he would be working on his project.

"What about my family?" Kirk whispered, his cheek rubbing against the hard metal.

"I'm going to show you," Baker said. "Don't try anything stupid, or they die."

The pressure of Baker's arm around Kirk's chest relaxed, but the muzzle dug deeper into his flesh. He could smell the cleaning fluid. Baker reached for his phone, glanced at the screen, and turned it toward Kirk with a triumphant smile.

"Here," he said. "Call off your FBI. Now."

Kirk stared at the screen—Aurora's and Peter's faces. Their mouths were duck-taped and their eyes telegraphed terror. Baker must have had his goons follow him. Kirk's stomach tensed. A hollow pain shot to his throat and took his breath away. He had to think. Fast.

"Okay," he said, showing open palms. "Take it easy. I understand. No FBI is coming in.. Let me message them, explain, or they'll never leave."

"Yell," Baker said. "We both know they're not very far. I need to see the fucking FBI crossing the street in the next five minutes. And tell them to leave my bodyguard alone."

"Stand down!" Kirk shouted. "He's got my family. Go away, now. He wants to see you across the street from the hotel within five minutes, or they'll kill Peter and Aurora. Please, go. Across the street! Leave the bodyguard alone."

Kirk's heart quickened. He took in a deep breath, ready to shout again. But a knock on the door told him Mulville had heard.

"We're leaving." Mulville's voice reached him from outside.

The periscope tip withdrew from under the door. Muffled steps followed, fading in the distance.

Baker nodded. Kirk was alone with a killer. His killer.

"Get your gun from the man outside." Baker pulled the gun away from Kirk's face. He used it to point at the door. "You have ten minutes to blow your brains out in front of the hospital. I'm watching you. If you're not a heart donor by 12 o'clock, your family will be ready to donate organs as well."

Kirk trudged to the door and opened it.

Baker glanced at his bodyguard lying on the floor. "Shit." The man moaned in pain, hands on his abdomen and genitals. "Give this asshole his gun so he can finish the job."

Kirk bent down and extracted his own gun from the man's belt. He couldn't see his phone.

"Remember," Baker said, his gun pointed at Kirk's head. "You shoot yourself right in the temple. Any other place and your family is dead."

Kirk ran toward the elevator. His mind groped for a plan to save his and his family's lives. He looked at his watch. Ten minutes until the 12 o'clock deadline. His deadline.

CHAPTER 26
THE DONOR

Outside the hotel, in an alley just off the main street, Bloom and the SWAT team stood in a circle facing Mulville. She raised her hand, clasping a cellphone. Mulville gave her a puzzled look.

"Got Miner's phone from the guard," she said. "While I uncuffed him. I don't think he noticed. Too busy with his privates."

All eyes turned to her.

"I'm working on accessing Aurora's location."

She activated Siri and used a few steps to hack her way into Kirk's phone without a passcode. She located Aurora's cell number. No one spoke. The noise and smell of traffic filled the air. Using a cell phone tracking application, she typed the number into her phone and held her breath. In a few seconds, a map appeared. A red dot stood still near the center.

"Got her. About five minutes from here, by car."

Mulville turned to one of the men. "You, stay here. Watch the hotel entrance for Miner. If I'm right, Baker will send him on a suicide mission. That was the purpose of the kidnapping. Don't do anything. We'll call you as soon as we have his family so you can tell Miner he can stand down. Let's hope we can do it in time."

They ran to the SWAT van Mulville and his men had parked half a block away. Passersby moved away to make room for the armed team on the New York City sidewalk. Some people stopped and took videos with their phones.

They loaded into the van and sprang forward before they had time to lock their seatbelts in place. Sirens blared from the roof of the vehicle for the next few minutes, until they reached a location a block from the signal Bloom was following on her phone. The sirens went silent. The team exited the van and hustled in straight-line formation behind Bloom's to a narrow alley. Bloom felt her pulse hammering in her throat as she arrived at the signal's location.

The pavement was dark and damp, shielded from the sun by tall and blackened brick walls. A smell of urine, garbage, and mold permeated the air. The red dot pointed at the center of a large dumpster. Bloom pushed up the cover, holding her breath. She squinted in the dimness and let her eyes glide over the entire surface of the trash. The men approached the rim and looked inside.

"There!" Bloom said.

A pink-covered cellphone flickered beside the remnants of a hamburger meal. One of the men reached out for it and held it up.

"Shit," Mulville said. "Miner's fucked."

No. Bloom wouldn't accept it. While her eyes swept the ally for clues, she searched her memory for something useful Kirk might have shared with her about his family, A dot of yellow at the alley's end caught her eye and reminded her of something. She ran to retrieve a balled-up yellow sheet at the corner of a side street. She opened it up. Blank. She sighed and rushed back to Mulville and the other men.

"What was that about?" Mulville said.

"Wait," she said, waving the crumpled yellow page. "Kirk mentioned his son is very smart and always carries a yellow pad with him, to jot down ideas. I think he or Aurora left us a signal. Look for more yellow paper."

All eyes combed up and down the alley's pavement. She turned the corner. A store advertising pet grooming opened onto the sidewalk, followed by a coffee shop, followed by a Chinese dry cleaner. In front of the dry cleaner was another yellow paper ball.

She signaled Mulville, showing him the first paper ball and pointing at the second. "They did a good job, leaving signals."

After searching for more paper balls in the nearby alleys and finding none, Mulville gave orders, setting up his armed men around the store. Bloom pointed at herself and the store. Better lead with someone in civilian clothes, to catch the kidnappers by surprise and lower the risk of them hurting Peter and Aurora. Mulville understood and nodded. She asked for another taser. Mulville signaled one of the men, who handed his to her.

She approached the door but met a "closed" sign. The door was locked. Through the front glass, Bloom saw a moving figure inside. Not even noon. Shouldn't they be working at this time? Bloom and the team must be on the right track.

Four minutes to noon. Kirk stood in front of NYMC. His hand slipped into his jacket pocket and wrapped his fingers around the Glock's grip. He tried to slow his breathing. He looked around 360 degrees to see if he could pick out some familiar faces, not expecting to see any, hoping that his colleagues were working at rescuing his family. He hoped that Aurora and Peter were nearby. And they likely would be, unless they had purposefully been taken to some remote location.

If only he had his phone. Baker had watched him like a hawk while he had retrieved his gun. His only chance now rested on Bloom finding his phone in the guard's pocket. The girl was smart. His and his family's lives were in her hands.

His watch showed 11:57. Once he took out his gun, he couldn't hesitate. Otherwise, he'd attract attention. He had to shoot his temple. His thumb took off the safety, but his hand remained inside his pocket. He thought of Peter. No more driving lessons or chess games. And, if Kirk died today, he would miss Peter's college graduation. Sadness flooded his chest. Aurora would be devastated. He was letting her down. But he had no choice. He gripped the gun in his pocket, while a cold sweat spread down his back. He would never know if his death had at least saved his family. As a last rebellion against doom, he looked around one more time.

A man stood flat against the hotel wall, shielded by a column. On his dark blue sweatshirt, Kirk saw three golden letters: F-B-I.

Bloom banged her fist against the glass door. A frail-looking Chinese man appeared. He wore a powder blue shirt and black slacks. He didn't smile. Bloom saw sweat stains on the shirt's armpits. Unusual for a laundry clerk. Not unusual for a terrified one. He fingered the store's "closed" sign.

"I need to pick up my laundry!" she shouted through the glass.

"Closed." The man pointed at the sign. "Come back tomorrow."

"I need it now," Bloom said, tapping her palm against the locked door. "Please."

A burly Caucasian man in black sweats appeared. Several religious tattoos decorated the visible parts of his muscular forearms. Bloom touched her phone screen, sending Mulville the signal to proceed to the back of the store.

"Miss!" the burly man shouted, opening a crack in the door, "what part of *closed* don't you understand?"

The Chinese man stepped back, head bent, as if bracing for violence. Bloom stuck her foot into the opening, grabbed the stun gun from her pocket, and fired it at the burly man's chest. The man fell to the ground, moaning and convulsing.

The sound of stomping feet came from the back of the store. Then a woman's scream filled the air.

Kirk stared at the FBI acronym. Under ordinary circumstances, the letters would bring hope and reassurance to good people in danger. But his situation was anything but ordinary. The presence of the FBI man could mean Mulville was working on the rescue. But what could Kirk do in the meantime?

His hand, still hidden, still clenched the hard cold gun, ready to fire to preserve his family's lives. But something stopped him. The FBI man had his hand out in a calming gesture, or more like a signal to delay. Perhaps he had heard word from the team. Kirk sighed. He needed more than this to risk his family's survival. And he needed it now.

His watch showed 12:00. A fleeting pang of sorrow for Bloom washed over him. From what he knew about her, Kirk's suicide, undeservedly, would burden the young woman for the rest of her life. Would she even accept his heart? Might he die for nothing. No, not for nothing. To save his family.

He looked again at the FBI agent, searching for answers to his burning questions. Hair stood up on the back of Kirk's damp neck as his hand tightened again around the Glock's grip and he began to pull it out of his pocket.

Having already reached for her weapon and handcuffs, Bloom shoved the door open against the stunned thug's writhing mass, stepped into the store, and handcuffed the burly man. The Asian man stood frozen as she stepped past the counter and burst into the back room. Mulville's imposing frame stood near the back door, eyes watching everything, phone glued to his ear. The SWAT team hovered around Aurora and Peter, removing duct tape from their mouths, releasing both wrist and ankle ties. Aurora, tears streaming down her face, hugged her son. Bloom saw pride in his dark eyes. He knew his cleverness had saved his family. He reminded her of his dad.

Bloom lowered her gun, leaned against the wall, and wiped sweat from her forehead. Was Kirk still alive? Had Mulville reached the left-behind FBI agent in time?

Baker watched the street through the 9th floor window. He had seen the SWAT team walking away. Now Kirk Miner stood on the sidewalk in front of NYMC, his hand still in his pocket. What was he waiting for? *Shoot your fucking brains out and get it over with.* Baker checked his watch. 12:01. Time was up. Miner might well be rushing back to the hotel.

Baker grabbed his phone from the table and dialed. The phone rang but went unanswered. Someone knocked. Baker's eyes went to the door. He let go of the phone, grabbed his gun, removed the safety, and checked the peep hole. Just as he feared, Miner stood there. Alone. His face in a grimace. Fucking idiot! Was he going to cry?

Now Baker had to go back to Plan A. The bodyguard's plan. Where was his man anyway? Baker hadn't heard from him. He seemed to have woken up from the stupid attack, but why would the moron have left?

Baker pointed the gun as he opened the door. The elevator whirred in the distance. From his right side, a hand came down like a knife and shattered Baker's wrist. The gun flew to the carpet. Baker howled in pain. Without the gun, the man was no match for Kirk. Kirk's arm came around Baker's neck in a chocking stranglehold. Dots of light appeared in front of Baker's eyes as he was dragged inside the room.

The tightening relaxed. Baker gasped. But the muzzle of Kirk's gun was against his temple. Then the floor vibrated with footsteps outside the open door.

A bulky FBI agent with eyes like slits ran in, followed by four men in uniform. All had weapons in hand. Red laser lights danced everywhere. A young woman in scrubs followed. What was she doing here? Had they brought a nurse for the wounded?

"Don't shoot!" Kirk shouted. "I got him."

The bulky agent stared at Miner for a moment. He smiled.

"Son of a bitch," he said. "You're alive."

"Clear!" one of the men said.

Another man pulled Baker from Kirk's grasp, read him his rights, and cuffed him. Baker was kept stable on his feet. They needed him alive.

CHAPTER 27
D3

Through the one-way observation window, Bloom stared at the poorly lit FBI interrogation room. A single bulb hung from the ceiling. Three gray walls surrounded a plain metal table and three straight-back chairs. The set-up screamed gloom in her head. Gloom fostered talking.

Handcuffed to a metal ring protruding from the top of the table, Baker leaned forward on his chair, his elbows resting on the gray metal. His hands were joined as if in prayer. His eyes seemed to have gotten baggier in the few hours since his arrest. His double chin stood out, sandwiched between his drooping head and caved-in chest. He looked deflated.

After letting him "marinate" as Miner and Mulville called it, alone in the gloom for more than two hours, director and detective now faced the prisoner from the other two chairs. Mulville still wore his dark-blue sweats. The director's unusual attire, which contrasted so greatly with Backer's expensive-looking suit, gave Bloom the impression that interrogator and prisoner had changed places. Only the yellow large FBI letters on Mulville's chest testified to his actual role.

"Let's have a no-lawyer discussion." Mulville's hand swept the top of the table in front of Baker's hands. "See what we've got. No recording."

"I want a deal." Baker's chin pointed up. "And I'm gonna need serious protection."

"Sure." Mulville pushed forward a paper with a pen lying across it. Bloom knew what it was. The temporary waiving of his rights to an attorney. "You need to sign. Before we can discuss anything."

Mulville waved his hand. A guard in uniform entered the room, approached the table, and uncuffed Baker's right hand. Baker rubbed his wrist, glanced at the paper, picked up the pen, and signed without hesitation.

Putting down the pen, he spun the paper and slid it back to Mulville. Mulville nodded. The guard recuffed Baker's hand to the table.

Bloom was surprised by the steadiness of Baker's hand. She also figured he might have valuable information to sell, with an important part concerning her relationship with Montepulciano. That's why she had ignored Mulville's and Kirk's insistent prodding to go home and rest. Bloom needed to hear what Baker had to say.

And what about Kirk? She couldn't leave Kirk alone with Mulville. She trusted him and his good intentions, but the PI might think he was doing her a big favor by telling Mulville about her heart condition, on the theory that it was appropriate in order to save her life. She hadn't dared leave the FBI quarters, not even to shed the sweaty scrubs and change into her regular clothes. She needed a shower. But she needed even more to hear Baker's interrogation. She stepped closer. Her palms left a film of sweat on the glass.

"Tell us everything you know about the heart chain," Mulville said, his hands flat on the metal surface. "How you got into it. From the beginning."

Baker turned up his hooded eyes, a sheepish expression on his face. The fingers of his cuffed hands intertwined. He cleared his voice.

"My wife," he said, shaking his head, "got sick with her heart. I told her so many times to ditch those damned drugs. Fucking movies. Everybody's an addict. She was a half-decent screenwriter. She could've had a career. Instead, she messed up her heart so bad she needed a new one. That's when she finally got off the stuff—too late, though. That's when we signed up for the chain. She got a heart, but something went wrong during the surgery. Now she's dead. End of story."

Mulville listened, his finger twirling in small circles. Several times during Baker's monologue, Bloom noticed him taking a breath to interrupt, then exhaling in silence. She knew what was coming.

"Listen, Baker," Mulville said, leaning forward, his face inches from Baker's, "when I said the beginning, I meant the beginning. As in, did you help Montepulciano hack into the MYMC records last year? That's the *be-gin-ning.*"

Baker's eyes drooped in defeat and resignation. His hands separated in surrender, at least as much as the cuffs allowed. A loud sigh could be heard, then a spark lit up Baker's face and the droopy eyelids rose.

"Wait a minute," he said. "You couldn't prove anything about that, let alone that I was involved."

Mulville's mouth stretched into a grin. By now, Bloom could read her mentor's face like an open book. As a matter of professional survival, she had to learn his skills.

"How would you know *that*?" Mulville said.

Baker faltered. His forehead shone brightly under the scarce halogen light. His eyes darted around the room as if he was looking for an answer.

"From the news." Baker's voice trailed down with uncertainty.

"The details of this investigation weren't public knowledge." Mulville shook his head. "Either you know it first hand, or the only one who could've told you is Montepulciano himself. Is Montepulciano's protection worth your taking the rap for murder?"

Baker cradled his shiny forehead into his cuffed hands. "I need a lawyer."

"If you want to change your mind, stop here, and get your lawyer, that's your call," Mulville said. "But right now we're talking about Santo Montepulciano. This is your last chance to help us out. Lawyers have a habit of spoiling the fun. Did you help Montepulciano with the hacking?"

Mulville pushed back and balanced his weight on the back legs of his chair. Baker's eyes swept the room again. A trapped animal looking for escape.

"I . . ." Baker said, his forehead shining under the light. "I might have. Some. But the whole messing with the chain was his idea. At first, he hijacked the hospital website and network just to make money with the ransom. But then he saw the opportunity to run a transplant racket. Soon he started to make some real money."

Baker paused. Mulville nodded. Kirk seemed deep in thought. Bloom understood. Coming close to death did that to people. Baker went on.

"He's a ruthless son of a bitch. No friendship or loyalty. Only business. My wife was dying. What was I supposed to do? I signed up for the damned thing. Paid good money too. I figured we were friends. He wouldn't really expect me to commit suicide. I mean, I'm not like all the other poor bastards he screwed. But no, everything turned to shit. First my wife died. That alone should've released me from the fucking deal, right?"

"You're asking me?" Mulville said, pointing at his own chest. He slumped forward. The chair thumped against the floor. "Tell me what happened."

"Montepulciano threatened to kill me if I didn't replace myself as a donor," Baker said.

"So you killed Amy Winter, the young woman in front of the hospital," Mulville said, "and made it look like suicide."

"I want my lawyer now." Baker sat back, stretching his arms.

"Never mind," Mulville said. "Tell us what happened with Margarita Herrera, who was supposed to get Amy Winter's heart."

"Lawyer!"

"You waived the lawyer, and you're helping us," Kirk said. "Your cooperation will be taken into consideration."

"Okay." Baker sighed. "Montepulciano made me lean on Herrera to make her refuse the heart. I had no idea what was going on. All of a sudden, a VIP patient needed the heart at all cost. But the donor died and I became a sitting duck. Again. The only available match for the freaking VIP. And the detective here told me the VIP was no less than Montepulciano's daughter. How screwed could I be?"

No sympathy came from Mulville or Kirk. Bloom's palms pressed against the cold glass. Mentioning the word "daughter" triggered the ominous pounding of her heart.

"The mobster wants a heart for his daughter without his having to kill himself first," Baker went on, as if talking to himself. He snorted. "Santo's rules for the chain don't apply to him."

"Margarita Herrera was highest priority for transplants," Kirk said. "She was in the hospital, on inotrope drips—medications to keep her heart going and her blood pressure up—but she refused the heart so Montepulciano's daughter could be next. You probably gave her an offer she couldn't refuse. Baker, what did you tell the poor woman? That she had a higher chance of dying with the transplant than without?"

Baker shook his head. "No. It wasn't like that."

"Right," Kirk said.

"After all this," Mulville said, his hand making a sweeping gesture, "what I want to know is: Who's the daughter?"

The glass felt icy cold against Bloom's forearms. This was the moment of truth. She hoped Kirk could somehow take the conversation in a different direction. She had once read that being blind enhanced your hearing. She closed her eyes. The glass vibrated under her head.

A banging at the door startled her. The door of the observation room slammed open. She turned, ready to protest. Her breath caught.

"What are you doing here?" she said.

Zayne stood in the open door, dark green scrubs under a black down jacket, computer bag in one hand and hospital ID in the other. He hadn't bothered changing since she fled the hospital. He must have rushed out as soon as he had a chance. A muscular, uniformed guard had his hand tightly wrapped around his arm. Bloom winced.

"Sorry, ma'am," the guard said. "He wouldn't listen to reason. He said it was a medical emergency and needed to talk to you, in person. Do you know this guy?"

Zayne shook his head and looked at her. He cared so much. Warmth spread throughout her body, despite all the dreadful implications of the doctor's visit.

"He's my doctor," she said. "Let him in."

"I don't know, Agent Bloom," the guard said. "Shouldn't it be the director's call? I can't take responsibility."

"The director is busy now." Bloom pointed at the window of the interrogation room. "I called the doctor. I'll take responsibility."

The guard nodded, released his grip, and left. Bloom grabbed Zayne's hand and pulled him into the small room. She waited in silence until they no longer heard the guard's steps.

"What are you doing here?" she asked again. "Good way to get yourself arrested. We're in the middle of an interrogation. Kirk almost got killed today."

"I'm glad he's okay," the doctor said, his chin pointing at the glass window. "I came for you. To take you back to the hospital. Do you realize you nearly died and are in no condition to be working?"

"I'm not going anywhere," she said. "Not now. This is how I graduate from probie to full-fledged FBI special agent."

"This," Zayne said, his tone serious, his finger pointing at the glass window, "is how you graduate to dying. I can't believe you just got up and left. We need to get you back into the hospital and get you a heart before the tumor kills you for good."

He took a step closer, cradled her shoulders with his strong arm, and directed her toward the door. The contact of his body made Bloom wish to give in. How good it would feel to just lower her guard, relinquish responsibility, and accept his help. And everything else he was ready and able to give her. But Bloom stood fast. She shrugged off his hug.

"No," she said. "I have the right to refuse treatment. No matter what. And don't you dare tell anyone about me. You're bound by doctor-patient confidentiality. You can't tell anything to anyone without my permission."

"Calm down." Zayne sounded like a doctor talking to an insane patient. "Have you forgotten the ultrasound images I showed you? The tumor mass bouncing up and down, pushed and pulled by the heart muscle like a small ball bouncing on a player's knee? *Your* tumor. The goal is the mitral valve. If your tumor scores, if the mass gets stuck in the mitral valve opening, the circulation will stop cold. You'll die instantly. This time for good."

"You have to go." Bloom shook her head, as if she could no longer hear what the doctor was saying. "Now. Before Kirk and Mulville see you here. They may arrest you. Civilians cannot witness interrogations. I'll call you when we're done."

"You can finish listening to this interrogation"—Zayne pointed at the window again—"if it's so important to you. But then you've got to listen to me and come back to the hospital. I don't want anything to happen to you. I—care about you. Not just as a patient."

Bloom saw his gray eyes grow shiny. She turned toward the glass. Baker was alone in the interrogation room. What had happened in these past few critical minutes? Had Kirk thrown her under the bus, revealing her secret to Mulville, the way the doctor might? Couldn't everyone just take care of themselves and leave her alone?

Zayne's arms closed around her. His mouth found the side of her neck. Two primordial instincts clashed inside Bloom. The desire that burned every inch of her body fought against her survival instinct. Kirk and Mulville might show up at any time. Her hands closed into fists and pushed on the doctor's chest.

"No!" she shouted. "Go away!"

Bloom gazed past Zayne, at the opposite wall and the closed door. The handle dropped, the door opened, and the director stepped in, followed by Kirk. Bloom freed herself from Zayne and shoved the doctor back and to the side, far enough for him to see Kirk and Mulville. Zayne stepped aside, but not before Mulville had the chance to take in Bloom and Zayne's interaction. The burning of desire turned into sizzling shame and rage. Bloom hoped for her tumor to score goal at the center of the mitral valve, so she could die immediately, avoiding what was coming. She stepped back against the glass. She was cornered.

"What the heck?" Mulville stopped in the middle of the room, fists on his hips. "We're in the middle of an investigation here. Doctor, you can't be here. You could be arrested just for showing up. Bloom, what's going on?"

"Director," Bloom said, her voice cracking, "it's not what you think."

"It isn't?" Mulville said. "Would you two like to take it outside, or better, get a room?"

"Dr Wilder…" Bloom said.

"Yes, Bloom," Mulville said. "Tell me what Dr Wilder is doing here, in a highly classified FBI location. Tell me what you aren't telling me. Remember that bullshitting me is much worse than anything you may be afraid to tell me."

"Bloom left the hospital a.m.A," Zayne said. "Against medical advice."

Bloom's legs felt weak. She stared at the gray floor waiting for the axe to fall on her career. Her heart seemed energized by the burst of anger toward Zayne. She looked up and stared at Zayne as if her intense look could transmit her feelings and thoughts. *Don't do it.*

"Against medical advice?" Mulville said, looking straight at Bloom.

"Thanks, Bloom. For lying about your discharge from the hospital."

At the sound of her name, Bloom's gaze turned to Mulville. What she saw in Mulville's eyes made her stare at the floor again.

"I was hoping," Mulville said, directing his comments at Zayne, "that you could teach her some sense. I guess I was wrong. She passed out and you let her rush away before it was safe? What the fuck is wrong with you?"

Zayne's shoulders dropped. The doctor looked pale under the scant light.

"And now you show up here, at the risk of getting arrested, as if it's an emergency," Mulville said. He pointed at Bloom. "How sick is she, *really*? She shows up for duty, like nothing has happened. Is she going to die on us? Give me a good reason why I shouldn't arrest you."

The only way Zayne could defend himself was to tell the truth. That she was deadly ill and totally irresponsible and needed major surgery requiring months of rehabilitation. Add that to a great resumé. Right below her mob connections. Great credentials for a never-to-be FBI special agent. Bloom clenched her teeth.

Kirk stood still behind Mulville, facing Bloom and Zayne. Bloom lifted her eyes to him. She bit her lips and stared. *Please, do something.* But the PI wanted her in the hospital as well. So what was the use?

"She has—" Zayne said, his eyes meeting Kirk's.

The PI's head, very slowly, moved side to side a fraction of an inch. Zayne directed his attention to his computer bag and fumbled with the zipper. Bloom lifted her head and held her breath.

"Charlotte, I mean Agent Bloom, forgot her computer." Zayne's hand reached inside his bag and pulled out Bloom's laptop. "I thought it was urgent for her to get it back, so she could continue to do her job."

Zayne's voice trailed off, as if the doctor had given up. Bloom was home free. She let her breath out. But at what price?

"Why in hell did she pass out?" Mulville went on. "That's what you told me when you called me. Explain how can she be running around now, after signing out of the hospital freaking a.m.A."

All eyes turned to the doctor. Everything was still in jeopardy. Bloom's anger turned into fear.

"I forbid you to talk about my medical problems," Bloom said. "You're bound by doctor-patient confidentiality."

"Confidentiality my ass." Mulville turned to her, red faced, saliva spraying from his mouth. "You're relieved of all duties until the doctor releases you. Go home. Now. Even better, go to the hospital. Doctor, take care of her, will you?"

"No, please." Bloom took a step closer to Mulville. "Don't do this. I'm able to work. I proved it to you today, didn't I?"

Mulville looked at her with that inappropriate paternalistic stare she knew so well. Why and how had she become the daughter he never had? Was her career resting on this role? If so, she wanted no part of it. Charlotte Bloom would stand or fall on her own merit.

"You did good," Mulville admitted, a flicker of rare and precious pride in his narrow eyes. "But now you're on sick leave. Until your doctor tells me you're not."

"At least tell me what happened with Baker," she insisted. "How did you end up with him?"

"Don't concern yourself with that," Mulville said. "You're on sick leave. Worry about getting better."

"With all due respect," Bloom said, "I'm part of this investigation. You assigned me to it. I'd like to know how it's going. Please."

Mulville stared at her. He nodded. He must have realized how important this was to her.

"Baker wants a deal," he said. "Best we can do is no needle. In any case, he's willing to be wired and talk to Montepulciano. Perhaps he was influenced by the fact that he has a fifteen-year-old daughter himself. Even if she will end up living with some relatives anyway, he wants to make sure she's set for a good life. Okay? Now go."

"But, sir," Bloom said, smoothing her voice like a gravel-flattening roller, "you may need me."

"If and when that's the case," Mulville said, "we'll call you. Don't call us. And remember, the first requirement for an FBI position is to be alive. Second requirement is not to piss off your director. One more word and you've failed to meet the second requirement."

All energy withdrew from Bloom's body like a receding tide, leaving only the painful throbbing of her heart, a reminder of the limited number of beats left. Only Zayne's squeeze on her shoulder kept her upright, but it did little to mitigate her resentment.

"May I have a word?" Kirk's voice broke the silence. Bloom looked up. The PI's finger flexed, inviting Mulville to a private conversation.

A forced breath escaped from the director's mouth as he dragged his feet through the exit, after the PI. Bloom took a cleansing breath, closed her eyes again, and concentrated on the soft rumble coming from the outside corridor. No intelligible words reached her. Only Mulville's gruff tone alternated with Kirk's calm and rational voice. Kirk got the last word. In her experience, an achievement in and of itself. Kirk came back first. Bloom wasn't sure if she imagined the slight grin on his face.

"Bloom," Kirk said, "we need to talk."

Mulville came in and stood at attention, rocking back and forth on his feet, hands intertwined behind his back. It was her turn to follow Kirk outside, into the corridor. She left Zayne's side and followed Kirk out the observation room. What were Kirk and the director plotting behind her back? Why were they treating her like an irresponsible child? Had Kirk betrayed her? Her hands tightened into fists.

"If you told him…," she hissed.

"Just listen," Kirk said. He stopped and turned to her, forcing her back against the cold wall, his finger crossing his lips. "If you don't listen to me, you're the one who's going to ruin everything for yourself."

She nodded.

"You're better off in the hospital."

She waited. More had to come. Kirk knew better than to talk to her that way. Just like Mulville.

"It's not just for you, so the doctor can treat you," Kirk said. "We *need* you there."

"Who's we?"

"Mulville and I," Kirk said. "You're part of the team. Baker is meeting with Montepulciano, probably tomorrow. He's going to tell him that I'm dead, that he killed me. And Montepulciano's daughter is getting my heart."

Wrinkles and sweat marked Kirk's shirt, testifying to all he had endured. Bloom guessed that Kirk wanted to be anywhere but there at the moment. Like in his Brooklyn home, with his wife and young son, who were waiting for him. A son who was recovering from kidnapping and a wife recovering from kidnapping and a gunshot wound. Yet Kirk was there, talking to her instead. Exhaustion suffused his deep, brown eyes. A dim light appeared at the end of Bloom's tunnel vision. They really did need her.

"Montepulciano isn't going to take Baker's word that you actually committed suicide," she said. "He's going to demand proof."

"Exactly." Kirk nodded. "You need to match the lie with the hospital's electronic medical records. Or better, the EMRs with the lie. Can you do it? Can you fudge the EMRs, just for a short time? Just enough for Montepulciano to check and confirm that I bit the dust and my heart is ready for harvest."

"I think I can," she said. "But why do I have to be in the hospital for this? I can do it just the same from home."

"That's the second reason we need you," Kirk said. "The one I *didn't* discuss with Mulville. To get a heart, you need to be in the hospital. It would look more real if you were lying on a hospital bed, strapped to catheters and tubing, instead of at home playing with your computer. I'm sure Montepulciano is watching you, or your apartment, or both."

It made sense. Baker would have to show Montepulciano proof she was lying in a hospital bed, covered with monitors and pumped with intravenous drips, ready to be rescued from the devil's clutches by a "fortunate accident."

"I understand," she said. "What did you tell Mulville, about me?"

"Are you two done screwing around?" Mulville's voice startled her from behind. She wondered how he had managed to open the observation room door and exit into the corridor without making noise. And for how long had he been standing there, a few feet from her and Kirk? "The doctor and I have better things to do than shoot the breeze and twiddle our thumbs."

"We're cool," Kirk said. "She's ready. Aren't you, Bloom?"

All eyes were on her. Even Zayne, who had joined them in the corridor, peeked at her from behind Mulville's massive back. The doctor had to stand on his tiptoes in order to see her.

"Okay," she whispered, wondering what she was agreeing to. But the need for self-assertion intensified inside her. "How are you going to wire Baker?"

"We'll manage," Mulville said. He gave her the waving sign with his stubby hand, as if her question had no importance. That was the marker of a final, never to be questioned, decision. Bloom had learned from experience not to challenge the waving. But today she would.

"If you're planning a regular wire," she said, "you may as well write *I'm wired* on Baker's forehead with a marker, so the mobster can put his bullet on the dot of the 'i'."

"What do you suggest?" Kirk said.

"A wireless loop-recording and transmitting device," she said, "You can implant it under the skin. Also, are you sure Montepulciano doesn't already know you're alive, Kirk?"

"Baker told us that he didn't share the details of his plan with anyone," Kirk said. "Montepulciano knew only that Baker planned to kill someone to take his own place. I believe him. If he lied, and if Montepulciano finds out Baker doesn't have a substitute donor, he'll kill him."

"Great." Mulville rubbed his palms. "Time to shove the wireless wire up Baker's ass. And, Bloom, I want to see you going. Right this minute. The good doctor Wilder can assist you with all the hospital medical record crap. We'll be in touch when we're in position."

Hearing his own name mentioned, Zayne lifted his head, his eyes widening. No time for objections, or mentioning the ever-sacred HIPAA. Bloom obediently walked to the elevators, Zayne following right behind her. They really needed her. Soon to be FBI full-agent Bloom. If she survived.

CHAPTER 28
THE WAITING

By eight o'clock that evening, Kirk's back had explored every lump and bump of the dirt-colored couch in the FBI meeting room. Given the job of faking his own death, Kirk had to postpone his return home to avoid being spotted by anyone. Kirk couldn't even have the luxury of talking explicitly to his wife about the plan, for fear that Montepulciano might have his phone under surveillance. Instead, the communication to Aurora had been done in person by uniformed agents, as it happens in the case of a death notification. He wondered how Aurora would respond to this development and what impact it would have both in their relationship and in his own future as a private investigator.

Kirk groaned and shifted in the darkness, searching for a more comfortable position. Stress had built up during the fight for his and his family's lives, the interrogation of Baker, the Mulville-Bloom mediation, and the final forging of tomorrow's plan. Exhaustion, kept in check by the necessity of focusing all his energy on crucial tasks, had at last won out, draining him like a leak in a sinking boat.

But Kirk couldn't give in to coveted sleep, not even for a few minutes. The excitement kept him awake. The most important event of his day had yet to come. Aurora was on her way. Kirk felt like a prisoner waiting for a conjugal visit.

A knock at the door, even though he'd expected it, startled him. His nerves hadn't yet recovered.

"Kirk." The intimately familiar voice eased some of the tension from his sore muscles. "It's me."

He jumped off the couch, found the light switch, and opened the door. Aurora stood in the corridor, accompanied by a uniformed FBI guard. Kirk searched her beautiful face for any sign of what she had endured. Her fresh-ly-washed blond curls were bouncing, but her dark eyes were still too shiny and surrounded by a bluish shadow. He took her hand and pulled her into a tight hug before she could begin to cry. Her sobs shuddered against his chest. He patted her back, swallowing his own tears. The soft light blue sweater she wore was one of his favorites.

He noticed some motion behind the guard. Kirk's muscle tightened up, as if called to action again, but soon joy filled him. Peter stood there. The boy smiled. Kirk wondered if he seemed suddenly older, or if perhaps Kirk had been away from home too long and too often to notice that his boy was growing up too fast.

"Peter." Kirk reached out for him and pulled him into a family hug. "You saved us today."

He felt him nodding against his side.

"That was so brave." Kirk squeezed him tightly. "When you're scared, it's very hard to keep cool and think clearly. Not many people can do it."

"You taught me." Peter looked up at him. "All the times you told me about your work."

Kirk had always been careful not to share the scariest part of his cases with his family. Luckily, Peter was smart enough to read between the lines. Today, Peter had showed him that he possessed courage that matched his brains.

They sat on the old couch and held hands, talking for another hour. Kirk was grateful for Peter's presence. It prevented Aurora from objecting to Kirk's continued involvement in the current case. The thought gave Kirk a pang of guilt. After more kisses and hugs, Aurora and Peter left him alone to wrestle the old couch again.

Sleep filled with dreams about tomorrow finally came.

Bloom sat on the hospital bed, still dressed in the stolen scrubs, her computer on her lap. She looked up at Zayne, sitting on a chair at her bedside. The digital clock on her screen showed 10:32 p.m..

"Can we at least hook you up to a monitor?" Zayne said. He pointed at the door. "The nurse wants to admit you. I need you registered as a patient in the hospital to be able to type my doctor's admission note. What do you have to do that's more urgent than making sure you stay alive?"

"You heard Mulville." Bloom sighed. "I have until eight o'clock tomorrow morning to get the medical records ready for the meeting between Baker and Montepulciano."

"Heard part of it," Zayne said. He looked beat. His corrugated forehead gave away his diminishing patience. Even his eyes had lost the sparkle she found so attractive. A morning crammed with surgeries, followed by rushing to her rescue, which put him at serious risk of getting arrested by the FBI. And now this was his free night.

"Can't say I like it," he said. "Sounds like you guys need me to falsify a bunch of medical records. I need to know the full plan so I understand why I'm going to lose my medical license once and for all."

Time was of the essence. She needed Zayne to cooperate. She was the FBI cyber expert on the case. Zayne was a regular civilian, albeit a medical doctor. Time to be professional with him. Bloom set the laptop on the bed cover.

"Baker," she said, "is a suitable donor for Margarita Herrera. And for me."

She shuddered, hearing herself say those words. She wasn't talking about a secret patient any longer. She was talking about herself. She was waiting for a heart. Or else. And this wasn't a human-imposed or-else, which a person could argue with, and perhaps act against. This was a nature-imposed condition. An absolutely non-negotiable one. If she didn't get a new heart, she would die.

Zayne clasped her hand. She hadn't told him anything new yet, but her earlier admission about her suddenly-discovered heritage, didn't seem to much affect him as well. To her, that was solid proof of how much he cared about her. Bloom hoped she would have the time and the opportunity to experience the doctor's affections again. Her face felt hot. She pushed the thought aside and explained everything.

"Now I understand why my poor patient refused the heart." Zayne sighed. "They forced her to go for an LVAD so the heart could go—"

"To me." A quiver shook Bloom's body. "But I would never accept a heart at the expense of another person."

"Of course. I wouldn't expect anything different from you." Zayne got up from his chair and sat next to her on the bed. His arm wrapped around her shoulders. "You have chosen a dangerous profession in order to serve justice and make a difference in the world. And you let nothing stop you, not even a deadly condition. Why do you think I care so much about you? I never wanted to save a patient so badly. I want you, Charlotte. With me. I want to spend time with you, to get to know you."

His lips found her mouth, her throat, her neck. Bloom wished Zayne would make love to her then and there, on the thin and slippery hospital mattress, the starched sheets, and plastic-wrapped pillow. But the clock showed 10:37 now. And tomorrow was the big day.

"Please," she moaned, easing herself away. "Not now. I want it also. So much. But I have work to do. By tomorrow morning, the hospital records need to reflect the fact that Kirk is a brain-dead heart donor and that I'm ready to receive his heart. This way, your heart chain will go back to being a tool to help patients get new hearts instead of a tool for the mob to get rich."

Zayne nodded. She watched him digest her plea. She needed his cooperation. And much, much more. She didn't want to lose him.

"I can access the medical records on my own," Bloom said. "This way it wouldn't be your responsibility. You wouldn't risk your license, or reputation. The FBI would be responsible."

"Really?" Zayne looked at her like she was an alien. "You can just hack into the medical records just like...like..."

"Like the bad guys," she said. "It's call ethical hacking. It's hacking by the good guys. Often using similar methods."

Zayne's brows lifted. Together with his amazement, she saw a new kind of respect from him. He nodded slowly.

"I can prepare a fake note about Kirk." Zayne stared at the wall in front of the bed, as if contemplating a solution. "That he received a gunshot wound to his head, was brought to the hospital in a brain-dead state, and was deemed a good candidate for organ donation.. etcetera, etcetera."

"Great." Bloom sighed in relief. "I can add it to the medical records, if you want. I'm able to show that you weren't the author. Can you do it now? It needs to be available for Montepulciano to see by tomorrow morning at the latest."

"What do you mean by *available*?" Zayne turned to her, his eyes wide. "Available how? As in hacking? Montepulciano is still able to hack the hospital records and look at patient charts as he pleases?"

"I'm sure of it," Bloom said. "That's how he manipulates the chain. He has free and unfettered access to the records. And I get the feeling Baker can do the same … and worse. We need to put an end to that by bringing them both down."

"Okay." Zayne leapt up from the bed. "I'll do my part. But according to your plan, you need to be officially admitted to the hospital. I don't want to hear any more objections. I'll take care of Kirk Miner's note. Meantime, you've got nothing to do but settle into your hospital bed so I can prepare your note as well, for real. In case someone needs to hack into it."

Bloom laid her head back on the lumpy pillow. She wouldn't be sitting in the surveillance van listening to the Baker-Montepulciano conversation tomorrow. No shouting "FBI!" while raiding the place with the SWAT. Bloom wouldn't be the one to apprehend the mobster either. She couldn't make any arrest in her own case. Unfortunately, in the deception they were fabricating, she was the only real entity. A *real* patient. In true *dying* need for a heart.

Bloom opened her eyes and looked at the wall clock: 12:10 pm. After a mostly sleepless night spent projecting worst-case outcomes for the coming Baker-Montepulciano meeting, she must've dozed off. Everything was ready on her part. According to NYMC medical records, Kirk Miner lay brain-dead in the intensive care unit, machine-pumped with oxygen and fluids with tons of tubes tethered to his body. The other piece of the transplant puzzle, she had been truthfully and officially admitted as a heart recipient. She had submitted to all patient requirements. Gown, intravenous access, sticky monitor leads, nurse's exam, and the totally professional doctor's exam. After confirming her readiness with Director Mulville and spending a few hours tossing and turning, she relinquished her consciousness to a sleep-inducing medication. And here she was, at the moment when Baker was starting his fateful meeting with Montepulciano.

Once more, she asked herself how she felt about contributing to the takedown of her father. Once more the answer was *nothing*. The word "father" didn't accurately apply to Santo Montepulciano. She shook her head. Inside her, the anxiety of uncertainty, of not participating in the live action, surged. These were matters which were crucial to her career, and even to her life. Yet she was relegated to the role of spectator. Powerless.

But she had a plan. At least, she didn't have to depend on others to update her with news, when possible and convenient, after the fact. She reached out for her laptop on the bedside table, dragged it onto her lap, opened it, and went to work. Soon the map of Manhattan appeared. A blue dot inched slowly along First Avenue—Baker, going to meet Montepulciano. She hoped the sound feed from Baker's device would work as well as the GPS. Involvement in Baker's wire setup was paying off. Bloom was going to watch the meeting after all.

CHAPTER 29
THE MOLE

As he trudged on First Avenue along with the rest of the Manhattan throng, Carl Baker thought of his wife and daughter. The years he had spent with them seemed to have passed by in a flash. No, that wasn't correct. The first ten years or so had gone quickly. The happy years. His wife was a work-from-home screenwriter, devoted mother, and housekeeper. She always had a hot dinner, a cold beer, and a hug, not necessarily in that order, waiting for him at the end of long days spent struggling to find clients.

For ten years, Baker had lived trying to meet his quota as an employee of a small brokerage firm. He had never excelled at his job. Baker sighed. He had always felt like a failure. His true love was sitting at a computer, coding, programming, manipulating data. Not much to manipulate twenty years ago. Baker was ahead of his time.

Yet, those years were happy, because his family life was based on truth. Unlike the next ten years. Becoming an independent stock broker seemed like a good decision. At least he didn't have quotas to meet. He struggled at first. Soonafter becoming the head of his mob family business, Santo Montepulciano, "invested" in Baker's private hedge fund company. Biggest mistake of Baker's life.... maybe until today.

Montepulciano made him rich. Baker's wife got jewels and a new wardrobe, not to mention a new home in ritzy Connecticut. His daughter was able to attend private school. All paid for by Baker's business which, in truth, was mostly money-laundering. All of it hidden from his family.

The women in his life had been outraged and shocked by the federal investigation. Luckily, Montepulciano had kept his word and Baker out of jail. But the relationship with the mobster was a sticky spider web from which Baker could never escape. Santo knew how to use him and his expertise. Turned out Baker's expertise was the reason Montepulciano had targeted him in the first place.

Baker had no choice but to set up the hacking of the hospitals' medical records. And then the takeover of the damn chain. It was either accept a full-time job with the mob or end up at the bottom of the Hudson in cement shoes.

Turned out his wife had a secret life too. Cocaine. Her scripts started selling. She travelled to New York, and then Hollywood, and got enough contact with the corrupt entertainment world to absorb the poisonous influence like a sponge. Nothing like the combination of money and movies. *Damn money killed her. My money. The money I made laundering Montepulciano's money.*

And now Baker was walking to a meeting with the mob. Did he fear that this might be his *last* meeting? Was this the reason his life had just flashed in front of his eyes? The possibility struck him as so plausible that he stopped in his steps a few blocks from his destination and felt his stomach go into a freefall. Despite the cloudy sky and the chilly autumn air, sweat broke out under his tweed jacket.

His hand went to the right side of his face. Fingertips massaged the still painful cheek. Inside, his tongue rolled over the small lump created by the injection of the wireless recorder. Damn Mulville didn't understand what risk they were all taking, messing with Montepulciano. The mobster was ruthless and relentless. Baker had been ready to talk, reveal all he knew. Wearing a wire, or in his case a wireless recorder, was a different ball game.

And for what? Life in prison instead of a death sentence? Only difference was that he would be able to follow his daughter's progress in life. From behind bars. Tears came to his eyes thinking of all those times he had dropped her off to school. Today, Baker had arranged for his sister to pick her up. He even had to tell his sister the arrangement might be for an indefinite time. He hadn't yet had the heart to tell his daughter the full truth. Maybe he'd never have the chance after today. Baker's only hope was to convince the DA that he had been coerced, at gun point, to commit all the crimes he had perpetrated. Money laundering. Hacking. Fraud. And even murder. Murder. Because of Montepulciano, Baker had to kill that beautiful young woman who was destined to become a doctor. A doctor who could have saved lives. It was her or him. What was he supposed to do? He had to get the bastard responsible for turning him into an unscrupulous criminal.

Baker resumed his walk and checked the address on his phone again. A small Italian food joint. Before turning the corner onto a side street one block away, he detected a familiar sight. Nestled among other anonymous tall buildings, the NYMC tower welcomed him from further down First Street. Until now, Baker hadn't realized that the meeting site would be just a block away from the hospital.

What did this mean? Was Montepulciano planning to kill him? Baker had requested the meeting. But Montepulciano had picked the location. A block from the damn hospital. Why not in his Manhattan office? Baker pulled out his pocket handkerchief and wiped his forehead. Baker had pulled the same trick with Kirk Miner. If only he hadn't missed the first time he had tried to take down the PI, instead of wounding the wife and missing Kirk entirely. And now Miner was Baker's only chance of convincing the DA that he'd always been unwilling to commit crimes.

Baker trusted Mulville as far as he could throw him. If it depended on the FBI's recommendation, Baker's chances of avoiding life in prison seemed as good as hell freezing over.

Giuseppe's Italian Take-Out was a hole in a wall. Through the glass front window, Baker could see two muscular men with dark hair in a net, standing behind a counter, dispensing take-out food to a handful of customers, mostly construction workers from a nearby site. They both wore a cook's white jacket and apron and scooped generous portions of sauce-laden noodles into take-out containers, pairing those orders with a choice of sausages and meat balls and large slabs of garlic bread.

Baker's saliva started to flow. For a moment, he wished he were there just for lunch. But today, his stomach couldn't accommodate any food, even if he tried. He saw no trace of Montepulciano. After confirming the address one more time, he waited for one of the patrons to pay for his order, then entered the store and approached one of the men in white.

"I'm here to meet Santo," Baker whispered. "Is he here?" Baker told him his name.

The young man's eyes gave Baker a once-over. Then, curling his index finger, he signaled Baker to follow him through a door at the side of the counter, into a poorly lit corridor ending at a second door marked "Private." The man stopped. He wiped his hands on his apron and opened his arms, indicating to Baker that he should assume the appropriate frisking position. Good thing he had left his gun home.

Soon his shirt was open, his chest exposed. No wires. His pants were next. After the fruitless search, he was allowed to enter a small windowless room. A wall closet and a wooden bench made Baker think that he stood in the staff coat room. The bench had been pushed against the closet door to make room for a table and two arm chairs.

Santo Montepulciano sat at a square table set for two with a red-and-white checkered tablecloth, white napkins, silverware, water, and wine glasses. He wore a black pinstripe suit, a black silk shirt, and a white tie. The black and white motif matched the smoothly combed hair and the perfectly groomed beard and mustache. Black with gray highlight, so perfectly symmetrical that Baker wondered if the mobster had sat at his hair dresser wearing silver foil to tint his hair and beard. He suppressed a nervous grin.

Montepulciano leaned forward to avoid dripping sauce on his shirt while stuffing his face with what looked to be chicken parmigiana. He didn't look up at Baker until he finished chewing and wiped the sauce-stained mouth with his napkin.

"Sit down," he said, folding the napkin and replacing it at his side. "Have some parmigiana. I'm afraid my nephew outdid my mother's recipe. Bless her soul."

"Sure. Thanks." Baker sat and, in case of an emergency, pondered how well his knife and fork would function as lethal weapons. By the same token, he hoped Mulville and Kirk Miner had a good vantage point. "But first I wanted to discuss the status—"

"Go ahead." Montepulciano relaxed back into his chair, picked up a calix of red wine from the table, and lifted it to his lips. He pointed at the bottle of Chianti on the table as an invitation. "Talk."

Baker picked up the glass of iced water in front of him and took a couple of sips. The cold liquid soothed his dry mouth. "I got a donor for your secret patient. Kirk Miner is dead. I mean, brain dead. And he's a good match."

Montepulciano replaced his wine glass on the table. His dark Italian eyes rolled up from under bushy eyebrows and he stared at Baker with full attention. Baker noticed a resemblance to the younger men in the front.

"The PI? Interesting. You finally did it right?" the mobster said. "How? When?"

"Yesterday." Baker said. "Made it look like my bodyguard did it, and in the process Miner shot him. In a room at the Fitzgerald. No witnesses."

"There's nothing in the press," Montepulciano said. Baker wondered if Montepulciano read every New York newspaper, cover to cover, every day. He hoped Mulville had done his job, leaking the fake news. "At least not in the Times."

"It's in the Post." Baker tried to keep his voice firm. "Local news page. Also you can check the hospital records. Your favorite patient should be in the hospital as well, since they have a heart for her."

Baker clenched his phone to stop his hands from shaking. His fingertip left a film of sweat on the phone. He prayed that someone had doctored the hospital records as promised. After finding Miner's name listed in the ICU as an organ donor awaiting harvest, he turned the phone over to Montepulciano. The mobster glanced at Miner's name, then remained silent while scrolling down with his finger. He stopped to examine a different page.

Baker sipped more water to alleviate the sandy dryness torturing his mouth. His mind tried to remember Mulville's instructions. He had to direct the conversation to useful, incriminating subjects. No matter what Baker's mind tried to focus on, only one thought kept on breaking through like a bulldozer demolishing sand castles. In order to move onto that information-ferreting phase, Baker first had to pass the test of trustworthiness, and thus remain *alive*.

Montepulciano smiled. His polished teeth shone in the dim overhead light. "Don't you think I already know all that?" He handed back the phone as if it were useless junk and poured more Chianti for himself and a glass for Baker.

"Have a drink, Baker. You look a little pale."

Baker spread his hands under the table to stop it from shaking. He told himself that Montepulciano hadn't known about Miner and the special patient until just now. To maintain the all-powerful veneer he needed to intimidate and rule, the mobster needed to lie about such things.

When he trusted his hand not to shake uncontrollably, Baker reached out for the wine glass. Montepulciano hoisted his in a toast. The clinking of glasses filled the quiet room. Baker gulped down half his glass.

"Well done, my friend," said Montepulciano after taking a small sip. "I knew you'd come through. I'm glad you can still be part of this business. It's getting very big. And I'm going to need you."

This was his chance. Baker had to watch his words carefully.

"I've always been loyal," he said. "Always followed your lead. You're the master planner, and I execute."

Montepulciano nodded. Baker needed more. He had to force the mobster to talk without getting himself killed in the process. Mulville had mentioned kissing the mobster' ass.

"Where did you even get the idea of getting into the hospital records?" Baker asked. "That was brilliant. Just brilliant."

Baker thought about fishing. During his happy years, he enjoyed launching line and bait into a river upstate. He couldn't think of the name now. His wife would pack these salami and hot pepper sandwiches for him. He would sit back and relax, waiting for the fish to bite. Just like now, except he was fishing now for information and, even with the wine, he wasn't doing too much relaxing.

But what was Montepulciano doing? Baker saw him take his phone out. He dialed a number. Baker muscles tightened. His heart rapped his ribcage in a frenzy. Was this the order to execute him?

"This is Santo Montepulciano," the mobster said into his tablet, pointing a finger at Baker and asking him to wait. Wait for what? A death sentence? "Please return my call as soon as possible. Thanks."

That was it? He needed to make a phone call in the middle of their conversation? It must be some sub rosa way, using some diabolical code, to give an order he didn't want recorded or repeated. The room suddenly felt air-tight. Baker's chest hurt from the effort of breathing.

"Taking advantage of the chain was a brilliant idea," Baker said, steadying his voice.

"I couldn't have done it without you," Montepulciano said, cutting a piece of chicken. "I needed you for the hospital hacking. And now that we've overcome that small glitch, we can continue to expand our influence. The chain will keep on growing, and so will the profits."

Montepulciano pointed his loaded fork at him. The sauce dripping from the pierced chicken reminded Backer of blood. "You may have to expand your business to accommodate the new funds. I'll help you. As I always do."

Baker couldn't believe what he had heard. His wife's death had been but a "small glitch" in the Boss' business? Baker's muscles contracted. He stared at his knife, one inch away from his fingers. Baker desperately wanted to thrust it into Montepulciano's neck, just above his collar, where his jugular vein bulged, and where it was compressed by the silk tie. He could imagine the blood spurting from severed vessels. Baker was going to jail, no matter what. What harm was another little murder anyway? Heck, Mulville would probably thank him. Baker's hand twitched. He ordered it to stand down.

"I'll tell you a secret, Baker." Montepulciano placed his phone in his breast pocket and gave him a wide smile. "I'm soon to become a *Capo-dei-Capi.*"

Holy shit. Montepulciano had once admitted to being in line for *Capo dei Capi.* Had Mulville heard this? Did the stupid FBI even know what that meant? That Montepulciano would soon be known as the boss of bosses of the entire Sicilian mob in the US of A. Usually this meant war among crime families until someone prevailed. Was that enough to nail him? Baker lifted his wine glass to the mobster to acknowledge his triumphant promotion and finished it in three large sips.

But his hand stopped in midair. Another thought crashed the party going on in his mind. The providing of all this information could be a sign that Montepulciano knew Baker was marked for extinction.

Montepulciano dabbed his mouth with the stained napkin, pushed back from the table, and stood up. Was the meeting over? Was it enough to incriminate? Baker stood as well. The future boss of bosses came around, his arms open. What was happening? Baker felt the wine come up from his stomach as a sour mouthful. Soon the mobster's arms were around him.

Oh! A hug. The sure sign of acceptance from a mobster. Baker was home free. He stood still, smelling Montepulciano's strong aftershave. In a few minutes, Baker would be out on the street, walking toward the FBI van. If only he could make a run for it now. But the police were hidden all around. Ready to pick up the Boss. There was nowhere for Baker to go but to jail. At least, he would have brought the future Capo dei Capi to justice, for turning him into a criminal, ruining his life, and contributing to his wife's drug-related death.

Baker saw the face with the perfect beard approaching. What was happening? Montepulciano wasn't just hugging him. The mobster's plump lips touched his left cheek. Italian mobsters were known for giving kisses to seal friendship and deals. Was Baker supposed to consider this an honor? He guessed it was. But now the face and the plump lips went to his right cheek. Two kisses, the Italian way. A stabbing pain shot to Baker's jaw and made him draw back. The recorder!

"What the heck?" Montepulciano pushed Baker an arm's distance away. "Your cheek is hard as a rock. What you got there?"

"No— nothing."

"You fucking liar. Let me see."

The mobster's hand went to Baker's throat and grabbed his trachea. Baker opened his mouth and gasped. Montepulciano shoved the index finger of his free hand inside Baker's mouth, scratching the soft mucosa with his manicured nails, while his thumb pressed against his cheek.

"You're fucking wired." Montepulciano pulled hard on the cheek. Baker screamed. "You and your family, what's left of it, will be very sorry."

The strong hands grabbed Backer's neck. Baker's chest muscle desperately contracted, but no air entered his lungs. Where were Mulville's people?

Didn't they know he was in trouble? They were supposed to extract him in case of an emergency.

Darkness with golden dots appeared in front of his eyes. He couldn't even say goodbye to his daughter. *Forgive me, sweetie.*

CHAPTER 30
RESCUE

In an alley a block away, Mulville, Kirk, and two uniformed FBI agents sat inside a plain van outfitted with computer screens and other electronic equipment. A narrow ledge all around the vehicle's windowless back supported keyboards, listening devices, binoculars, Kevlar jackets, and automatic weapons. A dripping coffee machine and an empty bag from a hamburger joint sat on a corner, the smell of coffee and grease mingling in the air. Mulville and the other agents wore FBI jackets and caps. Kirk had on his favorite black leather jacket and his comfortable sneakers.

"What the heck?!" Montepulciano's voice boomed.

"Shit!" Mulville said, swiveling on his bolted chair from the computer screen to face Kirk and the other agents. They all stood up and listened to the Montepulciano-Baker exchange.

"You're fucking wired." Gasps and crackles from the speakers filled the air.

"Holy shit," Mulville said "He's got him by the throat. The transmitter is getting slammed. Time to go."

He jumped up, pointed his finger at one of the other agents in a silent order to activate the nearby SWAT team, grabbed a Kevlar vest from the counter, and wrapped it around his chest. Kirk followed his lead and pulled his vest over his head.

"Where do you think you're going?" Mulville said. "Are you fucking suicidal?"

"I should come with you." Kirk finished adjusting the Velcro straps. "You may need me."

"Stand down." Mulville said. "If Montepulciano sees you alive, chances are he's going to immediately blow your brains out. I don't want you to show your face. We've got enough problems."

Mulville didn't wait to see Kirk's reaction. He unlocked the van, stepped out together with the two FBI agents, and met with two more men wearing helmets and bulletproof vests and carrying semiautomatic weapons. One man also held a crowbar. They ran, Mulville leading the line formation. along an alley smelling of urine and refuse. They stopped in front of a red wooden door in the middle of a discolored brick wall. The men flattened themselves against the wall at the sides of the door. Mulville talked into his wrist's microphone to confirm the position of the rest of the SWAT team at the front of the store. For the sake of innocent bystanders, he hoped to avoid a gunfight on the city street. He turned the doorknob from his side position.

"Locked," he whispered. Then he banged against the wood, weapon in hand. "Open up! FBI!"

He signaled the man with the crowbar. The lock gave way in the first attempt. The door splintered. Bullets from a semiautomatic weapon came through the open door. Everyone stepped further aside.

"FBI!" Mulville shouted again. "Drop your weapon and come out with your hands up. "You're surrounded."

A clang echoed from inside. Sounded like a weapon hitting the floor.

"Coming out now," a man's voice said from inside.

A man in his thirties wearing a cook's jacket and a white apron appeared at the door. He held both his hands up and looked side to side. One of the FBI agents took him into custody. Mulville pushed the door open and slammed it against the wall. He held his gun ready as he peered inside. A short corridor led to a second closed door marked "Private." He motioned to the team to follow him The doorknob turned freely and Mulville cracked the door open. No bullets. Only the sound of tapping feet and grunts filled the air.

"FBI!" Mulville barged in pointing his weapon.

Montepulciano stood next to a dining table. He had one hand wrapped around Baker's neck. The other hand held a gun to Baker's forehead. Baker's eyes were bulging and unresponsive. His neck veins protruded above his shirt collar. His skin had a pale-blue tint under the dim overhead light. If it weren't for the wheezing noise coming from his parted cyanotic lips, Mulville would have guessed him to be dead. Montepulciano held up the poor bastard by his trachea.

"Put down your weapon," Mulville ordered. "Let him go."

Four laser-light dots danced on Montepulciano's head, neck, and chest. He glanced at Mulville for a moment and refocused on choking Baker with the indifference of someone who had stopped caring about his own life and had nothing to lose. Mulville moved closer.

"One more step," Montepulciano said, "and I shoot."

Mulville stopped. He extended his arm to hold back the team behind. The lasers kept on dancing.

"Is Kirk Miner alive?!" the mobster shouted at Baker, shaking his hand holding the trachea. Baker's head bobbed like one of those bobblehead toys. "Is he?"

Mulville wondered how the mobster expected Baker to answer without being able to breathe. Baker didn't look good. And Montepulciano seemed irrational, possessed, and driven by anger. Not a situation conducive to negotiation. But brute force would only lead to unnecessary killing.

True, the two lives in front of Mulville were mostly wasted anyway. But he had made a pledge of Fidelity, Bravery, and Integrity. Mulville held his gun at Montepulciano's chest level. He had to resolve the conflict in the least bloody way possible.

Kirk slumped back on his chair but didn't remove the Kevlar vest. The speaker connected to Baker's recorder was still on. Kirk turned the volume nob to maximum. Wheezing alternated with static. Baker was struggling for his life. The man responsible for wounding Aurora and threatening Kirk's life was about to go down, but Kirk wasn't going to take part in the effort. An uncontrollable desire to spring to action infused him with energy.

The heart chain deal, with all the damage and disruption done to inno-cent patients and their families, was just a side venture—small potatoes for the next boss of bosses. A tip of the iceberg of his future crime empire. The man was a monomaniac who needed to be stopped. Kirk got up. Mulville had ordered Kirk not to show his face. And he wouldn't.

Without hesitation, he unlocked the van and stepped onto the side walk. As he rushed through the alley, a strategy molded in his mind. Mulville's plan, the plan that didn't include Kirk, was to approach from the back entry and to catch Montepulciano by surprise, while more men watched the front. Kirk decided to go through the front.

Kirk saw two SWAT officers at the front door of Joe's Take-Out. He had met them earlier that day. He hoped they weren't aware of Mulville's order to Kirk to stand down. He approached and nodded. The men nodded back. He saw no customers. A man dressed like a cook stood with a third officer in front of the counter. The man was in handcuffs. His black hair stuck to his forehead, his face was red and he kept on shouting about want-ing a lawyer.

"How's it going?" Kirk asked the officers at the door.

"No order to go in yet," the senior officer said. "Montepulciano has Baker and the director has Montepulciano."

The man had gray hair and a proud face. He seemed accustomed to following orders and to conduct his missions with expertise and diligence. Kirk nodded. He walked in past the officers, who looked at him without objecting.

Shouts erupted from the next room. Kirk couldn't make out the words. He took out his gun and walked toward the back and the next door.

"Where do you think you're going?" the third officer said. "We have orders to follow."

"I can assess the situation," Kirk said, his palm out in a calming motion. "It seems from what you said that it requires diplomacy more than brute force. That's why the director hasn't called for you yet. I've had contact with Montepulciano before. I know a little bit about how he thinks. Let me check things out without showing my face."

He heard no further objections. At least he intended not to show his face. He took a flexible scope out of his pocket and pushed the tip under the door behind the counter. He looked at an empty corridor. He peeked back at the SWAT team. The three men didn't budge. Kirk opened the door. Now he could understand what Montepulciano was shouting about.

"Is Kirk Miner alive? Is he? Is he?"

He gave hand signals to the officers that he was going in to observe. The senior man from the back door shook his head in disapproval. What was Kirk to do? He needed to get into the action. He swept up the scope and shuffled through the corridor to the next closed door. He shoved the flexible tip under the thick wood. Montepulciano's back came into view. He was strangling Baker and had a gun to his head. Mulville had his gun drawn, and the SWAT team had semiautomatic weapons pointed at Montepulciano, the red laser dots marking his black dinner jacket and the white shirt. The mobster acted as if he were unaware of the gravity of his situation. He kept on shouting as if on autopilot, "Is Kirk Miner alive?"

Mulville was right. If Kirk showed his face, his life would be over. Kirk couldn't gamble his life and the future of his family. But he couldn't let this go on either. The mobster had to be stopped. And Baker had made a deal. His life for his cooperation. Kirk had to protect Baker, despite how despicable a man he was.

He pulled the scope out and checked his Kevlar fitting. What good would the Kevlar vest do him? Montepulciano would never shoot him in the chest. Kirk might as well walk in without a vest. He placed his sweaty hand on the door handle and pushed down. His heart hammered inside his chest. He slowly opened the door and walked in, his gun pointed at Montepulciano's back. As he caught sight of him, Mulville's eyes widened in surprise. No time to figure out what was stirring in the director's mind. Kirk moved closer, his sneakers silent on the wooden floor, until the muzzle of his gun rested on Montepulciano's nape.

"Freeze," Kirk said. "Or you're dead."

The mobster shuddered against the hard metal. But he didn't budge. His hand remained in position around Baker's neck, his gun pointing at

Baker's head.

"Miner," Montepulciano said. "Nice of you to join the party. Thanks for answering my question."

Montepulciano's gun moved closer to Baker's temple. Baker shuddered, eyes closed, neck extended, mouth in a tight line. Kirk dug his gun deeper into the mobster's flesh.

"Drop it," he said.

"Miner," Montepulciano said, "only way to save this piece of trash is if I shoot you instead. Or just blow your brains out and I'll let Baker go. It's you or Baker. Either one is good, as you probably know."

The ringing of a cell phone broke the silence. Mulville looked side to side. Kirk knew It came from the mobster's breast pocket. The tip of a phone stuck up above the multicolored handkerchief. Montepulciano seemed more agitated now. What was going on? The mobster responded more to a phone call than to a gun at the back of his head.

"I'll surrender," Montepulciano said, his voice firm and almost pleased. No trace of begging or whining. "After I take this call."

"Lower your weapon," Mulville said. "Let Baker go."

Montepulciano let go of Baker's neck. Baker gasped and coughed. But Montepulciano's gun remained pointed at his head. With two fingers, the mobster pulled out his ringing phone, taking care to show his actions clearly. What was he doing? Kirk could think of only one person or persons the mobster would want to talk to in this critical life or death moment. His backup.

"Just answering the phone," the mobster said. "Then you can have me."

"Put the phone down," Kirk ordered. "Or I'll shoot."

"Hello, Doctor," Montepulciano answered. "I don't have much time. Send your team to Joe's Italian food, a block from the hospital. Address is in my message."

What doctor? Only one doctor the mobster could be talking to now. Dr. Wilder. Kirk understood. He had to stop Montepulciano at all costs.

"Don't do it," Kirk whispered, leaning toward the mobster. "What you're about to do won't help in any way. It'll make things much worse. Even for her."

Kirk saw in Montepulciano's head a tightening of the neck muscles and a hint of movement. A slight torque, as if Montepulciano had reacted to Kirk's words with surprise, and now wanted to ask Kirk how he knew his secret. It was just a moment.

Laser red dots still swirled on the mobster's chest. One strayed and crossed over Kirk's shoulder, stressing the fact that the PI was in the line of fire. Was Kirk hindering the take-down? He glanced at Mulville. The thick-necked Mulville gave him a barely perceptible nod of approval. Keeping his armed hand firm on the mobster's head, Kirk took a side step, hoping that his movement would place him outside the SWAT's aim. He also hoped the SWAT team had excellent aim.

Mulville stood firm, feet planted wide, right hand clutching a gun aimed at Montepulciano's chest. With his finger on the trigger, he took a calming breath, but his heart didn't get the message and kept on riding the high adrenaline wave, pulsating in his throat and temples. Kirk had disobeyed his order to stand down on this one. Mulville looked around the room. He clenched his jaw. He had to admit that the PI's move to catch Montepulciano from behind had possibly improved the odds of capturing the perp alive. Not that Mulville cared much about the life of the two murderers in front of him. The SWAT waited for his word to take Montepulciano out.

Kirk's presence complicated things. At least, the PI had stepped out from the line of fire. What was the delay now? Kirk should know the next move was his, unless the PI wanted to risk being blown up by SWAT. What was Kirk doing, allowing the stupid phone call? The mobster was chit-chatting with some doctor. A doctor he would soon need, if he kept up with this BS. Or perhaps a medical examiner.

Mulville suppressed a chuckle. If only Kirk would put an end to this stalemate. Montepulciano wanted a heart for his daughter. Baker and Kirk were both a match. And what Montepulciano wanted, he got. Mulville hoped that Kirk had followed the same train of thought and didn't hesitate. He had to shoot the mobster dead. Worst that could happen in the process, Baker could end up dead as well. So what?

"Stop," Kirk said. "Or you'll be dead before you finish your call."

"Okay, okay," Montepulciano said. "Don't shoot."

The hand carrying the gun lifted away from Baker's head and rose in the air. Kirk grabbed the gun from him and handed it to one of Mulville's men. Baker stepped away toward Mulville and the SWAT team. Mulville ordered the uniformed agent to arrest Montepulciano. Kirk moved to the side to make room for the arresting officers. One of them grabbed Montepulciano's hand with the phone. But Montepulciano's other hand was already inside his jacket. In a fraction of a second, the hand reappeared with a second gun. The muzzle pointed straight at Kirk's head.

"Gun!" Mulville shouted. "Hold your fire!"

"It's Miner or Baker," Montepulciano said, shaking off the arresting officers. "You give me Baker, I let Miner go."

"You don't have to do this," Mulville said. "This doesn't end well for you."

"Last chance to trade. Now."

"Stop!" a familiar woman's voice said. "If you don't drop your gun, I'll kill myself. Right now."

Someone stepped up from behind Kirk. Jeans, dark blue sweat shirt with large yellow letters on the front, flowing auburn air. Bloom! Mulville's jaw dropped, his mouth opened. Her hand held a gun pointed straight at her shirt's FBI logo.

As she tightened her sweaty hand around the Glock grip, Bloom's knuckles whitened. She took several deep breaths while her heart pounded and blood rushed to her face.

She had arrived in time.

After Zayne had left, she had followed Baker's journey on her monitor. She had listened to Baker's gasps and wheezes. Her life had become a cata-lyst for murder. Either Baker, or Montepulciano, or both were destined to die today. She had to prevent Montepulciano from killing anyone else on her behalf. Even if it meant her own death, from lack of a suitable heart donor. Even if it meant Mulville learning the truth about her and Montepulciano.

But there was more. Montepulciano shouldn't die either. She should bring him to justice, make him admit to Marsha Stevens' rape, and give her own mother closure. Bloom was the only one who could prevent both Baker and Montepulciano's deaths today.

Bloom felt glued to her hospital bed. She had hid her lethal condition, and her relationship to Montepulciano. Her mistakes had led to the situa-tion she was now facing. For once, she had to obey her orders and watch the action from the sideline. She inhaled and exhaled slowly, ordering her tense muscles to stand down, her heart to slow.

"Freeze!" Bloom heard Kirk's voice saying. "Or you're dead."

What was Kirk doing at the scene? His presence complicated things. In this volatile situation, Kirk was at high risk of dying. And Montepulciano was more likely to die as well.

A phone rang. Montepulciano talked to a doctor about his location. What doctor? Zayne?

After Kirk's order, Montepulciano agreed to surrender. Mulville then ordered the arrest of Montepulciano. Bloom gave a sigh of relief.

Then a shout from Mulville had jerked her back into full panic. Renewed adrenaline flowed into her veins.

"Gun!" Mulville said.

Montepulciano had a second gun.

"It's Miner or Baker," Montepulciano said, the sound muffled by Baker's distance.

The image of Kirk with a gun pointed at his head flashed into Bloom's mind. Kirk was going to die. Because of her.

She had sprung from her bed and peeled off her monitor leads. She connected her chest leads to a special port to her computer. A simulation of her heartbeat would fool both doctors and nurses into believing she was still hooked up to the hospital monitor. She retrieved the bag with her things from the locker in her room, stepped into her jeans and sneakers, and exchanged the hospital gown for her FBI sweat shirt.

She closed her hand around her badge and gun tightly wrapped in a pillowcase inside her locker. She rushed out of her room into a deserted corridor, down the stairs, and out of the hospital back exit, running as fast as she could, and arriving at Joe's Italian food store in record time.

Now she felt the pressure of the muzzle between her breasts, at the left side of the sternum, her pounding heart lifting the hard metal. The image of a shooting target flashed into her mind. The black silhouette of a man. A red oval at the center of the chest, the very site of the heart, infusing blood and life to the entire body. Bloom shifted the muzzle a few millimeters closer to the breast bone. Right on the black x in the middle of the red oval. A loaded and cocked gun, ready to fire a bullet through her heart. Her heart protested with a run of ventricular tachycardia.

"Santo Montepulciano!" she said. Under different circumstances, she might have just said Daddy. "Drop your gun. Let Kirk Miner go. Or I'll kill myself. And you'll be responsible for my death."

One of Montepulciano's hands still clenched his phone. Was the call still going on? Bloom could see the number. Zayne! Zayne was hearing everything that was going on. Zayne knew about her escape from the hospital. Her stomach sank.

"What the heck?" Mulville said, his eyes rapidly moving from her to Montepulciano and back, his gun still aimed at the mobster. "Bloom. What are you doing here? Are you trying to commit suicide? And for what? Have you gone insane? Put that gun down!"

"Bloom," Kirk said, his voice calm. "Stop what you're doing. It's not helpful. Move out of the way. Let us handle him. Please."

Montepulciano's eyes were on her now. The heavy eyelids drooped further. He seemed in a world of his own. What kind of journey had brought a ruthless, self-centered, seemingly heartless individual to care so much about his progeny that he was willing to throw away accumulated power and wealth, and even his own life, for her? Perhaps, at a certain age, even mobsters looked back, reassessed, and reevaluated their life's worth and legacy. In the end, she at least hoped this was the case.

"Stop killing for me. Now. I'm asking you." She took a deep breath. "As your daughter."

Bloom glanced at Mulville. He looked wide-eyed and suddenly pale, as if he could faint anytime. She forced herself to refocus on Montepulciano. His trigger finger was tightening. Bloom could see the tendons twitching, the knuckle withering. Montepulciano didn't believe her threat. He was going to shoot. Kirk would die. An ominous heat spread from her stomach to her neck. With a swift movement, Bloom removed the Glock's muzzle from her chest, pointing it at Montepulciano's head. The large hooded eyes became wider. Not fear. Surprise. He brought the phone to his mouth.

"Doctor," Montepulciano said, his tone hurried but calm, as if he was discussing business, despite Bloom's gun pointing at his head. "Come and harvest the heart of a scumbag. For my daughter. Charlotte Bloom."

Montepulciano's hand was still holding the gun tightly. The gun pointed at Kirk's head. Bloom shifted the Glock a little lower and to her right, making sure that her aim was clear of the arresting officers and of Kirk, yet still directed at Montepulciano. She pulled the trigger.

The blast boomed and echoed inside the small room. Montepulciano's neck burst. Blood splattered against the checkered tablecloth and the white wall in a shower of red particles.

CHAPTER 31
THE HEART

Montepulciano opened his mouth but Bloom's ears couldn't hear or feel his scream. His gun dropped quietly to the tiled floor. He fell to his knees, then collapsed, sprawled on the slick linoleum, blood pulsating out of his neck, surrounded by an enlarging pool of redness. The pungent smell of blood and gunfire filled the room.

All because of her. And she had caused it, let alone failed to prevent it.

"Hold fire!" Mulville shouted. He rushed to Montepulciano. Glazed eyes stared back at him. Mulville's fingers trembled as he pressed down on the neck wound. The warm liquid escaped through his fingers, soaking Montepulciano's black jacket, the white shirt, and the silk tie.

"He still has a pulse," Mulville gasped. Bloom knew a pulse meant nothing for Montepulciano's prognosis. "Getting weaker every passing second. Call the medics!"

Even tossed on the hard floor like a bag of useless merchandise, Montepulciano maintained an aura of dignity. Bloom stood frozen, gun still in her hand, at her side. She had just shot her father. Her FATHER. And she felt ... nothing.

Still holding Montepulciano's neck, Mulville looked up at her, his brow like a mountain, his eyes drilling into hers for answers she didn't want to give. She wanted her heart to shut down her mind.

Mulville fought a strong impulse to crush Montepulciano's neck, to squeeze the useless life out of him like remnants of toothpaste from an old mangled tube. It was all because of something that Bloom had said while she had her gun pointed to her heart. She had mentioned the word "daughter." This couldn't be right. Mulville would have to call his doctor, check out his hearing. Or perhaps this was just a nightmare he was experiencing, and he would wake up and go about his real life soon enough. But then why would Bloom have pointed a gun at her own heart? The only explanation, given that he wasn't having a nightmare, was that she was the reason for all this mess. Removing herself from the middle of it would have made everything collapse into place.

Montepulciano's last words registered as odd in Mulville's mind. Mulville replayed them, like a recording inside his head. Something about Montepulciano's daughter needing a heart. So what? He had admitted to having a daughter at the time of his alleged rape. Nothing new or surprising there. It was the name the mobster had pronounced that had made hair stand up on Mulville's neck. Charlotte Bloom. His daughter. Bloom was Montepulciano's bastard daughter whom Mulville was looking for.

Something burst in his chest and made it difficult to breathe. He forced air into his lungs. Why was everyone glancing at him now—Bloom, Miner, and even the SWAT team? What were those idiots doing? This was a take-down, for God's sake, not the time for a distraction. Mulville's girl. Yes, Mulville had to admit he regarded Bloom as the daughter he never had, and maybe never would have. The same beautiful, smart, honest, dedicated young woman carried in her veins the blood of a murderous scum of the earth. And she was so sick that she needed a new heart to survive.

But she had never, ever, mentioned any of these incredible, abominable facts to him, her mentor, her boss, her...whatever. A fist of pain lodged in Mulville's chest and spread to the rest of his body, making him weak. He glanced at Kirk. He didn't seem surprised. Only sorry. Sorry that Mulville had to learn the truth in such a freaking way? Miner, the doctor, Bloom—

they all had known the truth. Except for Director Mulville.

"Makes sure she gets the heart." Distorted soft, words exited from Montepulciano's mouth, his cheek flat, hugging the bloody tiles. "We're both in the chain."

Mulville's fingertips continued to maintain pressure on Montepulciano's neck. Kneeling on the hard floor, trying to avoid the sight of blood, Mulville looked at his own badge, clipped onto his belt. Fidelity, Bravery, and Integrity. A cold sweat coated his skin. Mulville went back to the moment when he could and should have unleashed his SWAT team before Bloom had shown up. Had he hesitated on purpose?

The truth crept up from under the avalanche of rationalizations cluttering his brain. Kirk could have died because of his hesitation. The blood from Montepulciano's neck had slowed down to a trickle. Mulville couldn't feel pulsations any longer. Lifeless eyes stared back at him. And Bloom would have to live with the consequences of killing her own father. No. Bloom would have to die now, because of the lack of donors. The pain and pressure in his chest receded, leaving behind a strange emptiness.

Deafening sirens announced the medics' arrival. A man and two women wearing bright orange jackets over white scrubs stomped into the small room carrying a stretcher and bulky equipment bags. Mulville relinquished his hold on Montepulciano's neck, pushed himself up from the floor, and stretched his knees. He took two decisive steps toward Bloom.

"You're going with the medics," he said. "Now."

"I'm…I'm sorry," she said, her eyes lowered to the ground. Sheepishly, she put the gun back in her waist-high holster, as if Mulville had caught her committing an infraction. "That you had to find out this way."

"We'll talk about," he said. "Afterwards."

"But I want to explain…"

"You go back to the hospital," Mulville said, speaking with clenched teeth. "Now. It's an order."

He watched Bloom turn away and approach the woman paramedic uninvolved in Montepulciano's rescue. The two talked for a moment, then Bloom followed the medic outside.

Mulville withdrew to the wall to give the medics space—and to lean on something solid, something reassuring. Radio communications with the supervising physician and calls for the necessary medications, blood, and procedures filled the room. He sighed, relieved that, for the time being, the responsibility for decision making had shifted onto different shoulders. He looked for Kirk Miner in the cramped cube of a room.

Kirk stood a few feet from Montepulciano. The PI seemed deflated, which was unusual for him. Mulville remembered, with a tinge of shame, his early resentment at Miner's seemingly permanent proud posture. Who did he think he was? But he had come to know and admire Miner during their collaboration. Kirk approached him.

"Sorry," he said. But his eyes weren't sorry. Given the circumstances, and despite the outcome, Kirk had acted in the only rational way for a law enforcer. "I had to barge in. Are you okay?"

Mulville took a breath. Last person Mulville wanted to talk to now. But what right did Mulville have to criticize or blame anyone?

"Can't talk about it now," Mulville said. He shook his head and put out his hand to keep Kirk away. "We'll have to talk about this one to one. Soon. Just you and me."

But Kirk wouldn't listen. The pain in the ass PI kept coming closer. What did he want now? Soon Kirk's arms were around Mulville's shoulders. And Kirk was strong, despite his lack of bulging muscles. His arms could barely encircle Mulville's massive chest. What was going on? This was a hug. Kirk was hugging him, his hands patting Mulville's back, his chest against Mulville's chest, separated only by Kevlar. Mulville could smell Kirk's sweat. Too much contact. Nobody had done this to him since—Mulville couldn't remember when.

"It's not your fault," Kirk whispered in his ear. "I should've taken him down. Way before Bloom showed up."

Mulville pushed against the rough Kevlar. His breath came with difficulty.

"I don't need fucking absolution," Mulville hissed. "Not from you, for sure."

"I hesitated." Kirk let go of him and looked Mulville in the eye. "And I didn't have any excuse about possibly hurting anyone, not like you, with me in the line of fire. Perhaps, unintentionally, we both wanted the same outcome. To make sure Bloom got a heart. Her showing up sure messed things up."

"Shut the fuck up!" Mulville shouted. "It was my call. And you know it. Bloom almost died. So did you. And now, if she survives, she's probably looking at years of shrink time. All because of me."

The medics were lifting Montepulciano onto a stretcher and the uniforms were taking Baker out into the corridor. Techs rushed in to work the crime scene.

"We're doing more hindering than good here." Kirk motioned toward the door. "Let's go to the hospital. Together."

Mulville obeyed. He extricated himself from the oncoming investigators, bumped into the last uniform leaving the crime scene, and mouthed a few final unnecessary orders to the techs, before walking toward the exit. He felt like he was still in a trance. Only one thought dominated his mind and, despite his efforts to suppress it, kept repeating in his mind like a broken record. He had wished and waited for Montepulciano to kill Baker. Mulville would have caused less damage if he had killed Baker, cut out his heart, and presented the organ to Charlotte Bloom on a silver platter.

"Wait up." Kirk was still there, walking behind him. "What did Montepulciano tell you? I overheard something about making sure his daughter got the heart."

"If only the son of a bitch had pulled the trigger earlier," Mulville said. "Before Bloom showed up. And while he's dying, he's blabbering about her getting a heart. The moron doesn't realize that he hasn't shot anyone. That Baker is still alive and well, and on his way to jail, instead of to the hospital. And now what's going to happen to Bloom without a donor? She's going to fucking die. That's what's going to happen."

"Montepulciano also mentioned that he and Bloom were in the chain," Kirk said.

"So what? Nothing new. He can hack and manipulate anything in the database, jumping in and out of the chain as he pleases."

"I need to speak with Dr. Wilder," Kirk said, reaching for his phone as he rushed toward the hospital. "Now."

CHAPTER 32
THE RECIPIENT

Not even four o'clock in the afternoon and Bloom was back in her hospital bed. She had been gone less than two hours. Yet, life-changing events had taken place in that short time. Perhaps not all favorable to her life. The ambulance had dropped her off at the NYMC's emergency room. The ER doctor, after hearing her story, called Zayne, her doctor, and Bloom was immediately re-admitted and brought back to her hospital room.

But Zayne had yet to appear. What would his reaction be to her deceit? Add that to the list of reasons he could hate her. Maybe he was waiting to see her until he could control his anger. Or maybe there was no reason for him to rush to her bedside. She had no donor. And without a new heart, she was going to die. She took a calming breath.

The door swooshed open, and Zayne Wilder stepped into her room, eyes dilated, mouth agape.

"What were you thinking?" he said, pulling a chair near the bed and sitting down, his feet planted wide on the floor No more sitting on her bed. "After all that I did to help you as a patient, and as an agent."

"I'm so sorry."

"You didn't think you could confide in me?" His neck veins looked engorged. His jaw contracted. But in his eyes, locked into hers, the anger was fading into pain.

"Would you have allowed me to go?" she said, immediately regretting her rhetorical tone.

"Are you insane?" he said. "In your condition, you want to participate in a SWAT take- down? You were lucky last time. Your director ordered you to be here, in the hospital. And he's going to hold me responsible for your escape. Again."

"I thought I could make a difference," she said. Her stomach clenched. "Avoid loss of life."

"At the expense of your own?"

"My life was the reason for all the killing ..."

"No. Montepulciano was the reason."

"But I made it happen," Bloom said.

"Montepulciano called me." Zayne swallowed. "He left me a message to call him back ASAP. When I did, he first told me to send my team to that restaurant. Then, he sounded like he was giving up. But then…"

"I didn't expect the second gun," Bloom said. "He was going to kill Kirk. I had to go."

"After a while," Zayne said, "I heard your voice saying that you would kill yourself if Montepulciano didn't stop what he was doing,"

Bloom knew what was coming and didn't want to relive it. But Zayne needed to talk. And she needed to listen. She sighed. "Then," Zayne said, "Montepulciano volunteered that I would have a heart to harvest."

Bloom stared at the doctor, waiting. His face looked pale. Drops of sweat shone on his forehead.

"Then there was a shot," he said. "I thought it was you!"

Bloom understood. What she was witnessing wasn't just Zayne's anger at her escape from the hospital. Much more was coming.

"I listened to screams, shouts of orders, stomping of feet, moans," he said. "But not your voice. Someone had gotten shot, and I didn't know who."

Bloom had stood in silence. And Zayne didn't know. Until when? She couldn't fathom. She shivered.

"Suddenly, the call ended," Zayne said. "Maybe the phone had become evidence and gotten bagged up in the process. I called everyone—you, Miner, Mulville. Nothing. Could only leave messages. I dispatched the medics. And I waited. I waited to see what came in. Hoping that it wasn't your dead body. Now. Do. You. Understand?!"

Yes. Bloom understood. During those stressful moments following the shooting, she had not thought of calling Zayne, too afraid of how he'd react to her deception. Not considering what he'd think at the time. And what about her silenced phone? She had been too distraught to even look at her phone. Everyone she cared about disapproved of her actions. She had been anything but eager to check her messages, to find out if relationships had survived, if trust had been mangled without any chance of healing. If she still had a career… or a life.

"I'm sorry," she said. Tears welled inside her lids, blurring her vision. "I was so focused on my own problems that I didn't think of what you were going through. I really feel for you. I hope you'll be able to forgive me."

"You could have at least taken the time to let me know you were alive."

She reached out for his hand. Cold and still. He had every right to be mad. It showed how much he cared about her.

"I didn't realize," she said. "I didn't even think about it. I stood there. Only thing I could think about was that I had failed. I had tried to stop him but couldn't. And now Montepulciano is dead, by my hand. He was trying to kill Kirk, on my account. I had no choice."

She fought her tears, but it was no use. She might as well let go of her anguish while she had a chance. Zayne came closer. He sat on her bed. She found her spot in his arms, head on his shoulder, and let go, sobbing with the relief that only crying can bring. But Zayne didn't let her weep for long.

"Charlotte, listen.," he said, patting her back after the sobbing had subsided and only silent tears were streaming onto his scrub shirt. "We'll have to continue this discussion later. When you're in better shape. We have to get you ready for surgery."

"What are you talking about?" she said, letting go of him. She took a new look, with newly skeptical eyes. "I don't have any donor."

"You do," he said. He looked at her as if worried about how she'd reaction to what he would say next. "Montepulciano is your donor."

"What?" she said. "Him? Isn't he …dead? He looked dead when the medics arrived."

"When the paramedics brough him here, Montepulciano was in cardiac arrest and probably already brain dead from exsanguination. The ER doctor was ready to stop the resuscitation attempts, but Kirk called me. He told me that Montepulciano, with his last breath, begged Mulville to make sure you got the heart."

"What heart?"

"The only heart available. Montepulciano meant his own heart. Kirk figured it out just in time and called me. Instead of sending Montepulciano to the morgue, I placed him on a heart-pump machine to keep his organs alive. We're ready to transplant his heart into you. Montepulciano is a perfect match."

"But how can you know he's a match?" she said. "You didn't have any time to do the necessary tests. He just arrived."

"True," Zayne said. "Montepulciano did his own tests. He's a better match than Baker and Kirk would be. Not only the blood type, but also the HLA markers are as good a match as you can get. When he signed himself up on the chain as a donor, with you as the patient, he placed the results into the electronic records."

Bloom shook her head. "I never agreed to be in the chain," she said. "Least of all with him."

"But you *are* in the chain," Zayne said. "You were admitted to the hospital last night. All your information was available in the records. It was easy for Montepulciano to add you to the chain. As you said, he still had access."

The circumstances were the result of so much deceit and trickery that, while working to catch a perpetrator of blackmail and murders, she had played into his hand, according to his very own plan. She had become an accomplice in procuring her own heart. Charlotte shook her head again.

"Under no circumstances," she said, "will *I* be part of *his* plan. If I accept his heart, I'll be doing exactly what Montepulciano wanted. I'll be sanctioning a murderous mobster."

"Shush." Zayne had his palm out in a calming gesture.

"Besides," she said, "Margarita Herrera should get his heart."

"Herrera isn't a good match for Montepulciano," Zayne said. "Fortunately, with her LVAD, she's in stable condition and not in any immediate danger. We let her know that it's now safe for her to get a transplant—that no one is going to hurt her or her family when she does. She'll likely accept a donor's heart as soon as it becomes available. You, on the other hand, can die any time. And a LVAD is not an option for you. It won't prevent death from the bouncing tumor and from arrhythmias. You're officially next in the chain. Besides, there's no other patient sicker than you now on the general waiting list. And this is the best heart *for you*."

The door slid open and Kirk stepped in, together with the last person Bloom wanted to see at the moment. Mulville, the mountain of a man she had hoped would always be on her side, looked as if he had eaten a volcano that was ready to erupt. In the past, when she had assumed her director was mad at her, she had been mistaken. Bloom realized she had never seen the director angry … until now. She lay back on her bed and pulled the covers up to her mouth. Her eyes glanced at the heart monitor. Would she survive?

Mulville looked at the auburn hair spread on the pillow. Also the brown eyes staring at him from under thick dark brows. Bloom's eyes always looked too large for her face. Today, they looked even larger. From fear.

"How is she?" Mulville asked Dr. Wilder, as if Bloom was unable to answer. Or unworthy addressing.

"Why don't you ask her?" the doctor said. Bloom lifted her chin above the covers. "She's as stable as she can be, given the circumstances."

"Now can you tell me what's really wrong?" Mulville said, staring at the doctor. "No more BS about fainting. The truth!"

The doctor looked at Bloom. Mulville turned his narrowed eyes to her. She nodded her consent to the doctor.

"She has a heart tumor," Wilder said.

Tumor. Tumor meant a swelling. A lump. But that wasn't usually what doctors meant when they talked about a tumor. The ridiculous euphemisms doctors and people used to avoid calling it by its fucking name. Mulville felt a heaviness beginning to outweighing his anger.

"Cancer?" he said. "She's got heart cancer? And none of you thought I should know about this? I'm her boss. I'm sending her out to dangerous assignments while she's dying."

Kirk looked at the floor. Bloom closed her eyes. Zayne looked at the heart monitor.

"We don't know if it's cancer," Zayne said. He seemed relieved to dive into a professional conversation. "According to our ultrasound expert, it's probably benign, which means it's not spreading to other organs, as when you have metastasis. But its position causes major problems. It's too big to cut off. There wouldn't be enough of her heart left to be able to function. That's why her only option is a heart transplant."

"What really happened when you told me that she fainted?" Mulville looked at Zayne, then at Bloom.

"She had a bad arrhythmia," the doctor said. "Ventricular fibrillation."

"English."

"The heart basically stops pumping," Wilder said, looking at Bloom. "So, she fainted from lack of blood to her brain."

"Do you mean she had v-fib arrest?" Mulville said, his voice screeching. "In the movies, people with v-fib arrest are like dead. Explain how she could be running around with my SWAT team, after signing out of the hospital fucking A.M.A. After nearly dying!"

The doctor looked at Bloom's monitors.

"I had to," Bloom said, pulling down her covers and sitting up. "It's my job. What I signed up for. What I want to do for the rest of my life, no matter how short it may be."

"I treated you as—" Mulville went on, his face flushed, his voice unnaturally calm, "as family. I trusted you like I never trusted any subordinate. My mistake. We're done. With everything. How could I ever trust you again, in the field, where lives depend on you, when you don't give a damn about yours, or how your problems may affect your performance?"

Mulville didn't wait for an answer. He couldn't stand to look at Bloom. The feelings he had repressed during the many months of her training were spilling into his guts like champagne pouring out of a shaken, then uncorked bottle. He was so angry he had to leave, before he behaved in a way unbecoming an FBI director. He stormed out of the room.

His steps felt as if his feet were weighed down by lead and he had to fight for every move. He reached a waiting area near the elevators and sat in an armchair in front of a low table covered with popular magazines. His face was in his hands, and the heat of his face scared him. In all his years as an agent, facing deadly adversaries, lethal weapons, and danger around every corner, he had never felt so scared and uncertain about choosing the right course of action. What was happening to him?

He had trusted Bloom. The bond they had developed working together during extreme circumstances, Bloom's drive and competence, exceptional for her young age, had wiped out his defense mechanisms and opened himself to dangerous, uncharted territory. For the first time in his life, Mulville had experienced what it meant to have a family. Not the penitentiary-like family imposed on dumb and doomed people by blood ties. Instead, the privileged, chosen family only long-tested trust and life-or-death challenges can forge. Yet, here he was, holding an empty bag. The trust was gone. But whose fault was that? He only had himself to thank and to blame.

His fist tightened and moved as if independent of the rest of his body, landing on the wooden table. The cracking of concrete blocks and wooden boards during his martial art training came back to him. The table made an ominous crunching sound.

"Jack." Kirk's voice reached him. "Breaking furniture isn't going to fix anything."

Mulville looked up. Kirk stood at his side. The table sagged in the middle, held together by threads of wood. Sports magazines and women journals slid toward the center. Kirk sat across from him on a matching chair.

"Talk to me," Kirk said. "And hurry up, because we need you to go back and talk to Bloom again."

"Trust me," Mulville said, looking up at Kirk's deep eyes. "I'm the last person she would listen to. I've used up all my fuck-ups for a while, and maybe forever. Bloom was the worst mistake in judgment of my sorry life."

"I think you're wrong," Kirk said. "You were right to trust her."

"Bullshit."

"With all due respect," Kirk said, looking at him in the eye, as if monitoring his chances of getting punched on the face, "she had no choice."

Kirk had nerve. Mulville had to admit that. Both of them knew how a fight between them would end.

"Explain," Mulville said. "Before I treat you like this table. And remember, my jury isn't out on you because you didn't level with me about Bloom's problem."

"What was she supposed to do?" Kirk sat back, placing as much distance between them as he could. "If you had known about her heart problem, what would you have done?"

"I would have taken her out." Mulville heard his words as they flew out of his mouth. He was behaving as if he was in a drunken stupor, squeezing undesirable truth out of him, preventing any evasion. "So she wouldn't have died. She *died*, didn't she? Or have you fucking forgotten that she actually did die. Did you know about *that*?"

"Are you listening to yourself?" Kirk looked at Mulville as if he had him trapped. "That's why she *had* to conceal it from you. You treat her like family, not like an FBI agent. She had to throw that fact into the equation. It was her career versus being like family to you. She tried to have both, by not telling you about her disease. You left her no choice in the matter. She needed you. And she needs you now."

"What about you?" he said, pointing an accusatory finger at Kirk. "You knew. And you never mentioned it to me. You even knew about the daddy-daughter relationship with Montepulciano. And don't deny it. I saw it in your puppy eyes. You weren't surprised by the dramatic soap-opera revelation."

"I knew about both," Kirk said, nodding. "But not because she told me. I found out on my own. And I couldn't tell you, without disobeying your order to watch over her. If Bloom had known that I knew the full truth about her, she would have slammed the door on any useful communication between her and me. I was following your orders."

Mulville couldn't find an appropriate answer. He suppressed the urge to finish off the table.

"The way I see it," Kirk said, "Bloom was so brave, and cared so much about her career, that she clenched her teeth and went on in the face of death. Even after VF arrest, she came right back to work. She kept on doing her job. Kept on risking her life."

Mulville had to nod.

"And who inspired her to care so much about her work?" Kirk asked. "Who gave her the opportunity? You. You are her mentor. And much more, in fact. Some part of your relationship may be awkward on the job. You have to learn to leave it out, and not to interfere in her assignments. But please, use everything you've got to convince her to undergo the heart transplant. She's refusing the heart. And without the heart, she'll die."

"Whose heart?" Mulville said. "Baker is still alive, for God's sake. She has no heart available."

"Montepulciano is a match for her," Kirk said. He paused, as if waiting for a reaction from Mulville. "Not too surprising, since he's the biological father."

"She'll never accept it," Mulville said. He bit his lip. "What about her doctor? He's also her ... her ... whatever. If he can't convince her..."

"Not even Dr. Wilder can. He tried, believe me. He has a lot invested. I'm sure he cares about her, in more than one way."

Mulville got up. He was operating on automatic pilot again. Step after more difficult step, he walked back toward Bloom's room. Kirk followed him in silence. When they got to the door, Kirk stopped. He tapped Mulville's back.

"You got this," he said, as if he had completed his mission. "You don't need me here. And I have to go home. My family needs me."

Mulville nodded. He glanced at the bed inside the room. Bloom lay still, her eyes closed, as if in a world of her own.

Bloom opened her eyes at the sound of the door sliding open. Her hand felt limp in Zayne's hand.

Mulville barged back into the room, marched to Bloom's bedside opposite Zayne, and stood straight like a rod. What did the director want now? Bloom's hand tightened around Zayne's.

"Take the heart," Mulville said, his tone that of an FBI director talking to a recruit. "It's an order. How else are you going to perform your duty as an FBI special agent? As I've said many times, the first prerequisite is being alive."

Zayne stared at him. At first, he looked surprised. But then he turned back toward Bloom and nodded, squeezing her hand.

"You want me to accept the heart of a man I killed?" Bloom said, sitting up. "Let alone the heart of a monster?"

"You did your job, as you said you wanted to do," Mulville said. "Today, you were the only one who didn't hesitate to do what needed to be done. Thanks to you, Kirk Miner is alive."

The heaviness that had weighed down her chest for most of the afternoon became lighter. "Still, I can't accept Montepulciano's heart," she said.

"Montepulciano *wanted* to be killed," Mulville said. "To give you his heart."

Bloom stared at Mulville, searching for evidence of trickery. He held her gaze, with his unblinking clear blue slits.

"How can you possibly say that?" she said. "You want me to believe that **someone like him wanted to give his life ... for *me*?**"

Mulville reached out for a chair from the bedside, pulled it as close as possible to Bloom, and straddled his legs across the seat, leaning his forearms on the back

"At first, I believe he wanted to kill Baker," Mulville said.

"At first when?"

"Today," Mulville said. "Montepulciano wanted to kill Baker, but you showed up and wrecked his plan. You were the only one who could stop him.

And you did. So he went to Plan B."

"You think he had a Plan B?"

"Absolutely," Zayne said. "In case Baker didn't die, he himself was Plan B. Why, otherwise, would he have done his own genetic testing?"

"He had himself tested?" Mulville said. "I'll be damned. So I'm right. He *had* planned for the possibility that he might be stopped or caught. He, in effect, committed freaking suicide by cop."

"He wanted *me* to kill him?" Bloom said. "Another good reason why I shouldn't accept his heart."

"I don't think he wanted *you* to kill him," Mulville said. He was probably hoping that I, or somebody from the SWAT team, or even Miner, would do it. But you're the only one who didn't hesitate."

"Lucky me. I still don't understand why he would do it."

"Montepulciano changed his plan when you showed up. He figured he was looking at life in prison for rape, murder, cybercrimes, and all the other unproven charges he had accumulated. So he decided to end his own life, and to make it worth it. He looked for Baker again, but he was already with the SWAT team, so he went for Miner. He figured that, any of three ways, you would get a heart—from Baker, Miner, or Montepulciano himself."

"He would have shot Miner," Bloom said. "I had no choice."

"Of course," Mulville said, nodding. "But I'm not even sure he particularly wanted to shoot Miner. I don't think he wanted to go back to jail for the rest of his life. This way, by giving you his heart, he leaves a legacy—you."

His legacy. Last thing Bloom wanted to be. Montepulciano's legacy.

"But," Bloom said, her eyes wide open, and suddenly feeling alive. "What about the rest of my probation time? I still have longer than a month to go."

"You completed the FBI probation requirements," Mulville said.

He had said it like an officer on the verge of handing out a diploma. Did that mean that she still had a career? Despite her illness, her cover-up, her disobedience, her connection to the mob?

"Despite the fact that, on several occasions, you disobeyed my direct orders, you proved beyond any doubt that you have bravery and integrity," Mulville said. "As for Fidelity, you need to do some work, especially when it comes to truthfulness in your relationship with others, and most of all with me. But, given the circumstances, your probationary period is officially over. Your badge will be waiting for you when you wake up. Now, go to surgery, or I'll have to find a replacement. And before you say anything, remember the second requirement: Don't piss off the director. Which you've done quite enough lately."

FBI Special Agent Charlotte Bloom. The words resounded in her mind over and over. She was going to be a *real* agent. But the catch was she had to stay alive. And in order to do so, she needed a heart. That was Mulville's dirty deal. She looked at the director. "Blackmail" was too strong of a word to describe his proposed exchange. He looked pale, as she had never seen him before. His eyes looked at her expectedly. The tight jaw, the stretched mouth. He was waiting to see if his words had changed her mind. He didn't want her to die. Bloom was sure her mother also didn't want her to die.

At last, Mom wouldn't have to worry about Montepulciano coming after her any longer. Bloom wished she could have gotten a confession from Montepulciano. An admission to the rape. The fact that he was a perfect match for his and Marjorie Silverman's—AKA Marsha Stevens'—daughter would have to do.

"Okay," Bloom said. "I'll accept the heart."

She didn't want to die either.

CHAPTER 33
KIRK MINER

Kirk stopped the car and looked at his house. The two-story white building with the dark roof had never looked more inviting. A few days before, for an interminable ten minutes, he had been certain he would never set foot in it again. Today, he had come close to dying as well. When he had called her after the Montepulciano's shooting to reassure her of his well-being, he hoped that Aurora wouldn't guess the truth from his tone.

He got out and locked the car. While walking toward the front door, he noticed the weeds. His front lawn needed attention. From the plant bed at the side of the front door, he touched one lonely red geranium. Somehow it was surviving, even though it was fall.

The barking started the moment he entered the code in the front door panel. The door clicked open and Brutus's wet muzzle stuck out. The mutt pushed the door open and jumped on Kirk, tail tapping on the concrete.

"Wow, Brutus," he said stroking the dog's head and gently pushing it down.

"Dad's here!" Peter said, standing at the threshold.

Kirk stepped in and took Peter into a tight hug, Brutus was still trying to place his paws on Kirk's legs and Buddy, his tail in a frenzy, was trying to step into the action by pushing his muzzle between Kirk and Peter. Aurora appeared behind Peter, smiling, her injured arm still in a sling, the other arm up and waiting for him. Kirk let go of Peter and went to her. Her able arm held him in a hug too tight and too long. She had to know the danger Kirk had endured.

"I love you," he said.

He felt her hand stroking his head and back. They all walked inside. Kirk was grateful she wasn't asking him for the details of the take-down in front of Peter.

In the living room, Kirk declined his favorite over-stuffed leather chair and opted instead to sit on the couch with Peter at his side, the two dogs on the alert sitting on the carpet. He placed his feet up on a stool and released a long deep exhalation.

Aurora went to the kitchen and returned carrying an open bottle of red wine. He wondered how she had managed to pry open the cork with just one hand. She must have gotten one of those electric openers. She was adapting to her temporary disability. And his absence. The second thought made him shudder. She placed the bottle on the coffee table and went back to the kitchen for two glasses, which she carried holding them together by the rims. She poured the wine and picked a glass up by the stem. Kirk did the same. She sat next to him.

"To us," she said, pointing at Kirk and Peter and herself. "Here. All together."

They toasted. The cool wine soothed Kirk's dry throat. Soon it would soothe his weary mind. Peter petted both Brutus and Buddy and smiled.

"Tell us what happened, Dad," Peter said after a short time.

"Not today," Aurora said. "Daddy needs to relax now."

"Tomorrow," Kirk said. He knew the answer wouldn't apply to Aurora. Before the end of the day, he would have to face her in private,. "Peter, why don't you walk the dogs before it gets too dark?"

Peter looked up at him from below his thick brows. Just like Kirk's, only several shades lighter. In between his and Aurora's hair color. Peter's look was of understanding. A "do-you-think-I'm-stupid" look. He stood and walked to the door. Brutus and Buddy immediately got up on their fours and rushed after him. The jingling and clicking of the leashes resonated, then a gush of cold air marked the opening of the front door. As he was grabbing his jacket from the closet, Peter turned and shouted, "Don't tell mom anything while I'm gone."

The door closed after Peter. Kirk placed his glass on the table and turned to Aurora. She took one more sip of wine and placed her glass next to his. She turned to face him. No smile.

"I signed up to be a wife," she said, touching his forehead with her good hand, combing his hair with her fingers. "Not a widow."

Kirk nodded. He controlled the impulse to give her a quick answer. He knew when Aurora needed to vent.

"We made a deal," she said. "Almost ten years ago, when Peter was a young kid. You said you wanted to see him grow up, so you quit the force for that reason and went on to become a private investigator."

"I did," Kirk said.

"Working with the police and the FBI, you're risking your life as often, if not more often, than before." Aurora sighed. "This has to stop."

The last four words crushed something in Kirk's mind. The life that he had carefully built for himself during the past several years crumbled and flattened like a house of cards.

"You know I can't possibly survive or enjoy my work just investigating cheating couples or similar stuff. It's not me."

"I know," she said. "You need excitement. But Peter and I can't pay for it. You haven't even had the time to properly discuss what's going on at college with him. He needs you. And I need you too. Alive. Here."

"But I *am* here."

"Did you risk your life today?" She looked him straight in the eye.

"Not really," he said, forcing himself to maintain eye contact.

"No one pointed a gun at you?"

Kirk swallowed. To quench his dry throat, he reached out for the glass and finished his wine in a few sips. He then turned to Aurora.

"Someone did," he said. "But it was just so the FBI would kill him. He didn't really mean to shoot me."

Now it was Aurora's turn to look at him from under her light brows.

"If it weren't so potentially tragic," she said, "this could be comic."

She let go of a sad chuckle. Kirk placed his arm around her and pulled her close. The fresh scent of her conditioner gave him a jolt of excitement. She shrugged his arm off, straightening her back.

"You can't dismiss what I'm saying," she said. "Not anymore."

"Okay," Kirk said. "What do you want me to do? You know you and

Peter are the most important things in my life."

"It's what I *don't* want you to do," she said. "I don't want you to take part in take-downs or gun fights. Leave those to the police, or the FBI. You're there to *consult*, not to shoot or get shot."

"I'm willing to try that," he said, taking her hand.

"This time," she said, "it has to be for real. For good. Not just trying."

"I will not participate in take-downs or gun fights," Kirk said. "Unless it is to save you and Peter. Then I'll do everything I need to do."

"I hate to say it, but all our risks and dangers come from your job."

"True," Kirk nodded. "I'm going to keep that in mind at all times."

"I need some time off," she said. "Time off from *your* job, not mine."

"Great," Kirk said. "How about a family vacation? Something like Disneyland. What do you think?"

She couldn't resist smiling. His arm reached for her again. This time she allowed him to pull her close. He turned to kiss her, just as the door opened and Brutus, Buddy, and Peter barged in.

CHAPTER 34
AGENT BLOOM

After the death-like sleep of anesthesia, Bloom's first sight was of Zayne. He stood at her bedside, clad in official blue scrubs and white coat. But she was only aware of his smile, the most reassuring thing she had encountered since the day she'd discovered her life-threatening condition.

"Welcome back." The squeeze of his hand told her how happy and relieved he was. Then he gave her the good news she now expected. "Everything went well."

"The heart is in?" she said, her voice hoarse.

Zayne pointed at the bedside monitor. The EKG tracing dominated the screen with pulsing spikes, a prima ballerina among the chorus of lines and scrolling numbers. The rhythm appeared regular and steady. No awkwardly-shaped beats or scary accelerations.

"Has been for two days," he said. "Not a beat out of tune."

Montepulciano's heart was beating in her chest. The heart of a criminal. A criminal she had shot dead. The gift from Santo Montepulciano, occupation mobster, rank Capo Famiglia. No longer to be Capo-dei-Capi. Her FATHER. Bloom looked at the monitor. The spikes reminded her of the waving of a hand. A salute. She took a deep breath and winced, a sharp pain spreading from both sides of her chest.

"Easy now." Zayne's fingertips caressed her cheek. "The chest tubes will come out soon. You can press the button of the pump attached to your IV. It lets you release pain medicine whenever you need it."

Not now. Not while basking in the joy of being alive after surviving such a life-threatening condition and the most major of major surgery. She smiled, wondering what had endangered her life more, her illness or her job. Then she remembered something else.

"What about the tumor?" She braced for the answer, which was destined to trim and shape the rest of her life. "What did it turn out to be?"

"Benign." Zayne beamed. "A very unusual fibroma, not a sarcoma. It means that it's gone forever and won't reappear anywhere else anytime soon."

She nodded as a weight she had learned to live with for so long lifted from her cracked chest and left her free to plan her future.

"Thank you," she said, "for taking such good care of me, even when I wasn't too cooperative. Thank you for rescuing me, and bringing me back to the hospital. And thank you for pushing me to accept the heart."

The squeeze Zayne gave her hand was his acknowledgment of her mea culpas. "I have to go now, but I'll be back after my next surgery."

He kissed her on the lips, turned to go, and walked away.

"Wait," she said. Zayne turned in front of the open door. "I need to see Mulville. About my badge. And my final diploma."

Zayne's smile faded. He seemed hesitant, as if he wanted to leave the room to avoid uan ncomfortable conversation. What was the doctor so afraid to tell her?

"Mulville was here earlier," Zayne said. "He's been here every day. I'll tell him you're awake."

The doctor was gone well before the door finished closing. The burning question came to Bloom's lips a moment too late. Her badge she would get. But when would she be able to actually get back into action? Would she be relegated to a desk for the rest of her career? That was the question Zane wanted to avoid, or so it seemed. He wanted Mulville to deal with that. Mulville to take the blame for an answer she probably would not like.

With Zayne gone, washing his hands of the responsibility for bad news, Bloom had nothing to do but wait. She looked around for her phone. Not there. Her computer. Not there either. She sunk her head into her flimsy hospital pillow, pushed the pain medication button, and closed her eyes. In the dreams that followed, Bloom lived and rehearsed the dreaded forthcoming conversation.

"How're you doing?" The familiar voice shook her awake. Bloom opened her eyes. Director Mulville stood at her bedside. "The doctor said you were awake."

This was real. The time had come. Mulville stood in his tight blue suit with the small American flag in the lapel. He held a letter-size brown envelope and a new FBI badge in his hand. The badge was shiny gold and blue. The usual eagle at the top. At the bottom were the words: "Cyber Police." Bloom sighed.

"Here," he said, placing the polished shield on her bed covers, next to the pain pump button. "As I promised."

Was she still dreaming? She had read how morphine could turn bad dreams around. That was why it was so addictive. Bloom reached out for the badge and clasped it within her hand. Cold, hard metal. Solid. Real. She was awake.

"Thanks." She smiled.

Mulville smiled as well. A rare event, in her experience. He turned for the door.

"Someone is here to see you," he said. He stepped aside.

Marjorie stepped into the room. She wore an old tan coat Bloom was very familiar with. A black pocketbook, too large for her small frame, dangled from her forearm. Marjorie looked at Mulville, and immediately she removed the coat, as if to avoid parading the faded color and the worn-out elbows. But then her gaze moved to Bloom, and she stopped fidgeting with her coat, dropped her pocketbook on the floor, and in two quick steps reached Bloom's bedside. She bent down and took her daughter into her arms. Bloom felt her muscles relax at the comforting touch of the fuzzy old wool. Her mom's old coat around her was exactly what she needed at this moment.

"Charlie, Charlie," Marjorie said. Then she straightened up and held her at arm's length. She looked at her. Tears filled her tired eyes. She hugged Bloom again. Bloom patted her back.

"I'm fine, Mom," Bloom said. "I'm doing well. Thanks to you."

Marjorie shook under Bloom's arms. Bloom stroked her back.

"Mom," Bloom said, after Marjorie stopped sobbing, "I want you to meet Director Mulville, my boss."

"Your mother and I met outside," Mulville said. "I called her a couple of days ago to let her know you were graduating to full-fledged Cyber Agent. She told me she wanted to be here when I give you your new diploma, just as she had attended the ceremony when you graduated from the Academy."

Marjorie let go of her and stood back. A dark green silk dress, her Sunday outfit, contrasted nicely with a strand of pearls adorning her neck. She stood at attention, waiting and staring at the shining badge on Bloom's bed covers. Mulville handed the brown envelope to Bloom. She ripped the top open and pulled out a paper document bearing the FBI seal and signed by Director Jack Mulville. She had officially completed her probationary period. She was a full- fledged FBI Special Agent, Cyber Division.

But something was still unknown. And Bloom savor her triumph until she found out if and when she would be allowed to perform her duty. Mulville's eyes studied her, as if trying to decide if she could take what he had to reveal. Now might be the best time to lay down ground rules. Bloom clenched her badge with all her strength.

"Do you promise you won't interfere with my duty," she said, "and won't treat me differently than other recruits?"

"Damned Kirk." Mulville shook his head and sat on the bedside chair. "Couldn't he just screw around with his PI cases and leave the FBI business to me?"

"Kirk didn't say anything," she protested, "But the doctor left in too much hurry not to be hiding something. What is it? It's about my recovery and downtime, isn't it? When can I come back to work? I mean *real* work"

"At least eight weeks." Mulville stared at her, waiting for the effect. "For regular duty. That's what the doctor said."

She was going to be a regular agent. In two months. Mulville had given her the answer she was hoping for.

"You can do your computer stuff as soon as the doctor discharges you," Mulville said.

"So, do you promise," she said, echoing the pledge she had to take at her graduation. "You won't interfere with my duty, and won't treat me differently than any other recruit?"

Mulville raised his right hand. "I do."

Under the circumstances, the lack of sarcasm seemed unnatural. She had never seen him so serious. Evidently, he meant what he said.

"Will you be able to compartmentalize your—"

"What …?" Mulville said. His eye twitched, like an uncontrollable tick. "Good God, I have to get out of this room. Who do you think I am?"

Bloom remained silent. Mulville's eyes widened, showing parts of irises and corneas Bloom—and maybe nobody else—had ever seen before. But she didn't detect any astonishment.

"Yes, Agent Bloom," he whispered. "I will."

He lifted his hand from his side, moved closer, and placed it atop hers.

ACKNOWLEDGMENTS

I'm very grateful to my husband Peter, my alpha reader, for his great patience, skillful editing, and unwavering love.

Much gratitude to Charlotte Cook, for the expert teaching I will carry with me throughout my writing career—I can hear you prompting me as I write. FYI: I named the protagonist after you.

Thanks to my great friend, Dr. Steven Lansman, who provided me with inspiration and education in the area of cardiothoracic surgery.

I couldn't have done it without my family: My husband Peter; my children Christopher, Francisco, and Aurora; my sister Silvana; and my extended family: Monica, Alan, Helane, Bob, Marsha, Lucy, Ben, Jonah, Jesse, Kimberly, Alexandra, Keith, and my life-long best friend Patrizia —your unwavering encouragement cheered me on during the difficult journey to publication.

A loving thanks to my grandson Zayne Wilder LePort for inspiring the name of one of the main characters.

Thanks to my agent Bob Diforio, for believing in me, and for his work and dedication to make my novels successful. Sincere appreciation to designer Tracy Copes for a creative cover that my publisher and I love.

A very special thanks to Bruce Bortz, publisher of Bancroft Press, for his great editing, which paved the way to a much-improved book, and for his contagious enthusiasm. You are making it all happen. Your appreciation of my work is a great and continuing source of inspiration. Finally, a heartfelt thanks to all my readers for taking the time to enter the world I created and meet the characters I invented.

ABOUT THE AUTHOR

D r. Cristina LePort is a multifaceted personality whose journey from a vibrant childhood in Bologna, Italy, to becoming a celebrated cardiologist and author in Southern California, encapsulates the essence of determination, intellect, and creative prowess. Born into a family where education and the American dream were revered, Cristina's early exposure to literature and her father's admiration for the U.S. profoundly influenced her path. Graduating summa cum laude from the University of Bologna School of Medicine, she embarked on a challenging yet rewarding medical career that led her to the shores of the United States, despite the hurdles of language and cultural transition.

After completing her residency in Internal Medicine at Long Island College Hospital/Downstate in Brooklyn, NY, Cristina's insatiable quest for knowledge and specialization in cardiology took her to the prestigious corridors of UCLA for cardiovascular research, culminating in a fellowship at the West Los Angeles VA/UCLA program. Her contributions to the medical field, particularly in aging and chronic diseases through her co-founded biotech company Genescient, underscore her commitment to advancing medical science.

However, it is Cristina's transition from a medical professional to a fiction writer that unveils the richness of her talents. Inspired by the medical world's inherent drama and complexity, she has penned gripping medical thrillers that not only entertain but also provoke thought about the ethical dimensions of medicine and science. Her debut novel, "Dissection," and its successor, "Change of Heart," are testaments to her ability to weave intricate plots that explore the high-stakes environment of medical crises and political intrigue.

Cristina's writing is infused with the authenticity of her medical expertise, drawing readers into the visceral realities of the operating room and the ethical dilemmas faced by those in the medical profession. Her narratives are a bridge between the worlds of medicine and literature, offering a unique perspective that challenges the boundaries of both fields.

Residing in Orange County, California, with her husband, Peter LePort, a general surgeon, and surrounded by a loving family, Cristina embodies the dual spirit of a dedicated physician and a storyteller. Her journey from an immigrant with dreams to a respected cardiologist and author is a compelling narrative of resilience, passion, and the pursuit of excellence.

Through her novels, Dr. LePort invites readers into the exhilarating and precarious world of medical thrillers, where the stakes are life itself. With each page, she reaffirms her place not only in the annals of medicine but also in the rich tradition of doctors who turn to writing to explore the moral and existential questions at the heart of human life.